THE ENCAMPMENT

THE ENCAMPMENT

A Novel

STEPHEN DAVENPORT

Cover image: Lifestyle Travel Photo/Shutterstock.com

Library of Congress Cataloging-in-Publication Data

Names: Davenport, Stephen, author.
Title: The encampment / by Stephen Davenport.
Description: [Berkeley, CA] : West Margin Press, [2020.] | Series: Miss Oliver's school for girls ; book 3 | Summary: "There are only two rules at Miss Oliver's School for Girls that lead to automatic expulsion: stealing, and permitting a male who is not a family member into a dormitory. The head of school's daughter breaks both when she meets a homeless man on the street. The third installment of the Miss Oliver's School for Girls series, *The Encampment* follows high school senior Sylvia Bickham as learns to navigate between the rules of society and the morals of the conscience"—Provided by publisher.
Identifiers: LCCN 2020004225 (print) | LCCN 2020004226 (ebook) | ISBN 9781513263069 (paperback) | ISBN 9781513263076 (hardback) | ISBN 9781513263083 (ebook)
Classification: LCC PS3604.A9427 E53 2020 (print) | LCC PS3604.A9427 (ebook) | DDC 813/.6—dc23
LC record available at https://lccn.loc.gov/2020004225
LC ebook record available at https://lccn.loc.gov/2020004226

Published by West Margin Press®

WestMarginPress.com

Proudly distributed by Ingram Publisher Services

WEST MARGIN PRESS
Publishing Director: Jennifer Newens
Marketing Manager: Angela Zbornik
Project Specialist: Gabrielle Maudiere
Editor: Olivia Ngai
Design & Production: Rachel Lopez Metzger

To the memory of my parents,
Stephen and Mariana,
and my brother Henry.

Yes, we'll gather at the river,
The beautiful, the beautiful river.
—Robert Lowry, traditional hymn

ONE

On a Saturday afternoon early in September, Rachel Bickham, Head of School, was in her office alone, eyes closed, sitting perfectly still, emptying her brain of details so that she could think. What had happened in the last week she needed to consider more, what left unsaid that should be said, and to whom? What part of the Big Plan should she pay attention to this coming week, what shoe was about to drop, what potential blessing should she recognize and cultivate? For all nineteen years that she had been the head of school, she had devoted an hour every weekend to this, a meditation akin to prayer she never had time for during the week because she led by walking around. She had always emerged from the hour energized and centered.

But this afternoon, her mind wandered to a dark place of dissatisfaction. She felt an emptiness, a hollowing out of herself, that had become familiar, and the whispered question: *Is this all?*

She opened her eyes, giving up her meditation—maybe she'd try again tomorrow—and glanced out through the big French doors at the huge copper beech tree that stood just yards away, a motherly presence. For years, this ancient tree, under which Pequot Tribespeople had once sat to catch its shade, had radiated its calm to her. And there also, as always to reassure her, was the school she was in charge of that she wore around herself like a coat. This view of the tree and, beyond it, the curved row of white clapboard buildings, graceful in their Grecian proportions, mildly Puritanical in their affect, and the green lawns beyond them sweeping down to the woods and then the Connecticut River, had always said to her: *You were born for this.*

Relieved again, Rachel stood from her desk, opened the French doors. The scent of fresh-cut grass rushed in. Girls were walking on the paths. Someone had parked a shiny green bicycle on the top steps of the library.

Just then, her daughter, Sylvia, and Sylvia's best friend and roommate, Elizabeth Cochrane, emerged from their dormitory. They walked past the music building where a big golden retriever raised her head and thumped her tail on the grass in greeting. Amazed as always by how different the two girls were from each other, Rachel watched them continue side by side toward the driveway that led to the front gate.

It was Saturday afternoon and they were free to go—but only as far away as the village of Fieldington, a very safe place. Rachel had a sudden desire to join them, as if to experience the world with them, seeing in it what they saw, would also calm her emptiness; but of course that was her imagination being overactive, and besides, she didn't think she should intrude. Instead, she watched them until, like ships slipping over the horizon, they were out of sight.

TWO

Sylvia Perrine Bickham loved being part of the community of Miss Oliver's School for Girls in which each person was embraced. She admired the school's mission, the empowerment of young women, was even inspired by the concept once in a while, and she had felt the blessing of the school's affectionate inclusion at the core of her being for as long as she could remember. Other girls, the ones who were lucky anyway, had a mom and a dad and maybe several siblings. But Sylvia, from infancy, had had a whole community whose values, articulated over and over in print, in meetings, in classes, and on the athletic fields, included compassion, empathy, and kindness to others.

And she was keenly aware of how special it was that the campus stood on ground once occupied by a village of the Pequot People. Their artifacts, left behind in their defeat, were prominently displayed in the Peggy Plummer Library as evidence of how various the ways of humans are. For as long as she could remember, Sylvia had imbibed these ideas, and she had been free to roam over this expansive campus where everybody stopped to say hello to her.

And on top of that, her mom was the boss.

But once she became a ninth grade student and official member of the community, she had begun vaguely to sense that she didn't really belong and that, if she were not the head of school's daughter, she might not have been accepted. She, who would get into one college or another because she was a gifted athlete, sometimes actually felt sorry for friends who stayed up all night studying subjects that were not intrinsically interesting to them and whose contents were doomed to be forgotten, just so they could get into a college which, in Sylvia's not entirely inaccurate opinion, was deemed to be one of the best only because enough people declared it to be. It was not satisfying to study hard to prepare for a future life whose purpose was still unknown. She needed a purpose for her present life, the one she was living *right now*.

That Elizabeth Cochrane, her best friend, already did know her purpose, that she knew exactly what she would become, is one reason why Sylvia had gravitated toward her, why she had wanted to room with her, to be her sister and confidant. Elizabeth, who would apply for early admission to MIT, planned, and expected, to be first a widely read author of highly literary science fiction, and then, using her fame as a platform, to be president of the United States. That she said this with a perfectly straight face and no one ever laughed was another thing about the school that Sylvia loved.

SYLVIA AND ELIZABETH walked straight to Rose's Creamery, praised for miles around Fieldington for being the first to serve only organic fare and where you can still trace the development of the automobile just by looking at the black-and-white photos on the walls. Elizabeth ordered an ice cream cone with a double scoop of rocky road and cherries on top. Just as Rose handed it to her, Sylvia blurted, "You really gonna eat all of that?"

"So, Rose, whaddaya think? Should I?" Elizabeth said, her sarcastic tone close to an act of aggression. She crossed her feet, bulky ankles touching, and assumed a pose, like a model on a runway, slurping at her cone and somehow making herself look even bigger and rounder as she wiped her mouth with the back of her hand. She then turned around with little mincing steps and, with the hand not holding the cone, gave herself a pat on the rear. "I might be just a wee bit too fat here," she admitted, "but it's great for sitting down."

Rose looked at her blankly.

Elizabeth turned to Sylvia, miming surprise. "Rose has no sense of humor at all!"

Rose sniffed, glanced impatiently past the two girls at the lengthening line of waiting patrons, then turned back to Sylvia. "And you? What will you have?"

"It'll be itty-bitty, whatever it is," Elizabeth said.

Sylvia ordered a double scoop of chocolate. She had planned to order something low calorie, but she didn't want Elizabeth to be right. She already regretted not keeping her mouth shut. Elizabeth felt far more vulnerable about her bigness than she let on. She had come to Rose's because she was hungry. Sylvia had come because she was bored.

For Elizabeth, her life at Miss Oliver's School for Girls was much too new and fresh and liberating to ever be boring. She had been plucked out of her little town in Oklahoma because of her smarts by an alert alumna on the lookout for special talent to enrich the student composition of her beloved alma mater. The alumna had intended to participate in a rally for a woman who was trying to unseat a senator who had been in office for several terms. But the alumna got the dates wrong and discovered she was actually at a rally for that very senator, whose policies she detested. She found herself sitting next to a large girl who couldn't have been a day older than fifteen, all alone, unaccompanied by parents. On her thick right leg just above the ankle was a purple tattoo of an oilrig with an X crossed over it. The alumna had been about to leave the rally, but she decided to stay and see what happened.

The senator in question, a tall person who looked as if he might be quite intelligent, took the podium while everyone cheered and clapped. He raised his hand and there was silence. He announced that he devoutly believed global warming was a hoax, perpetrated by the liberal media for the benefit of pointy heads on the coasts, and paused for acknowledgment. Everyone nodded their heads, and in the silence Elizabeth said, "It's a free country." Many in the audience turned to her, nodding their heads still more. They had missed her sarcasm. Elizabeth stood up and informed the senator that hearing him say such a thing would be like attending a math class at MIT and hearing the professor insist that two times two is one-hundred and seventy-six—except on Thursdays, when it's only five. The senator smiled tolerantly. After all, she was just a child. Then he proceeded to suggest that the current president of the United States was an illegal immigrant. Elizabeth managed to restrict her critique of the rest of the senator's talk to acerbic murmurs, and when the evening was over at last, the alumna turned to her. "Young lady, can we talk?"

Where Elizabeth came from, people weren't supposed to be so lucky. If her senator had been a normal person instead of, in

Elizabeth's opinion, one of the biggest assholes in the world, she wouldn't have gone to the meeting to let him know that what he was, and she'd still be going to a school where to let it out she expected to be the president of the United States someday would brand her as crazy. Or maybe a comedian. In fact, it had never even occurred to her to aspire so high as a published writer, until she'd arrived at Miss O's where the teachers demanded high aspirations. That's what the school was *for.* That's what *empowerment* meant.

Elizabeth thought of that moment, two years ago, as the luckiest thing that had ever happened to her. She was a senior now, like her roommate, Sylvia, who had convinced her parents she should live her senior year in a dormitory instead of the Head's House so she could have the same experience all the other girls had.

Licking at their cones, the two girls came out of Rose's and strolled along the pristine sidewalk of the village's central street in their cut-off jeans and floppy sandals, while their reflected doubles glided beside them on the storefront windows. They stopped for a few heartbeats at a women's clothing boutique to stare at two mannequins dressed for success in blue serge pantsuits before shaking their heads and moving on. Everyone they passed knew they were Miss Oliver girls. Sylvia was dark skinned, her mother African American and her father, like Elizabeth, as blonde as hay and Euro-American. Except for Oliver students, such a pairing was seldom seen on the elegant streets of Fieldington, whose buildings wore a studious New England Colonial look.

Finished with their cones, the two girls headed back to the campus on the east bank of the Connecticut River. The varsity soccer game, in which Sylvia would have played, had been canceled. They were glad to have the free time all the long afternoon and to be able to postpone until Sunday doing the burdensome load of homework the teachers insisted on assigning on weekends.

They came around a corner. Up ahead, a man stood by himself as if waiting for someone, but as they came closer, they saw his filthy clothes and realized he was a panhandler. "In *Fieldington*?" Elizabeth whispered. They were so surprised they stopped walking and stared, but only for a second because now he was watching them and they had no desire to be impolite. When they were next to him, about to pass, Elizabeth stopped again, and so Sylvia did too. They could smell him now: pungent news that he hadn't washed or changed his clothes for days and days. He had vacant eyes and long, dirty yellow hair. Elizabeth put her hand in the pocket of her jeans and pulled out her money: two quarters, two one-dollar bills, and a five-dollar bill—the change from the ten when she'd bought the cone. Sylvia watched the panhandler watching Elizabeth decide how much to give. He had a beard and moustache and his face was encrusted with dirt. She couldn't tell whether he was young or old. A couple with two little kids gave them a wide berth as they passed by.

Elizabeth shrugged and dropped two dollars into the greasy baseball hat at the man's feet. Sylvia, noticing that the hat was sitting on his sign, thought, *What's the point if no one can see it?* She bent down to move it off the sign. He bent down too, their heads almost touching, and in a flash she realized he was protecting the sign, the only one he had. Before his hand reached it, she slid the hat off the square of brown cardboard. There was just one word: *HOMELESS!* She was relieved it didn't say *GOD BLESS*, but she didn't know why. She stood up, resisting the urge to wipe her hand on her jeans, and wondered where he got the marker to write it. She expected they would look at each other, but he was staring down at his hat as if surprised she hadn't taken it from him.

"Come on, Sylvia, let's go," Elizabeth said.

They moved on. Trying not to sound defensive, Sylvia said, "My father says we should give to organizations that support the homeless, not to individuals."

"Yeah?" Elizabeth snorted.

"Yeah," Sylvia said. She was sure Elizabeth was about to say something sarcastic. She didn't want to hear it. So she turned around and went back to the panhandler and, bending down again, also dropped two dollars in his hat. Their eyes locked when she stood up straight again. Enveloped in the smell of him, she was shocked to see, through the beard and moustache and encrusted dirt, a young man's face, and to sense his lean, animal body beneath the filthy sweatshirt and jeans. "Thanks," he murmured, and then he averted his eyes.

All the rest of the weekend—and even during the week, when she was normally so busy she could hardly think—Sylvia kept seeing the shame on his face. She knew that's why he had looked away. He must have felt how surprised she was that he was where he was, in Fieldington, near Rose's Creamery, across the street from the wine shop where her father bought high-end Bordeaux, instead of the end of an exit ramp in Hartford. The homeless people there stared right back at her when she watched them from behind the locked doors of her mother's car.

THREE

A few days later, in the middle of calculus class, Sylvia thought about the young homeless man, remembering that he hadn't looked away from Elizabeth when Elizabeth had dropped *her* two dollars in his hat. It was a stunning revelation, as if the homeless man was making those few seconds in Sylvia's life happen all over again so she would focus, this time not on when he'd looked away, but when their eyes were locked. She was back again, enveloped in his pitiful, disgusting smell, miles and miles from utterly meaningless calculus questions, and he was looking at her as if he had seen her already some terrible place. She thought he must have believed he recognized her as someone he knew and that person had caught him being homeless, a mere beggar, surrounded in Fieldington by every sign of success. That's why he'd been so ashamed.

Yes, and no, she thought. Yes, and no. It was more than that. What else did he see? Her tall, very acceptable thinness? Her dark skin, rare in Fieldington, suggesting she didn't belong there either? Or didn't even want to? Did he see another girl in her face? It was as if he recognized something in Sylvia still unknown to herself. A question posed in a *calculus* class to which she wanted the answer! She would remember this moment the rest of her life.

On Sunday, when she and Elizabeth went downtown for ice cream again, Sylvia admitted to Elizabeth she wanted to see if the homeless man would be there again, but she didn't say why. That was much too private to share, even with Elizabeth.

The monthly farmers' market occupied the central street of the village on that Sunday. Big white-canvas canopies shaded the counters and stalls; the street and sidewalks, empty of automobiles, were crowded with people, dogs on leashes, baby strollers; there was the sound of many conversations, the smell of barbecuing meat. Sylvia had forgotten it would take place and was annoyed. She threaded her way through, sure the homeless man would not station himself in the midst of such a hubbub—if it were even allowed. Elizabeth lingered behind. She bought a long, shapely baguette, organic and locally baked fresh that morning. One end stuck out of its recyclable paper bag. She held it out for Sylvia to smell. Sylvia sniffed impatiently, then hurried on, past where the farmers' market ended.

And there he was, just past Rose's Creamery, standing in the bright hot sun!

He was facing away from her. She saw that his clothes were cleaner than last Saturday, and a surge of gladness for him lapped over her. She was relieved he was facing away, that she could watch him without being watched in turn. She wished she had the nerve to tell him to move to the shade of the trees that lined the street.

A Miss O's senior, Mary Callahan, came out of Rose's, carrying an ice cream cone upside down in a paper cup and a little wooden spoon. She headed in the direction of the homeless man, wearing big dark glasses, a top that didn't quite come down to her belly button, and shorts. Her sandals flopped on the sidewalk as she walked just ahead of Elizabeth and Sylvia. The homeless man turned his head. He and Mary looked at each other. Behind her dark glasses, Mary's expression was unreadable, but he scowled as she turned her head and hurried away from him. His beard and moustache were gone. His face was clean. His hair was shorter, chopped off, ends chaotic, obviously self-cut without a mirror.

The homeless man turned the rest of the way around and saw Sylvia and Elizabeth approaching. He seemed to be frozen for a second, recognition showing on his face, then turning around again, he walked away as fast as he could without actually running.

"Wait, your hat and sign," Sylvia called. She picked them up with the tip of her fingers, holding them out to him. There were two dollar bills in the hat. So, why wasn't he coming back? He took several more steps, then stopped, still for an instant, and turned back, keeping his eyes averted. He closed one hand around his hat, the other around the sign. She held on to both for a second, keeping him there. He tugged. She let go. He turned and fled.

Sylvia and Elizabeth watched as he looked back over his shoulder every few yards to see if they were following.

"Why'd you hang on like that?" Elizabeth asked, frowning. "You scared me."

"I don't know. I just did."

"You just did? It was *his* hat and sign. Suppose he got angry?"

"Maybe I wanted him to look at me," Sylvia admitted. That was as much as she was willing to say.

"But he wouldn't ever look at you. Couldn't you tell?" Elizabeth said. "He was too ashamed."

Sylvia shrugged.

"And what is it about us, anyway? He didn't run from Mary."

Sylvia shook her head. "I don't know."

"He thinks we came back to mock him?"

"Maybe. But he's changed his clothes. Did you see?"

"I don't think so. They look like the same ones to me."

"Where would he wash them in Fieldington?"

Elizabeth cocked her head, smiled her sarcastic smile. "Maybe he's a commuter. He spends the night somewhere so downscale you can actually find a public laundry. He takes some quarters out of his hat and puts them in a washing machine. In the morning he takes a bus to Fieldington. Wouldn't you? It's where the money is."

"Yeah, I know, where there's no competition," Sylvia said. "Someday I'm going to visit your hometown and make fun of it."

"Too easy. We're all rednecks," Elizabeth said. She pointed with her chin at the retreating homeless man. "Where do you think he's going?"

Sylvia sighed. "I guess it's none of our business."

"Whose is it then?" Elizabeth said.

IN ROSE'S CREAMERY, Elizabeth bought a hot fudge sundae. Sylvia wasn't hungry, but she bought a sherbet cone anyway to keep Elizabeth company. It did seem okay to spend their money on ice cream, instead of giving it to the homeless man. They would have had to chase him down the street to put it in his hat. They ate in silence in the heavily sweet smell of the place until Elizabeth blurted, "Jesus! Where does he go to the bathroom? Can you imagine living like that?"

"Maybe we should try it."

"What? Living like he does? Sleep in a doorway someplace?"

"Why not? Do it for a week. Learn how it feels."

Elizabeth put her hands out above the table, pretending to type. "Dear Mom and Dad, guess what I've been doing lately—helping my roommate with her term paper. The subject is really imaginative: where do homeless people crap? Experiential learning, three credits."

"It's not that bad an idea," Sylvia said. "You know it isn't."

"No, it's a great idea. The whole school should do it. We all move out and sleep on the sidewalks in Fieldington, and all the homeless people move into the dorms. You could write about how everybody in Fieldington just loves the idea."

Sylvia giggled.

"Yeah, I know. Funny, isn't it? But if it actually happened, it wouldn't change a thing."

The bell over the door rang, and a clutch of Miss Oliver ninth graders—freshwomen, in Oliver parlance—trooped in before Sylvia could think of her answer. They said hello, shyly, to the school's smartest scholar and to her friend, the premier athlete, and proceeded to order at the counter, babbling among themselves about some song they liked or didn't.

"Let's get out of here," Sylvia said.

Elizabeth picked up the bowl, slipped the remains of her sundae into her mouth, swallowed, grinned, and burped for everyone to hear. The bell over the door rang again as they left.

Outside, the farmers' market was being dismantled. The white canopies were spread out on the ground, like fallen clouds.

There is a kind of gloom that comes over the Miss Oliver's campus in the late afternoon on Sundays, when the relatively leisurely hours of that day are almost done and the relentless schedule of classes and assignments loom. Sylvia had sensed this on Sunday afternoons long before she'd been old enough to move from the status of faculty child to actual student. The feeling was most acute in the winter term when it was dark by five o'clock, but this Sunday, returning to campus, she felt the darkness even though the sun was still high and the leaves on the maples lining the paths had only begun to turn. She glanced at Elizabeth walking beside her. Did she feel it too?

The big clock in the library steeple said it was six o'clock. The girls were coming out of the dormitories and the library, heading for the dining hall. On Sunday nights, Sylvia and her mother always ate dinner with her dad in the Head's House. Right after dinner, her father would leave for his apartment in New York where he stayed during the week to be near the home office of Best Sports, the business he'd founded before Sylvia was born.

Starting the very first Sunday after she'd moved into the dorm, Sylvia had found herself wishing she could avoid this ritualistic family togetherness over dinner. Even though the dorm was only several hundred yards from the house she'd grown up in, she felt as if she were returning from a long trip, to parents who refused to recognize she'd ever left. And she was growing weary of trying to predict what would go on between her mom and dad as the time he would leave grew closer. Sometimes it seemed they couldn't wait until they could part and get on with their busied lives; other times they were just plain sad; and others it seemed that their resentment of each other's career dominated the mood they were both trying so hard to mute.

This evening Sylvia especially wanted a buffer between herself and their emotions. She knew that this had something to do with how she felt about the homeless man, but she didn't have time to figure that out because Elizabeth was about to leave her for the dining hall. "Would you like to eat with my parents and me tonight?" she asked suddenly.

Elizabeth looked doubtful. "Maybe they want to have you all to themselves."

"No, they'd love to have you too."

"All right. If you're sure," Elizabeth said.

SYLVIA, WITH ELIZABETH in tow, went through the big kitchen of the Head's House and then the even bigger living room, both designed to accommodate large groups, straight to where her parents would be: the little room behind the kitchen. Her dad had given it that name, the Little Room, with capital letters. It had its own fireplace. On a ledge of a bay window was an array of family photographs. Sylvia's father had inherited the rug on the floor. It was old and tired and didn't match the color of the walls, but he liked it there because, unlike this house, it belonged to him. The Little Room, where school-related functions never happened, was the only truly private place downstairs.

As they approached the closed door, they heard Sylvia's father talking. They were too far away to hear what he was saying, but they heard an excitement in in his tone, his voice rising. He just got an idea, Sylvia thought. Just this minute. And he's selling it already. She loved that about him. That's how he founded Best Sports and got rich, by coming up with ideas. Boom boom boom, one after another.

A few seconds later, when Sylvia and Elizabeth were almost at the door, the floor under Sylvia's step made a creaking sound, and he suddenly stopped talking. In that pregnant silence, the two girls looked at each other. "We're interrupting something," Elizabeth whispered. "No way I'm going in there."

"No! Stay!" Sylvia whispered. She took the last few steps to the door and pushed it open.

Her parents were sitting at opposite ends of the sofa, facing the door, rearranging their expressions from intense to neutral. "I invited Elizabeth for dinner," Sylvia announced, and, as if an afterthought, to hide the real reason she added, "She's tired of eating in the dining hall."

"Well, that's nice," Sylvia's father said, his tone failing to hide his frustration at being interrupted. Then, catching himself: "I mean, it's nice you're going to eat with us, Elizabeth, not that you're tired of eating in the dining hall."

Bob Bickham was a big man, not quite entirely bald. Sylvia thought him handsome and her mother absolutely beautiful, tall and thin, still a jock at age fifty-three. Sylvia was proud that her dad was white and her mother Black and that she was therefore both. Just the same, she was annoyed that, despite Elizabeth's presence, she'd have to face up to their moods. Glancing at the TV, which was not on, she said, "Dad, it's football season. How come you're not obsessing over the Giants game?"

"Because your mother and I were talking."

"Well then, I really do think I should leave," Elizabeth said.

"Absolutely not!" Sylvia's mom said, standing up. She seemed relieved, as if a danger had been thwarted. "You stay right here and eat with us."

Sylvia's dad stood too. "That's right, you stay. You're always welcome here, Elizabeth, you know that," he said, sounding to Sylvia almost too apologetic for his earlier reluctance. "There's tons left over from the fundraising thing last night. I hope you're hungry."

"I'm starving," Elizabeth said, grinning. "Haven't eaten since breakfast."

"Right," he, said, smiling now. "When Rachel told me you two went downtown, I knew you'd go right past all those yum yums in the farmers' market and not even stop to smell."

"I was in my office," her mom said. "I told your dad that if you had not been already so far away, I might have hurried to join you." She glanced at her husband, and added, shaking her head, "But then I thought, *helicopter parent.*" She put her hand up to her chin. "I've had it up to here with them. I wasn't about to become one. I stayed put."

"Is that really what you were talking about just now?" Sylvia asked. "How you didn't want to be a helicopter parent?"

"Partly," her dad said. "Yeah, that's *one* of the things we were talking about." He looked at his wristwatch. "Right now, let's help your mother get the dinner together. I have to leave for the city pretty soon."

"And Elizabeth and I have to get back to the dorm and study," Sylvia said, preparing the way for an early departure.

"That's right," he said. "Otherwise, Harvard, Yale, and Princeton will have a nervous breakdown."

"Oh Bob, not again," her mom murmured.

Her dad smiled. "And all the people in admissions departments all over the world will commit suicide."

Her mom raised her eyebrows at Sylvia and Elizabeth and headed for the kitchen.

In the kitchen, her dad made martinis for his wife and himself; then he poured two glasses of red wine for Elizabeth and Sylvia.

Sylvia saw her mom look away. They'd had this argument before, and he'd insisted that in their own house—even though it wasn't—on a weekend or a vacation, it was *their* rules, not the school's. They ate leftover appetizers from last night's fundraiser, slim pieces of cold smoked salmon on even thinner slices of cucumber, while they heated luxurious dinner remnants in the oven: filet mignon, potatoes au gratin, string beans. "Last night the menu was a la Francaise," her dad said. "Tonight, it's American. Red meat, cheesy spuds, and beans."

"And no speeches," her mom added. The martini had softened her mood.

They carried the food on trays into the Little Room and ate on their laps. Her dad was the first to speak. "What other amazing thing happened in Fieldington this afternoon besides your not eating?"

"Well, we met a homeless guy," Elizabeth said. "That's pretty amazing."

"In *Fieldington*. Did you give him money?"

"No."

"That's good. It's better to give to—"

"I know, Dad," Sylvia interrupted. "You've said that before."

He grinned. "Yeah, another lecture from dear old dad."

"We wanted to though," Elizabeth said. "But the minute he saw us, he bolted away."

"That was weird," Sylvia said. She drew a breath to explain, but in the presence of her parents she discovered an even stronger aversion to talking about the homeless man. He was her and Elizabeth's discovery, theirs to think about, no one else's.

So Elizabeth told instead. Her tone suggested that this was one of those things it is easier to talk to someone else's parents about than your own—and yet she managed to keep it matter-of-fact. She told what happened the first time, but when she told about the second, she left out that Sylvia had held on to the homeless man's hat and sign, making him tug, before she let go of them.

Her dad turned to Sylvia. "You called after him?"

Sylvia nodded. "He'd forgotten everything, Dad. His hat, his sign."

"The poor guy," her dad murmured. He pointed to his temple.

"He's probably not right up here. Of course you were right not to chase after him."

"But why do you think he wanted to get away?" her mom asked.

"I don't know, Mom."

"Of course you don't," her dad said. "You'd have to be a mind reader."

Silence then. There seemed to be nothing more to say.

"WHY DID WE get let her get away so fast?" Rachel asked as she and Bob stood in the doorway, still watching the girls walk away. The smell of the honeysuckle on the trellis did not reduce her anxiety. "It was like we didn't want her to be home with us."

Bob didn't turn his head to Rachel, his eyes still on the disappearing girls. The dormitories, clothed in white clapboard, green shutters framing the windows, and the library with its steeple seemed far away in the evening's fading light. When the girls had interrupted him, he'd been trying to sell Rachel on the idea that had just that moment come to him: that they each take a sabbatical from their work and go away someplace together. "So we can think," he'd said. "Certainly we don't have to stay home for Sylvia. Not now that she lives in the dorm, away from her parents, like every other girl in the school."

His idea had seemed to frighten Rachel. Her answer was an immediate no. He'd been about to push—"the school will still be here when you get back"—when he'd heard the footsteps on the other side of the door.

Now he was glad for the interruption. Dinner had given him time to realize something even more surprising. He didn't need a sabbatical, even a sabbatical he'd never taken. No, that idea was a disguise, prettying up the boogieman staring *him* in the face: maybe he needed to walk away from his business altogether. Sell it and start a whole new chapter in his life. He wouldn't bring *that* idea up again. And even if it were a good idea, he wouldn't bring it up now, just ten minutes before he and Rachel would say goodbye to each other.

Every weekend this moment came, the most relentless aspect of their lives. For the past nineteen years since Rachel had been appointed head of school, they been saying to each other, *It's only for a week*, but their time together was only for a weekend. With so little time to work things through, to feel their way like other couples who get out of the same bed every morning, how could their marriage not be in a permanent state of arrested development?

"I asked you a question," Rachel insisted. "Why were we in such a hurry to send our own daughter back to the dorm?"

"Because we want her to be a successful student at Miss Oliver's School for Girls, that's why." His tone was only mildly ironic.

"That's not what she wants though, is it?"

"She doesn't know what she wants, Rach."

Rachel turned to him. "You know what? Sometimes I don't either anymore."

She looked surprised by what she said. Then as if she'd realized she'd given him the opening he needed, she turned away from him and headed toward the kitchen. He stepped back from the doorway and closed the door. Now instead of the honeysuckle, he smelled the wax on the tiles of the floor and his heart went out to her. She'd surmounted everything that being Black in America, and a woman too, puts in the way in order to gain and, even harder, hold on to a position that had been so encompassing and so fulfilling—at least until recently—that she'd wonder who she was when she finally surrendered it.

So he'd say it to her back. Gentler, that way. She'd have time to prepare her expression. He followed her. Just as she entered the kitchen, he said it. "So maybe it's time to quit and find some other job."

She didn't turn around. But she did stop walking. "No!"

"Well then?"

He passed her and went through the cavernous living room, which he hated for being so huge, for hosting big groups, for raising money, keeping alumnae happy, for everything but being a home, and went to the Little Room, where he gathered the dishes and brought them to her in the kitchen. His *Well then?* hung in the air while they loaded the dishwasher together. Now the dishes were done. There was no task remaining for her to pretend to be focused on. He waited.

At last, she spoke. "There's something wrong. Something

missing. All these busy kids. Busy busy busy. That's what our daughter doesn't want."

"Yeah," he said, eager to agree. "I watch them hurrying here, hurrying there. Bent on success. They look like grown-ups already." He grinned. "Sometimes I'm surprised they're not wearing suits."

"Busy about what?" she said, ignoring his joke—if that's what it was. "Our daughter meets a homeless man. A human being who sleeps under bridges and gets his food in dumpsters. She's so disturbed she can't talk to us about it. And we send her back to do *homework*?"

"Well, it *is* a *school*." Just then the phone rang. He ignored it. "Maybe you want something more now—after nineteen years."

But he'd already lost her. There on the calendar posted on the wall just above the phone in big red marker letters: *7:30–8:30 Conference call, Executive Committee.* It was her Head of School phone, for school business. The other landline was private, almost never used. "Oh damn!" he said.

"Sorry, I thought you'd be gone by now, and I'd forgotten all about the call."

He heard in her tone how sorry she really was, but he saw her attention turn entirely. Her expression grew composed, attentive, empty of pain.

"Yes, this is Rachel."

He went upstairs to their bedroom, picked up his suitcase, which he'd already packed, and returned to the kitchen.

"Just one minute," she said, into the phone. "I have to say goodbye to my husband." She held the phone away from herself with her right hand and entered his outstretched arms, touching the back of his neck with the fingers of her left hand. He imagined the five people on the other end of the line listening, so he only brushed his lips on her cheek. Then he released her and she put the phone against her ear again and waved to him as he walked away.

On the drive back to the city, his mind too turned to the coming week, a focus, an eagerness, under which the darkness floated. He, too, had crossed a demarcation, like a line on a map, into a world of his own.

And tonight, Rachel would sleep in the single bed in a guest room down the hall from the master bedroom where, without his knowing, she always slept when he was away. It felt less lonely not to sleep in the place where they slept together—when they could.

LIKE ALL THE others, the dorm room to which Elizabeth and Sylvia were headed was small. This because the disease which Miss Edith Oliver, who founded the school in 1927, considered most pernicious to her students was affluenza. There would be no luxury in any of the accommodations—except for the Head's House, where commodiousness was necessary for raising money, and where she had lived in the servants' quarters. In the dorms, Sylvia's and Elizabeth's room on the first floor was narrow, like a section of a hall. Along the right wall were two bureaus and two desks. Along the left was a small closet and two bunks, one above the other. Sylvia, being more agile, slept in the upper one. There was a white curtain made of heavy material that could be closed in front of the bunks so one girl could sleep if the other stayed up late with the light on to study. Directly opposite the door, a small window gave out on the campus. More often than not, during the winter, after the maintenance department had removed the screens, the girls came and went through the window. It was fun to imagine being a burglar, and it was more direct than coming through the front door and then walking down the hall

That evening, in that tiny room, Elizabeth read way ahead in her history text, stopping every once in a while to help Sylvia with her math. They went to bed very late. In the dark, Sylvia remembered how matter-of-fact Elizabeth had been when she told about their transactions with the homeless man. She was hiding their feelings about his presence in their lives from Rachel, the head of school, so they could have further transaction with him. But what would those transactions be?

Just before Elizabeth fell asleep, Sylvia said, "Thanks for not telling how I held on to his hat and sign."

"I almost did," Elizabeth said. "Then I thought, whoops, that might complicate things. So I didn't."

"You're probably right, it might have," Sylvia said. She was glad she'd had Elizabeth's company when she'd been so close to human wreckage she could smell it.

But only minutes later, Sylvia heard the steady rhythm of Elizabeth's breathing and knew she was asleep. Sometimes Sylvia was jealous of her friend, maybe even a little bit angry at her, for knowing how to get through every day with so little fuss.

ONE THING ELIZABETH couldn't do anywhere near as well as Sylvia was run—not even if she wanted to. Sylvia had inherited the passion from her mother, along with her long legs and skinny hips, though if you asked her, she wouldn't call it a passion any more than her mother would. It was a need, one that for Sylvia soccer almost satisfied in the fall and basketball in winter, especially the wind sprints after practice, and track in the spring.

On an afternoon in the first week of October, the soccer coach ended practice early because the players were exhausted. It was midterm exam week and none of them had had enough sleep. But to rest her body was exactly what Sylvia didn't need. So she started to run across the soccer and lacrosse field to where a trail led through some woods down to the Connecticut River, and then along another trail that ran beside it. For both her mother and Sylvia, it was a favorite run.

She ran along a bluff above the river, breathing easy, feeling the smoothness of her stride, the soothing rhythm, and release of tension. The woods around her were yellow and gold. Her mind turned off. She wasn't happy or sad or tense or relaxed. She just was. The trail descended from the bluff to the level of the river, and she ran on and on, beside the river, past the time when she knew she should turn around if she wanted to get back to school in time to shower and get to dinner. Up ahead, a hundred yards or so, a big blown-down tree reached out into the river, obscuring her view of it. She would stop and turn around there.

But she didn't account for reducing her stride to slow down so she could turn, and she ran a few yards past the tree before she stopped and turned and saw a man rinsing himself in the river. He was naked, facing away, scooping a handful of water with his left hand up to his right armpit in the privacy of the space behind the tree. His skin was pale and hairless. There was a dark smudge of dirt on his back where he couldn't reach to wash. She saw the outline of his ribs. His buttocks, the crack between. About him there was none of that protective neutrality that enveloped ancient Greek statues, mere images in her Arts History course.

In a wave of embarrassment, she turned to escape before he would know, but he turned to walk out of the river at that same instant, and they stared at each other and he covered himself with his hands. He had that same shamed look on his face, intensified a hundred times over. "Oh, I'm so sorry!" she said, and turned and ran.

FOUR

That look on her face, when she'd dropped the dollars in. She smelled him. That's why he washed now. Every day. And a mother and father and two little kids walking past as far away as they could.

His clothes were still wet from washing them too, this second time. He'd hung them on branches to dry in the sun. He hoped she hadn't seen them. Everybody has to get naked to get clean. *Really clean. Really clean.* But underpants hanging on a branch? He'd shitted himself once. Browned his underpants. That's why.

Outside of Fallujah. They hadn't even gone in yet. But he'd already killed the girl, ran his truck over her to avoid the sniper fire, and he was remembering. That was why. There were lots of things he couldn't remember. Concussive brain damage, they said. Anger problems and loss of memory. From IEDs. But killing the girl he would always remember. She was tall and thin, like the one who'd just seen him naked, standing in a river, trying to clean himself. It was happening all over again.

Then he walked out of the river. Then he went to his lean-to. Its roof and sides and floor he'd made by weaving pine tree branches together. Then he went in. Then he unrolled his sleeping bag. Then he got into it. One thing at a time keeps you calm. He'd wait in the bag until his clothes were dry. But in the bag, he felt more naked than outside in the air. He wasn't surprised. When you are brainfucked, the only thing that surprises is that you're not. He crawled out of the bag and pulled the woven pine branches across the opening to shut himself in. He liked the piney smell of the lean-to; it made him think of the smell of balsam, which he liked even better. *On Osgood Pond near Saranac.* He would think about that. That's what he would think about. He'd think about that to keep himself calm. He got into the sleeping bag again. Tomorrow, if the weather looked like it might last long enough for a sleeping bag to dry in the sun, he'd wash that too.

On Osgood Pond near Saranac. He said it aloud to hear the sound. Saranac. Saranac. It didn't need notes to be a song. In the evening the wind always died and the lake would still, and the barn swallows would start to fly. Uncle Ray would say, *Take the Adirondack guide boat, Chris. It glides, you can row it sitting forwards, it's a canoe married to a dory.*

But when he told the VA doc all the things that had happened in just one instant and the doc said, *Yes, time slows down in combat,* he'd jumped up from his chair. "How the fuck do you know? You never been there." And he never went back.

Even though Uncle Ray would've liked the guide boat for himself. *No, that's all right, Chris. You take it tonight. I'll fish at dawn. I love to watch the sun come up.* He knew the girl who'd seen him naked wasn't the one he'd run over. She was the one who'd bent down to move his hat. He wasn't so crazy he didn't know what was happening, why every girl who looked like she was about to be a woman was the girl he'd run over. But now it was only this one, tall, thin, like the one he'd killed. And why he'd been sure she and her friend had come back again to punish him, to make it happen all over again, again, when they probably just happened to be at the same place he was at the same time because they wanted ice cream so maybe he wouldn't have hurt her to make her stay away—but not the other one, her big blonde friend, she hadn't seen him naked, he wouldn't need to hurt her, and he said aloud over and over the words: *Uncle Ray would say. Uncle Ray would say.* Because those words soothed him too—until he was sure his clothes were dry, or dry enough, and he wouldn't be naked anymore, and he crawled out of his sleeping bag and left it unzipped for tonight and moved the woven pine branches aside from the opening and went out. And gathered up his clothes. And put them on. As fast as he could.

"YOU SURE?" ELIZABETH said.

"Yes, I'm sure. I'd recognize him anywhere," Sylvia said.

"Yeah, but without any clothes on? That's a shock. You could be associating. You know what I mean?"

"But I saw his *face.*"

"First?"

"Yes, *first.* I told you. And *then* he put his hands down there. Whaddaya mean, 'associating'? Associating with what?"

"You know. We've been thinking about him, wondering where he lives. So you see some guy who's maybe just taking a swim."

"I keep telling you, I saw his face. How many people do you know who'd go swimming there? And without any clothes on? He was *washing* himself."

"All right. If you're convinced, so am I."

"Why did it take you so long? You think I make stuff up?"

Elizabeth shrugged. "No, but people do imagine stuff. You think he lives there? In a cave or something?"

"I don't know. Maybe."

"Well, I know how we can find out: put some food near where you saw him. If it's gone when we come back, then we'll know."

Sylvia didn't speak for a moment. She couldn't come up with a better idea. The one thing they couldn't do was just pretend she hadn't seen him. "Canned food," she said. "So animals can't get it. And a can opener."

"Right. And I think a grill to put over the fire so he can cook."

"Yeah, definitely a grill and can opener," Sylvia said. "Those are things he can keep."

"After that, we'll stop. Right?"

"Stop?"

"Bringing him food," Elizabeth said. "Just one time and then we'll stop. We don't want to be all alone in the woods with him. We should drop the stuff and get out of there. But he probably doesn't live there. The food will be still there when we sneak back. How many people do you know who live in the woods like a hermit?"

"Okay, we'll drop the stuff and run. We can always give him money in Fieldington."

"Yeah," Elizabeth said. "Right into his hat. Just don't tell your dad."

CHRISTOPHER TRIPLETT, DURING one of his more stable mental states, thought that one of the weirdest things about his situation was how worried he was that the food he ate at McDonald's would clog up his veins. And the other weird thing was that it didn't do any good to know he was being weird. Instead of worrying about starving right now, he worried about having a heart attack twenty years hence all through the whole long walk from the ice cream shop in the middle of the village to the McDonald's on the outskirts of town, where the money he'd begged for bought a Big Mac (for the protein) with tomato and lettuce (because vegetables were good for you) and a paper cup of milk (because milk was calming). Another thing about being brainfucked: he could actually see his veins, ruby-red pipes and yellow sludge. He could see the transparent plastic cups of yogurt topped with fruit they served in Starbucks too, and he didn't stink because he'd taken a bath and washed his clothes, but the barista would know where he got the money. She would look at him across the counter while he handed it to her and he would see the girl through the windshield, just before he ran over her. The look on her face wouldn't be her fear, not even her disappointment. It would be realization. *I am about to die. And this is how.*

Several days after the girl had seen him naked in the river, Christopher Triplett, early in the morning, the sun just risen, was taking a piss downhill, well away from his lean-to like any good camper, and remembering how he and his friends in seventh grade used to make their yellow initials in the snow where they hoped the girls would find them, when suddenly he caught a glimpse of two girls through a screen of bushes. He froze, wished he was through; and when he was, he crouched and slithered further away from them, uphill toward a big outcropping of granite to hide behind. Had word gone out that there was a guy hiding in the woods? Was this the girl who'd watched him taking a bath, bringing her friend in hopes of watching again?

He couldn't see them anymore now, nor hear their movements, nor what they said—only the insistent clack of a woodpecker hammering in a tree above him, and the smell of dead leaves and wet earth he crouched in. His craziness hadn't blossomed until he'd come home to the never-never land of post deployment when you didn't have to be at the ready, on the lookout every minute. Now it was a strange relief to be in that hyper-alert state again, calmer than when he wasn't. He waited a while, then he slithered on his stomach down the hill to get close enough to see them. Instead, he saw the sun glinting on something metal. He stood and approached whatever it was, wondering if the girls were watching and laughing at him, and found they had left something. A can opener. A lighter. A can of tomatoes. A can of beans. Of minestrone soup. Clam chowder in the red and white of Campbell's, like in that famous picture.

They were mocking him!

He starts running up the trail to catch up with them, yelling, *Stay away! Stay away or I'll—* They stop, turn around and laugh. He runs toward them, the axe that he'd built his lean-to with raised over his head in both hands, ready to chop down into the exact center of the top of the tall, thin one's head, splitting it in two, like a log on a tree stump. Their laughter turns to astonishment. There is a sudden darkness, as if he'd closed his eyes. He stops running.

Then it was light again and the girls were gone.

His hands were empty. He was still standing by the food they'd left. His axe was sunk deep into a tree stump by the firepit, where it belonged. He didn't have to turn around and see it there to know. *Take comfort in that,* he thought, *comfort in that. And take comfort in what I take comfort in.* He turned back and piled leaves over the food and the other things the girls had left for him. Then he walked the few yards to the edge of the river and watched it flow. After a while, he was sane again.

FIVE

At Miss Oliver's School for Girls, all new students, which include the entire Freshwomen class, are required to join at least one of the several clubs. The choice must be made during orientation days, which precede the start of regular classes. For Elizabeth, future politician, the Debate Team had been an obvious choice. For Sylvia, who thought she might like to learn to sing and who loved outdoor sports like canoeing, hiking, and rock climbing almost as much as she loved soccer, basketball, and track, the choice had been between the Capella Chorus and the Outdoor Adventure Club. She had flipped a coin—heads, Capella; tails, Outdoor Adventure. It had come up tails. Now, four years later, she was proud to be the recently elected president of the Outdoor Adventure Club, overseer extraordinaire of events, scheduled, like those of the other clubs, on the fourth weekend of each month. On that fourth weekend, no team games were scheduled so that everyone could participate in a club event.

But lately Sylvia had begun to regret not having joined the Capella Chorus. What she hadn't known when she'd flipped that coin was how unusually talented and inspirational the recently arrived choral teacher would turn out to be. What Sylvia also was ignorant of—because her mother wouldn't talk about such things with students—was how she, as head of school, made her decisions about which teachers to retain and whom to ease out, gently if possible, of course; newly hired teachers had three years of probation to grow from "excellent" to "unusually superlative." As Eudora Easter, the unusually superlative chair of the Art Department, often said: *People don't know what superlative means until they see it. You have to surprise them. Then they know.* The chorus teacher who had been in place the year before Sylvia's freshwoman year had not made that progress, and so Rachel had eased her out of Miss Oliver's employ, supplying truthful recommendations describing her excellence, so that she was immediately hired by a prestigious coed school where it was said she was much admired—and quite content.

The new chorus teacher's positive impact on the chorus was obvious from the beginning. Sylvia attended every performance. Her schoolmates' assembled voices, floating out from the stage into the auditorium, struck a bell of yearning in her that she wouldn't even try to describe. Never mind that as soon as the performance was over she forgot. She would experience it again at the next performance.

Looking back at that time she'd been so childish she flipped a coin rather than making a decision, she was a little embarrassed with herself. Elizabeth, in contrast, had been decisive. And right away, she'd been a star debater. Hands down, she'd blown away the opposition in her first debate, proving beyond the skills of everyone else that the Miss Oliver's School for Girls' community service program was a shadow of what it should be, mere window dressing, precisely because students got credit for it. "If the reward is academic credit, how can service be the purpose?" she had asked. The rebuttal, according to the judges, had failed to persuade.

Now, as Sylvia was president of the Outdoor Adventure Club, Elizabeth was president of the Debate Team. Sylvia loyally attended every debate, and Elizabeth, while refusing to go on even the least adventurous outdoor adventure, often accompanied Sylvia in doing her presidential work: organizing, inventorying equipment, and doing the bookkeeping. Gloria Buchanan, faculty advisor to the Outdoor Adventure Club, was so impressed by Sylvia's leadership that she'd delegated the responsibility of keeping track of the finances to Sylvia.

On the evening of the same day that Sylvia and Elizabeth had left the food and can opener in the woods for the homeless man, Sylvia recorded the expense of the recent purchase of a dozen brand-new black down jackets in the club's accounting book. A chill swept through the room, so Elizabeth got up from her desk to close the window. On the way back, she looked over Sylvia's shoulder and said, "You should be doing your homework. Let Gloria do that boring stuff. She gets paid." Then, noticing a number Sylvia had just recorded: "Holy shit, two hundred and fifty bucks for each down jacket! And there's twelve of them?"

"Yeah, I know, but they're for snow camping," Sylvia said, trying not to sound defensive. She knew what Elizabeth would say next. The thought had come to her too. How could it not have after what they'd done just this morning? But she'd pushed it away. After all, when you sleep outdoors in the snow, you could die of hypothermia without the right clothing.

"We just left food in the woods for a guy who sleeps outdoors because he has to," Elizabeth said. "And this school buys two-hundred-and-fifty-dollar down jackets for kids so they can sleep outdoors because they *want* to. How fuckin' crazy is that?" She landed hard on her chair, her face tight. "Most of the kids already have down jackets. They need them when they go skiing in Switzerland on Christmas vacation."

"Don't get bitter on me, okay?" Sylvia said. "It could get boring."

Elizabeth shrugged her shoulders and turned back to her work.

SYLVIA HAD NEVER been a dreamer. Deep, eventless sleep had always been a place she entered effortlessly. She took this for granted. Why else go to bed? But on the August night she had moved into the dorm, a feeling of expectancy, of waiting for something to happen, had clicked inside her. Now, several weeks later, she still had the same strange feeling of having moved a long distance away from where she nevertheless still resided. It was a kind of limbo, made of contradiction, that she was vaguely aware of, like background music in a movie, subtly dreamlike in itself. She'd lie awake long after Elizabeth had fallen asleep. Often, as Elizabeth's alarm clock would sound in the morning, Sylvia would awake from a dream, at once feeling rescued from its weird vivid logic and wishing she could remember it. What surprised her was not that this was happening. It was that she was glad for it.

In the early morning of the day after she and Elizabeth had left the food for the homeless man, Sylvia dreamed she was standing by the river watching him bend down to scoop water with his right hand up to his left armpit. Her heart lurched. She yearned to offer soap, a towel. Then he turned around. Their eyes met, and the space beside the blown-down tree became the most private place she'd ever been. Elizabeth's alarm shattered the moment, and Sylvia awoke.

The next night, when the dream returned, long before dawn, Sylvia already knew what she was going to do when he turned and they looked at each other. She peeled off her sweater, unbuttoned her shirt, unbuckled the belt of her jeans, slowly, slowly undressing herself, until at last she was as vulnerable as he, no more, no less. She stepped naked into the river. The dream ended there as she woke up.

There was no way she could go back to sleep, and she was too restless just to lie in bed while Elizabeth obliviously slept on. She climbed down out of her upper bunk. "What?" Elizabeth murmured, then rolled over and was quiet again, and Sylvia tiptoed out into the hall and down to the common room and turned on the light.

The common room smelled of pizza. The grease-stained cardboard box it had arrived in sat on a coffee table next to two opened cans of Coke. Sylvia had never noticed before this moment how inanimate and mute and hostile a space could be when you are hyper awake, alone, in the middle of the night. She wished the furniture could move on its own. She turned off the light so she wouldn't have to look at the mess. Still, there was the smell.

Outside on the lawn, a yellow square of light from her dorm parent's window announced that Eudora Easter was still awake, working in her studio. Prodigiously talented as an art teacher, Eudora was like a second mother to Sylvia. She was short and round, wore floor-length dresses in vibrant colors and big earrings. She was one of Sylvia's mother's closest friends, and, like Sylvia and her mom, a person of color.

After a while the light from Eudora's studio went out. In a minute she would walk through the dorm, just in case a girl might need her for any of the reasons any girl might need a mother in the middle of the night—and also to make sure no one was breaking any rules. Eudora as dorm police was no worry for Sylvia. Sylvia didn't know any boy she cared enough about to sneak him into the dorm, or for that matter her own room in the Head's House, in the middle of the night, and she just didn't happen to be interested in drugs, or liquor. And only an idiot would want to smoke.

Nevertheless, she didn't want to explain to Eudora why she was awake in the middle of the night.

She moved from the window and nestled herself down into the sofa as far as she could, hoping Eudora would assume the common room was empty and not turn on the light. Seconds later, the door opened and then came the sound of Eudora's hand sliding around the wall to find the switch, and then the click, and the room was so suddenly bright Sylvia had to close her eyes.

"Ugh! Pizza. What a mess," Eudora murmured. Then she discovered she wasn't alone. "Sylvia! What are *you* doing up?"

Sylvia opened her eyes. Eudora stood just inside the door, a mother figure, round and soft and knowing.

"You all right, hon? I saw the light go on and then off. I thought I should check."

"I couldn't sleep."

"Your mom never told me you had trouble sleeping."

"I had a weird dream, that's all."

Eudora nodded. "That'll do it. Every time."

"But I'm good now." Sylvia stood up and crossed the room toward the door.

But Eudora put out her hand. "Whyn't you come into my place and I give you some warm milk?"

Eudora's square hand, brown like her own, was warm and soft and firm all at once, and her apartment was as familiar to Sylvia as the Head's House, a neutral space she'd been wandering in and out of since she could remember. Eudora's apartment was a museum for her work: murals created directly on the walls, painted over when a new urge came, ephemera being more interesting to Eudora than permanence—except for the four life-size, utterly realistic human models, two men, two women, dressed in evening clothes, who sat around the dining room table, arresting time for as long as Sylvia could remember. Sometimes, when Eudora had guests, she moved these aside. Other times, the guest joined them.

Sylvia now took a place among them. All the dining room windows were open and she was vaguely aware of the sound of crickets. Eudora went into the kitchen to prepare the milk. It was comforting to sit around the table with Eudora's guests, old friends, while she listened to Eudora in the kitchen, the hum of the microwave. If anyone of them had asked Sylvia right then who was the smarter, her mother or Eudora, she would have said her mother; but if the question were who was the wiser, she would have said Eudora—who was coming through the doorway now, with two big mugs of milk.

Eudora sat across the table next to the handsome middle-aged white woman, whose low-cut evening gown revealed just enough of her waxen cleavage to entice some to stare and others to look away. "Sometimes it's good to talk about your dreams," Eudora said.

Oh, all right, Sylvia thought. *I'll start at the beginning.* She told how she and Elizabeth gave money to a homeless guy in Fieldington and how surprising that was, and how they came back the next weekend. "To see if he was still there," she said, leaving out her revelation in calculus class. She hadn't even told Elizabeth. So why would she tell Eudora?

"And was he still there?"

"Yeah, he was. But as soon as he saw us, he practically ran away."

"He did? He didn't want your money?"

"It wasn't that. He must have thought we'd come back to mock him," Sylvia said, holding back that she had held on to the homeless man's hat. She remembered how grateful she was that Elizabeth had held that part back too. She went on from there quickly describing both dreams, confessing that the person without any clothes on washing himself in the river was the same homeless guy. She didn't reveal that she had actually seen the homeless man naked in the river.

"Interesting," Eudora murmured. 'You tell your parents any of this?'

"I told them about meeting him that first time and giving him money, and about how the second time he walked away as soon as he saw us," Sylvia said, then corrected herself. "Actually, Elizabeth told."

"You didn't want to? Too disturbing? Not to have shelter is a bit like being naked, maybe?"

"Yeah, I guess."

"And you certainly didn't tell them about your dreams."

Sylvia shook her head.

"I wouldn't have either. Not with a naked guy in them. Was he young?"

Sylvia had to think. "Yes, but he looked—"

"Like he'd done things you haven't?"

Sylvia nodded. She couldn't think of any better way to describe how young or old he seemed.

"Well, girl, it sounds to me like it's just hormones, that's all. They're really good at keeping folks awake."

"No! I just wanted to give him soap and a towel."

"Well, there's that too," Eudora said. "And anyway, I would have done the same as you."

"Really?" Sylvia asked. She would tell everything if Eudora said yes.

"Oh yes," Eudora said, "as long as it was just a dream. But in real life? Are you kidding? Take my clothes off and get in a river with a naked guy? Why do you think you stopped dreaming just as you stepped into the river?"

Sylvia didn't answer.

"Why?" Eudora persisted.

"Because I couldn't even imagine what would happen if—"

"That's it, hon," Eudora said. "People do things in dreams they'd never do in real life. Right?"

"Right," Sylvia said.

"Good. Now drink your milk." Eudora took a sip of her own.

Sylvia took one too. It did feel calming.

"Listen to those crickets. Aren't they something?" Eudora said.

Sylvia listened, surprised by how loud the sound was, a signal of the end of summer floating in through the open windows.

"You ready to sleep?"

"I'm ready," Sylvia lied, planting a goodbye kiss on Eudora's cheek. She understood now that she and Elizabeth were on their own. Every adult they knew, even Eudora, would tell them to keep their distance from the homeless man. She tiptoed back to the room and climbed into her upper bunk where she stayed awake, imagining a younger Eudora dreaming she was naked, about to step into the river. Would *she* know all the reasons why she dreamed such a thing? Sylvia didn't think so.

The guy was naked, after all. And instead of running, she took off her clothes too. To be equal? To be fair? Because why should he be the only one? And she did feel a twinge, didn't she? Of course, she did, just as curious as any seventeen-year-old who so far, anyway, was still a virgin. Yes, a stirring, standing on the bank of the river, like when she'd bent to put the money in his hat and then stood up and their eyes had locked and, even through the smell of him, she'd sensed his body.

And what did *he* see? Who was that other girl he recognized? If she had stepped into the river, instead of waking up, would she have learned?

She didn't know. But she did know that when the winter would come, he'd need warm clothes.

"SO WHAT ELSE is new?" Rachel asked herself, across the campus in her single bed. Who in her shoes wouldn't be sleepless in the middle of the night where a million bad things could happen to the three hundred girls in her charge? But that didn't work; it didn't calm her down and make her sleepy. Because before her daughter had gone away—that's how she thought about it: *away*, as if Sylvia had traveled to the other side of the world—Rachel never had much trouble sleeping. Now sometimes in the middle of the night, she wanted to get out of bed and cross the campus to make sure the copper beech tree outside her office—*her* copper beech, is how she thought of it—whose leaves had begun to look dry and crinkled to her, shriven of the juices of life, was still alive; other times, she wanted to go straight to Sylvia's dorm.

She got out of bed, went downstairs instead, and heated a cup of milk in the microwave, then sat in a chair and sipped it in the dark. That also didn't feel calming at all. Didn't taste good either. Like cold milk does. But she sipped at it anyway, gazing out the window at the night. When the milk was gone, she stood up to go back upstairs and try again for sleep.

Just then, the light came on in Eudora's kitchen across the campus. A big square of yellow light against the black. Much more calming than warm milk, vastly more reassuring. Thank God for beloved friends! Eudora was sleepless too, in her kitchen, warming milk at two in the morning. No one in the whole wide world did she trust more, no other two names, *Eudora*, *Easter*, ever matched a person so well.

The only other person who came close, at least since their father had died, was Rachel's sister, Marian. Rachel looked forward to her annual visit over the winter vacation. But Rachel did worry that Marian's absolute certainty about the rightness of the way she was spending her life as a community organizer—afflicting the oppressor, comforting the afflicted—would be hard to tolerate. Until lately, this sureness had been one of the traits they'd shared. Marian was a good example of Rachel's belief that, when you are lucky enough to have a choice of profession, what you choose is who you are.

Rachel sat back down in the chair, keeping her eyes on Eudora's window. Bathing herself in its glow, she went to sleep.

When she woke up—how long after, she didn't know—the light in Eudora's kitchen window was gone. Rachel climbed the stairs again into the upstairs hall. To enter the master bedroom she would turn left, but she turned right, of course, past Sylvia's empty bedroom, and entered her own, and though she knew she wouldn't fall asleep again, she got back into her single bed. So maybe helicopter parents aren't overanxious, after all, she told herself.

Maybe they're just lonely.

THE NEXT DAY while Sylvia played in an away soccer game, the last of the season, Elizabeth walked down to Colonial Hardware Store in the village to buy—with Sylvia's money—the grill the homeless man would put over his firepit. That is, if he *did* live near where Sylvia had seen him taking a bath in the river.

But if he did live there, how was he going to get food to cook after she and Sylvia stopped bringing it to him? Because they were going to stop, weren't they? Two girls alone, deep in the woods, with a homeless guy who could do anything he wants to them? Or at least try to. They'd have to revert to putting money in his hat on weekends. Two dollars each, four bucks total, maybe three each, and count on other people to put the rest in his hat so he could buy food and carry it himself into the woods and cook it on the grill.

She also bought a few more cans of food since they were going out there anyway.

She took a cab back to the school because she had chosen, out of several, the most solid, most durable grill with thick rungs. It was too heavy to carry all the way back to the school, and besides, if anyone asked her, *What are you doing with that?* she wouldn't have an answer. Once word got out there was a homeless man living in the woods, then other girls would want to join her and Sylvia and bring him stuff too. Everybody would think, *Look how kind we're being!* And then the teachers would find out because nobody keeps a secret. *Then we'd be made to stop. Yes, I know: we're going to stop anyway.* But it's different when you decide for yourself.

Halfway home, it occurred to her that if the homeless man didn't live near where Sylvia had seen him, he would have to carry this load to wherever he did live—and who knows if you can even cook there? What good is a grill on a sidewalk? And maybe he really does actually live in a shelter someplace and takes a bus to Fieldington every morning. The grill would stay there in the woods. Someday, long from now, someone might come across it and wonder who had cooked here, and why in *this* place?

The cab driver offered to help her load the things into the dorm. She told him thanks, but men were not allowed. He seemed embarrassed to have asked. She managed to sneak the grill and cans into the dorm and shoved them under her bunk where, since they were only going to be there for one day, they wouldn't be seen. That evening at dinner she told several students she'd made a pre-New Year's resolution to get in shape, become a great runner like her roommate, so when she and Sylvia were seen running toward the river, people wouldn't ask questions. Maybe she'd even keep on after they quit with the homeless man and actually get in shape.

Bullshit! She was sick and tired of wishing she was built like a fucking Barbie Doll. From now on she was going to be like Eudora Easter, who obviously reveled in being exactly what she was: soft and round and fat. Elizabeth was going to make Extra Large the thing to wear as the first big, round female president of the United States. Legs like redwood trees, tummy like a barrel, arms that jiggled when she waved to the crowd. Robustness as power. After *her* eight years in the White House, there wouldn't be one girl, not one in the whole United States of America, who wished she was built like she had tapeworms.

And there wouldn't be any homeless people either. There would be a warm, safe place to live for everybody. Everybody! She'd see to that.

AT FIRST LIGHT of the next day, Elizabeth huffed and puffed beside Sylvia as they jogged across the campus. "Slow down," she said through gasps. "We don't have to go this fast to be convincing." But even with the grill strapped to her back under her sweat suit where it couldn't be seen, Sylvia kept running just as fast.

When they reached the woods and were out of sight, Elizabeth stopped running and bent over.

Sylvia stopped too and said, "Stand up straight. When you bend like that, it compresses your lungs and makes it worse."

"I'm bending over so I won't puke on myself."

"There's nothing to puke. You haven't had breakfast yet."

Sylvia waited until Elizabeth got some of her breath back, and then they walked the rest of the way. They put the grill and the cans down where they would be easy to see, next to a pile of leaves. One of the cans they'd left the first time was sticking through the leaves. They brushed the leaves back and saw that everything they had brought was still where they had left it, untouched. "So he doesn't live here," Sylvia said. She felt a keen disappointment.

Elizabeth didn't answer. She was looking away, up the hill. Sylvia followed her gaze. "Oh, but he does!" Elizabeth said, pointing, and Sylvia also saw the lean-to. It was green because of its sheath of pine boughs; and though it was fairly big, about four feet high and six or seven feet wide and just as deep, it blended with its surroundings. The two girls crouched down so as not to be seen. "He must be still asleep," Elizabeth whispered. "Let's get out of here before he wakes up."

"Wait," Sylvia whispered. She wanted to see him come out of his lair into the morning.

"Don't be crazy!" Elizabeth squirmed backwards, still on her stomach. "Come on!"

Sylvia stayed a few seconds more, watching the lean-to before she too squirmed backwards on her stomach. She kept her eyes on it, hoping for a sight of him, until she came up against a screen of bushes. She squirmed around them and stood up. Elizabeth was waiting there, shaking her head. Then, careful to make no noise, they headed back.

Just before they came out of the woods and began to jog again, straight to the dining hall, Elizabeth said, "I know why he hasn't eaten the food. Winter's coming. He's saving it for then, like a squirrel."

That evening they decided that what he also needed, when the winter came, was a down jacket, warm gloves, a wool hat, and a pair of boots. Then he would be fully equipped to live without their help and they really could stop.

"You're the president of the Outdoor Adventure Club," Elizabeth said, as if Sylvia didn't know. "You've got the key to the shed."

SIX

At two o'clock the next morning when they hoped everybody would be asleep, Elizabeth opened the door to the room a small way and stuck her head out into the hall.

"All clear?" Sylvia asked. Her right hand, tucked into her pocket, gripped the key to the Outdoor Adventure Club's equipment shed. The only other person who had one was faculty advisor to the club Gloria Buchanan, and thinking about her brought up the questions all over again for Sylvia. Was Elizabeth as surprised as she was that they were actually going to do this thing?

But Elizabeth was already out into the hall. Sylvia followed, rounding her shoulders, stooping low.

The hall was brightly lit as Eudora Easter insisted: *In an emergency, we don't want to be stumbling around in the dark looking for the light switch.* The two girls tiptoed in that glaring light, carrying their sneakers in their hands past the closed doors of their dormmates' rooms and through the front door into the darkness outside. Avoiding the lighted path, they forgot to put their sneakers on until a few steps on the dampness of the not-quite-frozen lawn alarmed them. They stopped and crammed their feet into the sneakers, bending down to tie them as fast as they could, then hurried on, seeking the darkest way. The campus was alien in its silence. It seemed to be holding its breath.

The gymnasium loomed before them in the dark. The equipment shed was on the far side, affixed to the back wall at the edge of a parking area. They ran down the side of the building and then around the corner into the parking lot and stopped. Ahead, the shed was in a bright pool of light, shining down from lamps on the gymnasium roof. No sane burglar would dare step into that light, and there was no way of knowing when the security patrol car would come by here on its rounds.

"You didn't know about the lights?" Elizabeth whispered. She left the rest unsaid: *You live here. Your own mother's the head.*

Sylvia was embarrassed. "How would I know? I've never had to be in the shed after dark."

"Well, you still want to?" Elizabeth said.

"Do you?"

Elizabeth hesitated.

"Come on! We have to decide. We stand here much longer, the sun will be up."

"All right, here goes!" Elizabeth ran toward the light. Sylvia sprinted past her and got there first. The shed was painted white. The light bounced off it. Any brighter and they would have to squint.

Sylvia reached in her pocket for the key to the padlock. It caught on the pocket's lining as she tried to withdraw it. "Hurry up!" Elizabeth whispered. Sylvia tugged hard, and still the key wouldn't come out. She reached across her hips with her other hand and with both hands in her pocket, ripped the key out, tearing the cloth. She held the key up triumphantly to Elizabeth, a wisp of cloth dangling from it like a tiny banner.

"Look what I found!" she announced, giggling.

Elizabeth stared at her for a second; then she giggled too.

Sylvia poked the key into the padlock. It wouldn't go in. "I got the wrong key!" she whispered.

"No you don't. It's upside down."

"Oh!" Sylvia turned the key right side up. It went in easily. The padlock snapped open. She pulled the door open. It made a loud scraping noise. Sylvia giggled again, turning to face an imagined audience. "Thanks for making me president of the club." Holding up the key for everyone to see. "It makes it so much easier to steal things from it." She put the key back in her pocket. Elizabeth shoved her chest and Sylvia entered the shed backwards. Elizabeth followed.

If the security guy came by, the first thing he'd see was the open door, so they pulled it shut, and now they were in the pitch dark, totally blind. "Turn on your cell phone light," Sylvia said.

"Oh shit, I forgot it! You too?"

"Yeah, me too!"

Elizabeth opened the door partway again to let the light in. "Some burglars we are!"

Sylvia knew where everything was stored. It didn't take them long to gather one of the new down jackets, which Elizabeth donned so it would look like hers if anybody saw them, and a wool cap, and a pair of gloves, which she put in the jacket's pocket. She grabbed a pair of larger boots, there for when a male teacher helped Gloria and Sylvia lead an adventure. She took off her sneakers and stuffed them into the top of her jeans beneath the down jacket to hide the bulge, and put on the boots for the same reason. Then she saw a first-aid kit and a Swiss Army knife in a box of tools, and put those in the jacket pocket too. They left the shed, snapped the padlock closed, and escaped the pool of light, heading across the campus toward the river and the homeless man, relieved to be in the safety of the dark.

A hundred yards later, Sylvia stopped running. "Wait. I've just thought of something."

"No you haven't! Keep going."

"Thermal underwear. He'll need that too. Why didn't we think of it?"

"Maybe because we were in a hurry?"

"I know right where it is."

"Oh no. We're not going back, are we?"

"You wait here. I'll be right back." Sylvia grabbed the key out of her pocket, turned, and sprinted back toward the parking lot, holding the key at the ready. Again, the light bounced off the shed and into her eyes. She poked at the lock with the key, missed the slot, and dropped the key on the ground. Panicking, she picked it up and poked at the lock again, but the key was upside down again and wouldn't go in. She inverted it, took a big breath, and, forcing herself to slowness, slid the key into the lock and turned, but the lock resisted. She turned the key the other way and at last the locked popped open. She let out her breath, put the key back in her pocket, and entered the shed, once again leaving the door open for the light, and went straight to where she remembered the thermal underwear was stored in cardboard boxes on shelves in the back.

They weren't there. Somebody had moved them. Or maybe she remembered wrong? She felt her panic rising again, sure the security guy would come and catch her. She told herself to leave. *Right now!* The down jacket, the wool hat, the gloves, the boots were enough. But she felt a stubbornness rising too, and so she looked on all the other shelves and saw the boxes piled one on top of the other in a corner of the shed. Just as she opened the box on the top of the pile and began to pull out one of the suits of thermal underwear, she heard a car entering the parking lot. She left the thermal underwear halfway out of the box and lunged toward the front of the shed pushed and the door shut and was instantly in absolute darkness again, totally blind.

She stood still so as not to make a sound. Through the thin plywood walls, she listened to the car approach—its door close—footsteps—and then she realized the padlock was still open. It was hanging on the door fixture in the gleaming light for the security guy to see.

In the pitch dark, she moved her hand across the door until she found its hinges and then moved up against them, so if the security guy pushed the door open, it would shield her from view. When he stepped far enough into the shed, she'd slip behind him and out the door, and sprint away into the darkness.

The footsteps stopped. She guessed he was deciding whether to close the padlock—because someone had forgotten—or to push the door open and enter the shed and look around. Then the door swung open, making the scraping sound and flooding the inside of the shed with light, and his shadow played weirdly in front of him. She put her hand on her side of the door, resisting, hoping he would assume it was the shelves preventing the door from opening all the way. She could hear him breathing just inches away on the other side of the door. His shadow grew until it was huge, its bottom half silhouetted on the back wall, its top half, after bending at right angles, on the ceiling. In one more second, he'd take another step and she'd slip behind him. If he turned and looked behind the door, she'd duck below his arm.

But the door swung away from her hand, his shadow backed out of the shed, the door made the scraping sound again as it closed, and she was so relieved she almost sat down—but then she was blind again, listening to the metallic rattle of the padlock as the security guy reinserted it through both fixtures and snapped it shut. *The key is in my pocket! I'm locked in!* She heard his retreating footsteps, the car door shutting and the car driving away.

Then, seconds later, footsteps and a whisper in the blackness. "Syl? You there?"

"Yeah, I'm here. What took you so long?"

"Whew! I thought he'd taken you away."

"He might as well have," Sylvia said aloud. There was no point in whispering anymore.

"What? He took the key!"

"No, it's right here in my pocket."

"Whew!" Elizabeth said again. "Can you slide it under the door?"

"Are you kidding? There's no space. I can't see any light."

A silence. A slight rattling of the door. Then: "Fuck! You're right."

"So what are we going to do now?" Sylvia said.

"We'll have to get the other key."

"How?"

"I think you know."

"Oh shit!"

"Exactly."

Another silence. "Elizabeth?" Sylvia said.

"I'm still here. I was just wondering. Should I go straight to Gloria Buchanan because she's got the other key, or your mom first?"

"Oh God, I don't know. Straight to Gloria, I guess."

"You sure?" Elizabeth asked, and when Sylvia didn't say anything: "Okay. Gloria. You'll get out sooner."

"And the other key's right here in my pocket!"

"Yeah, I know, I know. But why worry?" Elizabeth said. Her footsteps faded away.

In the blind dark, Sylvia couldn't find anything to sit down on while she waited and thought about how different it would have been if the security guy had arrived while they were still trying to get into the shed, before they stole anything. They would have thought fast and said they were too restless to sleep and so they decided to take a walk and were cold and they just wanted to borrow some warm clothes until they went back to the dorm. The consequence for being outside of the dorms after lights out would be something mild, probably not being allowed to leave the campus for the rest of the semester (except for athletic trips), and a letter home to the parents, absurd in Sylvia's case. Or if they did confess why they were going to steal the stuff, people would say it was just a dumb way of being kind and generous. Seniors should know better. *Thank God we caught them before this went any further!*

The desire to help a helpless person. *That's the reason we did it*, she and Elizabeth were going to say, now that they'd been caught. *You have a problem with that?* To do something about homelessness in the richest country in the world. It was too late to do anything about slavery and Jim Crow—or killing the Native Americans—or the fucked-up war in Iraq. She heard in her head how self-righteous that would sound, how comic, and the little pulse of justification she'd felt melted to nothing. She waited and waited and waited.

At last, footsteps. It didn't sound like two people. Of course! Gloria would order Elizabeth back to her room and come by herself.

"Guess what?" It was Elizabeth's voice!

"What? Gloria let you come back? Where is she?"

"A Swiss Army knife. I just happened to put it in the pocket of this down jacket and there it was. I'd forgot I'd stolen it. It's got a screwdriver. I'm going to take the hinges off."

"The hinges off!"

In the pitch black, the door moved in its frame, then the sound of the screwdriver engaging with the screws and the sound of their turning and then, after another forever, a space bright with light, as the door hung only from the padlock. Sylvia squeezed out of the shed. She could barely see in the sudden brightness. She and Elizabeth were actually not going to be kicked out of the school! She *wouldn't* have to face her mother! She felt a rush of love for Elizabeth.

Who was already pushing the door back into its frame. *Suppose I'd been the one to see the Swiss Army knife and put it in my pocket?* Sylvia thought. It would have been just as useless inside the shed as the key was. But Elizabeth had been sharper and had seen it first.

Elizabeth finished a minute later. "Let's get out of here!"

They moved across the campus, keeping to the darkest shadows.

When they got away from the buildings onto the athletic fields, they began to feel safe. The night was windless and the black dome above them filled with stars. They entered the trail in the woods. Soon there was the sound of the river, and a few minutes later, its dank and fecund smell.

As they neared the lean-to, Elizabeth insisted they go very slowly and make no sound. "We don't want to wake him up," she whispered. Sylvia agreed, though she didn't say so. If the homeless man would figure out who had brought the gifts, she'd be content, at least for now, but she didn't say that either. They left the stuff beside the food that was already there and put a rock on top of the jacket to keep it from blowing away. There was no sign of rain to wet the down jacket, the gloves, the wool hat, the boots, the Swiss Army knife.

Finished, they moved backwards, facing the lean-to. They could barely see it in the dark.

Just as they reached the same screen of bushes they had hid behind before, they saw his dark shape crawl out of the lean-to and stand up. He swiveled his head toward them, obviously searching for the source of the sound he must have heard. It was too dark to see his face. Neither girl breathed. Above their heads, pine branches trembled in the breeze. At last, he swiveled his head away, knelt down again, and crawled back into his lean to.

The girls turned, tiptoed away, then walked, then, when they were sure he couldn't hear them, started to run.

SAFELY HOME, ELIZABETH said, "Don't worry, he didn't see us."

"How do you know?"

"Because if he had, he wouldn't have gone back into his lean-to."

"What would he have done?"

"Who knows?" Elizabeth said.

It wasn't until they were in their beds just before dawn that Sylvia realized they'd left the thermal underwear in the shed. "All that for nothing!" Elizabeth said, and promptly fell asleep. Sylvia did too, a few minutes later. This time she didn't dream.

CHRISTOPHER DREAMED THE tall, thin girl visited him, appearing near the doorway of his lean-to, backdropped by stars. He went out of the lean-to to meet her. *What do you want?* she asked. *Who do you want me to be for you?* He didn't know how to answer her. So he went back into his lean-to, got back into his sleeping bag, and pulled its hood over his face.

Then she went away.

In the morning, he woke up starving. He hadn't eaten since the day before yesterday. Hunger hurt less than shame. Why not just stay in the sleeping bag until he starved to death? Yes.

But he imagined the girl and her friend coming back along the river to find his rotting flesh melting into the fabric of the sleeping bag, and he got the familiar whiff. There was more shame from that than from begging.

So, instead, he crawled in his skivvies and T-shirt out of the sleeping bag into the autumn cold and went outside, shivering, to take a piss, watching it steam against the ground. Then he came back into the lean-to and grabbed his thin cotton shirt and his jeans, almost worn through at the knees, and his sneakers, whose soles were getting thinner and thinner, and brought them outside where he could stand up without having to stoop way over and put them on; and when he was dressed, still shivering, he went back into the lean-to to get the *HOMELESS!* sign. He couldn't find it. Where did he leave it? Maybe outside? He came out again and walked all around the lean-to and still couldn't find it, and then it occurred to him he didn't need it anyway. Everybody knew.

He was cold. Half the leaves were gone from the trees. It must be almost November. But he wasn't homeless. He'd built the lean-to. Just like Uncle Ray would have: high enough to stand up in it if he stooped way over, and wide enough for his sleeping bag and clothes. And he had food. She'd brought food. She and the other girl. He'd left it where they'd put it because he was sure they brought it to mock him. But then why didn't he hear them laugh? Maybe they didn't. He went over there to get the food, still shivering.

The down jacket was on top. A rock on top to keep the wind from blowing it away. He picked up the jacket and put it on against the cold. In the pocket he found gloves, a hat. He put those on too.

He picked up the boots and carried them into the lean-to and stored them in a corner for when it snowed. Then he came back out and gathered up the cans of food, the lighter, the Swiss Army knife, and carried them back to the lean-to and stored them in a different corner. Then he went back and carried the grill to his firepit and placed it carefully on the surrounding rocks, like a bridge. There was too much here for just one girl to carry. She'd brought her friend. *Friends*, he corrected. *Friends. Not just one.*

He took a can of corned beef hash and his axe outside into the gray November air. He built a very little fire with very dry wood so it would make very little smoke, and opened the hash and put a small amount of it on the side of his axe blade and laid that across the grill to fry. The burning wood, the frying hash was the smell of Uncle Ray's place on Osgood Pond.

And he was warm.

THE NEXT SUNDAY was cold and windy and the sky was gray when Sylvia and Elizabeth walked to the village to see if the homeless man would still be begging. They didn't see him near Rose's where he'd been before. They walked to the outskirts and looked in the McDonald's. He wasn't there either. They walked back to Rose's Creamery, where they both ordered hot fudge sundaes so it wouldn't be obvious what they were really there for, and Elizabeth struck up a conversation with Rose behind the counter about what a great location the Creamery was in for doing business, where everything was so nice and so clean and safe, into which she managed to insert a question about the whereabouts of "that guy who begs." Rose answered she had no idea, making it clear with a shrug that she didn't care, and reported that he hadn't been around for at least a week. "Well, that must be a relief," Elizabeth said, failing on purpose not to sound sarcastic.

They finished their sundaes quickly and went outside where they could talk. "So he must be eating the food," Elizabeth said.

"It looks that way." Sylvia said. "We better bring him some more."

Elizabeth sighed and they stared at each other.

They walked straight to Stop and Shop and bought two shopping bags of food with the rest of both of their allowances and carried them back to the school. They'd hide them under Elizabeth's bunk for a few days and then carry them down river. "I can't believe we're still doing this," Elizabeth said.

"Well, then why are you?"

"I don't know. Maybe because you are and I'm like that guy who hanged himself to keep his best friend company."

"No. We're doing it because he's hungry, that's why. Besides, how do you know it was a guy who hanged himself?"

Elizabeth didn't answer. In this most feminist of places, she'd concede the last word to Sylvia: yeah, it *could* have been a woman who hung herself. Plus, she *was* doing this to keep Sylvia company. But she wasn't about to say the homeless guy reminded her of where people, including her own parents, might not be homeless now, but who knows when? Meanwhile, they shop in pawn shops and dollar stores and hope the next tornado doesn't blow their world away. Where Elizabeth came from, Sylvia wouldn't be allowed to be half white, half Black—even if her mom ran a hundred schools all at once. She'd be one hundred percent Black, living in the part of town that has a red line around it. Elizabeth wasn't about to explain this—not even to Sylvia. She didn't want anyone to label her the self-pitying poor kid from the wrong side of the tracks who appears so often in prep school novels. That was nowhere near original enough for Elizabeth. No, she was the girl with the tattoo on her ankle: an oil rig with an X over it, who only wore socks when it was very cold.

A few minutes later, they were back on campus. She was missing said socks very much. The wind had increased. It smelled like snow and blew into their faces, causing their eyes to water. "I can't wait to get inside and take a hot shower," Elizabeth said. "Even the trees look cold."

SEVEN

You keep looking out there at that tree, we'll never get these letters done," Margaret Rice, Rachel Bickham's administrative assistant, said. She was in her sixties, a woman whose once-blonde hair had turned silver years ago. "When spring comes, those old leaves that stay there all winter long because it's a copper beech will finally fall off, and new leaves will either bud again or they won't. Until then, there's nothing you or I can do about it."

Still, Rachel gazed out at the copper beech tree just yards away, willing herself to believe it was merely hibernating, like bears do in the winter.

The snow that had seemed to be coming on Sunday night had been rain instead. It had rained all day Monday, a light but steady pouring until early this morning. Now the sun cast a pallid light on the tree's stark trunk, and beyond it, the dead brown grass of the lawns. It was nine o'clock in the morning, but no one was walking on the paths. Everyone was sleeping in because last night at dinner, feeling in her bones the community's depressed mood, like her own, Rachel had declared the palliative would be a morning free of classes.

It hadn't taken more than a few seconds for everyone to notice her when she stood up to announce her declaration. When Rachel Bickham stood up, everyone always stopped talking. She was well aware that whoever followed her, someday, as the new head of school, would have to own that presence too, or she wouldn't last beyond a year.

Her announcement was followed by a roar of applause—though several of the teachers were annoyed. They'd had big plans for tomorrow's classes. If any of them had complained, Rachel would have said, "So did I, but I changed them," well aware that she would have been less impatient earlier in her career when everything was still new.

And, in fact, she had not changed *her* plans. She was right here in her office, right on schedule, dictating letters to this tall, large-boned woman, whom she loved and had depended on to keep her organized for all of the last nineteen years. Margaret had also served Rachel's predecessor, Fred Kindler, who'd lasted only a year, and, before that, the second half of the celebrated Marjorie Boyd's long tenure. Margaret could write a book, Rachel knew, several of them, a whole saga of what she'd witnessed and known more about than she ever let on, *The Saga of Miss Oliver's School for Girls.*

At last, Rachel dragged her eyes from the tree—and discovered that Margaret was looking at it too. "Where were we?" Rachel asked.

"What?"

"I asked, where were we? Where did I leave off? Don't tell me your mind was wandering too!"

Margaret turned her gaze to Rachel, nodding her head. "I confess."

"You too?"

"Me too. I've been working right next to it even longer than you."

"Of course you have. Does that mean if it does die, you'll—"

"Quit?" Margaret shook her head. "No."

"Good. Because if you did, I'd feel twice abandoned."

"And if it were the other way around?" Margaret asked. "Do you think I wouldn't? Besides, I'm too old to break in another head."

"So you'll stay as long as I?"

"That's right, as long as you do."

The two women stared at each other's surprised expressions, until Rachel finally broke the silence. "I wonder why you and I never talked about this before."

"No, you know perfectly well why. Because neither of us could imagine being in any other job."

"I know," Rachel admitted. "Let alone wanting to be."

"But now we can," Margaret said. "It had to happen someday. It does for everybody, you know. We really knew that all along."

A few minutes later, Margaret turned her head to the tree again, apparently incapable of getting its fate out of her mind. She looked surprised. Rachel, naturally, followed her gaze and saw Sylvia and

Elizabeth running across the lawns from the direction of the river toward their dorm. Actually, it was Sylvia who was running. What Elizabeth was doing, yards behind, was a mix of jogging, waddling, and wheezing.

"What in the world do you think that's about?" Margaret asked.

"I have no idea."

"Maybe you'd better ask."

Rachel nodded. They both knew Elizabeth wouldn't run anywhere if she didn't have to, especially instead of sleeping in!

The two women watched Sylvia stop, turn around, and wait for Elizabeth before they both disappeared into the dorm. Rachel resumed her dictation, but she couldn't focus on the task. Margaret didn't seem surprised. "I'll come back later," she said. She went back to her anteroom, leaving Rachel alone, staring across the campus at the dormitory's closed front door.

Maybe you'd better ask.

It was a feeling, an intuition, not a thought Rachel could explain: that Sylvia had been running to home and safety from some place she'd traveled to so she could find out who she was going to be. That was what kids her age were supposed to be doing, wasn't it? Finding out who they were going to be? And isn't it a school's job to help them with that? *Or do they arrive already knowing, like Elizabeth, and we just polish them up?*

Rachel would have asked her father who'd been an educator too, the president of a small liberal arts college, until he'd got fired for not being a disciplined enough politician to suffer fools gladly, a skill especially important for Black Americans. *Dad, did you ever wonder what the college you presided over was* for? But her father was dead.

Rachel thought Elizabeth was tagging along with Sylvia, keeping up as best she could, because that's what friends do. It took a mother's intuition to sense that the two girls running together had more to do with Sylvia's being so disturbed by a homeless man that Elizabeth had had to tell about it than Elizabeth's sudden desire to be in shape. And a mother's intuition, too, to guess that for Sylvia, it was more complicated than the need to help one helpless person out of so many.

Just a few months ago, Rachel had watched her daughter and Elizabeth disappear beyond the gates and had a sense that if she followed after them, she would learn what she needed to know to fill her own emptiness. Now, she'd watched them returning—from who knew where? She had that same fluttering vision again, remembering how, the evening of that Sunday, in the smell of honeysuckle, when her husband was about to leave again, Sylvia and Elizabeth had crossed the lawns, retreating from them both in the fading evening light, disappearing behind the same closed door. Sylvia hadn't needed to be urged to leave at all. She'd been in a hurry.

Rachel turned her gaze now from the tree she hoped was not dying to the painting of it in health, on the far wall of her office above the sofa. Nineteen years ago, in her first year as head of Miss Oliver's School for Girls, and not long before she became pregnant with Sylvia, a girl named Claire Nelson, who had just discovered her prodigious innate talent as an artist at the hands of Eudora Easter, had given the painting to Rachel in thanks, she said, for the school's admitting her in spite of her troubled past. Claire told Rachel she felt sad every time she thought of the ancestors of Sarah Warrior, the only Native person in the school then, sitting under the tree. Did they, whose village had occupied the ground now occupied by Miss Oliver's School for Girls, know what was going to happen to them? She had painted another picture: what she thought Sara's people would see sitting in snow at night in the middle of the winter looking up through dead leafless branches bare against the sky. Claire never showed that painting to anyone else.

Claire had found out who she was going to be at Miss O's and now was a well-regarded artist, one of the legion of distinguished Oliver alumnae. That the perspective of the painting in Rachel's office was slightly off, Claire's talent not yet fully instructed, gave the painting a spontaneity that moved Rachel every time she gazed at it. She had recently asked for extra locks and an improved security alarm to be installed in the Administration Building because the painting had been valued in the mid five figures, the prime example of the artist's juvenilia. That it was worth so much money was a disappointment. It meant that Rachel would be expected to give the painting to the school when she resigned. To live without the painting—that would be another emptiness.

THAT EVENING RACHEL toured all the dorms, stopping to chat with the girls in the common rooms, poking her head into rooms to say hello, to ask how things are going. Being present for the girls was a critical part of her leadership, the part she liked the best. She visited Sylvia and Elizabeth's room last.

Sylvia was lying in her upper bunk, reading her history text. "Hey," she said, looking surprised and sitting up. On the other side of the narrow room, Elizabeth was sitting up straight at her desk.

"Hey," Rachel answered. She glanced meaningfully at Sylvia's desk. "I thought I'd stop by and say hello." Sounding to herself like someone she didn't know.

"Hi, Rachel," Elizabeth said.

"Hi, Elizabeth. You really surprised me this morning."

Elizabeth stared.

Rachel looked away from Elizabeth to her daughter. "How'd you manage to persuade Elizabeth to go on a run?"

"Oh, you saw us?" Elizabeth said.

"Yes, from my office."

"A holiday for everyone but yourself!" Elizabeth said.

"I didn't persuade her. She decided on her own," Sylvia said.

"Really? Elizabeth! I think that's great," Rachel said.

Elizabeth shrugged.

"Well anyway, I just wanted to know how everything's going," Rachel said, sounding even more off-key to herself.

"Fine," both girls said in unison.

"Good, I'll leave you to your work." Rachel glanced meaningfully at Sylvia's desk and made to leave; then she had an idea and turned back. "I'm going on a run tomorrow morning before breakfast. Do you two want to come?"

Elizabeth shook her head vigorously. "No thanks. One day in a row is enough. I don't want to get carried away."

Rachel turned to Sylvia. "How about you?"

"I can't, Mom. I've got too much homework."

"Really? I'm going by the river. Our favorite run."

Sylvia shook her head again. Elizabeth turned in her chair, facing away from Rachel. She raised her eyebrows, an almost imperceptible gesture.

"Oh okay, I'll come," Sylvia said. She climbed down from her upper bunk and crossed to her desk, carrying the history textbook.

"Good. I'll pick you up here at six-thirty," Rachel said. She left the room, closing the door behind her.

BOTH GIRLS WERE wide awake at six-thirty the next morning when the knock on their door came. They were too nervous to sleep. Suppose her mom insisted on running *down* river toward the homeless man when Sylvia said she wanted to run *up* river, in the other direction, this one time? What would happen if they met the homeless man? Would her mother be afraid and turn around? Would she stop and talk to him? When the clothing was discovered missing from the shed, would she put two and two together? Sylvia was in her warm-up suit because it was cold. Elizabeth was still in bed, pretending to be asleep.

Outside it was still dark, just a hint of gray. A rime of frost on the grass. In spite of her nervousness, Sylvia felt a rush of joy to be running with her long-legged mother, smooth and easy, cruising, long deep breaths, light feet, rhythm, rhythm, rhythm. Once up and past her sleepiness, she loved the dawn, and she was glad to be free of the thudding heavy sound of Elizabeth's feet meeting the ground behind her, her labored breaths. Sylvia and her mother ran on and on, speeding up as they crossed the soccer and lacrosse fields in the growing light, and then into the still dark woods where the ground was softened under their feet by the cushion of a whole season's fallen leaves. As they neared the river, Sylvia put on a burst of speed so she would be ahead of her mother when they reached the river and she would turn *up* river, away from the homeless man, not down river where her mother preferred. But her mother said, "Oh. Okay," meaning *Sure, let's go faster*, and she quickened her stride too, and they remained side by side, bumping shoulders on the narrow trail as they came to the river, and Sylvia had to sprint now, to leave her mother a few yards behind, and she headed left at the juncture of the trails. "Why?" She heard her mother say behind her. Sylvia ran on and didn't answer, slowing gradually to their former pace.

They ran on, beside each other again. Sylvia forgot her worry. This joy she had in common with her mother. The sun was all the way up by now. The world was bright. Mist rose from the river. The bare tree branches were silhouettes against the sky. They spooked a deer. At last, they turned around and ran back. Only because they were running out of time. They sprinted across the athletic fields again, and slowed to a walk in the center of campus where they would part. They stopped and turned to each other and embraced. Sylvia felt her mother's cool cheek against her own. They breathed together.

"I'm glad we went the other way," her mom said. Her tone was as much a question as a statement.

RACHEL GOT TO her office just in time for a meeting with her administrative team. The minute it adjourned, she called Bob.

"Hi," he said, sounding surprised. "What's up?"

"Nothing. Just felt like talking."

"Really?"

"Yeah. Guess what Sylvia and I just did."

"Oh? You had a talk?"

"No, we went on a run together."

"Yeah? So? Was it nice?"

"Beautiful."

"That's good."

"We went up river."

"Up? What's that mean? Besides the opposite of down?"

"That's the point, Bob. We always go down."

"Maybe she just wanted to explore."

"I don't think so."

"Variety then, a change of scene?"

Rachel didn't say anything.

"Rachel?"

"I had this strange feeling she was leading me away from something she didn't want me to see."

"Or maybe *to* something she *wanted* you to see?"

Rachel thought about that, taking it in. "Maybe. It just seemed strange, that's all."

"I suppose. But anyway, you enjoyed it, right? That's what counts, you know. Running is something you and she have together."

A long pause here. Then from Rachel: "Yeah, you're right. So what's going on with you?"

"Me? Hmm."

"Yes, Bob, you. What was that 'hmm' about?"

"About how what's going on with me is changing the subject all of a sudden. I mean, you don't usually call me in the middle of the morning. You go on a run with Syl and right away you want to talk. So, I'm right here."

"You mean you're actually going to work me in to your schedule? Your secretary won't disapprove?"

No answer from Bob

"I'm sorry. I didn't mean to go there."

"It's okay. I deserve it—but then, so do you."

"Yeah, I do. It's just that I'm worried about stuff I never used to be. Like the tree, for instance. And I felt like talking."

"What tree?"

"What tree! *The* tree. Outside my office. The leaves look sick."

"Of course they do. It's a copper beech tree, Rachel, you know that. Its leaves hang on all winter. They don't fall off till spring. So of course they look sick."

"I suppose so. But the tree *is* getting old."

"Well, how long do copper beech trees live? Do you know?"

"Of course I know. Oh dear!"

"Well, how long? What are you 'oh dear'-ing about?"

"Margaret just poked her head in."

"Well, tell her to poke it out."

"I can't. She's pointing at her wristwatch. My physics class starts in two minutes."

"And the world will come to an end if you're late, right?"

"Bob, I have to go."

"I know. The boss sets the example."

"Well, don't you?"

"Of course I do, Rach. Goodbye"

"Goodbye, Bob."

"Thanks for the call, Rach. Try me again sometime."

Rachel chose not to respond. She hung up and rushed to her class.

"Maxine, tell us a little about yourself," Eudora said that evening in the brightly lit dining hall where the flags of many nations hung from the ceiling. The big windows were black with the early November night, and there was the noise of many conversations. Table assignments had just been switched. Maxine Tisdale, a freshwoman, was relatively new to the school, unknown to her tablemates, including Sylvia. For the next two weeks, they would eat dinner together on white tablecloths at the table over which Eudora presided.

Clearly feeling shy, Maxine hesitated.

"Where are you from, Maxine?" Sylvia asked. As a senior, her job was to be helpful.

"Florida."

"Florida! How do you like this cold weather?" Sylvia expected a stock answer to her stock question, and though she wanted to listen to it anyway, she couldn't keep herself from replaying her morning run with her mother, living again the moment when she speeded up to get to the river trail first, but her mother stayed right with her, their shoulders bumping.

"I like it okay," Maxine said. "Have you ever been to Florida?"

Just then, Sylvia, whose place at the table faced the entrance to the dining hall, saw Gloria Buchanan's tall, muscular form appear in it. *She's late*, Sylvia thought. *That's not like her.* Gloria swiveled her head, clearly looking for someone, until her eyes met Sylvia's, and Sylvia quickly looked away. Every day since she and Elizabeth had stolen the stuff from the equipment shed two weeks ago, Sylvia had expected Gloria to come to her with the news. But it hadn't occurred to her that Gloria would do so in *public*.

"Sylvia?" Eudora said. "Maxine asked you a question."

"Who, me?" Sylvia said, turning to Maxine. "No, I haven't been to Florida"

Now Gloria was standing beside Sylvia's chair. "Sylvia?"

Sylvia looked up at Gloria as if she hadn't known she was there. Gloria seemed to be taller than she ever had before. She was clearly agitated, her broad shoulders hunched up toward her ears, her mouth open, as if she were about to announce *Fire!* The conversation at the table stopped. Gloria hesitated, seeming to enjoy being distraught.

Then she stood up very straight, as if peering over a podium, and in a tone worthy of announcing the beginning of World War Three: "Someone's broken into the equipment shed!"

"Really?" Sylvia stood up from her chair. The only way she could think of to act surprised.

"Yes. There's all kinds of stuff missing."

"That's terrible!" Sylvia said.

"First I thought you'd just rearranged things, but I looked some more and still couldn't find—" Gloria lifted her eyes to Eudora. "Who would do such a thing?"

"It must have been someone from the outside," Eudora said.

"But the padlock was *locked*."

"So what?" Sylvia said. Maybe a little too aggressively? "Professional burglars have master keys."

"Do they?" Gloria said.

"That's probably what happened," Sylvia said. She wondered if everyone could hear her heart pounding. "But I'll report it in Morning Meeting tomorrow anyway."

"Just in case, right?" Maxine Tisdale said in a hopeful tone.

"Yes, just in case, Maxine," Eudora said. "Please don't worry. People don't steal at Miss O's."

"Yes, Sylvia," Gloria said. "You're the president of the club. The announcement's better coming from you." She left, heading for the table over which she presided, mission accomplished, and Sylvia, sitting down, was quick to change the subject.

But only for a minute. Everyone at the table seemed to want to talk about stealing. Mary Callahan told how a cop in Oakland, California, where she lived, told her the one about Hondas: how there are two kinds, the ones that have been stolen and the ones that are about to be, and her father's Honda had been stolen twice—"and one other time, he looked out the window and saw this Black guy trying to get into it, right in the middle of the day." Everyone glanced at Eudora, then at Sylvia. "I'm sorry, I know it doesn't make any difference what color he was," Mary said.

"To you it does," Sylvia said, relieved to have this to focus on. Feeling a convenient anger, she added, "You know it does."

Mary flushed. "I'm sorry, I really am. But he *was* Black." She looked around the table for support. Everyone looked down, or over her head. Then, angry too, she turned back to Sylvia. "I'm no more prejudiced than you are."

"If he was white, would you have said a *white* guy?"

"I told you, I'm sorry."

"Would you or wouldn't you?"

"Let it go, Sylvia," Eudora said. "Mary's learned her lesson."

"Yes, and I said I'm sorry!" Mary started to cry.

Sylvia threw her napkin down, got up from the table, stared at Mary, still sustaining her anger, and marched out of the dining hall. In the dark outside, she let out her breath. She didn't feel any guilt at all about stealing from the equipment shed. But she did feel guilty for using Mary's ignorance as a shield instead of addressing it for real. Just the same, if Mary wanted to apologize, she could, but Sylvia wasn't about to, ever.

MORNING MEETING, INAUGURATED by Miss Edith Oliver who had founded the school in 1928, was deep in the culture of Miss Oliver's School for Girls, a time for the whole school community to gather not just the students, faculty, and administration but also the kitchen crew, secretaries, janitors, and groundskeepers. It was a sacred communal togetherness and, for many alumnae, these gatherings in the Marjorie E. Boyd Auditorium functioned as the anchor of their remembrance of their time at the school.

On that Thursday, Sylvia sat in the front row of the auditorium in a catatonic trance of nervousness, waiting for the time for announcements. They usually came first, but today she had to wait while her nervousness blossomed because for this particular Morning Meeting, Galway Kinnell, Pulitzer Prize–winning poet, had graciously accepted the poetry club's invitation to read from his collected poems and then to spend the rest of the day working with the club's members—an opportunity so special that the members were excused from their classes. Sylvia loved poetry, especially when it wasn't part of an assignment, but today, though she did absorb some incantation of grief, joy, wisdom, and surprise, the words and their specific meanings flew right past her. Almost everyone else in that audience was moved, and those whose minds were elsewhere were politely careful to appear attentive.

Galway Kinnell read for half an hour, ending with "Freedom, New Hampshire," about two boys who speculate that the grass is especially green behind a barn because a cow was buried there. Early in the poem several girls in the row right behind Sylvia were moved almost to tears because they loved New Hampshire, where they were counselors in a beloved summer camp called Cragged Mountain Farm, and, many verses later when it became obvious that the poem was elegy for the poet's brother, they actually did cry, and even Gregory van Buren, advisor to the Poetry Club, famous for his ability to keep his emotions under control, appeared to be distraught.

When Galway finished, there was a long silence during which several girls decided they would spend their lives as poets no matter what, and other girls decided to be teachers of English, and then there followed a full sixty seconds of loud applause, and then the president of the Poetry Club, who would discover almost too late in life she had no talent for writing poetry, stood to thank Galway Kinnell. Then he sat down and it was time for announcements. Sylvia climbed up on the stage and turned to face the whole school.

"Yesterday Gloria Buchanan told me that the shed where the school's outdoor equipment is stored was broken into and stuff was stolen," she said, keeping her gaze above the audience so she wouldn't have to look in any person's eyes, especially Gloria's, in the front row, or her mother's, standing in the back—or Elizabeth's, three rows from the front. Sylvia thought she heard a tremor in her voice, but no one seemed to notice. Apparently, everyone was still in New Hampshire hearing words contrived to break their hearts. "It was probably burglars," she went on, "but Gloria and I thought you should know so we can all be on our guard in case they try to hit someplace else." She paused and forced herself to bring her eyes down level with theirs. They were paying attention now. "Gloria and I have the only two keys to the padlock," she said, precisely because the guilty person would never say that in public. She paused and then added, "At least as far as we know."

"Tell us what was taken," Abby Caballo said, a sophomore, sitting in the third row, right next to Elizabeth, and immediately all the items appeared in Sylvia's head, in the order in which she and Elizabeth had grabbed them. She drew breath to list them in response, looking directly at Abby, but next to Abby, Elizabeth's eyes grew big and Sylvia remembered just in time that Gloria hadn't told her *what* was stolen, only that stuff was. She was dumbstruck for a very long couple of seconds, then recovered and looked for Gloria in the audience. "Tell us, Gloria."

Gloria stood up and turned to the audience. "A down jacket, the best kind, very expensive," her voice full of amazement that such a thing could actually happen. "It could keep someone from dying by hypothermia," she scolded, looking straight at Sylvia because Sylvia had asked the question. "Whoever it was also stole a wool watch cap and a pair of gloves, a first-aid kit and also a Swiss Army knife, and a pair of boots. And let's see, what else." She looked at a pad of paper in her hand. "That's all, but there might be more," she said, looking up at Sylvia again. Then she cast her eyes around the auditorium, and it was clear that she didn't think burglars from the outside had done this thing. "It appears that whoever it was started to take some thermal underwear too and then decided not to."

"Thank you, Gloria," Sylvia said. "Let's hope it never happens again. Next announcement?" Sweat was running down from her armpits into her blouse.

"I'm not finished yet," Gloria said. "If any of you did this and comes to tell Sylvia or me, you'll be forgiven. Everyone makes mistakes. This is one that can be undone."

"Thank you, Gloria," Sylvia said. "Next announcement?" *Please please please, no more announcements!* she prayed. There was a second or two of silence. At last! The meeting was ending. Sylvia headed toward steps down from the stage.

But no one was getting up to leave. Sylvia turned and found out why. Her mother was coming to the front. Of course! When something big happens, everybody wants to know what the leader thinks. Sylvia already did.

Rachel Bickham turned when she reached the front and faced the audience. Even then, Sylvia marveled at her presence. When her mom walked into a room, everybody turned to face her. Now everybody was waiting to know what she was going to say.

"I have to make one thing very clear," her mother said, her head of school's voice ringing out over the auditorium. "It would not be fair to you if I did not. But first, please think again about what it means that there are no locks on your rooms in the dorms. Nor on the doors of the apartments where your dorm parents live. We don't steal at Miss Oliver's. Our community is built on trust. If we put locks on the doors, what would that say to you? The only reason there is a lock on the outdoor equipment shed is that it is exposed to the outside. So, while I appreciate and respect Gloria's offer to forgive a theft if the stolen stuff is returned, I need to be clear: if there ever is a theft by a student here, I will make the decision about the consequence alone. The usual protocol does not apply for theft. It is clearly stated in the handbook that the consequence for theft is expulsion; I can see no reason why I would decide to make an exception. I hope that's very clear. Nevertheless, I'm just as sure as you are that whoever stole the equipment was not one of us." She held up two fingers. "I've been head for nineteen years and am now in my twentieth, and I've only had to make that decision twice. Are there any questions?" She looked around.

There were none. Sylvia watched her mother deciding whether to end the meeting or—while she was at it—remind the school about the one other crime for which expulsion was unequivocal: allowing a male other than a parent or a sibling in a dorm room. Everybody agreed with the one about stealing. But not about that one. Sylvia did though. In her mom's very first year, a crazy rightwing radio nutcase almost brought the school down by broadcasting half-truths about the school's admitting a girl—none other than the now celebrated alumna Claire Nelson—in spite of her scandalous past, thus suggesting that Miss Oliver's was not a safe place for nice girls. Her mom had decided: never again. That the school was a safe place for girls had to be totally clear.

"Our meeting's over then," Rachel said. Sylvia knew why. Two messages at the same time, nobody hears either of them.

Rachel thanked Galway Kinnell again for inspiring us all, and Galway Kinnell acknowledged her thanks and said it had been a long time since he'd been to such an interesting meeting, and then Morning Meeting was over and everyone trooped off to class, comforted by the belief that the theft was, most likely, the work of burglars, professionals, from the outside, not one of them.

But if it was burglars, there really is something to worry about. Maybe the next time, they'd come right into a dorm. Maybe we should put locks on our doors, after all. Maybe that tradition's time is over.

It was kind of scary.

THAT AFTERNOON, A week before the deadline, Elizabeth sent her Early Decision application to MIT. She was just as sure as Miss O's college admissions counselors were that MIT would offer a full financial aid package to a person of her background—compellingly described in her personal essay—who also was a possessor of a 4.0 GPA, earned mostly in honors level courses. In that same personal essay, Elizabeth explained exactly why she chose the Massachusetts Institute of Technology over all other colleges or universities: she needed a four-year, deep immersion in the sciences as preparation for creating realistic science fiction—dystopia versus paradise as a metaphor for our nation to choose the best way forward—and also as preparation for her later career in politics. She didn't need institutional help with the humanities at which she was naturally gifted. And the essay itself was proof that, thanks to her ingrained talent and Gregory van Buren's coaching, she had developed a distinctive voice as a writer.

That evening, Elizabeth coached Sylvia in preparing her applications to a variety of colleges. Though Sylvia's standardized test scores and grades were nothing to be ashamed of, they were clearly not competitive enough for her to apply for either Early Decision of Early Admission. "I wish I knew which college I wanted to go to," Sylvia said.

"Don't worry," Elizabeth said. "You'll know when you get some acceptances."

"What makes you think so?"

"Because then you'll have to decide."

"How do you know I am going to get in any place I'd like?"

"Because once you do get in, you will have to like it."

"That's what my dad says. He'd never stepped foot on his college campus until the day he arrived to begin his freshman year, and he keeps saying he turned out all right. My mom, though. She knew all along she'd go to Smith."

"Of course she did," Elizabeth said. "But so what? And anyway, lots of college coaches will want you."

"Yeah, if I could only decide which sport I want to specialize in."

"What are you worrying about that for now? Wait until you get the acceptances. Decide then—or if you think you can get away with it, tell them you're going to play all three."

EIGHT

Late in the Tuesday night before the Thanksgiving recess which would begin the next day at noon, Rachel, drifting to sleep in her single bed in the room just down the hall from the master bedroom, heard tires on the gravel driveway. She was so close to sleep she wanted to pretend she hadn't heard the sound or was just dreaming it. Someone had lost his way and was turning around in the driveway.

In the middle of the night? Who? The police? Because something terrible had happened in the dorms? A bad trip? A rapist breaking in? *Please, not a suicide!* It had happened at a colleague boarding school last year. She jumped out of bed and looked out the window.

The black surface of Bob's BMW glistened in the yellow porch light. He was already almost to the front door. Flooded with relief and surprise—he'd told her he would arrive *tomorrow* night—she ran down the hall in her bare feet, hearing the front door open, and got into their king size bed. Seconds later, she heard him coming up the stairs. She rolled over so her back would be to him as he entered the room.

"Rachel?" A whisper in the dark, behind her. She didn't answer. His footsteps toward the bathroom. The toilet flushing, then water running in the basin. Then silence, while he undressed. Then an instant of light she perceived through her eyelids. Then the click of the bathroom light switch, then darkness again, his footsteps padding, and the slight chill on her back as he lifted the covers, and she turned over toward him, still pretending to sleep, nestling, as if by instinct her chin into his neck, while his arm came over her shoulders. "Surprise! Surprise," he whispered. And indeed it was: he'd skipped a whole day of work to have an extra day with her and Sylvia! She pressed herself more tightly against him. All was well! All was well! And they both drifted to sleep.

In the morning, before he awoke, she lifted his arm from her shoulder, rolled over away and got up as quietly as she could out of bed, and went down the hall to the room where she slept when he wasn't home and made up the bed. Just in case he went in there and wondered who'd been her guest. Even though he'd never gone in there. Not once in nineteen years. There was no reason he would.

She went back down the hall to their room and rejoined him in bed. "Thank you," she said, not whispering now. "Four whole days together, not just three!" Expecting they would make love. But he slept on, exhausted, she was sure. She waited some more. He still slept on.

"Bob, wake up," she said, not quite loudly enough. Because the head of school should be at breakfast to wish the girls a happy Thanksgiving. And remind them of how much they had to be thankful for. She got out of bed, hoping he would awake before she was finished dressing, but he slept on. Disappointed with herself, like an addict incapable of refraining, she left him for the dining hall.

IN THE EARLY afternoon, after parents' cars and the buses to the airports and Amtrak had carried the students away for the long weekend, Rachel drove in her green Subaru station wagon to the Stop and Shop in Fieldington to shop for Thanksgiving dinner. Bob sat beside her in the passenger seat. "I wish I'd woken up on time," he'd said. She'd forgiven him, of course.

Sylvia sat in the backseat between Elizabeth, who was staying with the Perrine-Bickhams because Thanksgiving break was too short to go all the way to Oklahoma, and Auda Hellmann, an exchange student with red hair from the Salem School in Germany who was also staying with Rachel's family, Germany being even further away than Oklahoma.

On that same afternoon, Christopher Triplett stood at the edge of the parking lot of the Stop and Shop, waiting for the bus to Hartford. He would buy the ticket on the bus with the panhandling money he'd saved up because he didn't need to buy food anymore. He hoped his aunt would be glad to have him. He would've called her to tell her he was coming, but he'd lost his cell phone. He'd have to take the chance. Maybe she would forgive him for the way he'd treated her last summer—showing up at her door, needing shelter, accepting her hospitality and her offered affection, and then suddenly disappearing.

It was a cold morning, but the sky was blue and cloudless and the air was fresh. He was almost happy, but nervous too, on edge. Like when you expect something good to happen—if something very bad doesn't happen first.

Even though he was not panhandling at that moment, some people coming in and out of the store must have recognized him. Because they walked right past him as if he were not there, and others glanced at him and then quickly away. The tug of war between his hope his only living relative would forgive him and the fear she would slam the door in his face made him more and more agitated. He couldn't stop himself from checking the rooftops and all the windows. His hands felt empty without a weapon in them, so he put them in his pockets.

A silver Prius came toward him across the parking lot, stopping so near him he had to step back, and a fat teenage boy, wearing a baseball cap backwards, got out and slammed the door. Christopher jumped at the sudden noise. The kid stared at him. Like he'd never seen anything like that before. "I'm waiting for the bus, shithead," Christopher said. "You got a problem with that?"

"Why would I give a fuck what *you're* waiting for?" the kid asked, and turned and sauntered away across the parking lot.

Christopher starts after him. He's going to reach around the kid's head and poke his forefingers into each eye and pry them out, hear the sucking sound the eyeballs make, feel the wetness on his fingers. And know the justice.

Then the darkness came. Did he close his eyes? And then it was bright again. The kid strolled into the store, utterly ignorant of what had been about to happen to him.

A few minutes later, while he was still imagining the shitstorm he would be in if he hadn't stopped himself, an elderly lady in a brown coat paused in her walk across the parking lot, and searched his face with kind gray eyes. "I wish you a happy Thanksgiving," she said. Her voice was firm, her manner formal.

"I thank you," he said. It was a moment of grace.

She nodded her head and reached in her purse.

"I don't need money," he said, gently. "I'm not begging."

She flushed, withdrawing her hand from the purse. "I'm sorry, the other day, near the ice cream store—"

He shook his head. "I don't need to do that anymore, but don't be embarrassed. Everything's fine."

"That's good. And you have a place to stay?"

"Yes, ma'am, I have a place to stay."

"I'm glad!"

"It's by the river."

"And they're feeding you?"

"Yeah, they're feeding me." He was feeling shy. And yet he wanted to tell her everything. If there was a bench, he'd ask her to sit.

"What organization is it? I'd like to know. Maybe I could volunteer."

"What do mean, organization?" he said, sad all of a sudden. And a minute ago he'd been almost happy! She was trapping him into telling her where his camp was. That was her job. Then they'd come and pull it apart.

"I mean where they're feeding you. Where you sleep."

He shook his head.

"All right, I'll leave you alone," she said, speaking softly, and he understood she was respecting his privacy. "But I am glad you have a place to stay." She stepped past him. He felt a surge of regret, wanted to call her back, to say he was sorry for being so wrong about her intentions.

She stopped, stood very still for a second, like she'd suddenly thought of something. She turned around. "Then why are you standing here?"

"I'm waiting for the bus."

"The bus?"

"The one to Hartford."

"There's no bus to Hartford."

"What do you mean, there's no bus to Hartford? What's this?" He pointed to a bus schedule on a placard affixed to a light pole.

"Oh dear! That's outdated. They should have taken it down.

There's no bus to Hartford anymore."

"No bus! How can they do that? Just cancel a bus?" He was genuinely amazed. He really didn't know anymore how anything worked.

"I'm so sorry. How will you—"

"You think I'm a nutcase, don't you?"

She looked at him gravely. It seemed for a very long time. Then she shook her head. "It's the world that's crazy. Not you."

He thought about that for a moment. "I didn't say the world wasn't crazy," he said. "It was crazy of me though, to think I should go to Hartford when I have a place right here." The words surprised him. He was just making them up. But now that he'd said them, they almost felt true.

"And they'll give you a nice Thanksgiving dinner?"

He thought about the cans of food the two girls had provided him. "Nice enough," he said.

"I'm so glad," she said. "God bless you"—and she turned to cross the parking lot toward the Stop and Shop.

He stood very still, fighting off the urge to run after her and tell her everything. Instead, he realized it was getting warm, and took off his down jacket and stuffed it into his backpack resting by his feet. He didn't see the car with a couple in the front and three girls in the back.

Elizabeth and Sylvia saw their homeless man standing near a silver Prius. The down jacket he wore was like a flag. Would Rachel recognize it? Had Gloria proudly shown them to her when she'd bought them for the club? "What are you staring at?" Auda Hellmann asked.

Then the homeless man took off the down jacket and stuffed it in a backpack that was by his feet, and Rachel steered her car into the slot between a silver Prius and a ragged man standing in a thin tattered shirt with a backpack at his feet. She moved her glance from him to the rearview mirror to look into Elizabeth's and Sylvia's eyes. "Is that your homeless man?"

Elizabeth said, "No. That's not him." Sylvia looked away,

releasing her breath.

Then the homeless man picked up his backpack and put it on and walked away. Everyone in the car watched him go. "Why are there so many homeless people in America?" Auda asked. "I saw them everywhere when I was in New York."

In the front seat, Bob said, "That's a good question. We better damn well figure it out."

"Or what, Dad? If we don't, what?" Sylvia said.

He hesitated. "We just won't like ourselves very much, I guess. Some of us already don't."

"I'm glad you said that, Dad," Sylvia said.

"I'm glad too," Rachel said, turning now to Bob beside her in the front. He was looking out across the parking lot. He'd made his remark to the whole wide world.

IN THE STORE, Sylvia's parents took half of the shopping list and went off toward the produce. Elizabeth, who'd accepted the second half, tore it into three parts, glancing meaningfully at Sylvia, and then the three girls separated, until Sylvia came as if by chance to where Elizabeth was pretending to ponder which kind of bread crumbs to choose for the stuffing.

"You think your mother recognized the..."

"Jacket?" Sylvia finished. It was the first time she'd ever seen Elizabeth look so worried. "No. She never even saw it. I was watching both. She was looking straight ahead."

"And then he took it off?"

"Yeah, then he took it off."

"I hope you're right."

"She probably wouldn't have recognized it even if she did see it."

"Maybe not. But then why did you keep quiet when your mother asked if he was the one?"

"I didn't want to lie to my mother."

"Really? What do you think you were doing at Morning Meeting?"

Auda came at that exact moment. "What do parsnips look like?" she asked. "We don't eat them in Germany."

That night, Rachel dreamed she was in some kind of boat. Ahead of her was a harbor, empty of ships, save one far away against a dim horizon. The boat made no sound, propelled over the water through a mist by neither engine nor sail.

Behind her, out of sight, she felt the solid brown land slipping further away, and then the mist and the water of the harbor joined and everything was liquid, without form, except the ship toward which she was flowing. It got bigger and bigger until it was a massive cliff looming over her with a ladder coming down. She put her right foot on its bottom rung, and the boat, with her left foot still on its thin gunwale, began to part from the ship. Her two feet moved further and further apart. She saw each separate little wave jar against the side of the ship and turn to froth, she saw the stipples in the red rust above the waterline. At last, just as she was about to make a clown's pratfall into the water between the ship and the boat, she moved her left foot off the boat's gunwale onto the bottom rung of the ladder and climbed upward and was finally on the deck. A tiny person whose gender and age she could not determine, dressed in a piercingly bright white sailor suit, reminded her she was still the captain.

"We are days and days and days late in getting started, and no one but you knows how to start the engines."

"I don't," Rachel said, "but please weigh anchor anyway."

The little sailor disappeared and soon she felt the ship moving. It was gigantic, she couldn't see the end of it in either direction and the funnel above her was a tower, but the ship glided as soundlessly as the little boat out through the narrows, and now she could see the land slipping by in sharp focus. Like a magnified photograph. Buildings, trees, cars of every color, people walking on streets. The ship glided faster and faster stern first, silently, toward the open ocean. She watched a green buoy leaning with the current, and then she woke up.

In the morning, lying beside Bob, she told the dream to him and asked him what he thought it meant. He waited for an irritatingly long time, staring up at the ceiling, pretending to be thinking hard. He turned his head to her and said, in his most gentle voice, "I think it would be best if you figured that out for yourself." He kissed her forehead. "I know you will." He got up and took a shower and left her in the bed.

"If I wanted to figure it out myself, I wouldn't have asked you," she murmured toward the closed bathroom door. But still, he'd said he was sure she'd figure it out, and anyway maybe Freud, or whoever it was, was wrong and dreams didn't mean anything—just random vivid craziness we cook up in our heads—and there were a million *real* things that needed to get done for the Thanksgiving dinner.

Like when should she wake the girls up so they could help?

NINE

This year, Rachel and Bob had invited Eudora Easter and Reverend Michael Woodward, Rector of the Episcopal Church in Fieldington, to their Thanksgiving feast. Michael was a small man with a very pale complexion who wore such big glasses that he looked as if he were surprised by everything he saw. Rachel admired him for stubbornly trying hard to believe what he professed. He wasn't wearing clerical clothes today, having changed to an old brown sweater over a white shirt after the morning service. Eudora wore a flowing blue robe of velvet that came down to the top of her shoes. She and Father Woodward were close friends. Sometimes Rachel caught herself hoping they would marry, like now as they sat beside each other on one side of the table. Sylvia, Elizabeth, and Auda settled on the other, Bob and Rachel opposite each other at the ends.

The conversation around the table that afternoon would have been even more lively if Dean of Academics Gregory van Buren were in attendance, but he had declined in favor of a splurge of theater-going in New York City. Gregory was brilliant and powerful in his position. Rachel adored him. For years she'd been wishing he would find a woman to share his New York City jaunts, a fellow lover of good food, great wine, theater, and, of course, sex and romance, but Gregory had adhered relentlessly to his monkish lifestyle and had reached an age that, for conventional thinkers, especially the young, romance is difficult to imagine and sex on the verge of disgusting. Some thought he was gay. Gregory explained to Rachel that the reason he refused to correct them was that if he did, it would appear that he didn't approve of being gay.

After Bob had carved the turkey and before anyone began to eat, he said, his voice rising with enthusiasm, "Just think how implausible it is, how many related events had to occur, to make the universe and this little dot within it that supports life against all odds; and then think about how all the events that had to happen for each of us to be born, and on top of that to be together, here, now."

"I bet the turkey wishes a couple of events didn't happen," Michael said, "but that was a very nice grace."

"Right. I said it because I figured you needed a break. Auda, would you like to add anything as our guest from Germany?"

"I'd like to thank God," Auda said.

Eudora got up from her chair, saying something about making sure the pies weren't cooling too fast, and went into the kitchen. She had converted to atheism when her husband drowned in a swamp during a Reserve Marine Corps training two weeks right after their honeymoon. She preferred no god to one so incompetent as to allow such an obscenely calamitous event.

Auda went on for several minutes, thanking God in better English than many Americans ever achieve, and ended by asking Him "to make us ever mindful of the needs of others" just as Eudora returned.

"Amen to that," Eudora said in spite of herself after Auda finished, and Sylvia and Elizabeth, thinking of their homeless man, glanced at each other.

"Sylvia, would you like to add anything?" Bob asked.

Sylvia shook her head. She didn't look at her father. She wondered how much turkey, cranberry sauce, and stuffing would be left over and how much she and Elizabeth could take to the homeless man without its being discovered.

"Elizabeth?"

Elizabeth smiled brightly at Bob. "I never thought of myself as a coincidence before."

Silence.

"This is wonderful cranberry sauce," Michael said, saving the moment. Everyone started eating.

All the rest of the day, even past the time when Elizabeth and Auda went upstairs to the guest room they shared, Sylvia tried to find a moment to be alone with Elizabeth. It never happened. Auda was always there.

In her own room, in bed, with the lights out, Sylvia didn't even try to sleep. What was the homeless man doing in the parking lot? In the stolen down jacket and his clean clothes, he was almost too well dressed to beg. It couldn't be that he was waiting for someone. She felt a flicker of jealousy. Who? To do what? To go where?

Sylvia was well aware of her confusion. She pitied the homeless man, was afraid of him, wanted to help him, was curious about him, attracted to him, and disgusted by him, all at once. Her various versions of him paraded in her head: the one who was her and Elizabeth's project. Keeping him alive was something to get done, like finishing a term paper. He was also the one she had smelled before she dropped the dollars into his hat; and the one up to his knees in the river, facing away, his skin so white; and the one who turned around, whom she would have the right to join only if she took off her clothes too. Or the version crawling out of his lean-to into the dark and swiveling his head to find her while she held her breath. *Here we are*, she imagined calling to him. *Over here.* What would have happened next? If Elizabeth had not been with her, maybe she would have called out to him. Oh yes, he could hurt her and Elizabeth—yes, they were maybe falling into his trap. And yes, every once in a while, she felt a pulse of attraction to him. Just knowing that was in itself fascinating. What amazed her so was how alive she was. She didn't even want to be *un*confused.

"Sylvia?"

For an instant, Sylvia was in the shed again, Elizabeth on the other side of the door. Unscrewing the hinges.

But this door was already open. "I can't sleep," Elizabeth whispered. She tiptoed into the room and sat down on the side of Sylvia's bed. Her ungainly form was a silhouette against the paltry light. "What was he doing in the parking lot?"

"I don't know," Sylvia said.

"Maybe getting ready to steal something from the store?"

"Why? We're bringing him food."

"Cash maybe. Who knows?"

"It's the middle of the day. He could never."

"I know."

"So you think he's crazy?"

"I don't know. But he does live in a lean-to. You and I wouldn't."

"We don't have to."

"Well, why does *he* have to?"

"Okay," Sylvia said. "So maybe he *is* crazy. So what? Let's bring him Thanksgiving dinner."

"You know that's insane."

"Why? We had ours. Why shouldn't he?"

Elizabeth didn't answer.

"Come on! Is Thanksgiving for everybody, or isn't it?" *That* was what to say to Elizabeth.

Elizabeth put up her hands, palms out. "Okay, okay, okay, we'll do it. We might as well. We're in deep shit anyway. I'm much more afraid of getting kicked out than I am of him. And your mom has made it clear we can't undo what we're going to get kicked out for, if someone figures out we are the ones who stole the stuff."

"Good!"

"But that's not the only reason, is it? We just like to take chances. And it's not even just that. We're sticking our middle fingers up, flipping the bird."

"I suppose we are. But to what?"

"I don't know. The universe your dad was talking about?"

Sylvia giggled. "Whatever."

"Besides you're in love with the guy, right?" It was Elizabeth's turn to giggle.

"Very funny," Sylvia said. "If you don't make it as president, you can try being a comedian." Then, switching the subject as fast as she could: "How are we going to bring dinner to him without Auda knowing?"

"We'll figure that out in the morning."

"Okay. Think you can sleep now?"

"Probably not." Elizabeth stood up and moved to the door. "See you in the morning."

SYLVIA WOKE UP around ten o'clock to a silent house. Cold, damp November air came in through the open window, smelling like dead gardens. She got out of bed, reluctantly, and closed the window. Outside, the campus was shrouded in mist. By the time she was dressed it had begun to rain.

Elizabeth was waiting for her in the kitchen. She told Sylvia her mother had gone to her office to catch up on work, and her dad was driving around visiting stores where Best Sports stuff was sold. "Pretending to be a customer," Elizabeth added, shaking her head. "We need to get going before they get back and Auda wakes up." She crossed to the refrigerator and took out the big container holding the remains of the turkey.

Just then, Auda appeared, sleepily rubbing her eyes. "I'm starving. What's for breakfast?"

"Granola, yogurt, and fruit," Sylvia said, forcing herself to sound glad to see her.

"Goody," Auda said. "At home it would be cheese and meat. Yuck. Everything we eat in Germany is brown. But why's the turkey out?"

"There's a homeless man we're going to bring some to," Elizabeth said in her most casual tone.

"Oh?" Auda didn't look sleepy anymore. "Can I come?"

"It's raining hard out," Elizabeth said. "So if you want to stay inside, it's cool."

"I don't mind a little rain. I've got a great raincoat. Besides, we'll be in the car." Auda turned to Sylvia. "Your parents coming?"

"Actually, we'll be walking," Elizabeth said.

"My parents are both working," Sylvia said. "They won't come."

"On a holiday weekend?"

"Yeah, Americans work even harder than Germans," Elizabeth said.

Auda shrugged.

Elizabeth glanced at Sylvia as if to say, *Your turn.*

"I feel like I'm giving a quiz," Auda said. "Why don't you just tell me what's going on?"

"He lives in the woods," Sylvia said. "In a lean-to."

"A lean-to? What's that?"

"It's like a shack he made out of pine boughs," Elizabeth said. "It's pretty cool."

"Why doesn't he live in a shelter? Aren't there any shelters?"

"In Fieldington? Are you kidding? Nobody around here needs a shelter. They were all born on third base," Elizabeth said. "Besides, maybe he wants to live in the woods."

"Third base?"

"Never mind. Let's get going before it starts to rain even harder," Sylvia said.

"Okay, but how do you know where he lives?"

"He told us," Sylvia said.

"You talk to him?"

"Sometimes," Elizabeth lied.

"That's nice. What's his name?"

"It's not like that," Elizabeth said. "We didn't get *introduced*."

Sylvia cut three slices of white meat from the carcass of the turkey and two dark from a drumstick, and put them into a plastic container while Elizabeth spooned stuffing and cranberry sauce in another. "Does your mother know we are doing this?" Auda asked.

"No, but she won't mind," Sylvia said.

"Just the same, let's not tell her. Okay?" Elizabeth said.

Auda nodded. "My parents wouldn't want me to be hanging out with a homeless guy either."

"And if she notices there's less, we ate it for lunch," Elizabeth said.

THE ROOF WAS leaking. Christopher reached up to tighten the weave of pine boughs, and a cold stream ran down his hand, across his wrist and into his sleeve. He started to yell a swear word but stopped himself. He didn't want to hear his own voice swallowed in the drum of the rain and the burble of the swollen river. He was disappeared enough already.

So he just moved from under the drip and went on thinking about the lady in the brown coat. That was another reason he didn't swear when the cold water ran down his arm: she'd said, *God bless you*, and it was the world that was crazy, not him, and now he was watching her walk away again across the parking lot into the store on her little black shoes, with their short, square heals. They kept her steady as she walked.

After a while, he couldn't sit there anymore. The drip was getting bigger, a steady wet percussion. He crawled out of the lean-to into the rain. His axe was embedded in a tree stump near the door. Like Excalibur in its stone in the stories Uncle Ray used to read to him. He pulled it out and carried it to a tree whose lower branches he chopped off, and then he trimmed the smaller shoots off and he brought them back to the lean-to and put them on top of where the leak was, and then he did this again and again, weaving the new boughs into the whole roof—and not just the leaking part, because, even though he was getting wet and cold because he wasn't wearing the down jacket because down loses its ability to keep you warm when it gets wet, working like this, treading back and forth over the sodden dead leaves of last summer to fix his lean-to, soothed him, and he explained to himself, because explaining things to himself was calming too, that the reason the pine boughs leaked after a while was that the needles died.

He crawled back into the lean-to, took all his wet clothes off, and got into his sleeping bag. When he was warm, he'd put on dry clothes and maybe even the down jacket. One step at a time. Think about each one while you do it and about nothing else. That's how you stay alive.

He was still in his sleeping bag, half an hour later, when the rain started to come down harder and then even harder, and then a wind came up, blowing through the woods. He told himself it was just pure luck that he had re-sheathed his lean-to just in time, and then he heard footsteps. He scrambled out of his bag. His axe was outside in the stump. Where an enemy could reach it first. How did he get so careless? An instant later, he was in his lean-to again, the leap from one place to another so explosive he would be better off to be still in Iraq with his friends; and then he figured out whose footsteps they probably were and he made another explosive leap, to the same upwelling of the sudden happiness he'd felt when he remembered he hadn't heard them laughing at him and realized they were *friends*. And not just one, but two!

He put on his dry clothes as fast as he could and even combed his hair with his fingers to make himself presentable, then he went out into the storm and there they were, three of them this time. Three! By the food cache. They didn't see him yet.

The tall, thin one was taking off her backpack and putting it on the ground. She took off her raincoat and covered the backpack with it. "But you'll get all wet," he yelled above the noise of the storm. "You'll freeze! Can't you see it's raining out?"

The wind was blowing the rain sideways now. They stared at him though the torrent of it. Like wet kittens someone had tried to drown. "Get in," he commanded, a sergeant again, taking care of his troops. He pointed to the opening of the lean-to. "Where it is dry." He stepped forward, picked up the raincoat and the backpack, and pointed to the lean-to again with his other hand. "Out of the wind," he yelled. "Otherwise you"—pointing at the tall thin one, her shirt and jeans soaked through, clinging to her like another skin—"will get hypothermia. Hypothermia," he repeated, and he stepped around them so he was behind them, and spreading his arms he shepherded them in.

There was just enough room in there for the four of them to sit in a circle. The other two girls, the big blonde one and the small one with red hair, were still in their raincoats. He put their backpack in the middle of the circle and reached behind himself into his own backpack and pulled out the down jacket and handed it to the tall, thin one where she was sitting across the circle, shivering hard in her wet clothes. She stared at the down jacket, like someone deciding whether or not to reject a gift. Then she reached for it and put it on over her wet shirt.

In that cramped space, the sides of the other two girls, the tall, thin one on his right, the big blonde one on his left, touched his shoulders and hips. He leaned forward to make a space, sure they didn't want their bodies to touch the likes of him, just as, very near, there was the huge cracking sound of a tree trunk breaking. The girls' bodies stiffened. They looked up, as if they could see through the roof. There was the roar of the tree falling down through the branches of other trees and the final dying crash, and then even in the wind it seemed very quiet and he realized the rain had stopped. "Don't worry, no tree is going to fall on us," he said. It was total bullshit. There were two huge trees even nearer that were just as likely to fall on the lean-to and squash them all like bugs, but he wanted them to feel safe.

The backpack they had brought sat in the center of the circle. The big blonde girl and the tall, thin one looked at each other. “Now?” the big blonde one asked. The tall, thin one, still shivering, nodded, and opened the backpack and pulled out two square plastic containers, placing them before him in the center of the circle. The other two girls watched, their eyes going back and forth between him and the tall, thin one. She popped the covers off. He smelled the turkey, the cranberry sauce, the stuffing even before he saw them.

“Happy Thanksgiving,” she said.

“For me?”

“Yes, for you,” the tall, thin one said. “And by the way, my name is Sylvia. And this is Elizabeth,” pointing at the big blonde one, “and that’s Auda.”

“Sylvia,” he repeated. “Sylvia.” A flush came on her face. He turned to Elizabeth and said her name, and then to Auda and said hers too.

“Aren’t you going to tell us yours?” Sylvia said.

“Christopher,” he said, turning his face to her. “Christopher Triplett, Sergeant, US Marine Corps.”

They were silent.

“I’m not in the best of shape,” he said, not sure whether he was warning them, or just stating the fact. “Maybe you can see?”

Auda frowned.

“I don’t see anything wrong,” Sylvia said.

“Iraq? Or Afghanistan?” Elizabeth asked.

“How did you know?”

“I didn’t. I guessed.”

“Iraq. Four times,” he said.

“Four!” Elizabeth said.

He shrugged.

“Well anyway, we’re glad you don’t have to go there anymore,” Sylvia said. She looked straight at him.

I might as well be there, he almost said. Instead: “You’re still shivering. You’ll never get warm with your wet shirt on. Take it off and put the down jacket back on.” The sergeant again, taking care of his troops. “I’ll go outside while you do.” He crawled out of the lean-to.

The first thing he saw was his axe. Embedded in the tree stump. Beckoning. *We're glad you don't have to go there anymore. Because you won't be killing any more of us.* Looking straight at him. She'd come back to punish him.

He stands up and goes over there and puts his hand on the handle of the axe. He doesn't let himself see what he's going to do.

Below his eyes, the rings marking the age of the stump when it had been killed are as clear as lines for rivers on a map. Then darkness came.

INSIDE THE LEAN-TO, Sylvia unzipped the down jacket.

"Don't!" Elizabeth said.

Sylvia took the jacket off and hung it over a pine branch on the side of the lean-to.

"This is fucking crazy!" Auda said. "He's trying to get us naked. We need to get out of here."

"If he wanted to hurt us, he already would have," Sylvia said. She took off her shirt and put it down beside her.

"Jesus, leave your bra on at least!" Elizabeth said. She moved to the door to stand guard until Sylvia put the jacket on.

Sylvia shrugged. She put the down jacket on over her bra. "I already feel warmer," she said. "You can leave if you want."

"Oh sure!" Elizabeth said. "And leave you behind."

"I'd go. I'm not crazy. But I don't remember the way," Auda said.

"Relax, everybody," Sylvia said. "It's going to be fine."

CHRISTOPHER WATCHED AN ant crawl across the stump. Crossing the rings, one by one. For hours and hours and hours, it felt like, until the ant reached the axe blade, a wall before it. It stopped, crawled to its left, stopped again, and crawled to its right. Christopher urged it to keep on crawling around the axe to continue its journey, but the ant stopped again and reversed itself. Christopher put his hand on the handle of the axe to pull it out of the stump and the ant's way, but something told him not to. The ant was on its own. Christopher turned away from the stump toward the lean-to, realizing, at last, he was hungry. "You ready?" he called.

"Yup," Sylvia called back.

He crawled back in past Elizabeth. Elizabeth returned to where she'd been sitting. "I'm not going to eat this alone," he said, a sergeant again, in full command of his troops—and of himself.

"We brought it for you," Sylvia said.

He shook his head. "We're eating together."

The girls looked at each other. Elizabeth nodded her head. She turned to him. "As long as you go first."

"All right," he said.

"Oh crap, we forgot the fork!" Elizabeth said.

"It's probably my fault," Auda said. "I should have thought of it."

"Who cares?" Christopher picked up a slice of turkey, pulled a piece of it off, dipped it in the cranberry sauce, placed it on the lid of the container as if it were a plate, put the rest of the slice back into the container, then picked up some stuffing and put that on top of the slice of turkey. He smiled and said, "Don't worry, I washed my hands last month," and put the turkey and stuffing in his mouth. He handed the lid to Sylvia, who tore off a tiny bit off turkey and put it on the lid, then did the same with an even smaller chunk of stuffing before picking both up and putting them in her mouth.

The other two girls followed, but they took big chunks and didn't bother to use the lid as a plate—to get this over with fast and get out of there, he understood. Because why shouldn't they be frightened of him? Even though he told jokes about washing his hands once a month. They went round and round, each in turn, until the food was gone. "That was the best Thanksgiving I've had in a while," he said.

Elizabeth said, "We're glad we came." She looked at Sylvia and pointed to her wristwatch.

Sylvia nodded. Her wet shirt was still hanging beside her on the side of the lean-to. Elizabeth stared at it. Sylvia turned to him across the circle. "Close your eyes."

Exaggerating, he closed his eyes, bent his head down, and put both hands over his eyes. His second try to let them know he could be funny when he wanted to be. Sylvia took off the down jacket and her damp shirt off its pine branch hanger, put it on, and shivered again, while Elizabeth put the containers into the backpack. "I'm finished now," Sylvia said. "You can open your eyes."

He opened his eyes and raised his head. She handed the down jacket back to him and reached for her raincoat to put it on. He nodded toward the jacket. "Thanks for this. And thanks for the dinner."

"We're glad you liked it," Elizabeth said. "We would have brought you gravy too, but you don't have a stove to heat it with." Then, flushing: "I'm sorry. I didn't mean—"

"It's all right," he said, softly. "I understand."

THEY CRAWLED OUT of the lean-to into the smell of woods after a rain. Right away, Auda started to run. Sylvia put her hand on Elizabeth's elbow, holding her back. "He's watching," she said. "Don't you dare insult him."

Auda was waiting for them at the edge of the athletic fields. "How did you know he doesn't have a stove?" she asked Elizabeth. "He has a down jacket and some other stuff."

"Oh, I don't know, I just guessed," Elizabeth said.

"Yeah, but he has a firepit with a grill over it. Didn't you see?"

"He does? No, I didn't notice."

"Oh well," Sylvia said, careful to avoid Elizabeth's eyes. "He didn't seem to mind not having gravy. The cranberry sauce was enough."

UPON THEIR RETURN, they found Bob Perrine raking leaves off the front lawn of the Head's House. "Where have you guys been?"

"Just walking around, showing Auda stuff," Elizabeth said. She wore her raincoat over the backpack. Sylvia had let her carry it because it was light now.

"In all that rain?"

"We left before it started," Sylvia said.

"Then why are you carrying your raincoats?"

Sylvia could tell by her father's tone that he wasn't suspicious. He was just mystified. She realized that if he were less trusting she would not feel the rush of sadness that descended on her while she gazed at his innocent face. She was drifting away from him, traveling to some place she needed to reach, where, because he was still mystified, she could not tolerate his company. She was halfway there, on a path she couldn't see, and she'd stopped to turn around and wave good bye.

All she had to do to keep him with her was tell him everything. Maybe the school wouldn't kick her and Elizabeth out for being kind. Maybe it was worth it to take that chance. She drew in a big breath and held it, on the thin edge of telling.

But they'd just brought Christopher his Thanksgiving dinner. Now they were going to tell where he lived? Those woods belonged to somebody. They'd tear down his lean-to and make him leave.

She let out her breath and said, "We took the raincoats just in case," supplying the only answer that came to mind, and waited for him to wonder aloud why they didn't wait till after the rain. But he nodded his head, satisfied, and resumed his raking.

THAT NIGHT, IN Sylvia's room, after Bob and Rachel had gone to bed, Auda said, "I started to figure it out when he thanked you for the down jacket. Because why would he thank *you* when *he* had lent it to *you*?"

"He was thanking her for giving it back," Elizabeth said.

"Like he thought you'd just walk away and leave him without it? Come on! And then you said he didn't have a stove when there's only one reason that you could possibly know. Why are you denying it? You think I would tell?"

"No. If we did it, you wouldn't tell," Sylvia said. "But we didn't."

"I hate this! I just hate it! You do think I would tell. Otherwise, why would you lie to me? You invite me to go with you. Like you want someone to know. You want to share, not just be alone in it. Then when it gets obvious to that someone, you pretend you don't know what she's talking about. That's crazy. You know what this means? It means you want to get caught, that's what it means. You want to get caught because it feels crazy to have to sneak around and pretend some burglar stole the stuff, when you did and everybody should be proud of you. The guy's homeless, he lives in a shack made out of dead trees in the woods because he has post-traumatic whatever from fighting in the stupidest war that ever was, and you bring him clothes and food and you're supposed to be *ashamed*?"

"Shh," Sylvia said. "My mother and father will hear."

"They should hear. Let's all three of us go in there and wake them and tell them. I'll say it was my idea. I'll tell them it was me who stole the stuff, not you." Auda shook her head. "What do I care if your mother kicks me out of Miss O's. I'm only staying the first semester anyway. My school in Germany would think I'm a hero. I'd probably get some kind of dumb prize named after some duke or other that somebody cooked up to salve his conscience. I live in Germany, remember. We're still living down the Holocaust." She paused. "And you need to stop going out there. He told us right to our faces he's not in the best of shape. He was trying to warn us he's crazy."

"I thought about telling this afternoon when my father asked us where we'd been," Sylvia said.

"And?"

"I decided not to. Because what would happen to him?"

"Somebody would take care of him."

"Bullshit," Elizabeth said. "Why do you think he's living in the woods? And guess what? Where he's living is on school property."

"What!" Sylvia said. "School property! It can't be. That lean-to is miles away from here."

Elizabeth shook her head. "I did the research. I thought I should find out. I told Mabel Walters—that's our business manager, Auda—that I wanted to find out how much land the school owned that it could sell to raise money for financial aid, and she got all excited and told me to bring it up in Morning Meeting and keep on talking about it until something happens. She showed me the deed and the map. She said, 'I've been saying for years we are a school, not a real estate company. Why are we hanging on to all this land?'"

"But suppose they do sell it?" Auda said.

"Are you kidding? It will take the board of trustees about seven hundred more years and two thousand nervous breakdowns to even be able to think about selling. You've read the brochure: *Surrounded by beauty*, blah blah blah. I told Mabel I'd bring it up at an opportune time. Meantime, the school owns miles and miles beyond the actual campus. We tell Sylvia's mom there's a guy living on school property—how's she supposed to know he's not crazy, maybe even has a gun? And how does she know other homeless people won't decide it's a good place to live and there will be a great big encampment? Can you imagine? Going to the bathroom all over the place? She'll have to bring policemen in to kick them off. Either get rid of Christopher or pretend she doesn't know he's there. That's her choice. Sylvia doesn't want to do that to her mom."

"I can speak for myself," Sylvia said. "But Elizabeth's right. You want to get Christopher out of his lean-to and us kicked out of our school, go right ahead."

Before Auda could answer, they heard footsteps approaching down the hall. Seconds later, the door opened. Sylvia's mom, barefoot in pajamas, said, "I can't sleep either. How about some pancakes?" The girls didn't answer. They had expected her to urge them to go to bed. "Pancakes in the middle of the night," she urged. "Wouldn't that be fun?"

Auda was the first to recover. "What a great idea!"

"Yeah, I'm starving," Elizabeth said.

"Wonderful! See you downstairs."

THERE WAS A gas fireplace in the huge kitchen, which was almost never lighted. But that night, Sylvia's mom struck the inaugural fire, after first searching through almost all the cabinets before she found the remote to light it with—as if having a fire in the hearth, even a fake one, was critical to this one occasion. Indeed, it did give off a warm yellow glow. Auda kept the conversation going—mostly about the mix of ingredients and what they would be cooking in the middle of the night if this were happening in Germany. Sylvia was grateful for this. They turned on the oven and put the cooked pancakes in it to keep them warm until there was a huge stack of them, and the kitchen smelled of sweetness and maple syrup, which they warmed in the microwave. When the pancakes were all done, they carried a platter of them to a big leather sofa which faced the fire and they sat there, snuggled close together, and started to eat.

Sylvia should have been shivering with happiness and pride in her family at such an intimate, cozy moment. But she felt again the distance she'd felt when her dad had asked, "Why the raincoats?" There was a removal—as if she were remembering what was happening while it still was. She ate her pancakes robotically, feeling a weird nostalgia and amazement. She was now a guest, like Elizabeth, and maybe even Auda. She pushed the thought away.

But then she heard her dad's steps on the stairs and he appeared, rubbing his eyes in his old rumpled pajamas and those raggedy slippers she'd put in his stocking ten million years ago, and said, "I smell pancakes," and precisely because he'd completed and perfected what was happening, the feeling that she had separated from her family returned with even more intensity. She couldn't wait until she could get away and be alone in her own bed.

TEN

Sylvia, are you with us this morning?" Gregory van Buren asked on the snowy Monday morning after the Thanksgiving break, during his famous class on Greek tragedy. Gregory offered it only to seniors—though he wasn't sure if even seniors had lived long enough to understand.

Sylvia turned from the window. "I was watching the snow fall." Her tone was matter-of-fact. She was in no mood to apologize.

Gregory nodded. "It is beautiful, isn't it? Why would anyone pass up a chance to gaze at beauty? And it *is* hard to focus the first day after a vacation—even a short one. My own head is full of the plays I saw during the break." He paused, just as surprised as his students. He was usually a fierce taskmaster. "So here's what we will do for the next few minutes this morning. Everybody, please, look out the window at the falling snow."

They all, including Sylvia, looked straight ahead at him in disbelief. "No, please," he insisted, pointing to the window. "Look!"

They turned and looked through the window. None of them were surprised to see that the girls walking on the paths wore no coats in spite of the cold. It was an Oliver tradition: to prove how much tougher girls are than boys, no Miss O's student ever wore a winter coat while on the campus.

"Now, don't tell anyone what you see," Gregory said. "Or how you feel, or what you're thinking about watching the snow fall. Keep it a secret. That's what the playwrights you are reading did: kept secrets until they built and built, and then they told. And even then, some part of their stories is still a secret. The ones who tell all are the ones we don't remember."

Everyone, including Gregory, looked out the window. A radiator rattled. The fluorescent lights on the ceiling hummed. Some girls did their dutiful best to follow Gregory's request. For some of them, it was a nice experience, one they even might remember. Others tried and failed. Their minds wandered to other concerns: *Where the hell did I leave my cell phone? How long are we going to have to do this?* For others, it was just Gregory being Gregory. They thought about that, not about the snow.

Sylvia thought about how impossible it was going to be to pretend to be going for a run when they would be sinking up to her and Elizabeth's knees, and almost all the way to Auda's hips, in the snow with every step. If it kept on snowing, they would have to make the trip at night when they wouldn't be seen.

She was still thinking about this when Gregory brought the class back to *Oedipus Rex* and *Antigone*, breaking them into four groups of four. *Would these plays say anything different to you if they were set in a Connecticut snowstorm instead of the bright, revealing light of Thebes? Yes or no, and why. Be specific and refer to specific scenes in either or both the plays. You have ten minutes. Then we'll put each group with another one to see if they agree—and if not, why. Then each of the two combined groups will report.*

For Sylvia, who didn't say a word for the rest of the period, the question should have been if Sophocles had a choice. He'd never been in a New England snowstorm. How could he know? Normally, she would have pushed the discussion in that direction: *We all do what we do because of whatever we inherit. Like I inherited this school. Or maybe we do whatever we want.* But not this day. In her mind she was watching snowflakes filter down through the trees and land on the green of Christopher's lean-to. And hearing the silence.

After the class, as she was trying to leave, Gregory put his hand on her elbow. "I've never seen you so distracted. Are you all right?"

"I'm fine."

"Really?"

"Yes, really."

He let go her elbow. She went outside into the falling snow. The world was mute. There wasn't a sound.

ON WEDNESDAY NIGHT, Sylvia and Elizabeth set the alarms on their cell phones at two in the morning and put them on vibrate. They put the phones under their pillows and got in their bunks, fully dressed. Neither was surprised by how long they lay awake, and when the phones buzzed beneath their heads, it felt as if they'd been asleep for only minutes. They got out of their bunks and, because they deemed their mission exempt from the no-coat tradition, put on the full array of cold-weather gear. In the dark, the clothes made them looked puffed up to each other, as if someone had pushed air into them with a bicycle pump.

The summertime screen had been removed from the window so they didn't have to sneak down the hall. Elizabeth went out first. Sylvia followed into the burnt almond smell of snow on a freezing winter night. There was no wind, no moon, no clouds, and lots of stars. They snuck across the campus to the kitchen behind the dining hall.

Auda, who lived in a different dorm, was there waiting. She was counting on her roommate, a sound sleeper, not to discover her absence for the two hours or so she'd be gone. She did have a story at the ready though, just in case: she had a boyfriend who had arranged to meet her in his car and take her to a party at his fraternity in Trinity College where he was a sophomore. She'd been very careful to tell her roommate about how she'd met him in Fieldington's only bookstore, Colonial Books. "He loves to read," she'd said, and even brought a book back to the dorm she claimed he'd urged upon her.

The school's head cook, Mr. Erickson, whose nickname was Leif, of course, was notoriously absentminded. He could be counted on not to lock all the windows. Hungry students had been sneaking into the kitchen in the middle of the night for all the years of his tenure to find what he had pretended to have forgotten to put away. It was exactly the same every night: a giant-size jar of peanut butter, a variety of cold cuts, a big loaf of bread, and even, sometimes, some pie or cake. Whatever it was, it was always set out on a counter with a light left on just above it.

That night it was all gone, consumed by earlier visitors. The three girls weren't surprised. They went into the storeroom and filled their backpacks with cans of food, then went back out into the night and labored across the deep snow toward Christopher's lean-to.

At the edge of the woods, about half the distance, Elizabeth stopped walking. She had to wait until she had enough breath to speak.

"What?" But Sylvia already knew.

"I'm sorry, I just can't."

Sylvia was surprised how angry—and maybe even a little bit contemptuous—hearing that confession made her. "Just do it!"

Elizabeth shook her head. There was a beseeching look on her face. Another surprise. "You go on ahead. I'll wait here."

"All right, we will," Sylvia declared.

"No we won't, that's nuts. She'll freeze," Auda said. "Let's hide the backpacks and we'll get snowshoes tomorrow and go the rest of the way tomorrow night."

"Where are we going to get snowshoes?" Sylvia said.

"Where do you think?"

"No way. I'm not going back there."

"Not the equipment shed, dummy! I'll buy them."

Sylvia turned to Elizabeth for her opinion, but Elizabeth looked away, embarrassed. She was usually the solution to a problem, not the cause.

"Come on, let's get to work," Auda said, pointing. "We'll bury the stuff in the snow by that tree over there."

They buried the backpacks and started the slog back to school. Before they were halfway home, Sylvia was tired enough to understand Elizabeth had been right. She could never have made it to Christopher's lean-to and back again. Even Auda was obviously exhausted. Sylvia got on one side of Elizabeth while Auda got on the other, and together they propped her up by her armpits, but they still moved excruciatingly slowly. They took a route that led them onto the campus a long way from their dorms and then to a path that had been cleared of snow so their tracks could not be traced. They got to Auda's dorm first. She gestured good night and disappeared into her room through the window.

Minutes later, Sylvia and Elizabeth did the same. They did not speak until they were in their bunks. It was easier to say things when they couldn't see each other. "I'm sorry I got so mad," Sylvia said.

She waited for Elizabeth, below her to say she was sorry too, for making them get only halfway, but Elizabeth said nothing. Sylvia said, "Not everyone is a good athlete," to appear to provide Elizabeth an excuse—but actually to rub it in.

There was a long silence. Just as Sylvia was going to end it by admitting that she was tired too, Elizabeth said, "I would have been able to get to the lean-to. I know that now because I got halfway there and also got back. But I couldn't have gone any further than we went tonight, counting both directions, so I also know that if we did get to the lean-to, I would have had to stay there overnight."

"Well, Auda and I would have stayed with you. I wouldn't be scared if there were all three of us."

"Yeah? Maybe I wouldn't either. But I sure as hell wouldn't let myself go to sleep. And suppose we did spend the night out there because I couldn't get back. We might have not got back in the morning on time for classes. Everybody would want to know where we'd been. That should make you glad we came back."

"Well, you should have thought of it since you're so smart. You could have said that was the reason to turn back."

"Instead of admitting I was tired?"

"Yeah."

"That's ridiculous," Elizabeth said.

It seemed like only seconds later that Sylvia heard the long deep breaths of Elizabeth sleeping. Soon she drifted off too and dreamed she and Christopher and her dad were in her dad's apartment in New York City. Her dad was wearing Christopher's black down jacket. Christopher was wearing a blue blazer and gray flannel sacks and was saying, "You can kill people and still be sane," and her dad was nodding his head.

The next day, the snow plows having done their work, Auda used the lunch period and her subsequent free period to walk into Fieldington and return with three pairs of snowshoes, which she bought on her credit card. "Thank God my dad is rich," she said, "or Christopher would starve." Then Sylvia suggested that since Auda had lots of money, they could buy the food at Stop and Shop and eliminate the risk of getting caught stealing stuff that Leif Erickson didn't plan to give away.

Auda was delighted with this plan. She seemed to have replaced her fear of Christopher with a newly discovered love of risk and adventure. Every other day she bought food at Stop and Shop, and every other night the three girls snowshoed out to Christopher's food cache. Auda was relentlessly cheerful and determined and seemed impervious to fatigue, unlike Sylvia and Elizabeth, who were worn down as much by worry as by the exertion of snowshoeing out to the lean-to every other night. "What do I care if I get sent home? I'm going there anyway, back to my own school when vacation starts," Auda said again and again, until one night Elizabeth said, "Why don't you just shut up about that, okay? We don't need to hear it again. And besides, if your dad weren't rich, do you think we'd let Christopher starve?"

"Elizabeth, what's wrong with you? Why're you picking on Auda?" Sylvia said. "You'd rather steal the food, wouldn't you? If you weren't so scared of getting caught and kicked out—and rejected by MIT."

"Yeah, and I'm stealing from my dad. Isn't that good enough?" Auda said. "Instead of being pissed off at me because he's rich, think of me as Robin Hood, come all the way from Germany just for you."

Elizabeth managed a half-smile. "Okay, fine. Keep on buying. Just don't buy Christopher anything he might actually like to eat, okay? If your dad were an American, he'd be a conservative, wouldn't he? I mean, he has something to conserve, right? Like money, for instance. Which he thinks he earned all by himself. He might not mind giving stuff away to Christopher. He just wouldn't want him to feel he deserves it."

They trudged out to Christopher's lair, returning tired, sleepy, cold. Then they would wake up, go through the rigors of classes, and do it all over again a few night later.

They left the food where Elizabeth and Sylvia had made their first cache for him, fifteen yards or so away from his lean-to. If he came out of the lean-to and charged at them, they could easily outdistance him on their snowshoes while he'd sink into the snow. It was scarier to be close to him in the dark of night than it had been when they'd brought him Thanksgiving dinner in the daytime. Even though they had actually gone into his lean-to with him. They didn't mention this to each other, but it was a wonder. How had they gotten up the nerve?

Working quietly, they buried the food deep in the snow to keep it from freezing and started the long slog back to school. One time he did come out of his lean-to, but he stood unmoving by the opening, watching them. He didn't seem to know who they were. In the dark, it was hard to see the expression on his face, but they sensed an aura of derangement or forgetfulness. Or maybe he was walking in his sleep? The woods and snow and his lean-to, and the river they could hear in the dark, was a world with different rules they had invaded. When they turned back and started for home, the sensation followed them until they were safely back in the dorm, where, in bed at last, trying for sleep, it seemed as far away as Mars.

Other times, that world, its black dome above them, spread with tiny stars and white snow beneath their snowshoes, contained an almost unendurable beauty—which their schoolmates, asleep in their warm beds, would never know.

STARTING THE FIRST week of December, the twenty-three girls who had applied for Early Decision went to the student mailboxes every day, hoping to find a thick envelope. The boxes were situated conveniently in a part of the dining hall building that everyone had to pass on the way to the dining hall, and the mail arrived at the school midmorning. Those who had a free period then would check their mail before lunch. They were too anxious to wait, and also they wanted the moment to be relatively private, especially if they pulled a thin envelope out of the mailbox. Elizabeth, who took more than the usual number of courses, had classes every period in the morning, so she had to wait for lunch.

On the first two days, her mailbox was empty; on the third it contained a check from her father for her monthly allowance of twenty dollars, and a short note saying how much he and her mother missed her and reminding her that her mother's birthday was a week hence. *So be sure to get a card into the mail right away.* "I already did, Dad," Elizabeth murmured. She knew her annoyance with him was actually just disappointment.

The next day when she pulled open the door to her box, the

thick letter—actually a small package—was there, looking strangely inert. She pulled it out, put it surreptitiously under her arm in a failed attempt to hide it from eyes both congratulatory and envious, and took it back to her dorm room, skipping lunch. Despite the thickness of the envelope, she suddenly wasn't sure anymore that MIT would admit into its hallowed precincts an overweight tattooed female from redneck country.

As soon as she was alone in her dorm room, she ripped the envelope open. Everything was there: the congratulatory acceptance, the needed financial package, and several pages of unctuously helpful information that, even in her rush of happiness, struck her as being way to full of itself, as if the glorious existence of MIT would save the world from perdition simply by being MIT.

All of this contingent, of course, on the successful completion of your secondary school course work and graduation.

Elizabeth sat down heavily on the edge of her lower bunk, overcome, as if she hadn't known this when she and Sylvia stole from the shed. In her head she saw the declaration in the student handbook that the consequence for stealing was expulsion; she heard Rachel Bickham reiterating that when she contradicted Gloria Buchanan in Morning Meeting. Elizabeth had a sudden desire to rush out into the woods right then and demand that Christopher give it all back so she and Sylvia could put it back in the shed and make the problem go away.

But of course she wouldn't do that. Sylvia wouldn't either. He'd freeze to death. Besides, there was no way they'd get caught. Even if Gloria Buchanan happened to see him wearing the down jacket. What was she going to do? Go up to him and say, *Where'd you get it?* There were lots of black down jackets just like it.

Just the same, next time they brought him food, they should leave him a note not to tell anybody ever where he got it.

Elizabeth stood up, telling herself not to ruin the moment by worrying that they were going to get caught. Because that wasn't going to happen.

And anyway, if it did, it did.

She put everything back in the envelope and put that in her desk drawer out of sight. She didn't want Sylvia to walk in and see it and think she was bragging. Now she was very hungry, but the lunch period was over. She left the room, closed the door, and hurried to her next class. On the way, using her cell phone, she called her parents and left a voicemail. "Hey, Mom and Dad. I got in."

As soon as her parents got home from work, they called back. "We are so proud of you!" her dad said. He said it again. And then again. Then her mother said it too, her voice a tremolo, on the verge of tears. "I never dreamed I'd have a daughter so smart."

That night after she and Sylvia were in bed, Elizabeth said, "By the way, I heard from MIT today."

Above her Sylvia sat up. "You did!"

"Yeah, I got in."

"Congratulations! I'm happy for you."

"Thanks."

"I bet your mom and dad are proud."

"They are."

"What did they say?"

"Just what you said. They are proud." She didn't tell Sylvia that her mother almost cried.

"I'm proud of you too!" Sylvia said. "Now we just have to be careful we don't—"

"I know," Elizabeth said. "Let's not talk about that, okay? 'Cause it's not going to happen."

There was a silence. Then: "Okay, it isn't. So congratulations. You're a star."

"Thanks," Elizabeth said.

AT HER GOING-AWAY party the night before the beginning of winter vacation, Auda promised she would return for a few days in February when Salem School would have a recess. "I wish I could stay here for the whole rest of the year," she said. "I hate going home to boring old Germany." Sylvia and Elizabeth wished so too, for a reason no one else at the party knew: Sylvia, Elizabeth, and Auda had become a team of three. Now they would be only two.

In fact, for the next two and a half weeks until the vacation ended and Elizabeth returned from Oklahoma, the team would be reduced to one. Elizabeth had wanted to offer to stay at the school in order to help Sylvia bring the food to Christopher (and also to leave that note). But her parents, who both worked for the same local trucking company, her father as a freight dispatcher and her mother a bookkeeper, would have been heartbroken. They had given up the company of their one beloved child during her most formative years only because of the superior education they believed a prestigious New England boarding school with a mission to empower young woman would provide. Besides, now that the pay-off for that sacrifice had been assured with the acceptance to MIT, they wanted her home so they could tell her to her face how much they loved and were proud of her.

Sylvia rode the bus to Bradley Airport with Elizabeth and Auda the next morning to extend their time together. Without talking about it, as if instinctively, they sat all the way in the back to separate themselves from the other girls who were talking loudly and laughing, glad to have two whole weeks of vacation in front of them.

At the security point for Auda's flight to Frankfort, which left before Elizabeth's to Tulsa, the girls huddled in a tight circle. "Text me every day so I know what's happening with you and Christopher," Auda said. "And remember, just leave the food and get away."

"I will," Sylvia promised.

Auda promised again she'd visit next year. She got up on her tiptoes and hugged Elizabeth hard and then hugged Sylvia a little bit harder and longer. She turned away and got in the line.

Sylvia wanted to wait until Auda got through security and then wave a last goodbye, but Elizabeth tugged on her elbow. "Let's not drag it out."

A few minutes later, at the domestic security lines, Elizabeth reminded Sylvia that she'd only have to take food out to Christopher twice because they'd planned ahead and taken large amounts out the last several trips. He should have plenty in reserve. "And without me you can go on your cross-country skis instead of snowshoes. And you can go in the middle of the day because people will think you're just going skiing for fun."

"I know. I'll be fine."

"Well, then don't look so worried. Just remember not to go

straight there, in case somebody follows the tracks—which probably nobody will." She paused, looking sternly at Sylvia. "And promise me you won't go into the lean-to with him."

"I already promised Auda I wouldn't go near it. What makes you think I'd go *inside*?"

"Are you kidding? We already did."

"Yeah, but there were three of us. I'll just wave and ski away. He'll understand," Sylvia said, imagining Christopher standing at the door of his lean-to, calling after her to come back.

"All right, see you later." Elizabeth gave Sylvia a brisk hug, turned, and started to walk toward the line.

Only a few steps gone, she turned back. "Whoops, I just thought of something. We can't text Auda about Christopher. Suppose one of us loses her phone, even for a minute. It will be right there for whoever finds it to see."

"I've never thought of that."

"Well, I almost didn't myself. Maybe e-mail instead." Elizabeth turned away. Over her shoulder she added, "If Auda's smart enough to delete."

BACK AT THE school, Sylvia went to her and Elizabeth's dorm room, where the silence now that all the girls were gone was overbearing. She packed a suitcase as if she had to travel as far as Elizabeth and Auda to get home, and carried it to the Head's House, which was quiet too, with the absence of her father, who was busy as usual in New York City, and her mother, just as busy in her office. Sylvia unpacked, putting things neatly in her bedroom where they belonged, only because she had nothing else to do. She sat down on her bed and texted Auda and Elizabeth. *Ur flites left yet? Miss u already.* She didn't get an answer so their planes must have lifted off. Wondering how she was going to fill her day, she went downstairs into the kitchen. Maybe she'd eat something. As soon as she opened the refrigerator door, she realized she wasn't hungry.

Through the kitchen windows she saw that the weather had turned warm. Melting snow on the roof dripped down from the eaves. The sky was blue, the sun was fierce, and the snow on the campus lawns a glistening white. Why did she have to come inside and look out a window to discover she wanted to be outdoors? She crossed the kitchen toward the door to the garage. Her cross-country skis and boots were stored there, right next to her mom's. It was vacation and besides, she was going skiing so it was permissible to wear her down jacket, but that would be too warm. Her woolen sweater was enough.

She had no intention, none whatsoever, she told herself, to ski out to where Christopher Triplett lived in his lean-to. He wouldn't need a resupply of food for at least four more days, and why increase the odds, however small, that someone would follow her tracks and figure everything out? She heard Elizabeth's voice: *He's killed people, probably. Once you do that, maybe you can do anything.* She didn't have Elizabeth and Auda with her to make it three against one. No, she would stay on campus. Its great big lawns and athletic fields were a good enough place to ski. And yet, what would it be like to be alone with him? *If he'd wanted to hurt us, wouldn't he have tried, even though there were three of us and only one of him?*

Maybe her mom would come skiing with her. Sylvia would be safe from temptation then. She could suggest going to one of her mom's favorite places, a trail on the other side of the campus from the river, through state-owned land, to a pond which she loved to ski across when it was frozen and covered with snow. Sylvia skied toward the big sliding glass doors that led from the campus into her mother's office.

Her mom was on the phone, frowning, obviously hearing something she didn't want to hear. She looked up at Sylvia and waved. Sylvia waved back and waited outside. And waited and waited. "Come on, Mom," she murmured, "just hang up." She waved again. Her mom nodded to her, distractedly. Sylvia put an imaginary phone up to her ear and mouthed *blah blah blah.* She stepped out of her bindings and entered the office, and sat down on the big sofa against the back wall. Above her head on that wall was the famous painting, given to her mom about a hundred years ago by a famous artist named Claire Somebody, of the ancient copper beech she'd just skied past to enter the office.

Her mom said into the phone, "Yes, I do understand. But I have to go. I'm late for an appointment. Thanks so much for your call." She hung up her phone and smiled. "Some people have to say everything twice."

Sylvia held her breath. She'd just thought of something: suppose her mother decided to take a *short* break and come skiing with her? There wouldn't be time to go all the way out to the pond. She'd have time to ski by the river though. Maybe that's why she was here in her mother's office.

"You're going skiing! I wish I could come," her mother said.

"You can't?" Sylvia let out her breath.

Her mom sighed and shook her head. "I wasn't lying on the phone. I have an appointment in Hartford." She stood up from her desk. "Let's go this weekend. You think we could get your dad to come too?

"Dad skiing with us? He'll never keep up," Sylvia said.

OUTSIDE, SYLVIA REALIZED she needed to tell Christopher to move his lean-to further away from the trail where her mother—or anyone else—wouldn't see it when she *did* go skiing there. And if her mother did see Christopher wearing the down jacket, she'd think he was the burglar—when he didn't even know it was stolen. Would her mother have him arrested? Why hadn't she and Elizabeth thought of that? Elizabeth would say because it was just natural to think of your own problems before the other person's, and Sylvia, heading for Christopher Triplett's lean-to, thought Elizabeth was probably right.

And Auda: *Don't go near him. Stay away. Especially when you're all alone.* But Auda's voice, coming from halfway across the Atlantic by now, was easy to ignore.

SHE THOUGHT HE must have heard the swish of her skis on the snow. Because he was crawling out of the lean-to to greet her. All Sylvia saw of him was his boyish yellow hair flowing down to cover his face. Then he stood up, and she saw a face so drawn she could almost see the outline of the skull underneath. Once again Elizabeth said, *He's killed people probably. Once you've done that—*

Still, she kept skiing to him. He didn't make any sign that he was surprised. She stopped beside him and planted her ski poles in the snow, her hands gripping their handles, her wrists in the loops.

"Wait," he said, as if he'd just thought of something, and knelt down again so he could crawl back into his lean-to. She thought he was giving her a chance to get away.

He reappeared, holding the down jacket out in front of himself for her to see. He said, "Take your sweater off when you ski and tie it around your waist." With the hand that wasn't holding the down jacket, he reached and touched the end of the sleeve of her heavy woolen sweater. "That way you won't sweat as much. Then when you stop and put your sweater back on, you won't get cold."

"Next time I'll remember," she said, too flustered by his touch to think what that might mean.

He held the down jacket out to her. He had the look of a person who had just made a decision. "Put this on," he said, reaching further to give her the jacket, but she kept her hands on the handles of her ski poles, her wrists in the loops. "Put this on," he repeated, sternly this time. "And come inside."

"That's your sergeant voice?"

He shrugged. "I just want to keep you warm."

She remembered before that she had just wanted to give him a towel and a bar of soap. She took her gloved hands out of the ski pole loops to receive the jacket. A talisman, she thought, remembering the word from English class. *Talisman.*

He knelt down and unclipped her ski bindings. Then he crawled into his lean-to.

She stepped out of the bindings, put the jacket on, knelt down too, and followed him in, staying close to the opening—just in case.

ELEVEN

He would tell her everything now, the one who would absolve him. Everything. Leave nothing out.

How the corporal always yells, *Speed up! Speed up!* lifting his weapon beside him in the shotgun seat, and then the corporal's face always explodes and he is covered by blood and bits of bone and brain, and then he sees the sniper in the second-story window on the right, framed like in a picture, and then more fire from more places on the right, and he yanks the steering wheel left suddenly so another round hits the corporal beside him again, and the corporal twitches and jerks as if he were still alive, and then he sees the girl standing where she should have been safe by the left side of the road, just as surprised as he is, and they look at each other through the windshield and he always sees in her eyes that she knows he's going to run over her and knows he knows it, and then the right front fender thuds into her and she disappears and he feels the bump of the front tire going over her and then the second bump when his rear tire does. It's always the same, and it's why he is alive.

"I WOULDN'T BE if I hadn't yanked the wheel to the left," he said. Because that was the point, the whole point.

"Wouldn't be what? I don't understand." Sylvia was staring at his face.

"Like I said," he began, and then he realized they hadn't even sat down yet. "How long have we been in here?" he said.

"I don't know. Fifteen seconds maybe?" Then, after a silence, "Are you all right?"

So he hadn't told her. He'd just lived it again. That's what *always* always means. "You know I'm not," he said. "I was going to tell you why and then I thought I had and then I knew I hadn't, and now I know I can't."

"Yes, you can. I'm old enough."

He shook his head. "Nobody's old enough."

SHE DIDN'T KNOW what to say now, having no experience to argue from. He seemed to be receding from her, floating away into some horror he'd tried to share with her and couldn't. Impulsively, she reached across the charged space between them and laid her fingers on his cheek. Trying to bring him back to this lean-to, a much safer place. He took a big breath and held it. "Please. Tell me," she insisted. "I'll be all right."

She waited. He let go his breath. He put his hand on hers, lifting it from his cheek and replaced it at her side.

"Well then, I guess I better go."

"Yes, you should go."

"I came to tell you that you should move your lean-to away from the trail."

"So no one will see it?"

"Except Elizabeth and me," she corrected, taking off the down jacket. She didn't bother to mention Auda. Did he even remember her? She handed the jacket to him and went outside.

He followed her out, as if maybe, in the bright sunshine, he'd change his mind and tell her what he hadn't been able to tell her, but he was silent. She waited for a few seconds but he still didn't speak, and so she stepped into her skis and bent down to snap the bindings on. He handed the poles to her when she straightened up. But she could see he was miles away.

She started to ski, feeling his presence like an actual pressure on her back, between the shoulder blades, until she was around a bend in the trail through the woods, and then she was free of him, skiing as fast as she could.

NOW HE WAS alone again, still unforgiven. What right did he think he had to give her his pain? Or maybe he just didn't have the nerve, he was too ashamed.

And the corporal is sidewise again so that his shoulders and his neck and what is left of his head fall in Christopher's lap where they stay all the rest of the way, and when he gets back to base the lieutenant has to pull the corporal off him, dragging him out of the driver's side door, the whole length of the corpse sliding across his lap. *I don't even know his name*, Christopher says. *He just bummed a ride.* The lieutenant nods and looks down. The corporal is lying beside the truck now, face down on the pavement—except he doesn't have a face. *That's okay, he's got dog tags*, the lieutenant says, and then the medics come and pull the corporal up out of the black tar of the pavement, which is melting in the sun, sticking to the corporal's uniform, and so at least he didn't get it on his face, and the lieutenant says, *You couldn't stop and take care of her. What good would that have done? You'd get dead and she already was, and what about the truck behind you?*

And he says, *How did you know?*

I was in the truck behind you. I'd be dead too. Now get out of that fucking truck and go take a shower.

"HOW WAS SKIING?" her mom asked. "Was it fun?" Sylvia had just put her skis away in the garage and entered the kitchen, still pouring sweat. "If we'd known how little time my appointment was going to take, you could have waited for me and we could have gone skiing together after all."

"That would have been fun." Sylvia pulled her sweater up over her head, choosing that moment to take it off so she could hide behind it. She tossed it casually on a chair, remembering how Christopher had reached and touched its sleeve. She'd forgotten all about his advice not to wear it while actually skiing. Next time she'd remember.

"Where'd you go?" her mother asked.

"All around."

"All around where?"

"On that trail you and I ran this fall."

"Up river?"

Sylvia hesitated. "Yes."

"That's a nice trail. I bet it was lovely today all covered with snow."

"It was, Mom." Sylvia escaped upstairs to her room, pretending she needed a shower right away.

Nobody's old enough. The way he'd said those words. So matter-of-fact, she couldn't doubt him. And from some place far away. He'd been about to take her there before realizing she couldn't come. Because nobody can. Not her mother. Not her father. No one. He was all alone.

TWELVE

The next day, when Aunt Marian walked through the front door of the Head's House to spend Christmas week with the family of her younger sister, Sylvia knew she would tell her everything. Of course she would! Why did it take until the most independent person Sylvia knew was right there, in the foyer, winking at her over her mother's shoulder while she and her mother hugged each other, to realize it? The family story was that as soon as she understood she had been named after a famous African American singer, Aunt M declared herself tone deaf. "So I can be me," she had announced, still a little kid, "not some other person." Aunt M was exactly the kind of person Sylvia could count on for absolution and advice.

Sometimes Sylvia thought she would model her life after her Aunt M's; other times she doubted she could ever be as pugnacious and sure of herself as she would need to be in the profession Aunt M reveled in. Aunt M was a community organizer, a protégé of a protégé of Saul Alinsky. She loved to tell Saul Alinsky's pancake story, almost as much as Sylvia loved to hear it.

"So Saul is having breakfast in a restaurant on a Sunday morning," Aunt M would say, starting the story exactly this way every single time. "A husband, a wife, and three little kids who couldn't have been more than a year apart come into the restaurant and take the table next to his. They're all dressed up. It's obvious they're going to go to church after they have their breakfast, it's a Norman Rockwell scene. Saul can just tell they've saved up to do this for weeks, because when they order their pancakes it's obvious there's nothing in the world they could enjoy more that morning than nice, hot pancakes with tons of maple syrup. The restaurant is crowded and the waitstaff are busy, but the family gets lucky and their breakfasts come almost right away: two big, grown-up stacks of pancakes for mom and dad, and three children-size for the kids. They pick up their forks, so happy that if they died right then it would be okay, but then they notice there's no syrup. The dad tells a waitress, but she's already speeding away. The dad senses Saul, who he doesn't know from Adam, watching. He sends him a furtive look. *What do I do?* Saul rolls his eyes and points his chin at another waitress working a table not far away. The dad raises his hand. The waitress doesn't see him—or pretends she doesn't. He sends his wife a shamefaced look. She looks away. The youngest kid whines, 'Where's the syrup, Daddy? My pancakes are getting cold.' The dad raises his hand again, waves it this time. No waitress responds. A minute or so later, another waitress goes right by their table. 'Miss?' he says, 'miss?' She ignores him, hurrying to take another party's order.

"By now the pancakes really are getting cold. Saul gets up and goes over there. 'You want some syrup, right?' 'Yes, we do. The pancakes are getting cold,' the dad says. 'And you're paying good money for them, right?' Saul asks. The dad nods, looks desperate, but it's clear he appreciates Saul's sympathy. 'How bad do you want to get the syrup?' Saul asks. 'Very bad,' the dad says. 'You sure?' 'Yes, why wouldn't I be?' 'All right,' Saul says, addressing the whole family now. 'You are gonna have your syrup in about ten seconds. Guaranteed.' Then Saul goes back to his own table, but he doesn't sit down at it. What he does instead is he gets up on the table. In fact, he's standing on his own breakfast, his two big wing-tip cordovans right in the middle of his scrambled eggs, and he yells at the top of his voice, 'HEY, BRING THIS FAMILY THEIR SYRUP RIGHT NOW! OR I'M GOING TO DO SOMETHING REALLY CRAZY!' Just about every waitress in the place and the manager and one of the cooks comes running over with syrup and now they have at least a gallon, and Saul figures that poor daddy has learned his lesson about how to deal with power.

"But guess what?" Aunt M always paused here because that's what Saul Alinsky did when he told the story. "The poor guy and his wife were so embarrassed they slinked out of the restaurant, and the kids had no choice so they followed their parents, and all those pancakes and all that syrup just sat there on the table—until a waitress came and took them away."

"You've been wanting to tell me something since I arrived, haven't you, sweetie," Aunt M said once she and Sylvia were alone.

"How did you know?"

"Oh my, how did I know! 'Cause it's bursting out of your ears maybe? Flying out through the top of your head? You got something in you that's going explode if you don't let it out. Something you don't want to tell your ma, which is why you are about to tell me. So I'm going to sit here on this sofa, and you're going to sit down next to me"—patting the cushions next to her—"and tell me."

"All right. Can I get you a drink first?" Now that Sylvia was about to tell, she was nervous. Fixing a bourbon on the rocks, Aunt M's favorite drink, would put it off for another minute or two.

"No, I've quit. I haven't quit swearing, and I still pleasure myself when I'm in the mood, and I continue to get about fifty new people, most of whom are white, to hate me every week. But drinking?" Aunt M shook her head. "I don't do that anymore."

"You're so different from my mom!" Sylvia said. "She would never say things like that."

"Wouldn't do them either. But yeah, variety's the spice of life. Now sit down. Let's hear it." Sylvia started to sit down on the sofa next to her aunt, but her aunt put up her hand. "As a matter of fact, let's have you sit over there, facing me." She pointed to an armchair only a few feet away. "That way I can see your face and know if you're leaving stuff out."

"I won't. I promise."

"I'll be the judge of that. Now go on."

"All you wanted was to get some ice cream." Aunt M repeated when Sylvia had finished. "But you did say you were bored. That should tell you something."

Sylvia was outraged. "That's not why we're doing this!"

"No, it isn't. It's why you went to get the ice cream. You didn't have anything better to do. And guess what happened? You found something better to do. Mission accomplished. So what's the big deal?"

"What's the big deal? You don't understand. We could get kicked out. And my mother would have to do the kicking out."

Aunt M nodded. "Like I said. What's the big deal?"

"And Christopher would starve, or feel so abandoned he'd maybe kill himself."

"Ah, now, that is a big deal." Aunt M had that look on her face that people get when they've been looking for something and finally found it. "So I'm going to tell you a story, hon. You ever been to Detroit?"

Sylvia shook her head. For the first time in her life, she didn't want to hear Aunt M tell one of her stories.

"Never mind," Aunt M said, making a dismissive gesture with her hands. "I don't know why I asked. Because even if you had been there, it wouldn't have been the part of Detroit I'm talking about." She paused for a second and then went on. "Think of a great big field that used to be a nice neighborhood. Single-family homes with front porches. People sitting on them say hello to people walking by. And there are trees. But now there is only one street, Hobart Street, and its right in the middle of that great big field, and all the rest is a desert. Packs of dogs roaming around. Every street except Hobart Street bulldozed away for urban redevelopment. So what if the people living there didn't want redevelopment? But the houses on Hobart Street are beautiful. Nice, comfy old Victorians, painted many colors in gleaming new paint. Picket fences and little front lawns. Rose gardens. All alone like that, the street looks like a movie set.

"And here's why. When the crew came to shut off the gas to the houses on Hobart Street, a woman named Mildred—can't remember her last name—got down in the hole with them with a lighted blow torch. A flamboyant gesture, don't you think? In more ways than one? Here's this very large, almost elderly Black woman sitting next to you with a lighted blow torch. Might just get your attention. And your sympathy too, especially since you are also Black. These guys from the gas company are not about to wrestle with her. They just leave. Maybe she won't be there tomorrow. But of course she is there tomorrow—and so are some reporters.

"I was just starting out, but I got wind of this and I hooked Mildred up with a pal of mine who taught in a private school like yours in the suburbs, and the three of us came up with a plan:

get some high school kids from the public school near Hobart Street and some kids from the private school, and assign them to write a plan for redevelopment of the area and see if they can get it approved by the municipality. In the meantime, fix up the houses so that they are no longer 'eligible' for redevelopment.

"So kids and parents, working on weekends and after school in the afternoons, with advice from plumbers and carpenters and electricians all over the place, completely reclaimed the houses on Hobart Street. Now, inside *and* out, it looked like that movie set. And those kids also submitted a redevelopment plan that mixed businesses with residences, the kind of place that works for families. Think about how much those kids learned about architecture, economics, the realities of welfare, the laws, the crafts—and in general how the world really works, like, for instance, one of the conditions required for the houses not to be eligible for the bulldozer was that the plumbing worked. So the city sent some goons in every once in a while to break the toilets in the middle of the night, and in the morning the kids would come in and install new toilets. Every kid in the project said they learned more in that experience than from all their school courses combined, and they were prouder for it too. They had a purpose in life.

"And here's the point of my story," Aunt Marian said. "I know you've been wondering. My teacher pal from the private school wanted other educators to know about the Hobart Street Project so they could learn from it. So he arranges for Mildred to come to a big important conference of private school educators, the National Association of Independent Schools, no less, and tell the audience, some four thousand people, about it. She agrees. It's all set up. On the big day, my pal shows up, ready to introduce Mildred; the audience fills every seat. Reporters are present and TV people. But not Mildred. She doesn't show up.

"You know why? There was an emergency in one of the families of the public school kids. She figured the people at the conference could get by without her, but the family at home could not." Aunt M stopped talking. She looked like every storyteller who has just come to the end and is waiting for a reaction.

"So what happened?" Sylvia asked.

"Oh come on! You know what happened."

"The teacher made the talk?"

"Yes, and a good one too. Probably better than the one Mildred would have made. He's a *teacher*. He's supposed to know how to be interesting. He made everyone forget that the prime mover wasn't there."

"So that's your point? Elizabeth and I keep on taking food out to Christopher and so what if we get kicked out?"

"And your mom is put in a terrible situation, don't forget that," Aunt M added. "You could also not wait to get caught. Just tell everybody you were the ones who stole the stuff. Get up in your Morning Meeting and say, *We did it because he was hungry and cold.* Now what's the school going to do? Why should you do this alone? Better yet, invite this Christopher of yours to dinner in the dining hall. Bang on a glass with your fork and get everybody's attention. Then introduce him. Maybe he could say a few words. You never know. With an audience like that, he might be able to tell what happened to him over there that he couldn't tell you. Why he's hungry and cold and deranged and maybe is going to kill himself or somebody else. That's what I'd tell you to do, honey, if I didn't love you and your mother. But I do, so I won't. People like Mildred have to do radical stuff. People like us can decide whether they will or not."

Aunt M paused. And then, as if it had just occurred to her, she added, "Besides, I have a better idea. We'll get him some help. It's not about you and Elizabeth, you know. It's about him. Let's you and I go to the VA office tomorrow and see what they can do for him."

IT WAS RAINING the next morning, snow everywhere turning to slush. The world was gray, but Aunt M's voice, the hum of the tires, and the steady, monotonous back-and-forth of the windshield wipers made the inside of Aunt M's rented car a cozy place. "He knows how to live in the woods so he must be a country boy," Aunt M said. "So we're going to the facility in Newington. It's almost rural there, less scary for a guy like that than the place in New Haven."

"That's a great idea," Sylvia said. "I never would have thought of that."

"You would have if you'd been doing this kind of work as long as I have," Aunt M said, launching into a story about an organization she had helped start for sheltering runaway children, how the smaller the shelters were, the easier it was to entice the children into them. "Over two stories high, we didn't have a chance."

Sylvia only half-listened. She was thinking about how normal her life would have been since September if after that very first day when Elizabeth dropped two dollars in Christopher's hat and started everything, Aunt M had been there to intervene.

"Now here's what we are going to do in the VA office," Aunt M said. "They are going to say that Christopher can fill out a form, VA 10-10EZ, online or by the phone, and he'll find out whether he's eligible within five to seven days. And we're going to explain that he can't fill out the form online or by phone because he's homeless and doesn't have phone or a computer, so we're going to bring him in in person and all we want now is someone to promise they'll be on the lookout for us, someone who'll be in his corner and go the extra mile. We're just smoothing the way today, that's all. And it will make us more convincing when we go out there and talk to him."

"What if he refuses to leave his lean-to?"

"I'm pretty good at persuasion. But if he still refuses, we'll think of something else. Whatever happens, you and Elizabeth will have to let him go. Something tells me that will be easier for her than for you."

Sylvia felt a flash of emptiness at the thought of letting go of Christopher, but just then Aunt M turned off the main road onto a long driveway that advanced in sweeping circles, as if toward a palace, arriving at a large, exactly square, utterly utilitarian building best classified as American Ugly, its redbrick walls monotonous with no adornment. Aunt M parked the car.

"That's it?" Sylvia said. "*That* building?"

Aunt M looked surprised. "What were you expecting, hon?"

"I don't know. Something less depressing."

Aunt M looked even more surprised. "Come on, let's go in and see if we can rustle up some help for your homeless guy."

Just past the entrance to the building, there was a security gate, like the ones in airports that you stand in with your arms up, but

Aunt M and Sylvia didn't have to go through it because it was off to one side. "So why have it then?" Sylvia said. Aunt M didn't answer. They crossed the lobby toward a sign: *INFORMATION.* Three white elderly men wearing baseball caps sat along one wall on folding chairs, waiting for something. They watched Sylvia and her aunt get in line. Sylvia returned their gaze with a knowing look. It wasn't the first time she'd been studied by strangers trying to figure out how a dark-skinned mom could have a lighter-skinned daughter. All three looked quickly away.

When it was Aunt M and Sylvia's turn, the woman behind the desk—Black, handsome, middle aged, in a trim brown suit and a modest gold necklace—gave them a welcoming smile. But she also looked concerned, like somebody's youngish grandmother. "I'm afraid you and your daughter have come to the wrong place," she said. "She needs to go there"—then she handed Aunt M a brochure and pointed to a door on her left. "The recruiting stations for the Navy, the Army, and the Marines are all there."

"Oh my dear, we didn't come to sign up!" Aunt M said.

"You didn't?"

"No."

The woman smiled, obviously relieved. Here was one child who wasn't going to get herself killed in a war some grown-up invented.

Sylvia was shocked. It had never occurred to her that anyone would take one look at her and assume she was "the kind of person" who would join the military.

"But thank you anyway," Aunt M. said. "Actually, Sylvia here is my niece, not my daughter."

"Oh?"

"Yes. Her mother is a very busy woman. And Sylvia couldn't find her driver's license this morning. I thought, why take a chance, you know? A young person of color pulled over without a driver's license—"

The woman glanced at Sylvia. It took her a second or two before she nodded, evidently convinced Sylvia *was* a person of color. Then, turning, smiling, to Aunt M again. "I understand. By the way, I'm Dorothy."

"Good morning, Dorothy. I'm Marian, and this is—"

"Sylvia," Dorothy finished. "And what may I do for you, young lady?"

Sylvia hesitated

"Sylvia?" Aunt M. said.

"I thought you were going to—"

Aunt M shook her head. "No. It's your story. You tell."

"Yes, tell," Dorothy said.

Sylvia couldn't think of anywhere else to start but the beginning. She said, "My friend and I met a homeless Iraq War vet."

"Met?"

"Well, we gave him some money."

"Oh, I see. Go on."

"And then we brought him some food."

"You brought him some food? And now you're coming here?"

"Yes. We thought—"

"Where was he when you brought him food?"

"His lean-to in the woods."

"Lean-to?"

"It's kind of a shack, but made out of pine boughs."

"Pine boughs! In the woods! Nearby?"

"No, actually, it's a little bit away."

"A mile? Two?"

"Three, I guess. Well, maybe four, actually."

"And you brought him food?"

"Yes, and then we brought him some clothes."

"You did!"

"Sylvia nodded. "It was getting cold."

"Yes, that's what happens in the winter. How many times was this Iraq War Vet of yours deployed?"

"Four."

"Four," Dorothy repeated. "And he's not well? That's why he's living in a… what'd you call it?"

"Lean-to."

"Oh yes, a lean-to. Made out of pine boughs. Does he have post-traumatic stress, you think?"

"I guess so. Maybe. I really don't know."

"You don't know. And you're here because…?"

"Because we"—nodding at Aunt M—"are going to go out there and persuade him to come see you."

Dorothy sat very still, gazing up at Sylvia.

"That's what we are going to do," Sylvia said. "Bring him to you."

"You bet you are, young lady! What's his name?"

"Christopher. Triplett. Christopher Triplett, Sergeant US Marines."

Dorothy bent her head down to write the name on a piece of paper. She looked up again and stared at Sylvia. "How long have you known Christopher?"

"What?"

"You gave him money. Then you brought food and clothes to him in his lean-to. How long has this been going on?"

"Since September."

"September. Three months ago. Why'd you wait so long?"

"I don't know."

"Maybe you should figure that out." Dorothy paused. "How long has your aunt known?"

"Since yesterday."

Dorothy nodded. "That's what I thought." She turned to Aunt M. "Thanks."

"No, it's the other way around," Aunt M said. "Thank *you*."

Dorothy shrugged. "I'm just doing my job. You really think you should go out there to his lean-to?"

"I've done scarier things," Aunt M said.

"Sounds like Sylvia has too," Dorothy said.

Aunt M smiled and raised her eyebrows.

"Well, then, I won't try to tell you not to." Dorothy stood, came around her desk, and shook Aunt M's hand.

"You're a good person," Aunt M said.

"Sometimes," Dorothy said. She turned to Sylvia. "I'll do everything I can for your Christopher. You can count on that. You just bring him in."

"Thanks," Sylvia said. "And I'm sorry—"

Dorothy put up her hand. "Don't."

Aunt M put her hand on Sylvia's elbow, tugging.

"So how come you let her walk all over you?" Aunt M said as soon as they were in the car. "Why didn't you defend yourself?"

"Let's just go home. I don't want to talk about it."

Aunt M turned the ignition on and started to drive. The windshield wipers swung back and forth.

"Okay, I couldn't think fast enough," Sylvia admitted.

"That's what I thought. But what would you tell her now you've had a few minutes?"

"That I didn't know he was a war vet until a month ago."

"You think you would have done differently if you'd known that from the beginning?"

"No, I don't think so," Sylvia admitted.

"So why *did* you do what you did?"

"Not just me. Elizabeth. And Auda too," Sylvia said, trying not to sound defensive.

Aunt M glanced at Sylvia. "Dorothy was asking *you*." She turned her gaze forward again. "And anyway, you didn't even mention Elizabeth and Auda."

"All right. It started because he needed help."

"That's why you dropped the money in his hat?"

"No, actually it wasn't," Sylvia said, remembering. "I didn't want to hear Elizabeth make a sarcastic remark, so I turned around and went back and dropped the dollars in his hat."

"Interesting. You didn't do it for him at all."

"Not at first, but after that I did."

"Because he needed help?"

"Of course!"

"And what did *you* need?"

"To know what he thought about me, I guess. Who he thought I am."

"He was curious?"

"I suppose so."

"Well, that's natural. Most people just walk right by people like him. What else?

"To be thanked, I guess. For him to be grateful."

"Was he?"

"No."

"Well, what was he if he wasn't grateful?"

"Shamed. It was obvious."

"So you made his condition worse? You shamed him by giving him what he asked for? It would have been better if you just turned away, like he didn't exist?"

"No."

"All right then. And you didn't just do it so Christopher would be grateful. Maybe you like to be a hero. You like to take chances. Most anybody worth her salt does. But basically you did it to make yourself feel good. You wanted to be the person to help him. That person, not the one that turns her head away. And what's wrong with that? Does Mother Teresa feel bad when she does what she does?"

"No, I guess not," Sylvia murmured.

"I didn't hear you."

"I guess not," Sylvia repeated louder.

"Good. Now let's stop at Macy's and buy your mom and dad some Christmas presents."

"I already did."

"I know. So did I. But if we buy them some more, we won't have to lie when they ask us what we did today."

IN MACY'S KITCHEN department, it required all of about ten seconds for Sylvia to be clear that she didn't want to buy Christmas presents for her parents. She wanted to buy something for Christopher. A fancy nonstick frying pan made in Italy, for instance. Or better yet, that coffeemaker over there that makes one cup at a time, espresso, latte, whatever, with a placard that says: *Everyone deserves the freedom to choose.*

Aunt M, who had been glancing contemptuously at an array of fancy knives for which her clients would not have room in their kitchens, let alone, she wished, the lack of good judgment to even want them in the first place, looked up and caught the stricken look on her niece's face. "Let's get out of here," she said. She put her hand on Sylvia's elbow for the second time that day and led her to the escalator. Moments later, outside on the sidewalk, she said, "Nobody has ever had too many books. Let's check out that bookstore over there," pointing across the street.

"My parents don't have time to read."

"Well, that's a problem you can fix. All you have to do is give them some books and ask them every day, 'Have you read any of them yet?' and look disillusioned—not disappointed, *disillusioned*—when they confess they haven't. After a while, they'll find the time to read one just to keep your respect."

"Do *you* read, Aunt M?"

"Are you kidding? I'm worse than them. You could include me in the program, if you want."

"All right," Sylvia said without conviction. But a moment later in the store, enveloped by walls of shelved books and their papery smell, she felt a pulse of calmness. After Macy's pornography of excess, here was silence and retreat.

She and Aunt M spent much longer than they had planned perusing titles, picking books up, feeling their physical reality, their actual weight against their fingers, and finally walked out of the store laden with books.

On the way home in the car, Aunt M told a joke by Groucho Marks which actually made Sylvia laugh: *Outside of a dog, a man's best friend is a book. Inside a dog, it's too dark to read.*

HER MOM WAS still in her office working even though it was Christmas Eve, and her dad was out doing the last bits of his Christmas shopping. Sylvia and her aunt had expected to have to wait for so perfect a time to go to Christopher's lean-to, where Sylvia would introduce her aunt to him and Aunt M would begin the process of gaining his trust. They set out right away.

They waded in the rain on snowshoes through deep melting snow. Fog rose upward. Buildings, trees, the tops of stone walls emerging from the snow were ghosts of themselves. The only sounds were the murmur of rain and their own breathing. Sylvia was not surprised that Aunt M kept up with her, stride for stride on snowshoes. Her aunt was a force of nature. Sylvia was surprised though when they had reached the trail beside the river not to smell the smoke from Christopher's fire. They came around the bend and

Sylvia was surprised again. It was the same lean-to in the same place; he hadn't built another further away from the trail after all, and its door was open, cast aside, green against the snow.

Inside the lean-to, they found a note on brown cardboard. It was placed on top of the down jacket, underneath which, neatly arrayed, were all the other things Sylvia and Elizabeth had stolen.

I don't need the stuff you brought to me anymore. Please take it back. I have gone back to my family. I will seek help. Maybe it will work. If it does, I'll go to college.

Christopher Triplett, Sergeant, US Marines

Once again, the first thing that entered Sylvia's mind was: *Where did he get the marker?*

Aunt M said, "Well, hon, it looks like now you're off the hook."

Sylvia reached out and touched the lean-to. The roof was level with her shoulders. She smelled the piney smell. It would turn brown soon and then, in a year or two, there'd be nothing left but a pile of sticks on the ground to mark where Christopher had kept himself alive. "It's all over now," she said, relieved of her burden, empty without it, and happy for Christopher all at once.

"Not quite, hon. There's one more thing to do."

"I know. Come back here and get the stuff and put it back in the shed."

"That's right. Then it really will be over. We're going to need a great big backpack."

"Except for the grill," Sylvia said, remembering. She pointed to the blackened grill over the firepit. "We didn't steal that. It doesn't belong to the school. We can leave it right where it is."

It was late afternoon by now, beginning to get dark. By the time they were almost to where the woods ended at the athletic fields, it was so hard to see the trail that they lost it and had to go by Sylvia's sense of direction, pushing through bushes and low branches. They came out onto the very northern edge of the athletic fields. "We almost missed!" Sylvia said. "Any further, we could have gotten lost."

"Well, we would have come to the road eventually," Aunt M said. "And anyway, you know what Dan Boone said when somebody asked him if he'd ever got lost: 'No, but I've been awful damn bewildered for two or three weeks.'"

Sylvia giggled. No more worries that she and Elizabeth would be caught and kicked out. Elizabeth especially was going to be happy. *MIT, here I come.* She'd never say it. But she'd think it. They had done the right thing. And now it was Christopher's family's job to take care of him.

Aunt M and Sylvia went straight to the Christmas tree in the Little Room and put their books under it, adding to the gifts already there. A fire was burning in the fireplace. Bright and yellow after the darkness of the woods. The tree gave off its Christmas smell. Sylvia felt a surge of happiness.

Bob and Rachel were in the dining room, setting the table for Christmas Eve dinner.

"Where have you two been?" Bob asked.

"We were doing a little more Christmas shopping," Aunt M said.

True enough, Sylvia thought. She escaped upstairs to e-mail Elizabeth and Auda.

She sat down on her bed and typed on her cell phone: *C gone. 2 family, maybe college. Remember 2 delete. Don't reply.*

She put the phone down and headed down the hall to take a shower and put on festive clothes for Christmas Eve.

When she was back in her room, getting dressed, her phone signaled that an e-mail had just arrived. Even though she had said not to reply and it was two in the morning in Germany, she knew it was Auda who'd sent it.

Syl,

You disappointed? It would be selfish, I know, since he's safer with his family than in a lean-to. Just the same, it was interesting, wasn't it? Hard to let go? Anyway, make sure you put all the stuff back into the shed. No one will care who the robbers were then.

And why can't I reply, since I'm going to delete?

Miss you

A

P.S. How'd you find out? You went out there? You said you

wouldn't. Typical, reckless you. But who cares now? You're safe.

Sylvia read it twice. The emptiness she'd felt at the lean-to reading Christopher's note came rushing back. She realized she had been expecting it. It did not push away her relief. It just sat beside it.

Auda
Sure, I'm disappointed. Yes, I feel empty. But relieved too, and I'm going to do my best to stay that way.
Syl
P.S. You didn't have to tell me to put the stuff back. I'm not dumb.

Another e-mail came.

Syl,
I meant to tell you, but I forgot: just dump the stuff in front of the shed door. That way you only have to be there for a second. Because how do you know when the security guy will come around?

Sylvia didn't reply. She put a check next to each of the messages and hit delete.

THIRTEEN

Even though he hadn't been able to confess and be forgiven, Christopher had begun to feel somewhat healed. Sylvia had come to give him the chance to confess because she cared. And he had held back because he cared for her. There must be some healing in that transaction. Besides, putting distance between himself and Sylvia prevented her from ever morphing into the girl he'd killed come back to punish him. He was going to be okay.

The proof was he was doing what he was doing right now: sitting in a SuperShuttle van heading for Bradley Field. Just like an ordinary person coming home on Christmas Eve. If he weren't okay, he'd never have been able to figure out how to get to his aunt's house—or even remember his Uncle Ray was dead so he had to go to Uncle Ray's sister's house in Hartford, instead of Uncle Ray's in the Adirondack Mountains where he really wanted to be.

Near Saranac.

The lady in the brown coat had looked so sorry when she'd told him there was no bus to Hartford. Walking to him on her worn-down heels to say God bless. He wanted to tell her now, make her stop feeling sad, how it wasn't a problem that there wasn't a bus anymore. *I figured it out*, he would say to her. *I didn't need to buy food, so now I have money to pay the SuperShuttle driver.*

He would tell her how he'd buried his axe under a fallen tree where no one would find it. Because he knew how strange it would look to be traveling with an axe. But he wouldn't tell why he was so relieved to be separated from it. He would tell how he went to the Fieldington Inn and called SuperShuttle, like he had an airplane to catch, and waited in the lobby because it was warm in there and he didn't have a winter coat and then the van came—because he had ordered it to.

Yes, he had ordered a thing to happen and it had happened, and he was on his way to Bradley Field, a person who could get things done in the world. At Bradley Field, he'd pretend he just flew in from some other city and tell a different SuperShuttle driver to take him to his aunt's home in Hartford.

He would ring the doorbell and wait for his aunt to come to the door. That would be the nervous time. She'd never come to the door without first peeking between the curtains to make sure the person waiting for it to open wasn't a burglar, or some guy wanting to hurt her just for the sake of dealing hurt. She was alone and elderly, a spinster—a virgin too, he was sure—so who could blame her? He'd feel her eyes going up and down over his body, inspecting him, while she decided whether to let him in her house. After how he had behaved the last time he was there—taking his car without leaving a note. He would have to fight the urge to run away.

If she did let him in, he would try hard to love her, but he never would understand how she could be so different from her own brother. *You're mine to take care of now, Chris. That's my blessing in all this grief,* Uncle Ray had said, when Christopher's mom and dad died in a car accident. Christopher had been so young, he hardly remembered them. Uncle Ray had taken their place.

He didn't believe it when he got the message in Iraq that his Uncle Ray had died, that his heart had stopped nine-tenths of the way between his front porch and edge of the bluff overlooking Osgood Pond. Better way to go than some, everyone said. And he loved the view from there. One more step and he would have rolled right down the bluff into the pond and maybe floated away. Which everyone also agreed that Ray would've said was a pretty good joke on somebody, he just didn't quite know who.

Later, his aunt called to tell him that his uncle died so broke that the estate sold his house and everything he owned—including his canoe—to pay off his debts. "Your uncle had no sense at all about money. He never took my advice." Miles and miles away in Connecticut to him in Iraq, she drew a breath to say some more about how now Christopher wouldn't have any inheritance at all, but Christopher didn't stay on the call to hear it. He just walked away from the phone while she went on and on and on and on.

There were lots of ways to get killed in Iraq, one of which was to be distracted by news from home you didn't want to get, and another was every once in a while since you got the news you didn't care anymore whether you got killed or not.

But when his hitch with the Marines was up and there wasn't anything to be distracted from anymore, he surely did believe Uncle Ray was dead. Uncle Ray had a saying for everything, including sadness. *The best place to be sad was in a canoe*, he'd once said, not because being in a canoe would make you get over being sad, it just meant what he said: *The best place to be sad is in a canoe.*

And he'd also said, Christopher remembered with perfect clarity, while even though he was in a SuperShuttle van because he had ordered it and it had come, his brain was beginning to go fast, repeating, repeating, Uncle Ray saying, *I've been reading about this waterway over in Maine. When you get out, let's go down it. You can go a whole summer without taking out.*

So that's what he did, he remembered now, while the panic surged and he wanted to jump out onto the highway to escape it… he's going down the Allagash. Without Uncle Ray because Uncle Ray is dead… and gets run over on the highway, run over run over, or maybe, instead, he puts his hands around the driver's neck and squeezes and squeezes and squeezes, watches his face in the rearview mirror, the big surprise… first down the Allagash all by himself, and then, because he learned all about the river he got a job guiding people down it, city people who might be nice but who Uncle Ray would say didn't know their assfromaholeintheground about canoeing in rivers.

Now the van was pulling up at Bradley Field. Just like he'd planned. He was halfway there already and he hadn't jumped out and his brain was slowing down. The day after tomorrow he'd go to Southern Connecticut State University and sign up for classes.

He waited for the driver to get out and walk around the van and open the sliding door. Then he waited for the fat guy sitting between him and the sliding door to get out first. Then he unclicked his seat belt. Then he stepped down out of the van onto the sidewalk and then he paid the driver. One thing at a time. "No, I don't have any luggage," he said. Then he remembered to give a dollar tip. Then he went inside the terminal and walked around and around and around until he found the SuperShuttle desk. Then he bought another ticket to his aunt's house on Farmington Avenue in Hartford. Then he went outside to where the sign was and waited for the van to come. He was calm now, everything was fine. And he hadn't jumped out and killed himself. He'd just thought about it, that's all. And anyway, maybe he would never have the nerve.

WHEN HIS HITCH with the Marines was up last spring, Christopher had gone to his aunt's house to get his car. She had stored it for him in her driveway the last time he was deployed. He had planned to spend a few days with her, his only living relative, before he went to Maine. But she wasn't there when he arrived. He hadn't dared let himself know how fervently he didn't want the company of anyone in close quarters until he felt the relief that she wasn't there; so, instead of waiting for her to return from whatever errand she was on, he took the spare house key from where he knew she hid it outdoors because she was always forgetting to take her regular key with her, and he went inside and rummaged around in her desk in the study until he found the keys to his car, and then he drove it to Maine. He didn't even leave a note.

He then spent the month of June in the Allagash Wilderness, proving that his Uncle Ray was right: the best place to be sad was in a canoe. He became a calm man again, in charge of himself, his devils contained.

So he decided he would spend the rest of the summer guiding groups through the wilderness, then return to Hartford in late August and matriculate at Southern Connecticut U. He would apologize to his aunt so he could live at her house for very little rent until he earned an associate degree in business. He'd specialize in retail. He had an idea that he'd find a job in a store selling fishing, camping, river-running, and backpacking equipment—everything but guns—until he'd learned enough to start a store of his own.

But his first guiding gig turned out to be a group of men, four canoes' worth, every one of whom seemed to him to be overweight and have a very loud voice. They wanted to fly in to Allagash Lake, spend a day there, and then run down Allagash Stream into

Chamberlain Lake, down to Round Pond, and meet the bush pilots there a week later. When he told them bush pilots weren't allowed to land on Allagash Lake and would instead fly into Johnson's Pond, near Allagash Lake, and run down a stream from there into the lake, they just laughed and assured him they could bribe the pilots into breaking the rules. Several of them pulled their wallets out and waved them in the air. He decided not to argue, knowing the pilots would refuse the bribe. The next morning, they showed up at the bush pilots' place, each one dressed in a camouflage suit, with too much gear to fit in five canoes, let alone four, and he had to sort through it all to extract the useless stuff and persuade them to return it to their cars. Then the pilots expressed their amazement that they were being asked to risk their licenses by flying into Allagash Lake, which they refused to do, so Christopher's clients were as irritated at him for being right as they were at the pilots for refusing to be bribed.

When they had finished unloading the planes at Johnson's Pond, one of the pilots sidled up to Christopher, and whispered, "How you gonna get through a whole week with these assholes and not kill at least one of them?"

Christopher pretended he didn't hear.

The pilot grinned. *Come on back with me. Just leave them here. I won't tell.*

Christopher forced himself to smile. "See you in a week."

CHRISTOPHER MANAGED TO get them safely down the stream from Johnson's Pond into Allagash Lake, and then across it to the premier campsite with a sandy beach at the head of Allagash Stream, which flowed into Chamberlain Lake. There, he soon discovered that not one of them had the slightest idea how to set up his tent. They'd each brought their own, but every tent had room for four people. They hadn't even opened the packages they'd come in. He suggested they double up and use fewer tents, but they insisted on their privacy. When it became clear they expected him to set the tents up, he told them he was a guide, not a butler, and, one by one, instructed them. When, at last, all the tents were set up, except his, they started to drink.

He gathered the wood, made the fire, and cooked the dinner for them, promising himself he'd let them know in the morning they were expected to do much of these chores for themselves. During dinner, they continued to drink. After dinner, none of them was willing to take off his shoes and wade into the lake to fill the buckets for dishwashing and rinsing; so he filled them, and, sure they wouldn't get them clean, he washed the dishes.

His first task in the morning was to shovel sand over the several places where who knew how many of them had vomited on the beach. He went to each tent and woke its occupant. When they had all staggered out, he instructed them in his sergeant's voice they were expected to participate in all the chores. He would not tolerate any more drunkenness. They had to be efficient and stay on schedule to arrive at Round Pond and meet the bush pilots a week hence. The plan for the day was to get down Allagash Stream and across Chamberlain Lake.

But they were too hungover to be efficient and it took them several hours to take down the tents, make breakfast and, load the canoes. And going down Allagash Stream, two of the canoes tipped over once; the other two tipped over twice. With each of these comedic disasters, Christopher, thankfully traveling solo in his own canoe, didn't even try to hide his laughter.

WHEN THEY FINALLY reached Chamberlain Lake, just as it was growing dark, he took them to the closest campsite, the Crow's Nest, infamous for its mosquitoes. He had intended to go past it, across the lake, not only to avoid those mosquitoes but also to stay on schedule, but it was too dark already for these incompetents to paddle, even if they weren't exhausted. They'd lose sight of each other and him in the dark. They'd be spread out all over the lake.

While last night it was drunkenness that, in addition to their lack of necessary skills, had caused them to take forever and ever to set up camp, this night it was their exhaustion and the onslaught of the mosquitoes. There was much slapping and waving of hands and swearing. Christopher, covered in insect repellent spray and a long-sleeve shirt, relatively impervious anyway, enjoyed their suffering.

Once again he gathered the firewood for cooking dinner so nobody would self-amputate some part of his body with his axe.

When that job was finished, he laid his axe down near the firepit and built a little teepee of birch bark and twigs to start the fire while his clients stood in a circle around him, watching and slapping mosquitoes. He assumed that one of them at least would reach for small sticks to lay on top of what he had started and then continue to build up the fire so he could set up his own tent.

But no one moved.

So he knelt again, next to his axe. Its handle, where he had shined it with the oil of his palms, reflected the glow of the little fire. He reached for his pile of wood, chose two small sticks, and placed them gently on top of the little flame, still teepee shaped. Above him one of the clients said, "These fucking mosquitoes are driving me crazy." Christopher put his right hand on the handle of the axe—to steady himself, he told himself—and leaned forward and blew on the fire. "Yeah, I've never been anywhere where there so many bugs," one of the other clients whined. "Why didn't we camp someplace else?"

Christopher stood up, holding the axe in his right hand. It hung, head down, alongside his leg. With his left hand, he pushed aside one of the men and walked to his canoe and laid his axe down in it. He was less frightened now that it was out of his hands. His tent and duffel were still in his canoe. All he needed was some food and some equipment to cook it with. He'd packed some wanigans—his clients called them chests—with food for breakfast, others for lunch and dinner, so it was an easy job to put what he needed into just one wanigan. He didn't hurry because he was sure they thought he was gathering food for their dinner.

"When are we gonna eat?" someone called from where the fire was now dying out.

"Whenever you finish cooking it," he called back, storing the wanigan in his canoe. "Don't forget to put the fire out when you finish." He pulled the canoe the rest of the way into the water, got in it and started paddling.

"Where you going?" said an astonished voice.

"Away," he yelled, raising his paddle above his head.

He was halfway across Chamberlain Lake to Lock Dam and

the portage into Eagle Lake, paddling in the dark under a million stars, feeling the intensity of his relief that he wasn't going to be a murderer, before he understood he couldn't go on to Round Pound. He imagined himself greeting the bush pilots there six days from then. *Where is everybody?* They'd want to know. So he changed course, steered down the lake, heading south, paddling all night, and the next day into Telos Lake and down that until he came to its southern tip. With a fisherman who let him put his canoe in the back of his pick-up truck, he hitched a ride to Millinocket, where he'd left his car. From Millinocket, still without sleep, he drove south toward Hartford.

NOW, SIX MONTHS later, unclicking his seatbelt in the SuperShuttle van, he remembered how much he had wanted the company of a caring person after being with the losers in their camo suits, but the closer he had gotten to his aunt's house, the more nervous he'd grown. He didn't feel nervous now at all though. But then? Maybe he had begun to want to split *her* head with his axe. Yes, maybe that was why, he explained to himself now in his calmness, getting out of the van, remembering driving right past Hartford, seeking country roads until he found one by the side of the Connecticut River. "No, I don't have any luggage," he said for the second time that day, handing the driver a dollar and remembering how, six months before, he'd parked his car by the side of the road. And went into the woods to build a lean-to to live in. With the same axe. Because otherwise he'd have to live in his car like a homeless person.

And now he was climbing the steps of her front porch, remembering how lucky he felt to have built the lean-to when he came to his car the next day and found it gone. Stolen. He didn't even try to get it back. Maybe now he would.

Through the window, he saw her Christmas tree in her living room, aglow with lights. He rang the bell, expecting to wait for her to inspect him up and down.

But the door opened right away. "Christopher!" Her arms flying around his shoulders and hauling him in. "Oh my, how I've missed you. Where have you been?"

FOURTEEN

Rachel surprised her family—and herself—when, just as they sat down to begin their Christmas Eve dinner, she announced her intention to go to church for the midnight service. Just seconds ago, she'd had no such intention—at least no conscious one. No one spoke. They were waiting for an explanation. So, shrugging her shoulders, she provided one: "To support Michael Woodward." At the other end of the table, Bob cocked his head and raised his eyebrows.

"Well, he is our friend, isn't he?" She resented his making her feel defensive. Why couldn't a person want to do something without knowing why?

"Well, if you're going, so am I," he said. If either had been looking, they would have seen Sylvia trying to hide her shock behind a slightly bored expression, a teenager surrounded by adult talk. Tonight would be the perfect opportunity to ski to the lean-to, gather the stolen stuff, and sneak it back into the equipment shed in the protection of the dark!

"But it's Christmas Eve," Aunt M said. "His church will be crammed. Why would he need support from *you*?"

"Because we know his secret," Bob said. "He doesn't believe. At least not the resurrection part. Makes him feel like a hypocrite."

"Oh, poor little boy," Marian said. "Maybe he could just get over it."

"Marian!" Rachel said.

"Or he could quit. Find some other way to make a living."

"He'd never quit. He loves his flock too much," Bob said. "He's a great guy. He's always there for them."

"Well, I take it back then," Marian said. She turned her head to look across the table at Sylvia. "We all need someone to be there for us, don't we, Sylvia?"

The question came out of left field. For cover, Sylvia turned to her mother, and said, "Can we start? Everything is getting cold."

"Especially when we're hurting, right?" Aunt M persisted, still looking at Sylvia.

There was a pulse of silence. Then, from her dad: "Where you going with this, M?" There was an edge to his voice. "She doesn't need a lecture."

"Sorry." Aunt M leaned back in her chair. She actually looked contrite!

"You coming with us, then?" her mom asked Aunt M.

"Yes."

"You *are*?" Sylvia said.

"Why not. In Rome, do as the Romans."

"Three guesses whether Sylvia will," her dad said, smiling at her. "The first two don't count."

Sylvia reached and touched the back of his hand and left it there. "You go first."

"You're staying right here. You've got better things to do."

Sylvia forced herself to look right at her dad. "That's right. I haven't finished wrapping presents."

Her mom picked up her fork: the signal to begin.

"WHAT WERE YOU doing? Trying to get me to *confess*?" Sylvia whispered in the kitchen. Her parents were clearing the table, just out of earshot.

"No, just giving you an opening, if you wanted one," Aunt M whispered back. "Your parents talking about being there for someone else? You might not ever get a more opportune time. Plus, it's Christmas Eve. You were being served a forgiveness special."

"I can't believe you didn't see what else it's an opportune time for."

"...Oh!"

"The minute my dad said he'd go too. We'll never get a better one. You really didn't see it?"

Aunt M shook her head. "I never said I was smarter than you, hon. Just older."

Sylvia's mom and dad were heading back to the kitchen now, laden with dishes. Aunt M dropped her voice even lower. "If they get bored and say they want to leave in the middle of the service, I'll say I don't want to leave. That will guarantee you enough time—if you really hurry."

SYLVIA WAITED FOR the sound of her dad's car leaving before she went to the garage. There, hung on a row of hooks on the wall, were three cross-country ski outfits, her mom's on the left, hers in the middle, her dad's on the right. She pulled her ski pants on over her skirt. Now the sight of the empty hook between her parents' outfits stunned her, as if she herself had been between them, safely protected by their loving care. She went out through the side door of the garage.

The recent rain had turned into snow again and then had stopped, leaving several inches of new, powdery snow. There was no moon, the sky huge, entirely black between the million stars. Yellow light spilled from the windows of the Head's House onto the snow. Across the campus, the row of dormitories in their white clapboard, the library with its steeple, the Administration Building where her mother worked, and the big copper beech tree her mother loved were almost invisible in the dark. Sylvia put on her skis and headed as fast as she could across the campus and athletic fields and onto the trail by the river, where she smelled the familiar musky smell. Did every river have its own smell?

She found the lean-to bowed down under the weight of snow. Soon it would collapse. The pile of stolen stuff in the doorway was sugared by the snow that had drifted in. The note was not there. It must have blown away. Somebody would come across it someday and wonder what it meant. She wished she and Aunt M had put the pine bough door back in the opening. It was the least they could have done. She filled the backpack with the stuff she and Elizabeth had stolen, stuffing the down jacket in last, and looked at her wristwatch. The opening into the lean-to beckoned. What was it like to live in there? No, she didn't have time.

She picked up the backpack, heaving it shoulder high to put

her arms through the straps. Then she dropped it on the snow and crawled into the lean-to. She would stay only a minute.

In the center of the lean-to, she turned around and sat facing the open door, wishing that she could close it as Christopher must have closed it in the wintertime, to make it almost cozy. It smelled of dying pine needles in there, and smoke from his cooking fire that had drifted in, and maybe his sweat, his clothes, maybe even his bug repellent, lingering from the summer. She lay down, closed her eyes, and tried to call up the sounds and the sights and smells of his war that he must have relived while he tried to sleep. Minutes went by, and by, and by, while nothing came but dim replicas of black-and-white photographs she'd seen in the *New York Times.* "Tell me," she said, closing her eyes. And waited. There was no answer. She opened her eyes. There was nobody beside her, of course. She felt empty and sad, and angry at him for not being there, and embarrassed at her own foolishness—because now she was panicking over the lost time. She crawled outside, clipped her skis back on, and as she hefted the backpack up she noticed the little berms of snow that lay on top of the rungs of the grill over the firepit. Long after Christopher's lean-to fell and rotted away, the grill would still be there, waiting for someone to come along and use it.

A half hour later, breathing hard, pouring sweat, she headed across the campus toward the bright pool of light that bathed the outdoor equipment shed. Almost there, she realized she didn't have the time to take off her skis, sneak across the lighted parking lot, open the padlock, unpack the backpack into the shed, and get home before her parents returned. Why did she even go into the lean-to, let alone stay there for so long? She turned around and skied home. In the garage, she hurried out of her skiing clothes as she heard her dad's car in the driveway and carried the backpack up the backstairs just as she heard her mother and dad and Aunt M enter the house through the front door. In her room, she hid the backpack under some spare blankets in her closet. Then she counted to ten and went downstairs.

Her father was already pouring eggnog. "Sylvia! You're up." He handed her a mug. Her mother nodded her approval. After all, it was Christmas Eve. He handed a mug to Aunt M, but she shook her head. "Oh that's right, you've given up drinking," he said, sounding a touch disappointed. He handed the mug to Sylvia's mother.

"How was church?" Sylvia asked.

"It was nice," her mother said, and went on to name the carols they'd sung. Sylvia only half-listened. It had just occurred to her that her mom might feel like trading clothes with her tomorrow morning. Ever since Sylvia had grown as tall as her mom, it had been happening whenever either one of them felt the impulse to wear the other's clothes. Her mom would open the closet door to make her choice. And guess what she would find?

Sylvia knew it was ridiculous, but the feeling still wouldn't go away that her parents and Aunt M were staying up late, talking just to make sure she wouldn't have time before the sun came up to sneak the backpack in her closet back into the outdoor equipment shed.

At last, all the eggnog was gone. "Isn't anybody getting sleepy?" Aunt M said. Everybody decided they were and went upstairs to bed.

THAT NIGHT RACHEL lay waiting, well after two, for Bob to finish his shower and join her in the big king size bed in the master bedroom—that other country she was a citizen of when he was home. He would have left the shower stall door open, as usual. Water would be flying all over the bathroom floor. It had been going on for twenty-five years. She would be disappointed if it ever stopped. "You grew up in a barn?" she'd joked the first morning of their wedded life, standing in the water he'd left on the floor, naked beside him, watching him spray toothpaste on the mirror which he was gazing lustfully at, her reflected breasts prominent there. The night before he'd said, "Yum yum, chocolate nipples. So much better tasting than strawberry ones," and she, who would still be a virgin for another few seconds, had wanted to ask *How do you know*, but didn't. "I'll mop it up, but first a little more of this," he had said, patting her ass with the hand that wasn't brushing his teeth.

Usually the sound of his shower while she lay waiting was a foreplay all its own: she was the queen of Sheba, he the adoring, glistening prince adorning himself with cleanliness so as to come unto her. But never on Christmas Eve. She thought of it as a family tradition: Christmas Eve was for thinking of the Christmas story—

which, she promised herself, she would learn to believe someday. It wasn't passion she craved, nor excitement; it was serenity. Everybody deserves a little serenity on Christmas Eve. That's the real reason she'd suddenly decided to go to church.

The absence of serenity. She'd been trying to ignore it since even before September when, at the end of the weekend, just before he left again, she'd dropped the news that something was missing and he'd wondered aloud if it was maybe time to think about some other kind of work, and she'd said *No!* and he'd said *Well then?*

That question had been in the air every weekend since then, but he had never brought it up, the subject too fraught for such small pulses of time. Guaranteed not to be resolved. Better to focus entirely on the pleasure of each other's company than on heavy considerations. It was the same with the copper beech: she could call an arborist to tell her if the tree was sick. Instead, she'd wait for spring when, like Margaret said, either the new leaves would replace the dry old shriven ones, or they wouldn't. But now, more than ever before, she felt that something scary was going to happen if she didn't resolve Bob's question soon.

When you can choose the work you do, then what you do becomes who you are. She was the one who had said that. Or was it her sister? Either way, it was true. She couldn't imagine herself as any other person than the Head of Miss O's, but she'd begun to think of the school as a person who would stay young forever. As if there was nothing remaining for it to become—while what she wanted was change, even if that meant getting old and wrinkled and finally dead.

The *shhhsss* sound of the shower stopped. She listened intently. The sound of his electric toothbrush. Like a little bee. It would last exactly two minutes. What did he think about all that time? It stopped at last, and she heard the water running. Rinsing his toothbrush. Now he was flossing. Naked, watching the mirror. Now he was putting on his pajamas. She knew because putting on pajamas didn't make any sound. Is this what it was like to get old: shivering in anticipation of a *cuddle*? Was he an artifact in her life and she in his? Could you really love someone as ardently and faithfully as they both believed they loved each other and that someone not be the center, pushed to the periphery by work?

The bathroom door opened. He was framed in the doorway by the light behind him. The light went out and he padded in the dark across the carpet. The mattress sagged down on his side of the bed and he lifted the covers. She turned away from him so he could press himself against her back, like two spoons cradled, his arms around her. He kissed her ear, then nuzzled his lips into the back of her neck. She felt his breath. It was safe now; he could ask that question again: *Well then*? He'd even help her answer.

"Something's going on with Sylvia," he said.

She was too disappointed to answer.

"I hope you'll talk to her."

"Not you?" she managed. "Not both of us?"

"It's about something that's going on at the school. Something you need to know. If not you, then Eudora."

"How do you know?"

"Because otherwise she'd tell us."

"You sure?"

"I'm a whole lot less sure of almost everything than I used to be. But we have to base our decisions about what to do and what not to do on one assumption or another."

"All right then, I'll talk to her."

"When school starts up again, right? Like for the other girls? They don't have to deal with the head of school when *they're* on vacation."

"If you say so." She rolled over on her back, put her hand on his chest, and pushed him gently away.

Nothing to do now but try to fall asleep.

IN HER OWN room, Sylvia got under the covers with her clothes still on and waited. She cared less whether her aunt was asleep than her parents—though she would hate to have her aunt know the reason she had failed to get the stuff back on time was her lingering in Christopher's lean-to. She'd keep that a secret forever.

When she was sure they were asleep, she got up, leaving the light off, picked the backpack up off the floor of her closet where it rested below the ankle-length green dress on its hanger that she was sure her mother would choose to wear in the morning, and tiptoed toward the door of her bedroom.

Out in the hall, Sylvia stopped. Was this one of the nights her dad couldn't sleep? But all she heard was the wheezing of the grandfather clock getting ready to ring the hour, then the tinny ring three times. She tiptoed down the stairs, across the hall, and out the front door. It was the farthest door away from her parent's room on the other side of the house.

Outside, the cold hit her immediately and she sucked in her breath. She carried the backpack in her hand so she could toss it away, out of sight if the security guy appeared. It was hard to carry that way, making her feel lopsided. She had to put it down and rest twice. She was breathing hard by the time she came around the gym, key out in her hand already. She was going to put everything back. Christopher had gone away; so make the crime go away too. She hurried across the wash of glaring light. It glinted on the padlock.

Which was a different one.

Of course they would have changed it! Why hadn't she thought of that? She tried to stuff her key in anyway. It didn't go. She leaned the backpack against the door and started to run home. The stuff was returned, that's what counted. It didn't make any difference whether it was inside or not when it was found.

She was almost all the way home when she remembered the backpack was hers, not the school's. *But this isn't ours*, Gloria would say, pointing to the backpack in her mom's office. Her mom would already know. She'd given it to Sylvia for her birthday.

Sylvia ran back into the glare of the light again and pulled everything out of the main section of the backpack, piling it on the ground, all the while listening for the security guy's car. Next she tried to extricate the first-aid kit out of the small side pocket into which she had crammed it into at Christopher's lean-to, but she could get only the tip of her fingers and thumb around the top edge of it and they kept slipping off. The kit was labeled *Property of Miss Oliver's*—she knew because she was the one who had done the labeling—and it wouldn't budge. She turned the backpack upside down and pushed hard against the bottom of the side pocket. The kit popped out, landing on the hard pavement, spilling its contents out in a fan. A bottle of hydrogen peroxide, glistening in the light, rolled away, making a hard brittle sound. In a rage of panic, she ran after it and picked it up and stuffed it with the rest of the contents back into the kit and pushed the lid shut, but it wouldn't close. She would have to take everything out and repack it all neatly, each item in its specified place. Instead, she plucked the bottle of hydrogen peroxide out and threw it across the parking lot, out of the light. She closed the first-aid kit and left it next to everything else. She laid the down jacket over the top of the pile as if to keep it warm. Then she picked up her empty backpack and ran.

Home again, she entered through the side door of the garage and returned the backpack to its place, and then, repeating the steps she'd taken earlier, went up the backstairs and to her room. The grandfather clock wheezed the half hour. *Only thirty minutes? That's all it took?*

Soon she was snug and warm, under a thick comforter in her bed, on the delicious downward slope toward sleep. She wouldn't re-enter the world until noon, at least.

But why hadn't they told her they'd changed the lock? She was wide awake again. Wouldn't the first person they told be the president of the club? And who were *they*? Gloria Buchanan? Mabel Walters, the business manager? The head of maintenance? The security guy? Did they just forget—or did they suspect her? Why hadn't she suggested they change the lock? Maybe when she didn't, they began to suspect her.

And if Christopher had just taken the stuff with him, wherever he went, wearing the down jacket to keep himself warm, she wouldn't have had to sneak it back. *Why did he think he had to give it all back?* After a while, the questions, endlessly repeating, were more boring than frightening. She fell asleep.

She woke briefly in the daylight. Her mother was tiptoeing out of the room with the ankle-length green dress. Sylvia turned on her side and went back to sleep.

FIFTEEN

For months Christopher Triplett had been waking up in his lean-to deep in the woods to the sound of the Connecticut River flowing by; so when he was awakened on Christmas morning by the sound of traffic on Farmington Avenue in Hartford, he had no idea where he was. It was a new kind of terror for him. The endlessly repeating wallpaper pattern, a stagecoach drawn by four horses past a stately New England house, didn't tell him anything. Nor did the casement windows through which the traffic sound continued, or the peaked ceiling above him that should have told him it was an attic room. The most foreign of all was the actual bed he lay in. For Christopher that Christmas morning, not knowing where he was soon transmogrified into not knowing *who* he was and, for a few unbearable seconds, not knowing *what* he was. It was tantamount to being born as an adult person who had no idea what a *person* was.

Memory returned to him, like an image rising from a negative in an old-fashioned darkroom, his aunt emerging as a small, gray-haired woman with sharp blue eyes opening a door, her braceleted wrist ushering him into a room. "It will be more private for you up here than on the second floor. There's a bathroom just down the hall. It's all your own."

Then, like a movie spooling backward, he was following her up the stairs again to the room, watching at eye level the hem of her skirt, the back of her legs in their brown nylon pantyhose, and her two feet pressing down against the steps in small black shoes. He would have been only slightly less flooded with relief if he'd awakened from a dream that he'd been sleeping in a dumpster, which he had imagined more than once. It had been only for few seconds that he'd not known what existence was, but during those seconds he hadn't known what time was either, and so those seconds had lasted forever.

He lay, reveling in the release from terror, under a down comforter in clean white sheets, naked because his aunt had taken his clothes to wash them. When he got up, he would write a note to Sylvia and Elizabeth and Auda to tell them he was safe. And how surprised he was that his aunt had opened the door to him right away. No, not Elizabeth or Auda, just Sylvia. She's the one who, when he was washing in the river, looked right through his nakedness, as if it were a suit of clothes. Then he remembered he didn't even know her last name, let alone her address. He'd go back to Fieldington someday soon—if he stayed healthy—and ask her.

He heard footsteps coming up those remembered stairs, and a knock on the door.

"Yes?" He pulled the comforter up to his chin.

His aunt opened the door just enough to put his clothes into the room, placing them in a neat pile on the floor, then stepping back, out of his sight on the other side of the door. "What would you like for breakfast, Chris?"

He hesitated, stunned by his good fortune.

"Corn beef hash?"

"Yes, corn beef hash. How did you know?"

"I remembered from when you were little. Come on down when you're ready."

She closed the door. Then, like leaving the house and then right after remembering something left behind, she opened it again. "Chris?"

"Yes?"

"You will take a shower, won't you?"

He didn't answer. He didn't know whether he was more angry than ashamed, or more ashamed than angry. Uncle Ray would have known better than to ask that question.

He heard her retreating footsteps and wanted to follow them and tell her how he never let himself get dirty, not his clothes either. *You just try washing in the river in the winter!* How he shaved too. Every day. By feel. Maybe he wouldn't take a shower. Let her smell him the way he was.

But only crazy people pass up chances to take hot showers. He got out of the bed, and even though he knew it was warm in the room, he was surprised to feel how good that felt. He stepped out of the room into the smell of brewing coffee wafting up the stairs. Carrying his clean clothes in front of himself to cover himself, even though no one was looking, he padded down the hall, the soles of his bare feet luxuriating in the carpet. The bathroom was shiny clean. He remembered it now, from last night when he'd brushed his teeth. He'd kept his head down while he brushed and spat so he wouldn't see himself in the mirror to learn how old he looked. He was proud of himself for knowing he wasn't ready yet. One thing at a time. One thing at a time. He did the same that morning.

Then he stepped into the shower stall—a whole room just for a shower!—and turned on the water. It came out cold at first because showers always do that, but he didn't wait for it to get warm because he wanted to feel it getting warm, and soon the hot water streaming down on the top of his head, over his shoulders, stinging his skin, soothing his muscles, and the soft hissing sound, melted his aunt's insult away like the steam rising around him. He was clean. *Really clean.* He stayed in some more, just for the feel of it. When he turned it off at last and stepped out, the whole bathroom was full of steam. He lifted his right arm and put his nose in his armpit and sniffed up the smell of soap.

There, on a chair near the stall, was a big white towel, folded neatly, and on top of that a washcloth. He had never used a washcloth in a shower, he just used his hands, but he wasn't about to pass up a gift so he picked up the washcloth and stepped back into the stall and took a shower again, cleaning every inch of himself with the washcloth. Then he stepped out and dried himself with the big white towel. Its nubby surface against his skin was a luxury too. He kept on wiping himself with it after he was dry and then he hung it neatly over the back of the chair.

He found his clothes already ironed, sharp creases pressed into his khaki trousers. He put them on, feeling like Christopher Triplett, Sergeant, US Marine Corps, but not enough to wear a uniform. Not yet. One thing at a time. When he went down to breakfast, he'd explain to his aunt why he wore khakis instead of jeans, how when jeans get wet they cling to your skin and lose their shape, especially in the ass, so you walk around looking like you had a load in your pants;

but that wouldn't interest her so he probably wouldn't tell her. He'd talk about something else instead.

The smell of coffee got even stronger as he went down the stairs. At the foot of them, in the big front hall—white, old-fashioned plaster walls, brown oaken trim—he also smelled the hash. The little window in the front door was stained glass, some kind of tree, a lawn, a sky, sun shining through right at him, landing on his face, clean shaven to prove he was a civilized man. In the dining room, a chandelier over the big round polished table, chairs all around as if talking with each other, a standing screen with a Chinese design in front of the door to the kitchen so nobody would see the maid who wasn't there anymore, while they talked about things she wouldn't understand. All these thoughts, like friendly bullets, zinging through the air into his brain. He was that alive!

He stepped around the screen, pushed the door that opened both ways, walked through the pantry into the kitchen and into the gaze of a little girl framed in the photograph on the opposite wall. He stopped walking, stood still. She was looking right at him in black and white. Below them, sitting at the kitchen table, so was his aunt. "Merry Christmas, Chris!" she said, standing up to greet him in a bright-red dress.

He shook his head. To clear the girl away. If he didn't, she'd grow up to be the one he'd killed.

His aunt frowned. "But we can make it merry."

His eyes still on the little girl, he shook his head again. To let his aunt know that's not why he had shaken his head.

"We can," his aunt insisted. "Oh Chris! I know it's hard. But you're home now. You're safe."

He looked away from the little girl to his aunt and shook his head again—up and down this time. So she'd think he agreed. And wouldn't talk like that anymore.

"Good," she said, though she didn't look convinced that he was convinced. She crossed to the stove. "Sit down, dear," she said over her shoulder, looking more like Uncle Ray than she did last night. He sat down at the kitchen table and watched her spoon a big, mounded helping of hash on a plate. The girl in the photograph was still watching him, but he kept his eyes on his aunt. She had a little hump high up in her back, and her hair was white with a hint of blue. He felt a twinge of affection for her. It made him wary.

She turned from the stove and crossed the room in her red Christmas dress with a plate of hash and two pieces of toast in one hand, a cup of black coffee steaming in the other, and put it down in front of him and sat down next to him and watched him eat.

He ate ravenously. He even knew that was the word to describe the way he ate, and though he missed the taste of wood smoke and the feeling of hot food going down inside him while outside him all around there was snow, it was as luxurious to eat breakfast in his aunt's warm kitchen as his two showers had been. When he was finished, he asked for more. His aunt leaned and kissed the side of his cheek and practically jumped out of her chair and brought the frying pan to the table and spooned the rest onto his plate, and he ate that too, and when he was finished, on a sudden whim which surprised him as much as anything else that happened that morning, he let out a long, loud, unseemly burp: what he would have done, right then, to make his Uncle Ray laugh, if his Uncle Ray weren't dead. He turned to his aunt and grinned.

He watched her deciding how to react. The silence went on, and then she squeezed his hand and said, "You could always make me laugh when you were a little boy." She glanced at the picture on the wall.

"You? His eyes followed hers to the picture.

"Yes, me. Who did you think it was?"

He thought, *If you were Uncle Ray, I'd tell you.*

"It's been there for years. You never saw it before?" She studied him. He made himself not look away. "Well, you just didn't take note, that's all," she said at last, standing up from the table. "I'm going to leave for church in a few minutes. You want to come?"

"Okay," he said, so he wouldn't be alone with the picture.

THE MINISTER, ROBED in white, looked down from her brown pulpit straight into Christopher's eyes, and read with a sonorous voice: "And in that region there were shepherds out in the field keeping watch over their flock by night. And an angel of the Lord appeared to them, and the glory of the Lord shone around them, and they were filled with fear."

Squeezed tightly against his aunt in a pew crammed with Christmas worshipers, it flashed to Christopher that the girl named Sylvia and the Angel of the Lord were interchangeable—and so maybe was his aunt.

Before he could make that thought into a vision of Sylvia, the angel, and maybe his aunt becoming each other, switching back and forth, the minister finished reading and climbed the stairs down from her pulpit. The congregation knelt and began to sing "Silent Night." He knelt too but kept his mouth shut, waiting for the hymn to end. If he explained to the people around him why he had no right to sing with them, they wouldn't understand.

His aunt nudged him and moved her hymnal toward him so that it was half under his eyes, and pointed with her finger at the words. He shoved it back toward her so hard it fell to the floor by her knees.

The people in the pew stopped singing. He bent and reached to pick up the hymnal, but his aunt's hand got there first and pushed his aside. He stood up, fumbled past her and the others in the pew, and rushed down the center aisle toward the doors, holding his breath, staring straight ahead, so he wouldn't meet the eyes of the kneelers as he passed. Outside, he let out his breath. He started down the steps. He'd go to his aunt's car and wait there for the service to end. If he knew the way to her house, he would've walked.

"Christopher, wait."

He turned and saw her coming out of the church. "Go back in," he said, remorseful now. "Finish the service. I'll wait."

"No, Chris, I'm not in the mood anymore. Please, get in the car."

They didn't speak to each other on the drive back to her house. He went straight to the attic and got up on the bed and pulled the comforter up to his chin.

He awoke several hours later, surprised that he'd fallen asleep. He couldn't just hide up there forever. He would have to go downstairs and apologize.

Still in her dress, his aunt was in the living room, sitting in a big blue armchair, watching him approach. The Christmas tree was behind her by the window, its lights turned on, and she had lighted a fire in the fireplace. He thought, *That's a job I should do, not her.*

He said, "I apologize, Aunt—" and discovered he couldn't finish the sentence. He couldn't call up her name!

The hurt recognition of this flashed in her expression, and he rushed on to cover up. "I'm not myself sometimes since I've been back."

She nodded her head. "I understand, Chris. Maybe you should see somebody."

He shook his head.

"All right, Chris. We'll talk about it some other time." She got up, went to the Christmas tree, and picked up a package wrapped in red. "When you were sleeping, I got you this. I would have preferred to give you a book, but bookstores are closed on Christmas day." She held the package out to him. He hesitated. "Take it," she commanded.

He opened his hands and she put it in them. He held it for a second or two and then unwrapped and opened it. A box of Whitman's chocolates. Each nested in its little cup of brown paper. He felt a wave of grief for her, trying so hard to make him happy.

"Try one," she said.

He put one in his mouth. Nougat wrapped in shiny dark chocolate. Delicious.

"Merry Christmas, Chris." she said. "Now I've got to get Christmas dinner ready." She headed toward the kitchen. At the screen with the Chinese design, she turned to face him. "By the way, my name is Adelaide." Then she disappeared into the kitchen.

DINNER WAS A great big steak, a ton of mashed potatoes, and a salad. "Fit for a Marine," Aunt Adelaide said, pouring a glass of red wine for herself out of a bottle that was half empty. She'd drunk two glasses while preparing dinner.

"Can I have some?" he said. He didn't like wine. He was a beer man. He just wanted to make her have to say no.

"Do you think you should—I mean—in your condition?"

"My *condition?*" Now he wanted to embarrass her by having to describe his condition.

She stared at the bottle. "Well it is Christmas," she said, sounding as if she were talking to herself. She got up from the table, crossed the dining room to the sideboard, and came back with a glass.

"Never mind," he said, regretting his meanness. "Keep it for yourself."

"There's more." She put the wine glass on the table by his place and filled it. "Remember to sip it, Chris. It's wine, not beer."

He grinned, drained half the glass in two swallows, reached for the bottle, and refilled his glass. She pretended not to notice.

They ate in silence. He drank some more wine, obediently sipping now, beginning to feel its glow. "This a great Christmas dinner," he said.

"I'm so glad not to be eating it alone!"

"You know, I'm going to go to college and get me a degree in retailing."

"Retailing?" She was sneaking a look at the bottle. There was one more glass in it.

"Yeah. Outdoor stuff. Canoes, fishing rods—"

"That's wonderful, Chris!"

"You think so?"

"Yes. Canoes, fishing rods, sleeping bags, tents." Her cheeks were flushed. "A store like that is right up your alley."

"I think so too. Maybe we should drink to it, Addy," he said, emptying the bottle into her glass. "Like you said, it's Christmas."

She grinned and got up and went to the sideboard again and came back with another bottle of red and an opener. He opened the wine. "Just one glass more each," she said. He filled her glass and then his own, and took a big swallow and had some more steak and another swallow and filled his glass and hers again, and he told her his plan to use the GI Bill to pay for college at Southern Connecticut State and get himself a secondhand car and his own apartment, and then the steak and potatoes and salad were all gone. So, they opened a bottle of white because that went better with the chocolates. "If I'd known you were coming, I'd have baked you a cake. But these chocolates are scrumptious if I do say so myself," his aunt said. They ate the rest while he told her of all the reasons—which came to him as he talked—of why there was a great big market for outdoor equipment, and with each glass of wine they both grew more enthusiastic.

In gratitude, he raised his glass to her and said, "Here's to you, Aunt Addy. We only have each other."

"That's right," she agreed, smiling brightly. "Everybody else is dead." And they both burst into drunken laughter.

ADELAIDE TRIPLETT WAS embarrassed the next morning to be still in her bathrobe as she scrambled eggs for her nephew's breakfast. What he needed after so much chaos was some formality in his surroundings, neatness and order, not the sight of an old slattern suffering from a hangover in her bathrobe and slippers. Last night, even though she'd been quite tiddly, to put it mildly, she had laid out her clothes for the morning before she went to bed: a wool skirt, a white blouse, her blue cashmere sweater. And most important, pantyhose to cover the web of blue veins on her ankles. She was a realist, a practical New England girl. When you are young and if you are pretty, show as much of yourself as you can get away with. When you're old, wear a lot of clothes.

But this morning she had awakened to the sound of his footsteps coming through the ceiling of her bedroom, and then she heard his shower going, and she got out of bed, threw on her bathrobe, and hurried downstairs. She didn't want him to come down to an empty kitchen and wait for his breakfast. It was important that he be greeted every morning by a cheerful smile and a breakfast of his choice.

She ascribed to Uncle Ray's careless upbringing of him that he didn't even notice she was still in her bathrobe—and to his youth that he could actually consume food after what they'd put away last night.

She brought his eggs to him now, cooked hard, the way he'd said he liked them. (She liked them that way too. They were chicken ovaries after all, disgusting when you thought about it, so she always cooked them to oblivion.) Heaped also on the plate were two pieces of toast and four slices of bacon. She'd already brought him his coffee and his orange juice. She sat down at the table across from him.

"Aren't you going to eat?" he said. She shook her head and shuddered.

But she loved to watch him eat. She longed to tell him how lonely it was to live all alone in this great big old house she and her brother Ray had inherited from their parents, and Ray living way up there in the Adirondacks, and they didn't like each other all that much even though they were brother and sister, and now he was dead. But the last thing Christopher needed was to know her neediness. It was the other way around. And one of the things he needed was some clothes.

She watched him finish his eggs, put down his fork, and pick up a slice of bacon. "I'd like to go to the VA today and get everything squared away," he said, and took a bite of the bacon.

Her spirits brightened. "Good!" She'd drive him there and help him navigate all that bureaucracy. Everybody knew the government made things more complicated than it needed to be.

"I'd like to borrow your car to go there."

"Oh?"

"I'll only need it for the morning. Why, do you need it?"

"No, I'm not going anywhere. But you've been under so much strain—"

"But I still have my driver's license. I even have a guide's license."

"It's not a good idea, Chris." she said, speaking firmly. "I'll drive you there. If the doctors say you can drive, then you can borrow my car any time you need."

"I'm not seeing any doctors! I'm going to get my enrollment squared away."

"All right then. We won't see any doctors today. We'll just take care of the enrollment." She paused. "But let's stop on the way and get you some new clothes."

"I don't have any money."

"Think of it as a Christmas present from me."

"You already gave me a Christmas present."

"Christopher! It was a box of chocolates. And I ate half of them."

It wasn't until Adelaide Triplett pulled into the parking garage at the corner of Pratt and Main where they would get two free hours of parking for Stackpole, Moor, Tyron, one of Hartford's finest clothing stores on Trumbull Street, that she realized her nephew had thought they were going to Walmart. "Would I get dressed like this to go to *Walmart*?" She was wearing the clothes she'd laid out last night. "This is where *I* shop, why would I take *you* some place less?" She used this ploy to appeal to his sense of justice and equity. As she expected, he got out of the car.

Adelaide felt grounded, as if the world was a sensible place where logic prevailed, as soon as she walked through the doors of quality establishments like this century-old clothing store where the pace of changing styles was judicious, where there was a refreshing dearth of things made of plastic, and where a well-dressed salesperson with good manners greeted you and served your needs rather than abandoning you to a wandering search in a huge featureless desert full of horrible stuff made by people who were getting cheated in some benighted faraway place, if not by robots. There was a predictability in this place, a quietness, unlike what she imagined was the random chaos of war. If she could clothe her fraught nephew in garments purchased here, she would gird him in calm.

She introduced Christopher to the salesperson, a tall, trim man wearing a gray suit with a vest, who managed to look simultaneously avuncular and young. "This is my nephew, just back from Iraq."

"I'm honored to meet you, sir. Thank you for your service," the man said.

Christopher flushed and looked away. Adelaide wanted to tell the salesperson to think before he spoke. She also wanted to reach for his lapel and feel the thick fabric of his magnificent suit between her fingers and thumb. Of course, she did neither. "He will attend university," she said, careful not to name which one so the salesperson would assume Trinity. Or even Yale or Harvard.

"Shall we start with a blue blazer?"

It went on from there, Christopher strangely compliant, Adelaide thought, until he was supplied with every kind of item he might need, including a very sporty, warm outer jacket in dark blue wool, suitable for both formal and informal occasions, and a handsome leather briefcase, like the ones executives at Travelers Insurance carried back and forth from home to work so their bosses would think they worked late into the night. When the tailor was brought in to measure Christopher for the blazer and the gray flannel slacks, Adelaide was shocked by how surprised Christopher looked when he saw himself in the mirror.

A few hours later, at the Veterans Administration offices in Newington, which Adelaide chose over the one in Hartford because it was easier to find a place to park in Newington, she stepped back to let Christopher complete his errand on his own. She didn't want to reveal to what she thought of as "the authorities"—though they were merely clerks—that he might be in need of more help than he was applying for.

A handsome Black woman about Adelaide's age actually got up from her desk when Christopher told her his name. She guided him to the person he needed to see and introduced him as if she'd known he was coming. When Christopher emerged only a few minutes later with the papers he would need to fill out, a confident look on his face, his mission accomplished, Adelaide was even more amazed. "Thank you very much," she said to this fine woman whom she longed to hug. She wasn't about to shake up her world by ascribing this event in which the government performed at a high level to anything other than the exception to the rule, but she was glad that Christopher was the lucky beneficiary.

Maybe she wouldn't have to cajole him into seeking medical help. Maybe going to college was the only medicine he needed.

SIXTEEN

Sylvia and her parents and Aunt M were gathered in the Little Room of the Head's House, reading the books they had given each other for Christmas. It was cozy and warm. Her dad had lit a fire. "I love reading together like this," he said. "It's how it used to be before central heating. Now everybody goes off to their own room."

Sylvia remembered back in sophomore year when Gregory van Buren had mentioned in class that Jane Austen wrote her novels in the living room surrounded by conversation and card games. Elizabeth had murmured from her desk, "Maybe that's why her books are so boring."

"What?" Gregory had asked.

Elizabeth had answered: "I really didn't care whether Miss Bennett and Mr. Darcy ever got married. He was a horse's ass, and she should never have persuaded herself that he wasn't. Like it implies in the first sentence, what is interesting is the economics of the time. That could have been explained in a short essay, not in a boring romance novel." Gregory had challenged her to write that essay and three days later she handed it in. It was so interestingly acerbic that Gregory read it out loud to the class.

Sylvia was trying to remember whether that was the moment she'd first been attracted to Elizabeth or if it was when she first noticed the oil rig on her ankle with the big X over it when she heard a knock on the front door.

Her dad got up and went to the door. Sylvia heard him say, "Merry Christmas and happy new year, Gloria. Come on in. Want some coffee?"

"No, thank you. I have some good news for Rachel and Sylvia, that's all."

"Good news? What a nice Christmas present! Come on in."

"I'm sorry to interrupt," Gloria said, a minute later, her large form almost filling the doorway to the Little Room. She was dressed in a wool shirt and jeans, no coat. Upholding the tradition even on vacation.

"That's all right, come on in," her mom said. "What's up?"

"Yes, tell us," Sylvia said. *Why doesn't she ever tell me when I'm by myself?* Aunt M was watching Sylvia over the top of her book. Her face was blank.

"Whoever stole the stuff brought it back."

"They did!" Sylvia said. "When?"

"I don't know." Gloria looked mystified. "Security found it early this morning. Someone left a pile of it by the door of the shed."

"Really?" her mom said. "That *is* good news."

"Someone stole something?" her dad asked.

"Yes," her mom said. "A while back. From the Outdoor Adventure Club."

"Oh?" He glanced at Sylvia. "I don't remember your telling us that. The Outdoor Club is pretty important to you."

"I didn't think it was that interesting," Sylvia said. "I mean, people steal things."

"Besides, you weren't home," her mom said, pointedly.

He flushed and stared.

"Sorry," she murmured.

Gloria frowned, looked confused.

"Well, anyway," Sylvia said. "It's a relief to know it was an outside job, since the stuff was returned on vacation when the students were gone."

Her mom looked surprised. "I never suspected it would be anything else."

"But why would anybody return the stuff?" Gloria asked. "If they wanted it bad enough to steal it, wouldn't they keep it?"

"It happens all the time where I live," Aunt M said.

"Really?"

Aunt M shrugged. "Even crooks can have a change of heart."

"This is really good news," Sylvia said. "I'll announce it in Morning Meeting the first day of school."

Gloria nodded. "Good idea. You announced it was stolen, so you should announce it was returned." She paused. "I'd appreciate it if you helped me get everything back where it belongs. You know better than I do about that."

"Now?" Sylvia said.

"No time like the present," Aunt M said.

"Okay." Sylvia put her book down, opened, on the arm of her chair, and followed Gloria out. Her mother and father watched. Aunt M was focusing hard on her book.

"By the way, you need a new key," Gloria said, unlocking the padlock. "Remind me." She opened the door. The security person on duty had delivered the stuff to her and she'd put it just inside the shed. She picked up the down jacket, rubbed a bit of dirt off a sleeve, frowned, lifted the jacket up to her nose and sniffed. "Somebody wore this for a while," she said, handing it to Sylvia. "We should have it cleaned, don't you think?

Sylvia lifted the jacket to her nose and sniffed. It smelled like wood smoke. She was in the lean-to again, taking it off, while Christopher looked the other way. "We don't clean them after the *girls* wear them," she said.

"Our girls aren't crooks."

"Maybe he isn't either."

Gloria looked at her.

"Or she," Sylvia added. "I'll put it back over there." She pointed to the place where the other down jackets hung neatly side by side.

"No, let's have it cleaned," Gloria said, reaching for the jacket.

Sylvia shrugged, pretending she didn't care. *Christopher's just as clean as you are. And you don't have to wash in a freezing river.* It would be worth saying it just to see Gloria's face.

Gloria turned and dropped the down jacket outside of the shed. "I'll take it to the dry cleaners. Better to be safe. We owe it to the girls."

They spent the next ten minutes or so returning everything else to its rightful place, while Sylvia's resentment of Gloria's unknowing insult to Christopher grew so intense she wanted to scream his story right in Gloria's face and tell her to shove it if she didn't like it. When the job was done, Sylvia fled, stepping past the down jacket, without so much as a backward glance or wave, leaving Gloria mystified by the door. She hadn't even said goodbye.

Halfway back to the Head's House, Sylvia pulled out her phone and e-mailed Elizabeth and Auda: *All stuff returned. GB agrees I report.*

By the time she was at the front door, Elizabeth had responded: *Good.* Then almost immediately: *All done.* Sylvia deleted both messages and emptied her trash file.

"WELCOME BACK," MARIAN said when Sylvia returned. She and Rachel and Bob were still reading by the fire.

"How'd they get in?" Bob asked her. "Was it a padlock?"

"Yes. Gloria's getting me a new key."

"Did they pick the lock? Or just pry the hasp off where the lock goes through?"

"Why so interested, Bob?" Rachel asked. "What difference does it make?"

"I don't know. Just curious, I guess. If the lock was picked, it means professional burglars. They fence the stuff. If it's just pried off, it's amateur. Poor people who need the warm clothes."

"Yeah," Marian said. "Where I come from, much more stealing gets done in the winter time. Makes me almost want to root for the robbers, you know? But I guess that's what charities are for. Like Goodwill. So people don't have to steal.

"Yeah, nonprofits," she went on when no one answered. "Goodwill for giving away warm clothes to people who would freeze to death without them. And Miss Oliver's School for Girls. For getting smart kids into college. Right?"

"Wrong!" Rachel said. "We do a whole lot more than that."

"Yes, you do," Marian said, nodding her head vigorously. "The empowerment of young women. Something that really needs to be done."

"Well, thanks," Rachel said. "I'm glad you approve."

"Oh I do. I do. I just wonder sometimes. Empowerment for what? Don't you?"

Rachel flushed. She stared at Marian.

"Mom?" Sylvia said.

"She does wonder," Bob said. "Every day. I know."

"That's right," Rachel said, still staring at her sister. "Every day. But you are not the one to tell me."

Marian nodded. A half-smile appearing. "You got that right."

"I get a lot of things right. In case you didn't know."

"Of course I know. You always have. You'll get this one right too, I bet. You'll find the answer—unless you wait too long."

"Glad you think so," Rachel said, her tone as testy as it ever got. "But right now I hope everyone will just mind her own business." She stood up. "And also, right now it's time for lunch." She moved toward the door.

Sylvia jumped up. Maybe a little too eagerly, given how interesting the conversation was? "I'll help you make it, Mom."

"Come on then."

"I am, sort of," Marian murmured to the backs of Sylvia and Rachel as they went through the door.

"Sort of what?" Bob asked.

"Minding my own business."

"Because she's your sister?"

Marian hesitated. "Yeah. You could put it that way, I suppose."

Bob nodded, apparently satisfied. He stayed in his chair. So did Marian. "But why would whoever stole it bring it back?" Bob asked. "That's what I also want to know."

"Me too," Marian said. "I'd love to ask that question. The answer would be really interesting." She stood up and headed for the kitchen.

Bob stayed in his chair for another little while. Still pondering.

IN THE KITCHEN, Sylvia looked at the e-mail from Auda on her phone. *Where's his family? Are they strong?*

SEVENTEEN

All day long, doors opened and closed to the dorms as girls returned from vacation. Classes would start tomorrow. The bleakest time of the school year was about to begin for the girls and for their teachers. Day after day they would get out of bed and trudge across the wintry campus to breakfast while it was still dark—and it would be dark again by four in the afternoon. It would be forever before spring arrived.

"You'll talk to her tonight then?" Bob asked Rachel at five-thirty in the morning at the kitchen table, eating breakfast. The day before yesterday, New Year's Day, Aunt M had gone home, her vacation over. In another minute, Rachel and Bob would say goodbye. He would get in his car and drive to New York, and because she was wide awake, unable to sleep, even if school were not about to start up again, she'd go to her office while she could still hear the sound of his car's tires on the gravel driveway. In her mind, she was already walking across the campus in the dark.

By noon, Sylvia would be up. But Rachel wouldn't talk to her then. She would wait until this evening, Sylvia's last at home, just the two of them, together. Bob was right: whatever was going on with Sylvia had to do with school. It was a student's problem, who just happened to be their daughter, and they weren't about to treat Sylvia any differently. So it was Rachel's duty to figure out. "Because otherwise Sylvia would have told us," he had said. That would be too painful not to believe.

"I hope whatever it is, it doesn't complicate your position too much," Bob said. He glanced at his watch, gulped coffee, pushed his chair back, and started to stand.

"Well, if it does, I'll give you a call," she snapped.

He sat back down. "Yeah, I know."

"You know what?"

"Maybe we should have enrolled her in some other school where her mom's not the head. You could have arranged an exchange of students with Miss Porter's or Emma Willard, where someone on the staff had the same problem."

"*I* could have?"

"Yes, *you* could have."

"We didn't even think about it. Why are you bringing it up now?"

"Because I was just thinking about it now. But I know. It was stupid. I'm sorry."

"You should be. It's lonely enough around here with you gone all the time."

"That's right," he said, flushing. "When you can keep your daughter home where she belongs, why would anybody want to send her away to a fucking *boarding* school?" He threw his napkin down.

Just then, Sylvia came into the kitchen, rubbing her eyes. She bent down and kissed him on the cheek. His scrambled eggs were still on his plate. "Aren't you gonna eat, Dad?"

He shook his head. "Not hungry."

"Yeah, it's much too early."

They sat at the table in silence while nobody ate until Bob said, "Syl, you want to walk me to my car?"

Sylvia nodded, still too sleepy for conversation. She got up from the table, picked up her dad's suitcase, and disappeared with it through the door to the garage.

Bob looked at Rachel. How to say you're sorry when you're not? She shrugged and looked the other way. He got out of his chair so fast he almost knocked it over. Striding across the kitchen, he followed Sylvia out to the driveway through the garage.

Rachel stayed in her chair, rewinding the scene. *This is how we end our vacations?* She got up, cleared the table, scraped the uneaten scrambled eggs that she had cooked for Bob into the garbage disposal, and went out through the front door on the other side of the house, listening for the sound of his tires on the gravel as she headed in the dark across the campus to her office.

When she returned that evening, she found a note from Sylvia: *Mom, I'm back in the dorms like everybody else.* Below that line was a big drawing of a heart.

"You don't have to whisper, the door is closed," Elizabeth said that evening when Sylvia started to tell her what had happened over the vacation. Sylvia agreed. No one had her ear to the door. No one suspected. Just the same, she couldn't make herself talk any louder. She was paranoid about being overheard for the same reason she had come back to the dorm instead of spending the evening alone with her mom, who had had that look this morning that said, *Can we talk?* Sylvia was afraid she'd say yes and tell her everything. Because why shouldn't she steal things for somebody who actually needed them? Elizabeth seemed to understand. She didn't ask Sylvia to talk louder again. She just moved a little closer.

When Sylvia got to the part where she entered *and lingered* in Christopher's lean-to, she found she couldn't tell it. It was none of Elizabeth's business. She explained about the backpack and the new lock. "First Auda e-mailed me to put the stuff back in the shed, then later she sent another email to just drop the stuff in front of the shed and run. I didn't want to, but that's what happened."

Elizabeth was surprised. "You wanted to put it all back in?"

"Yeah, I did," Sylvia said. Then, as if she'd confessed to wrongdoing, she added, "But I just said it didn't happen."

"Everything back like we never stole it in the first place?"

"I suppose so. It's hard to tell what I would have done, if I'd had the key."

"But the security guy could have come right then!"

"I know."

Silence. They both looked at each other, waiting for the other to say it.

Then Elizabeth said it: "Sometimes it feels to me like you don't care whether you get kicked out or not."

"Oh, I do!"

"You do?"

"Yeah, I do. But—"

"But what?" Elizabeth leaned forward.

"Not as much as you. You have more to lose. I've known that all along, I guess."

"You probably have," Elizabeth said, leaning back again. "I know I have." She seemed more vulnerable to Sylvia than she ever had. Except sometimes when she didn't know that Sylvia was looking—or when she was sleeping.

"How come we've never talked about this?" Sylvia asked.

"We didn't need to," Elizabeth said, brightening. "We've already gotten past bigger differences than that."

"Yeah, and we don't talk about them either—at least not much," Sylvia said, feeling a rush of affection. "Maybe someday we will."

"I suppose so," Elizabeth said. Then, as if she'd forgot to ask: "But the Christmas Eve service was that short? Where my parents go to church it lasts forever."

"This is New England," Sylvia said. "We're very businesslike." Then she told the rest of the story, ending with Gloria's insistence on having Christopher's down jacket cleaned.

"Of course she would. I would too," Elizabeth said. "Anyway, it's over. I'm glad, but I loved it while it lasted. We did the right thing. We're safe. And we can hope he is too." She turned her desk lamp on and opened her notebook. "Now I have to study."

"I might as well too," Sylvia said, turning her desk light on. "Now that there's nothing else to do."

IN HIS UPTOWN apartment near the FDR Expressway for rapid getaways to Connecticut, Bob Perrine couldn't sleep. Just the other day, in his office, after another sleepless night, he'd typed *sleep problems* into a search browser and was advised to get out of bed, read a book, take a little walk, or maybe look out the window—but whatever you do, don't watch TV. The blue light from the screen signals *Day Time, Wake Up!*

But that's what he wanted to do: watch TV. A talk show maybe, harmless blather in the middle of the night, a movie, even the stupid ads—anything to cure the buzzing in his brain that went on and on and on.

Obediently, he got out of bed and chose looking out the window from the options. He didn't feel like reading because then he'd have to turn on a light, and even a little walk in a tiny apartment is unrewarding. He'd get to a wall in about four steps and would have to turn around. So he went to a window.

And discovered another option: just stare at the night screen over the window. Its fabric was darker than the night, the color of ink. Just stare at it, instead of rolling it up. Just stand here like a blindfolded man and let calmness come.

Maybe he should sneak into his wife's office and install a nightshade like this one for those big sliding doors so every time she even begins to think it's time for her to move on with her life, she can't look out and see that big old copper beech and the campus beyond it and tell herself, *No way.*

Someday soon, he'll say to her: *Remember when I said let's take a sabbatical, and you said no, and I never said it again?*

And she'll say, *Yes. I do remember.* And he'll say, *Because when I get up in the morning and think of what I'm going to do that day, I don't rub my hands together anymore.* And she'll say, *Like a man who can't wait to get to work?* And he'll say, *Yeah, that's it, like a man who can't wait to get to work, but I don't do it anymore.* And she'll say, *Do you know what that's telling you?* And he'll say, *Yes, I do.*

He stared at the screen for another few seconds, and then he raised it up and looked down at the street. A man was walking his dog. Bob looked at his watch. It was two in the morning. Does that guy walk his dog *every* night?

There was no way to know.

But he did know he'd made a decision.

So he got back into bed and promptly fell asleep.

"Wait, your lunch," Aunt Adelaide said. Christopher was halfway out of her car, one foot on the sidewalk at the place where he'd catch the bus to Southern Connecticut State University. She leaned over to pluck the brown paper bag off the floor by the passenger seat where he'd left it and held it toward him. She'd got up early to make it for his first day of classes: a bacon, tomato, lettuce, and avocado on rye, two brownies, an orange, and a bottle of water. "You're just excited," she said. "That's why you forgot."

"Yeah, thanks for the ride," he said. He closed the car door and stepped into the shelter. Several people were sitting on the bench. He stood apart from them in his new coat. With so much snow on the ground, she was glad he was wearing his hunting boots rather than the brown cordovans she'd purchased for him. She waved goodbye, remembering how hard it had been for him to fill out the university's admission forms. But, she reassured herself, she wasn't so good at that kind of thing either. It runs in the family.

IT WAS ORANGES that Christopher Triplett was so surprised to smell when he heard the word *marketing* and read it as it now appeared in capital letters on the screen in the front of the classroom. The professor, a tall man in a blue suit standing to one side, aimed a little red dot at the words: *THE PRINCIPLES OF MARKETING.* Unlike Christopher's other classes which were spread out through two semesters, this one was intensely crammed into one semester, meeting five days a week.

Sitting in the first row so he wouldn't miss a single concept, Christopher heard Uncle Ray say, like he did every Saturday: *I'm going to the market today to get us some groceries.*

Christopher would always blurt, *Can I go with you?* as if he needed to ask, and on the drive from Osgood Pond to Saranac, Uncle Ray would always say, *It's a crappy little store, but the owner is a friend of mine. So, Mr. Kin-I-go-Widja, that's where we're going today.*

Even if they hadn't run out of groceries. Kids like to know what's going to happen next.

Inside the store, Uncle Ray would head straight for the oranges. *One for Mr. Kin-I-go-widja*, he would say, flipping an orange Larry Bird style behind his back in the general direction of Christopher who always caught it in the shopping basket. *And one for me*, he'd then say, this one a Magic Johnson jump hook. The next two were pure Uncle Ray: a zippereeno from underneath his armpit, and the finale, a weird underarm backward scoop over his head, from behind himself. That one always landed on the floor. Christopher would pick it up and put it in the basket with the other three. The four oranges, side by rounded orange side in his basket, were a sign to him that the world was right. The smell of orange would be on his hand the rest of the day.

"There are five marketing principles," the professor announced. "They are easy to remember. Think of the word FOCUS with the U made into a V: FOCVS."

The smell of the orange flooded out into the air from the brown paper bag on Christopher's desk. The classroom was large and exactly square, its walls painted gray, with no pictures to adorn them. About thirty students, sat in rows facing forward.

"F for first in category," the professor said. "O for being the opposite of the brand that is first in category—if yours can't be first."

Christopher reached into the brown paper bag and palmed the orange to stabilize himself. He'd come to this place to learn how to sell beloved things. He'd seen them in his head: canoe paddles made of ash, fly rods, binoculars, backpacks, tents. There wasn't one item he hadn't been able to see, arrayed in his imagined store. Now they were disappearing, melting away in the professor's voice.

"C for category dominance, which is different from being first. V for visual hammer because words are great, but pictures are greater. And S for second brands, now that you're a winner."

Christopher looked around the classroom to find at least one person to keep him company, somebody else who'd come to the wrong place. All he saw was the sides of faces, people looking intently forward at the professor, or head down, taking notes. Not one person turned to him.

He tried hard to follow, taking notes, using his brain, a delicate instrument, concussed by an IED blast he had no memory of. Words went in, ideas, conclusions, but they didn't assemble. The professor moved to the next concept in line while Christopher Triplett, the only person in that classroom who had killed a teenage girl, was still trying to find the words to write the note that condensed a concept the professor wasn't talking about anymore because he'd already moved to the next. And then the next. And the next. After a while, Christopher put his pencil down and told himself to be calm. One concept at a time. Just listen. *Just listen*, he repeated, drowning out the professor.

At the break, most of the students got out of their chairs and left the room. Christopher stayed in his. If he sat perfectly still, thinking hard enough, maybe he could retrieve the lecture.

The professor left the screen and approached the front row where Christopher was sitting. Christopher hoped he was heading for the exit, to go to the men's room, but no, he kept right on coming. *He's going to kick me out of his class*, Christopher thought.

The professor stood in front of Christopher's chair, leaning down. "Are you all right?"

"Yeah, I'm fine. Just haven't studied for a while."

The professor nodded, radiating sympathy. "It *is* a difficult transition from where you've been, Mr. Triplett."

Christopher didn't answer. This was worse than getting kicked out of class.

"I'm right, aren't I? You're going through a difficult time?"

"Yeah, I am," Christopher admitted. Now maybe the professor would leave him alone.

The professor glanced at his wristwatch. "It'll just take time, Mr. Triplett. See me after class. We'll set a time for an appointment." At last, he headed for the exit.

Christopher needed to go to the men's room. He'd drunk a lot of water. But he guessed that's where the professor was headed, so he stayed in his seat.

AFTER THE BREAK, Christopher focused so hard on each of the professor's words he was surprised his brain didn't hurt, but those words were disembodied sounds going out into the classroom over Christopher's head. He understood they were figuratively over his head as well. *I can't understand a lecture, but I can think in metaphor?*

He began to get angry, which showed just how crazy he really was. The professor wasn't some asshole in a camo suit. Still, Christopher wanted to jump up from the chair, charge the professor, knock him down to make him shut up. Afraid that he would actually do this, Christopher got out of his chair, grabbed his coat, and went out into the hall, right while the professor was still talking.

Now what was he supposed to do?

He'd go to the restroom first. Finally. Then he'd eat lunch.

That's what he would do. It would be embarrassing to go back into the lecture room to retrieve his lunch and briefcase. He'd get them after everybody was gone. So after the men's room he went outside and wandered around the campus until he found a place to eat and ordered a vanilla milkshake and a hamburger.

"We don't serve milkshakes here," the waiter said, his hair dyed red.

"Start now," Christopher said, crazy again.

The waiter went pale.

Christopher held up two fingers. "Two scoops of vanilla."

"Sir! We don't even *serve* ice cream."

"Make it three scoops then."

The waiter looked both frightened and disgusted. "I'll get the manager. You can talk to *her*." He crossed to the front of the café and whispered to an almost elderly woman in a blue serge pantsuit. She stared at him over the waiter's shoulder. Christopher was flooded with shame. He fled.

Outside in the cold sunshine, the campus seemed bigger than when he'd arrived. Across from him was the Elihu Burritt Library. He'd go in there and read. He couldn't make himself go to his afternoon class. The same thing might happen again, and it was too early to return to his aunt's house. She'd want to know why he wasn't still at the school. Tomorrow he'd explain to both professors: *All of a sudden, I began to feel sick.*

The reading room in the library was too warm. The air was dead. Someone had sucked the oxygen out. It was crowded with students. Their germs floated around in the air, spewing corruption. Every time someone coughed, he held his breath. He spent the hours reading back copies of *Field and Stream* and *Wooden Boat* and *Fly Fisherman.*

Around four in the afternoon, while reading an article about fishing for pike with an old-fashioned casting rod and reel like the one his Uncle Ray used, he looked up from the magazine, suddenly remembering reminiscing with his Uncle Ray, not long before he died. *Hey, Uncle Ray, remember that time you got really mad at me, really really mad? It was the only time. You caught that great big pike, remember? And put him in the bottom of the Adirondack guide boat, and I thought it had died so I picked it up and held it with both hands in the water. 'Look, Uncle Ray, I'm going to teach him how to swim,' I said, because I wanted to hear your laugh. 'Don't,' you said. 'Why not?' I said, and the fish twitched out of my hands and swam away. 'Oh!' I said. 'That's why.' Remember?* He looked around for Uncle Ray.

But he was in the library again. Surrounded by people staring at him. They'd been reading his mind? Or had he thought out loud? "So I'm crazy. Fuck you if you don't like it," he said under his breath, in his most matter-of-fact tone, standing up, putting his coat on calmly to show how sane he was. He walked slowly out of the library. He knew how funny this could be—from another perspective. Another sign that he was sane.

He could go home now. It was late enough that his aunt wouldn't know he had not attended his afternoon class. He'd go back to the lecture hall to retrieve his briefcase and uneaten lunch, and then get on the bus. He started to walk across the campus in what he thought was the right direction toward the lecture hall. It was getting dark. The buildings loomed. People he passed didn't even look at him. Berms of dirty snow lined the paths. A few minutes later, he realized he didn't remember the way. But sometimes he'd lost his way in big institutional places like this before he'd gone to Iraq, so that meant he wasn't really crazy, and he did remember the name of the building. That was important. And he was still able to read a map. That was really important.

Because there was a map of the campus posted near where he was standing.

It told him he'd been walking in the opposite direction. Ten minutes later, he was in the academic building, walking toward the big closed doors of the lecture hall, already sure they were locked. And even if they weren't, someone would have stolen the briefcase by now or turned it in to Lost and Found. Where was Lost and Found? Or maybe given it to the professor. *Have you got my briefcase?* he'd ask the professor tomorrow. *My aunt gave it to me for Christmas.*

There was a note taped to one of the big doors to the lecture hall: *Mr. Triplett, I have your briefcase. I'll be in my office until 4 pm. Take the stairs at the end of the hall, up one floor. Then turn right. Three doors down the hall on your left. Room 205.* It wasn't four o'clock anymore, but Christopher climbed the stairs anyway. Just in case the professor didn't leave at four. Just in case. Just in case.

I had to go home, the note on door 205 said. *I will bring your briefcase to class tomorrow...* and now the professor is standing in the front hall of a big house, a big, hairy dog bouncing toward him and shoving his nose into his crotch, followed by a boy and a girl the same age as Christopher was when Uncle Ray adopted him. Waiting for their hug. Then suddenly Christopher is in the doorway and the professor is the one watching. The wife waits demurely behind the children, waiting for her hug in a red wool sweater and tight jeans. She's got big breasts and is almost chubby, like those old paintings in museums, and he's trying to decide whether she is beautiful or not, but he could tell by the look on her face, not demure anymore, that she would rush him into bed and make love to him as soon as they read the kids to sleep. *But Christopher*, she says, *where's your briefcase, we can't without your briefcase...* and now he was standing at the office door again, reading the note.

Outside he ran for the bus, waving at it to stop, but it kept on going, spewing exhaust at him. It was his punishment for missing it, not being on time. He took the next one, an hour later.

Aunt Adelaide met him, as planned, at the bus stop where she'd left him off. He could tell she was working hard to pretend she hadn't been worried. She drove faster than her usual nice-old-lady pace back home, and when they opened the front door greasy smoke billowed out, smelling like burnt meat. The smoke alarm was screaming. Now he knew why she'd driven home so fast.

They rushed into the kitchen. He reached up and yanked the smoke alarm from the ceiling. "Oh Christopher, I wanted so much for you to have this dinner," she said in the sudden silence. The smoke hurt his eyes. The whole downstairs would smell like burnt grease for days.

Aunt Adelaide put on big oven mitts and pulled the oven door open, and another cloud of greasy smoke billowed out. She dragged out the roasting pan, a little tiny blackened chunk of meat in it, and rushed it to the sink and stuffed it down the sink disposal and turned it on. The grinder roared, filling the house with a sound like a broken outboard motor, while they rushed around opening all the windows and doors. The smoke oozed out the windows and the cold winter air rushed in.

Christopher ran away upstairs to the attic, too cowardly to stay and apologize. He'd have to explain why he was late. She called after him, "Let me at least make you a sandwich." He didn't answer.

Upstairs, surrounded by the horse and carriage and big house times a million on the wallpaper, he sat down at his desk and, to reassure himself that he was at least a little bit sane, tried to retrieve the professor's first lecture. This time the whole string of capital letters the professor had hung his concepts on reappeared in his brain along with a dim understanding. So what if it was maybe the rush of adrenaline from wading through the smoke? His spirits rose. He had some hope.

In the morning, when he came downstairs the stench of burnt meat carried also the smell of coffee, like a layer of snow covering the ice on Osgood Pond in the wintertime. Aunt Adelaide turned to him from the stove, attempting her Good Morning smile. She had opened all the windows again to let out the smell and was wearing a heavy woolen green sweater. He saw her for an instant as a little girl in a puffy green snowsuit, about to go out and play in the snow.

"Sit down, dear," she said, gesturing to his place at the table.

He sat down, more careful than ever not to glance at the picture of the girl on the wall. Aunt Adelaide brought him an omelet and thin slices of ham and four pieces of toast made with the raisin bread she's got up early to bake. "Your grandmother taught me how to make it," she said. "In this very house." He took a bite. It was delicious.

"But you're supposed to put the marmalade on," she said, reaching to touch his hand, stopping him from eating any more until he did. "It's fancy, from Scotland. I send away for it." She pointed to the center of the table where, on a shiny silver platter, next to the bowl of sugar with its special spoon and the breakfast salt and pepper shakers, stood the white crockery Dundee Marmalade jar. He picked it up and read *James Keiler & Sons DUNDEE MARMALADE*, surrounded by a wreath of leaves, like an ancient Grecian victory crown. Under it in smaller, more modest letters: *First Prize Medal for Marmalade London 1862.*

"The jars are so beautiful, I can't make myself throw them away," she said. "I have hundreds of them on a shelf down in the cellar."

He slathered some marmalade on his partially eaten slice of raisin bread toast and took a bite. It was even more delicious than the bread without it. He actually had to chew the orange rinds. "Don't put too much on, it ruins the taste," she said. He ate the omelet, two thin slices of toast, lightly rimed with the butter she'd warmed, and looked at the clock on the wall opposite to the picture of the girl. It was time to go, not enough time for her to make another two slices for him. She picked up her own spoon, not yet touched, spooned a bit of marmalade out of the beautiful white crockery jar, held it toward him. He opened his mouth leaning toward her and she fed him the marmalade, like a mom giving medicine to her little boy. It had happened in an instant, without any thought, just an impulse which flooded him with affection and embarrassed them both.

She drove him to the bus. Just as he opened the door to get out of the car, she said, "Where's your briefcase?" It was not clear whether she had just noticed he didn't have it or had been getting up the nerve to ask.

"I left it at the school on purpose. I didn't need it," he said, and tried to prove it by telling her how he sat at his desk last night and retrieved the whole lecture, and how the professor said that's the way to do it, to secure the knowledge.

She looked like she was about to cry. "Please don't lie to me, Chris. You don't need to. I'm on your side." Then she pushed the button to roll up the window so he couldn't tell her any more lies and drove away.

He walked into the lecture room along with several others. The class was about to start. Up front at the lectern, the professor saw him entering. He leaned down behind the lectern, picked up Christopher's briefcase with yesterday's lunch still in it, and showed it to him. Christopher went there to get it. Before he could think of how to explain, actually make an excuse for leaving it behind, the professor said, "You don't have to explain, I understand." Then, in a commanding tone. "See me in my office right after class. I can help."

The professor's lecture this time was understandable for Christopher: a straightforward statement, backed up by statistics and percentages, that business organizations, especially small ones, like family-owned stores, don't spend enough on marketing, getting known, creating a brand, because they get too wrapped up in operations.

After class, Christopher walked beside the professor, climbing the stairs to his office. On the way, several students and some colleagues waved to the professor or paused to say hello, and Christopher felt the professor's ease in the community—and his own foreignness.

The walls in the professor's office were lined with books. The professor noticed him noticing them. "Most of them are bullshit," he said. "They're just for show." Christopher wanted to know whether the professor was joking or serious. Because it was very important. But he didn't dare ask. The professor pulled his chair from behind his desk to prove how friendly he was and sat down in it, gesturing to a chair facing him just a few feet away. Christopher sat down. So he wouldn't run away. He was sure the professor was about to try to teach him stuff he'd never understand.

The professor cleared his throat, preparing to begin. Christopher leaned in. "That war was stupid," the professor said. "Which makes it all the more morally important that the people who had to fight in it deserve reward."

"Please don't tell me how you feel about the war," Christopher said mildly, politely, to this person who he was sure never had to fight in one, proving to himself once again that he was sane.

The professor looked disappointed. "I understand," he said, proving that he didn't, and Christopher felt a sudden rush of what he knew was a totally unreasonable surge of hope.

Then the professor, still looking apologetic, asked Christopher a lot of easy questions about the lecture, little softballs to make him happy, and Christopher answered every one.

"That's all for today," the professor said, sounding like the shrink who Christopher had wanted to kill. "We'll do some more tomorrow." Christopher's hope rose still more as he stood up to leave. But standing up, he was able to see past the computer and the mess on the professor's desk a framed photograph of the professor surrounded by his family, a dog, two kids, and a wife. They didn't look at all like the people he had seen when he'd been the professor standing in the doorway with the dog's nose in his crotch waiting for hugs from his kids, looking forward to making love to his wife.

"Goodbye and thanks," Christopher said, mildly and politely, hiding his relief that he was seeing what was really there.

He rushed to his next class, Financial Planning and Strategy. He managed not to be offended that the professor, a very small woman who had to stand beside the lectern because it was too tall for her, didn't notice his presence, which meant she didn't even know he was absent the day before. He understood her lecture, and she didn't look anything like the girl he killed.

The next several days went quite well. He managed to understand almost everything in both professor's classes. He came home each night to a sumptuous meal which his aunt had taken great satisfaction in preparing for him in her kitchen. It smelled only a little bit like burnt grease now. The first night was a pork roast—to make up for the one he'd ruined by missing a bus. Mashed potatoes, with a hint of cheese. String beans she'd frozen last summer about two minutes after she bought them from a local farmer. And for dessert: a cherry cobbler, still warm enough to melt the vanilla ice cream, her special kind from Philadelphia—"because you can see the little vanilla beans, that's how you know." The next night, two small roast chickens. She'd put a whole lemon inside each one, and little red potatoes roasted in the drippings—"which doesn't clog your heart, no matter what they say, because how could it when it makes you happy? Right, Chris?" Only one glass of wine because he had homework to do. "So I will only drink one too." (Not counting the ones she drank while she was cooking before he came home.) The third night, homemade pasta topped by her homemade tomato sauce, also frozen after being made right after she bought the tomatoes from the local farmer. But the ground beef and pork and little bits of sausage that were in it? "I bought those this morning right after I dropped you off at the bus."

The next morning, he went off to school full of energy and hope. The marketing professor must have sensed his growing confidence. He stopped his lecture and asked Christopher to explain his point by saying it in a slightly different way. It was no surprise to anybody in that class. He'd done the same thing to other students the day before and the day before that. But Christopher couldn't explain. The concept was there. But the words were not. Or maybe it was the other way around? The professor quickly moved on to save face for this student of his he felt so sorry for. That's what enraged Christopher. That pity.

All of a sudden, he is standing up and walking toward the professor. *Open your mouth!* he commands. The professor doesn't. So Christopher shoves the end of his rifle right through the closed lips, breaking teeth on the way to where the professor's words at him emerged. He stops before he pulls the trigger, though. He doesn't want to see the professor's head exploding.

Appalled by what he was capable of imaging, Christopher got up from his chair, sadly waved goodbye to the professor, and exited the classroom. First he took the same bus he would have taken if he were returning to his aunt's house. He arrived an hour before she would come to meet him. He waited another forty-five minutes for another bus to Bradley Field, getting away just in time. How long would she wait for him before she gave up and went home? Would she eat alone the dinner she'd cooked just for him? Or throw it away? Would she call the police?

At Bradley Field, he bought a postcard showing how it looked when he was just a little kid, and some stamps. *I can't do it, I tried hard. I'm not ready,* he wrote. *I'm going back to where I was until I am. Please don't worry. Thanks and Love, Christopher.*

He didn't say what else he was thinking: that he couldn't hang around her house until he was ready. She'd learn to hate him if he did. He might fly into one of his rages and hurt her. He simply mailed the card, comforting himself: this was an improvement. The last time he'd left her without even a note.

Looking like just one more tired and haggard business traveler in tasteful, if somewhat preppy, clothes, he took a SuperShuttle to the Fieldington Inn. From there, he headed on foot for his lean-to.

At the edge of the town, the sidewalks ended and the road narrowed. He was afraid drivers would not see him in his dark coat, so he walked on the left side of the road facing traffic, and each time a car came toward him, blinding him with its headlights, he stepped up onto the rim of plowed snow beside the road, sinking almost up to his knees to get out of the way. The light from the front windows of nearby houses helped him see where he was going, but the distance between them grew longer, until he came to a stretch where there were no houses and the only lights he saw were coming from the campus of Miss Oliver's School for Girls a quarter of a mile or so ahead.

On his trips from the village to his lean-to, he'd always walked past the campus, sticking to the woods on the other side of the road from the school. It was best to stay out of sight. As soon as he was around a curve in the road and could not be seen by anyone on campus, he crossed the road and cut directly through the woods to his lean-to. But now it occurred to him that, dressed as he was, no one would recognize him as the man who begged near the ice cream shop—the kind of person who would stir alarms in an all-girls boarding school, on guard against deviant intruders. If anyone saw him, dressed as he was, they'd think he belonged.

And anyway, no one would see him in the dark. Besides, this was a shorter route and he was exhausted. The driveway into the campus was now just yards away.

A car came around the corner, hugging the side of the road, blinding him again. It kept coming right at him, still tight to the side of the road. All the other cars had swerved toward the middle of the road, but Christopher had climbed up the rim of piled snow anyway to be sure to avoid being hit. Not this time. He stood still right where he was. The fucker behind the wheel was going to be the first to move. But the car kept on coming, still tight to the side of the road. Christopher took a step sideways to his right to get further out into the road and make the driver swerve so hard the car would go out of control and plow head on into a tree on the other side of the road. He could almost hear the sound of the car hitting the tree, the noise of the horn stuck on, and could see the front of the car accordion back into the driver's chest, blood erupting in a red flow from the nostrils. Instead, he watched the car turn into the school's driveway.

Christopher stood in the dark almost in the center of the road, watching the car's red taillights move up the long driveway. The rage that had filled him drained away. He was a crazy man for sure, frightened of himself, doubly sure now he had been right not to return to his aunt's house. She wouldn't be safe with him around.

He walked up the long driveway, his brain flickering with the notion that maybe he wanted the car to hit him, but then he came upon the white clapboard buildings of the campus. They were arranged in an arc, embracing an expanse of snow-covered lawn. No one was about. Everyone was tucked into one of these buildings. Their comely Puritan shapes were satisfying to him against the night. Lights from their big windows made squares of warmth upon the snow. Then voices. *Girls' singing voices*, floating into the dark:

This is my song, O God of all the nations,
A song of peace for lands afar and mine.
This is my home, the country where my heart is,
Here are my hopes, my dreams, my holy shrine.
But other hearts in other lands are beating,
With hopes and dreams as true and high as mine.

My countries skies are bluer than the ocean,
And sunlight beams on clover leaf and pine.
But other lands have sunlight too, and clover,
And skies are everywhere as blue as mine.
O hear my song, thou God of all the nations,
A song of peace for their land and for mine.

He didn't know that he was standing next to the music building where the Glee Club was rehearsing *Finlandia* for their participation in the Round Square Conference, an international league of schools, devoted to service, founded simultaneously in England and Germany soon after World War II. But he did know that he wished he could linger in this well-ordered place where young women sang songs of forgiveness. Reluctantly, he left it, the girls' voices, as they perfected their hymn, following him, softer and softer, as he headed under bright stars across the athletic fields into the woods.

Soon he would hear the river.

EIGHTEEN

Even though this was the third Sunday in a row, Eudora Easter was surprised to find herself in church. Yes, she was in the back pew, on the aisle, so as soon as the spirit moved her—which she had been sure it would—she could leave the church without attracting any more attention than she already had by being the only Black person in the congregation and get back to her studio, which was *her* church, where she belonged. Now she knew she wasn't going to leave before the service was over because she would attract the attention of her friend—her dear friend—Michael Woodward. He'd see her leaving and be disappointed. She had observed how surprised he was when he'd climbed up into the pulpit three Sundays ago and saw her there in the back pew—surprised and delighted, as if he thought she needed the support his church would provide her, when he knew as well as she did that it was he who needed support. She couldn't imagine how much spiritual energy it required to purvey a faith one doesn't share.

Eudora hadn't been a congregant long enough yet to know that Michael's parishioners loved him for doing exactly that. The way he had conducted himself as their rector for so many years had bolstered their faith more than it would have if he'd had his own belief to use as a crutch. *Trying* to believe day after day, and acting upon that belief—that was what was important. Michael Woodward loved dogs and kids. He breathed compassion and forgiveness. When you grieved, he grieved too, sometimes even more profoundly; and when you were glad, so was he. His congregation had come to understand that Love is God so God is Love, and all the rest is just theology.

Nineteen years ago, Michael and Eudora had watched their friend, the extraordinarily talented teacher, Francis Plummer, lose his mojo, run completely out of gas, and pretend it wasn't happening to him while all his embarrassed colleagues and students knew it was until, at last, he did the right thing, as Eudora had predicted he would, and retired before Rachel Bickham would have had to fire him in her very first year at the helm. Eudora would resign before that even began to happen. "Then what would I do?" she'd asked Michael over coffee one day during the winter vacation. "I don't know if I can do it alone."

"Not sure what *it* is," Michael, that subtle proselytizer, said, "but I do know you don't have to do it alone."

So here she was in his church.

When the service was over, Eudora was the first out the door where Michael stood to greet the parishioners. They both wanted to hug each other, but especially now that she was tinkering with the idea of joining his church, it was wise to keep private their indecisive and racially mixed courtship of one another. It had been going on for several years. If people knew about them, they'd grow more and more curious.

Eudora grew curious herself when, parking her car in front of Rose's Creamery where she would buy a butterscotch sundae to assuage the hunger the tiny communion wafer had stimulated, she recognized the youngish-looking man standing nearby as the one who had panhandled there most days in the autumn. His presence in Fieldington was even more anomalous than hers. She wondered where he had gone and why he'd come back, and why had he let someone cut that lovely blond hair, but most of all, she wondered where he'd got his nice new clothes, especially that smart blue woolen coat. And where was the hat people had dropped their money in? At his feet was a Styrofoam cup he must have harvested from a dumpster. Suddenly hungry no longer, she turned the ignition back on and headed for the school and her studio.

On the way home, Eudora decided that this person in his new attire had to be the same person Sylvia had come across. At the time Sylvia had been so disturbed she didn't want to talk about it, so Elizabeth had. It wasn't as if hordes of derelicts chose Fieldington as their base. So maybe it was the singularity of his presence that had disturbed Sylvia. Or was it the attraction of a likeness she didn't know how to talk about, their mutual anomalousness? It wasn't so very long ago that it would have been no less natural for the citizens of Fieldington to think of Sylvia as a half breed than to think of him as a beggar.

By the time she was halfway home, Eudora had dismissed her theory as the musings of an older woman who'd lived a history Sylvia had only read about. For all Eudora knew, Sylvia had never even heard that racist pejorative term, and she would never think of herself as an "exotic." Instead, Eudora began to think about how disturbed Rachel was when she'd told her about Sylvia's being closemouthed about her transaction with a homeless man. What degree of intimacy with him would rile her daughter so?

Eudora hadn't been worried at the time. She'd ascribed Sylvia's unwillingness to share her feelings with her mom as the normal desire of young adults to put distance between themselves and their parents. Now, as she turned into the school's driveway, anticipating entering her studio and transferring her attention to her work, Eudora began to think of the homeless man as an uninvited guest Rachel would have to make room for in her own life, as well as her daughter's. Otherwise, she would soon exhaust all the space around herself. That the homeless man had no idea of this didn't make it untrue.

It was strange: Eudora had started her day, postponed her work because she was worried about her future and needed the solace of Michael's church; and here she was, still postponing, thinking about *Rachel's* future. Well, they'd keep each other company, urge each other on to fulfill whatever that future turned out to be.

That decided, she got out of the car, pushed Sylvia, Rachel, Michael, and the homeless man in his new attire out of her mind, went into her studio, and resumed her career.

WINTERS SEEMED TO be longer in a New England boarding school. The days went on and on. Even the best of friends could get tired of each other, as differences, accepted, even celebrated, begin to rub.

Which is why Sylvia was somewhat less than a hundred percent enthusiastic when on a winter night she said to Elizabeth, "You're going to stay with us over the Washington's Day weekend when school closes down. So, let's make some plans." She was in her top bunk.

Elizabeth had just turned out the light and crawled into her bunk below. "Have you asked your parents?"

"I don't have to ask my parents. It's my house too. Why do you even ask?"

"If I wanted to bring you home to *my* house, I'd have to ask *my* parents."

"That's different."

"Yeah?"

"Yeah."

"Why?"

"Because you go to school *here*, that's why," Sylvia said.

"And you don't go to school in *Oklahoma*?"

"Obviously."

"Yeah, obviously," Elizabeth said in that knowing, sarcastic tone that grated on Sylvia, mainly because she couldn't match it and sound like herself. "Besides, it isn't Washington's Day," Elizabeth added. "That was years ago. It's President's Day."

"What's the difference?"

"Are you kidding?"

"I asked you what the difference is. Does that sound like kidding?"

"Okay. Washington owned slaves. You want to celebrate his birthday, you go right ahead."

"Whaaaat? Say that again."

"I shouldn't have to."

"Oh? Because—"

"Yeah, because." Elizabeth said. "Forget it, let's change the subject."

"Like maybe Washington owned my great grandfather?"

Elizabeth sighed.

"So I should be the one to not celebrate his birthday, not you?"

"That's not what I meant."

"It's what you said."

"Besides, we both know that's not why they changed to President's Day," Elizabeth said. "It was because Lincoln—"

"What about my dad?" Sylvia said. "Is it okay for *him* not to be pissed at George Washington?"

"Why don't you ask him?"

"Why don't you?"

"Fine, okay, I will. I'll make an appointment with his secretary."

"Oh shit, how'd we get into this?" Sylvia said. "Do you know how stupid this sounds?"

"Or maybe I'll write him a letter," Elizabeth said. "Dear Mr. Perrine. I have a question about George Washington. Was he a nice guy?"

Sylvia didn't respond. She'd just let Elizabeth wind down and then maybe they could go to sleep.

"I heard he killed a lot of Native Americans," Elizabeth said. "What do you think, Mr. Perrine? Was that okay?"

Sylvia made a loud snoring noise.

Elizabeth stopped talking.

Sylvia knew that in the morning, they'd both pretend this conversation never happened, but she remembered their wondering why they'd never talked about this stuff before and Elizabeth saying because they didn't need to. Well, Elizabeth was wrong. When you're sick of winter and tired of being stuck away in a boarding school with the same people every day, you take it out on people who will let you get away with it.

Like Elizabeth, who, as usual, was the first to fall asleep. Listening to her breathing, Sylvia wondered not for the first time what it would be like to spend the weekend with Elizabeth and her parents in Oklahoma rather than the other way around. She saw the same tall, skinny guy in a straw hat and red neckerchief she'd always seen standing in the doorway as Elizabeth introduced her. Behind him, trying not to look uncomfortable, Elizabeth's mother was a stout woman wearing a full-length apron and black flat-heel shoes. Sylvia knew that when she visited there someday, Elizabeth's parents wouldn't look like this at all, and she knew Elizabeth would be knowing enough to have warned them, but she continued to be sure they would be surprised anyway to see the dark skin of the girl who was their daughter's roommate actually standing at their door. Sylvia had the idea that males were less prejudiced than females. She hadn't read the polls. *Come on in!* the father would say, recuperating first.

He might even touch his hat.

SENT BY: BOB Perrine on 2/14/12; 10 pm

To: Rachel Bickham

Re: This weekend

Hey,

I've cleared my Friday afternoon, so BIG SURPRISE! I'll be at your place by late afternoon on Friday. Aren't you proud of me? Can't wait.

Love,

B

P.S. I won't leave until Tuesday morning.

SENT BY: RACHEL Bickham on 2/15/12; 7:12 am

To: Bob Perrine

Re: This weekend

Hey yourself,

Proud? YES! Ecstatic? OH MY! We'll be at the door waiting for hugs on Friday afternoon. And on Sunday night, Big Surprise, haha, we are having our usual double birthday party. Your 55th and Sylvia's 18th. Too bad I wasn't born in February. We could have a triple. And of course, the usual suspects are coming.

We have you all day Saturday, Sunday, and Monday! Three whole days! Can't wait for Friday night. *You will need to rest up on Saturday morning.*

Love,

R

P.S. It's your place too, by the way.

WHEN RACHEL WOKE up on Thursday morning, anticipating her husband's extended visit and the birthday celebrations, the weather outside her window matched her mood: sunny, blue skies, almost warm at fifty degrees. The school would close for the long Presidents' Day weekend at noon. In the early afternoon, she and Sylvia and

Elizabeth would go into Fieldington and shop for Bob's and Sylvia's Sunday night birthday party. Then they'd come home and have the rest of the afternoon to enjoy the intimacy and unguarded conversation that would happen naturally while preparing the dinner ahead of time together.

Rachel got out of bed, still excited by this prospect, but a few minutes later, while looking in the mirror to brush her hair, she thought of the actual work to prepare the dinner and realized she didn't want to do it. It was one thing to whip up a batch of pancakes in the middle of the night, another to go to the grocery store and buy all the stuff and then come home and actually have to cook it. Just the idea of work she seldom had to do as a boarding school professional who ate most meals in the dining hall brought a groan. Peeling potatoes, chopping carrots, incessantly checking the recipe in her one and only cookbook? Who was she trying to kid?

Besides, she had decided to give her daughter some space of her own, hadn't she? No, they were not going to have a cooking party. They'd go to Battastelli's Deli and buy everything pre-prepared and then come home and stick it all in refrigerator. The kids could do whatever they want and she would retire to the Little Room and read one of the books Sylvia had given her for Christmas.

BY THREE O'CLOCK, the campus was empty and silent. Clouds had covered the sun, a fierce wind had arrived, and the temperature had dropped to just above freezing. It was hard to know whether it was going to rain or snow. In this cold grayness, Rachel, Sylvia, and Elizabeth went downtown, with Sylvia driving.

Sylvia parked the car in front of Battastelli's, and Rachel tore the list of items to be bought into three parts to expedite the chore of shopping. After Battastelli's, they'd cross the street and buy the ice cream at Rose's.

Sitting in the front seat of the car on the passenger side, Rachel turned to her left to hand Sylvia her third of the list, but Sylvia was looking away to *her* left, at something across the street. A powerful tension was radiating from her shoulders. "What's over there?" Rachel asked.

"Nothing." Sylvia snapped her head and shoulders around to face forward.

Rachel leaned forward to see around Sylvia, instantly disliking herself for not trusting her, and saw several people entering Rose's Creamery. Another person stood by the door in a blue topcoat, the hood of which was pulled up, hiding the person's face so that Rachel didn't know whether it was a man or a woman. Why wait for someone there? Why not inside where it was warm? Sylvia was still looking straight ahead as if to look any other direction would cause her harm, her expression studiously blank. So this is one of the places kids get the drugs they bring into the school, Rachel thought. Makes sense for a dealer to hang out here: drugs and ice cream in one trip. Rachel turned to glance at Elizabeth in the backseat. Elizabeth returned her look, her face as blank as Sylvia's. Nothing could be clearer.

"All right, let's go shopping," Rachel said, and some of the tension flew out of the car. She would never use her own daughter as a spy to catch her fellow students doing wrong. That's a line no school professional would ever cross. Sylvia and Elizabeth both knew this. And they didn't do drugs, she was quite sure of that. For anybody who had worked in a boarding school as long as Rachel had, there were multiple signs, both of innocence and guilt, that most parents would miss. So all three of them were safe.

Rachel got out of the car first, leaving Elizabeth and Sylvia to say whatever they needed to each other, and entered the deli where it was bright and warm and the air was loaded with the scent of hams and cheeses, just baked bread, and olives. She felt a surge of happiness. She'd think about drugs and kids after the weekend.

Moments later, Sylvia and Elizabeth came into the store. She wanted to tell them not to worry. Instead, pretending she didn't notice their expressionless expressions, she handed each the third of the list she had been going to hand them in the car. The two girls went off to different aisles while Rachel went to the bakery section.

She felt another surge of happiness when the baker said, "Hey, headmistress, how ya doing?" and smiled at her like he always did. He was big and round, with lovely blue eyes, and looked exactly like a baker. She'd been buying cakes from him for years—for teachers' birthdays, anniversaries, retirements.

"I'm doing fine, John. And you're looking great."

She didn't know his last name and he didn't know her first. They were just two people who liked each other. "It's for my husband's and daughter's birthday," she said, pointing to the biggest, most expensive cake.

He smiled. "Really? Born the same day! How'd you manage that?"

"Magic, John. Pure magic."

He grinned and his eyes lit up. Then he put on a sad face, shaking his head. "Sorry. I'm saving that one for myself."

"Oh, your birthday too?" Rachel said, playing along.

"Nah, I'm just hungry."

Rachel giggled.

Smiling again, he bent down and took the cake from the glass display and placed it before her on the counter. "Your husband's a lucky guy."

She started to say, *I bet your wife is too*, but realized just in time she didn't know if he really had a wife. For all she knew, he was divorced, or never married, or had a wife who had died. "Thank you," she said instead, and while he placed the cake in a cardboard box, she imagined saying, *My husband and I live apart most of the time but he's going to be home for three whole days.* It was surprising how much she wanted him to know.

She began to wonder if Elizabeth and Sylvia would buy the ice cream right there in Battastelli's instead of across the street at Rose's as planned. They'd say it's just as good ice cream and more convenient since they were here already, and avoid passing close by, practically bumping into that drug dealer. But she knew they were too smart to try that ploy. As soon as Rachel got home, she'd call her friend Mo Comeau, Chief of Police, and ask him to keep an eye on this person.

Sylvia and Elizabeth stood beside her now, each carrying two full shopping bags. Several people had lined up behind them waiting to be served. "John, this is my daughter, Sylvia, and our friend Elizabeth," Rachel said. "She's coming to the party too." There was no need to tell him who was the daughter and who the friend.

"Well, that's nice, Elizabeth. And happy birthday, Sylvia. Wish your dad one from me too." He lifted the box with the cake inside it into Rachel's outstretched hands. "You all have a wonderful time."

They left the store. It was four o'clock, already getting dark, and it had started to rain and grown even colder. They put the purchases into the trunk and headed across the street toward Rose's. Rachel walked ahead so she wouldn't have to watch them pretend not to notice the drug dealer. The girls would have the same idea: they would lag behind her as far as possible without being obvious.

Just then, a man passed by the person in the hooded topcoat and bent down to drop some money in a Styrofoam cup on the ground. Rachel froze. She'd been so sure this was a dealer that she hadn't even seen the Styrofoam cup. She gathered herself, started walking again, and was soon right beside this person and he was looking straight at her the way people do when they are trying to figure out if they have met you before. In the dark, and with his hood covering much of his face, all she could make out was his yellow beard—and the dirt on his topcoat and the knees of his trousers that told her he lived outdoors. Of course Sylvia had been disturbed. How could she not have been? Rachel turned her face from him, imagining apologizing for thinking he was a drug dealer. *Maybe I wouldn't have wanted to talk about it either*, she thought as she entered the bright warmth of Rose's Creamery.

"WHY DID HE have to come back?" Elizabeth said, exasperated, when they were halfway across the street. She spoke in a whisper, as if Rachel, now entering Rose's, could still hear. "I thought we were finished!"

Something that's supposed to happen hasn't yet, is why, Sylvia thought. She'd say it out loud if it didn't sound so crazy. Why else leave a family who cared enough for him to give him that coat? The hollow feeling she'd been trying to convince herself was actually relief from the burden of responsibility for him had disappeared the instant she'd seen him, right where he had been standing the first time.

In another ten steps they would be right next to him. Elizabeth whispered, "Don't say anything to him."

"We have to. We can't just walk right by. My mom won't figure it out."

"What, you think she's stupid? We've risked enough. No more!"

They finished crossing the street and stepped up onto the sidewalk. The door to Rose's and Christopher were only a few yards away.

"Oh all right, I won't even look at him, if it makes you happy," Sylvia whispered. She put her right hand in the pocket of her slacks where her cell phone was. With her left hand, she gestured for Elizabeth to go first. "I'll just put a dollar in his hat."

"A whole dollar! Gee, that will help a lot," Elizabeth whispered, and walked past Christopher without turning her head. One step behind, Sylvia didn't look at Christopher either when she bent down and put the cell phone gently into his Styrofoam cup. "Elizabeth is on speed dial," she said, still not looking at him. "Call us when you need anything." She followed Elizabeth in.

"THAT'S YOUR HOMELESS man, isn't it?" Rachel asked the two girls once they entered Rose's, blinking their eyes against the sudden brightness. She had meant to wait for a minute or two to appear more casual than she felt, but the question popped out of her mouth with a will of its own.

"I don't know whether he is or not," Elizabeth said. "Maybe he's some other homeless man."

"I doubt that, Elizabeth. There's not a bunch of them here."

"Why wouldn't there be? This is where the money is."

Rachel shook her head. "Don't be sarcastic." She turned to Sylvia. "Is he?"

"He is." Sylvia seemed resigned.

Rachel nodded. "I can see why you were disturbed," she said. "It *is* very disturbing." Sylvia didn't answer. Elizabeth stared at Sylvia. "We'll put some money in his cup," Rachel said. "And give him some hot chocolate."

Sylvia shrugged.

"Yeah, I know. What good will that do? But get the hot chocolate for him anyway, all right?" Rachel said, wondering whether she wanted this for the benefit of the homeless man or Sylvia—or herself. She pointed to the dispenser and its array of throwaway cups. "I'll get the ice cream."

Rachel went to the counter and bought a gallon of Rose's vanilla ice cream, famous for the little black beans of vanilla that looked like pepper. She paid for that and the hot chocolate and they went outdoors. Sylvia carried the hot chocolate.

He wasn't there. They looked right and left and across the street. Light from the shop windows made silhouettes of people passing on the sidewalks, hunched over against the rain. There was no way to tell if he was one of them. "He must have gone to wherever he sleeps," Elizabeth said. Sylvia stared at her.

Rachel shivered. A bridge, a culvert, a doorway?

Sylvia poured the hot chocolate out, a misdemeanor in Fieldington to sully a sidewalk so. She watched the little steaming puddle form, then headed for the car. Rachel and Elizabeth followed.

A few minutes later, they pulled into the Head's House driveway and saw the rain on the black shiny surface of Bob's BMW glistening in the light pouring from the kitchen windows. They found him in the kitchen making martinis for Rachel and himself. He'd done even better than he'd promised and left a whole day earlier. Not three but *four* days away from his work to spend with his family!

NINETEEN

By midday, Bob had realized he couldn't make himself wait even one more day to share his news. For days and days he'd been on the verge of decision but hadn't wanted to tell Rachel. It was hard enough to tell himself. Even though he'd already decided that night when he had looked out the window and saw a man walking a dog at two o'clock in the morning and wanted to know, *Do you do that every night?* And as the days went by and he got used to knowing that he'd already made the decision, it got less scary and even more exciting, and then he caught the reproof in Rachel's postscript: *It's your place too, by the way.*

But it wasn't *by the way* at all, and it wasn't really a postscript either. Because it wasn't really his place too. It wasn't even hers. It was the school's.

He had planned to make the grand announcement over dinner, but when he saw Elizabeth too as the three came into the house, he changed his mind. This first announcement should be to family only. He'd tell Rachel later, when they were in bed. They both would tell Sylvia in the morning.

Now dinner was over and the girls were downtown at the movies, and at last he had his wife to himself. As she climbed into bed, he lit a fire in the bedroom's fireplace, one of the few aspects he liked of this enormous, too institutional house. It made this one room feel like a home they owned together. (It also provided just the right amount of light for making love.) He crossed the room from the fireplace and climbed into the right side of the bed. It was the side he'd claimed on the first night of their marriage, after Rachel had claimed the left. They had never thought of trading.

He hadn't even pulled the covers up when Rachel said, "Syl and Elizabeth and I went downtown today."

"So?" Now he'd have to wait even longer to tell her his news.

"We met her homeless man."

"*Her* homeless man?"

"Yes, hers. The one she couldn't talk about in September." Rachel went on to tell him what had happened: how Elizabeth had denied that it was the same homeless man and Sylvia had admitted it was.

Now he was feeling guilty for being annoyed. It was their *daughter.* "You say Elizabeth said it could be a different one?"

"Yes, she did. She basically told me that maybe he was or maybe he wasn't—you can't tell anymore. She implied that homeless people have figured out that Fieldington is where the money is so they're coming in bunches. I told her not be sarcastic. You should have seen how she stared at Syl when Syl said he's the one."

"What difference could it make whether it was the same one or not?"

"You tell me."

"Some kind of attachment? Maybe they meet him on a regular basis and give him money?"

"Maybe. But what's there about that for Elizabeth to want to hide?"

Bob gave Rachel a look. "Maybe they were afraid I'd find out and give them another boring lecture about not giving handouts to individuals."

"Yes, when you talk like that, you do sound a little bit like the people Elizabeth says she's going to offer free lobotomies to when she gets to be president."

He giggled. "She said that?"

"She did."

"She's got a tongue, that one."

"She does. It grates on Sylvia sometimes."

"Of course," Bob said. "It's always going to be Elizabeth who comes up with a line like that, and it's always going to be Sylvia who wishes she could. You ask Sylvia was this the same guy she saw last September and was upset enough not to want to talk about it, and she says it was. Why shouldn't she? What's there to hide? You ask Elizabeth and she has to make a smart-ass political remark."

"That's it? They're just different?"

"Yeah, except they both care. They're both kind. They've got that in common. We should be glad."

"So we shouldn't worry?"

He turned on his side, drew her close, foreheads touching. "Oh, we'll always worry. Even when she's a grown up. That's what parents do."

She was silent then, still thinking, he supposed. The firelight flickered on the ceiling. It seemed wrong, as if he didn't care about his own daughter, to switch away from talking about her to talking about himself. Should he wait until the morning?

No. He could not. "I've got something to tell you," he said, his tone casual, as if he were predicting the weather.

"About Sylvia?"

"No. I've decided to sell."

"Sell?"

"Yeah, Best Sports."

She sat up straight.

"I'm through," he said.

"Through?"

"Yeah," he said, sitting up too. "It's time."

She brought her knees up under the covers and hugged them.

"I know. We were talking about Sylvia. I shouldn't have changed the subject. It's just that I've been thinking about it a long time."

She turned to him, a look of amazement on her face.

"What?"

"When did you decide?"

"A while ago."

"A while ago?"

"Yeah, a while ago, while I was looking out the window in the middle of the night."

"But you'd been thinking about it a long time."

"Yeah. I don't know what I'm going to do, but ideas will come. Main thing is, though, I'll do whatever it is in Hartford, or maybe New Haven. I'll be home every night."

She didn't answer. Just kept looking at him, seeming even more amazed.

He frowned. "You can say you're happy now."

"I will be, I suppose—when I figure out what it means that you've been making one of the biggest decisions in your life and you didn't tell me one word." She lay back down, stared straight up at the ceiling.

"I thought you might point that out. Well, I'm not going to apologize. It's just the way I am. And you are too. All you ever told me is that something's missing."

"And you didn't prod."

"Nope. I didn't. And I think I won't. When you quit. Or don't quit. Or whatever, I'll find out after you've made up your mind and I promise I won't act surprised." He lay back down beside her. Watched the flickering glow on the ceiling.

"So we're in trouble?"

He didn't answer.

"Bob?"

"The only way not to be in marriage trouble is not to be married."

He waited for her to respond to that; and when she didn't, he said, "So, please, repeat after me: 'I'm glad we will be together all the time, not just weekends'—and then we'll go to sleep."

"I'm glad we will be together all the time, not just weekends."

"Thank you."

"I really am, you know."

"That's good."

"But that's not why you quit, is it?"

"No. I quit because I'd run out of gas. But I *will* be home every night."

"That *is* good," she said. "That's *very* good."

She reached for his hand. He took it in his, gave it a tender squeeze, and drifted toward sleep. But then, still holding her hand, he heard his own question again: *What's there to hide?* He remembered the weird feeling he'd had about Sylvia's reaction to Gloria Buchanan's news that the stolen stuff had been returned. And Marian's too. Like something was off-key It was just a tickle of suspicion, a little itch. Maybe more of an idea than an actual suspicion.

Nevertheless, he felt a tinge of guilt again for speeding through Rachel's news of Sylvia so he could get to his own. If he had waited longer, maybe he would have admitted that sometimes he could actually visualize Sylvia and Elizabeth stealing stuff to give away to a homeless guy. But then why would they return the stuff exactly as winter arrives? That there was no answer to that question should have been comforting enough to allow him sleep, but the surprise that he was disappointed that they were not the ones who'd stolen the stuff kept him awake—until his thoughts drifted to his satisfaction at having made the decision to sell Best Sports and his joy that he would spend every night—every night!—with his wife and daughter. Then he was finally able to sleep.

Rachel lay awake dealing with her realization that she'd known all along that when he went away on Mondays, it was to Mars. Now he wouldn't disappear anymore. Grateful, she drifted toward sleep.

But then was wide awake again. How did he do it? Best Sports was his life. He could just stop? *Could I do that? Will I still be able to focus on Miss Oliver's School for Girls with him around all the time?*

"You know the only way not to fall asleep while watching fantasy?" Elizabeth asked on the way home. They had just finished the movie and Sylvia was driving. "Or how not to laugh so loud everybody turns to you and tells you to shh and you're so embarrassed you wish you were dead? You just have to turn your brain totally off. Like, blank. Don't think of anything."

All the while Elizabeth was talking, Sylvia had been getting up the nerve to tell her about what she'd done. "I gave Christopher my cell phone," she blurted when Elizabeth stopped to take a breath. "He'll call you if he needs our help—which you know he will." But Elizabeth had been so totally into what she was saying, she didn't get it. "Shut up about the movie, please," Sylvia said, and gave her news again.

"You what?"

"You heard me."

"You put it in the *cup*?" Anybody who didn't know Elizabeth would have thought from her tone that she believed there was a better place to put the phone—like maybe one of Christopher's pockets? Or directly into his hand?

"And I know you liked the movie," Sylvia said. Anything to change the subject. "You were just practicing taking the opposite—"

"How do you know he won't sell it?"

Sylvia was stunned. "He won't. That's a terrible thing to even think." She turned the car into the Head's House driveway.

"Why? He needs the money, doesn't he? I bet you'd sell it in his shoes. And anyway, I know one thing that's true."

"Yeah, I know. When my mother asks me why I don't answer when she calls, I'll have to say I lost it." Sylvia drove into the garage and turned the ignition off.

"And guess what she'll do then."

"I know. The Find My Phone app. I didn't think of it when I gave him the phone."

"Well, your Mom'll think of it in about one second and she'll want to know why you didn't tell her you lost it right away, and then she'll want to go out there with you and help you find it," Elizabeth said, getting out of the car. "So you better hope he did sell it, preferably to someone about to leave for Australia." She went into the house and straight upstairs to her bedroom without another word.

"HELLO, SWEETIE. SLEEP well?" Sylvia's mom said, smiling from her chair at the kitchen table as Sylvia appeared in the doorway the next morning. Sun poured in through all the windows. Her mom and dad were still in their bathrobes. It was eleven o'clock. Elizabeth was still upstairs in bed.

"Umm," Sylvia answered.

"Want some eggs?" Her dad had a lilt in his voice. "I'll scramble you some."

Sylvia nodded.

"Well, sit down then, hon." He patted the table with his hand.

Sylvia pulled out a chair and sat. She hadn't slept well at all. What had made her so impulsive as to give her cell phone to Christopher? How was she going to get it back? And what was making her parents so irritatingly cheerful this morning?

"Shall I make them the usual way?" he asked.

Sylvia nodded again.

"How was the movie?" her mom asked.

Sylvia shrugged. "It was okay."

"Wow! She talks!" her dad said, grinning. He pushed back his chair and came around the table to Sylvia, bent down and kissed her on the cheek. On the way to the refrigerator for the eggs, he said, "How about Elizabeth? Did she like the movie?"

"She liked it okay."

"No diatribe about how stupid it was?" Sylvia's mom asked. "That's a surprise." Then, after a pause: "Anyway, your dad has something to share with you."

"He does?" Alarms went off. Her mother must have called. And Christopher had answered.

"Yes, but wait until I finish cooking these eggs," her father said, proving that telling her she'd been caught red handed was clearly too heavy for him while performing such an everyday task as scrambling eggs.

It was typical of her parents to try to make such a moment light by assuming cheerfulness. *It's how liberals do it*, she was sure Elizabeth would explain later. *Conservative parents would glower like it's the end of the word—which, for them, it would be.* In a minute the eggs would be done and her dad would bring them to her, a big smile on his face to show her *We love you anyway*, and wait until she'd had a few bites and then he'd say, *We called you last night. It seemed a little late for a movie to get out, and we just wanted to make sure you were okay. But a man answered and said, Hello? Elizabeth?* He'd stop right there and look at her mother and her mother would wait for her to say something, and when she wouldn't her mother would say, *We know who it was. It was easy to figure out: you and Elizabeth were the ones who stole that stuff.* And it would all be over. It would be done.

Her dad spooned the eggs from the frying pan onto a plate and put it down on the table in front of Sylvia. "You ready to hear it?"

"I'm ready, Dad," she said, forcing herself to look him in the face. She couldn't breathe.

"I'm going to sell Best Sports."

"...What?"

"I'm going to sell Best Sports. I'm not got going to live in the

City anymore," he said, just as Elizabeth walked sleepily into the kitchen. "I'm going to live right here with your mother and you." He reached across the table and clasped her mother's hand.

"Isn't that wonderful?" her mother said.

Halfway to the table, Elizabeth stopped walking. "I didn't mean to interrupt."

"No, it's all right, come on in," Sylvia's mom said. But Elizabeth waited for a cue from Sylvia.

Sylvia, by now no longer in disaster mode, ignored Elizabeth. "Dad! That's great!" She leaned across the table and kissed him on the cheek. So what if he didn't know the real reason she was so happy and how fast her heart was beating?

"Really, I can wait," Elizabeth said, standing where she had stopped. "You guys obviously have something to talk about." She was still looking at Sylvia.

"No, please, sit down," her mom said again.

Elizabeth sat. She glanced at Sylvia. Sylvia looked away. The phone was still out there. Waiting for her mother to call it.

"Bob just told us he's going to sell Best Sports," her mom said.

"Really!" Elizabeth said. She turned to Sylvia's dad. "You're going to sell?"

"I am." He looked proud.

"Well, good for you, Bob. I'm glad you knew you were the one who had to make the move."

He laughed. "Oh Liz! So glad you are going to run as a Democrat. As a Republican, you wouldn't have a chance."

Sylvia's mom, however, didn't seem amused. She looked thoughtful, maybe even perturbed. Her dad was quick to change the subject. "What should we do today?" he asked. "Whatever it is, let's do it together." For the next few minutes, while Elizabeth had another helping of scrambled eggs and another muffin, and Sylvia kept putting her hand in the empty pocket of her jeans, they discussed the options—until finally, with a barely perceptible impatience in her tone, her mom said, "Bob, why don't you decide?"

"All, right. Let's go to New Haven to the Yale Art Gallery, then to an ice rink to go skating, then out to dinner."

That's how they spent the rest of the day.

How do you fit seventy-three candles on a birthday cake? The answer Rachel came up with on Sunday evening: *Don't even try.*

Stick one big fat one in the middle? Everybody mentally does the arithmetic?—fifty-five plus eighteen. Maybe one of those funny ones that you blow and blow and blow on, spraying germs all over the icing, and the flame just gets stronger?

But she didn't have one of those candles. And it was too corny anyway. So she used the little tube of red icing her baker-friend John had put in the cake box to write *HAPPY BIRTHDAY BOB AND SYLVIA* on the white icing.

No. Too ordinary. She wanted to start over, but that would make a mess. Instead, she added the two words that flew into her brain, right then without her even thinking—*CARPE DIEM*—and immediately wondered why she wrote this on *their* cake. Bob had already seized the day. Maybe Sylvia had too, when that homeless man showed up. Rachel didn't want to answer that question right then, not in the middle of her husband's and daughter's birthday party.

She picked up the cake and marched into the dining room, where the only light was from candles on the table, and presented the cake with outstretched arms like a Pagan priest with a sacrifice, placing it in between Sylvia and Bob. She stood between them with a hand on Bob's shoulder, the other on Sylvia's, ready to start the singing. But the "usual suspects"—Michael Woodward, Eudora Easter, retired faculty members Francis and Peggy Plummer, and Gregory van Buren—all stared at the big red *CARPE DIEM*. "I know," she admitted. "Weird, isn't it? It's those martinis before dinner and all that wine during that made me write it."

"Yeah yeah yeah," Elizabeth mocked. "At my back I always hear. *Boohoo. Boohoo*," and everybody smiled. Except Bob, a mere businessman, who knew nobody expected him to know the reference. He glanced bemusedly at the cake, and then lifted his eyes to each face, one by one, around the table, beaming his thanks.

"Happy birthday to you," everybody sang. "Happy birthday to yooooou."

"We are so glad you were both born," Michael Woodward announced.

"Hear, hear!" Gregory said.

SYLVIA, WHO HAD been careful for the last two days never to get far enough away from her parents to cause a reason for them to call her, had lost track of the conversation long before her mother had gone into the kitchen. Until her mother reappeared with the cake, the picture in Sylvia's head of Christopher in his lean-to with the cell phone in his left hand and the forefinger of his right aiming at the list of contacts on speed dial had been taking more of her attention than any real scene she had been a part of.

But now Francis Plummer was asking her, "How does it feel to be eighteen?" sounding provocative, as if he were trying to help her discover a truth, the way he must have in class when he was still the most storied teacher in the school, if not the world, even more legendary than Gregory van Buren. She was sick of all those stories. And what did Francis want her to say? One day she's seventeen, the next eighteen, and it's some kind of magic passage?

She wasn't about to tell him she felt nostalgic already. For her dad's New York City apartment as her connection to the larger world "out there." And because you can't give shelter in a girls' school to a homeless man, especially one who is maybe crazy. She'd been imagining her father taking Christopher into his apartment to give him shelter there. Even though that was definitely crazy and would never happen. Now her father was going to sell the apartment, she guessed, since he wouldn't be needing it anymore. It wouldn't be there for her to escape to. *I feel closed in*, she would tell Francis—if she wanted to. Sealed in by walls all around in hermetic space. *Hermetic. Use it in at least three sentences, each differently structured.* Everybody at this table was a part of Miss Oliver's School for Girls. Even Francis who didn't teach anymore, a has-been, but still a legend. Now even Dad. Not one person from the outside. And she was still enclosed in the same old question: what college to attend? At least a month until the acceptances or rejections would be known. And then what?

Yes, her father had seized the day. Sylvia wasn't so sure she was glad. She glanced across the table at Elizabeth, wondering what her reaction was to such a strange admonition on a birthday cake, but

Elizabeth, still angry about the phone, refused to meet her eyes.

"In some states, reaching eighteen is when you are legally an adult," Francis said, still prodding, wanting to know what made her tick at this stage in her life. That's what had made him a legend, she supposed: caring about each kid more than about himself. So what? It was none of his business,

"In Connecticut?" Gregory asked, challenging Francis, like in all those old stories. He cared as much as Francis ever did about what made his students tick. "Let's look it up. Sylvia, you're never without your phone. Can I have it for a second?" He reached his hand out to her.

Sylvia froze for an instant while everybody at the table naturally turned to her, and she had no idea what to do. Then the idea coming, along with a huge relief, she patted at the back pocket of her slacks and managed to look surprised that her cell phone wasn't there. "That's strange. I must have left it upstairs."

"Here, use mine," Elizabeth said, handing her phone to Gregory.

"Actually, it's the idea I was getting at," Francis said. "Not which particular state."

Hearing that, Gregory seemed even more interested in finding the answer. He thumbed in the question. Francis sighed an irritated sigh while Gregory watched the phone, waiting for the answer to arrive. Then, nodding his head: "Yes, just as I thought: eighteen." He held up the phone toward Francis. "See?"

"So what?" Francis said.

"So congratulations to Sylvia, that's what."

Francis thought for a moment, clearly seeking a truce. "Well, I'll second *that*."

"And congratulations to Bob," Eudora said, as she and Elizabeth handed their plates to Rachel for seconds. "He's been a grown-up for a very long time."

AFTERWARD, AS THEY were clearing the dishes, Francis edged close to Sylvia and whispered, "Sorry, I didn't mean to pry." And later, in the kitchen while they were cleaning up, during another moment when they were out of everyone's earshot, Elizabeth asked Sylvia,

"Was that close enough for you? And by the way, what are your plans for getting your phone back before your mother calls you and the shit hits the fan?"

TWENTY

The next morning, when Rachel awoke in the dark, Bob was still deep in sleep. Good. He needed the rest.

She rolled on her side away from him. She would try to fall back asleep, but she knew she'd fail. School resumed tomorrow, and sure enough, a line of the anticipated events of the morrow paraded in her brain. Marching vividly in the front was the conversation, scheduled for ten o'clock, in which she would inform the parents of sophomore Kimberley Atkins, a girl she loved, that Kimberley's best interests would be served at a school whose academic demands were more forgiving. How many such fraught conversations had she managed? How many more would she have before she packed it in? The answer to the first question was vague, the second not forthcoming. She got out of bed, dressed quietly in the dark, and went downstairs. Maybe she'd go to her office and catch up on some work. No, she would have to sit down at her desk. She was much too restless.

She heard the soft thud of the *New York Times* landing on the stoop. She'd take it and a cup of coffee upstairs, and get in bed beside Bob and share the paper when he woke up. Easy because he always read the Business section first, which she never read at all.

Outside, before she even bent over to pick it up, she was struck by the early morning smells, free of pollution, cleansed by the night. Of snow, still dry in the biting cold of dawn. She spread her arms to the growing light. No way was she going back to bed. She would go skiing. That would cure her restlessness. By using it. On her favorite route beside the river. She'd be back in an hour, two at the most.

She carried the paper inside and left it on the kitchen counter for when Bob woke up. In the garage, donning her ski pants, she wondered if Sylvia would want to come with her. No, she'd want to sleep, might even be irritated to be woken up. It was the last morning free to sleep late. But the truth was Rachel didn't need anybody's company, not even her daughter's. She needed to be alone, to ski fast and headlong and without conversation.

Headlong was what she was when, a few minutes later, she saw the glint of the river up ahead and, reaching it, turned to the right on the trail, following the river on its southward tumble toward the Sound, her favorite route. Sylvia's too. Except that once.

A few minutes later, she smelled the smoke. She told herself it was just her imagination. Then she came around the bend and, surprised that she wasn't surprised, she saw him. Sylvia's homeless man. She stopped. He was squatting beside a fire, frying something on the side of his axe. He was even thinner than when she saw him last, his clothes so loose on him, like luffing sails. She thought of clowns. His yellow hair came down over his ears beneath a black watch cap. She still had no idea how old he was.

Then she saw his lean-to. It sagged, looked tired, ready to fall down, its covering of pine boughs flecked with brown. He turned and they looked at each other. His eyes were deep in their sockets, rimmed with shadow. He didn't speak, as if he wanted her first to note where he lived.

How cold you must be without a coat! she thought. He nodded. He must have sold it so he could eat. *Just a sweater over some kind of shirt?* He nodded again. This harmless, vulnerable man was waiting for her to say *I know who you are.* She shook her head. Because now she understood: it wasn't just Bob who was making a move; it was Sylvia too. Following her heart to wherever it would take her. Her own mother wasn't going to get in the way.

Astounded by her own decision, she turned and fled.

TWENTY-ONE

Christopher Triplett willed the woman to turn around. *Come back, come back, don't fly away.*

The same will which had enabled him to stay alive, to not shoot himself, instead to build a shelter of pine boughs against the cold and suffer contempt—his own as well as that of others'—for begging for his livelihood on haughty streets. When she had disappeared around the bend and he could not hear the swish of her skis on the snow anymore and knew she would not return, he put his hand in his shirt pocket, fingering the cell phone there as a person might a cross or a rosary, and willed himself to believe that revelations arrive in instants. They come and go in one beat of the heart. That's the mark of their truths. If he were a churchgoer like his aunt, a singer of hymns, he would know because the Bible told him so.

The revelation was the mercy he'd seen in her eyes, the worry there about how cold he was living outdoors. How could she know that he always kept the topcoat his aunt had bought for him in the lean-to, away from the cooking fire, so it wouldn't smell like smoke?

It took a powerful will for him not to believe it was his concussive brain damage bringing him an apparition: the mother of the thin girl named Sylvia and the mother of the girl he'd killed becoming the same. Others would call it faith, not will. Whichever, he was glad for it for saving him. If the woman had turned around and come back, he would have knelt in the snow and put his arms around her legs and thanked her for forgiving him.

He ducked inside the lean-to to get the coat his aunt had bought for him, which lay on his pine bough bed as a blanket, came outside again and put it on, and, placing his feet in the holes his prior steps had made in the knee-deep snow, made his way to his bathing place in the river. It was too cold there, away from the fire, to take off his clothes, to bathe all of himself and get clean, really clean, like he had in the summer when Sylvia had seen him here and he'd had nothing to hide any part of himself, nothing at all. He knelt by the edge of the river, made a cup out of his hands in it, and washed his face. It was sufficient ceremony, given the conditions. He went back to the fire and ate the rest of his breakfast.

RUSHING AWAY FROM the man through the woods, Rachel felt those hollowed eyes on her back, exactly between her shoulder blades. Not pushing her away. Just staring. Maybe even trying to pull her back. If she turned around, he would still be there. And the next day, and the next. Until whatever Sylvia and Elizabeth were going to cause to happen came to pass. What would she say to him, who would speak first, if she turned around? But of course she couldn't. That would make her complicit. She would have to resign.

There was no proof. That's why she could pretend she didn't know—that she hadn't half-known when he was panhandling in the parking lot the day before Thanksgiving and she'd seen the look on Sylvia's and Elizabeth's faces in the rearview mirror, and three-quarters known later when he was standing in front of Rose's Creamery and Elizabeth said no, he's not the one and Sylvia said he was. Sylvia had trusted her mother with that news: *He was.* Now it was time to return the trust. It would all come out in the end, but because Sylvia and Elizabeth caused it to, not Rachel. She wouldn't take that away from them.

The feeling between her shoulder blades didn't diminish until she was almost home, passing the edge of the woods into the shadow they cast on the athletic fields. When she was past that shadow into the glare, her own shadow slid on the snow in front of her. Elongated, ten feet tall at least, heading toward the campus. Now the feeling was on her chest, pushing against her to slow her progress. She wished for some other place to return to and tell Bob what she had just learned, a home of their own that had nothing to do with Miss Oliver's School for Girls.

But why in the world did Sylvia and Elizabeth take the stuff back? Couldn't they understand how cold he was without it? She had half a mind to go into the shed while no one was looking and grab a down jacket, and ski pants, and some gloves that stayed there unused ninety-nine percent of the time like yachts at their docks, and ski out to him with them.

She put her skis away in the garage, next to Sylvia's, and went into the house. Bob would be up. Making a mess in the kitchen.

HE WAS IN his bathrobe and slippers. "Good morning," he said. "I missed you."

"I'm sorry. I should have left you a note." She was right. A terrible mess. Pancake batter all over the stove.

"I thought you'd be hungry." He bent over to open the oven door.

"I'm famished. I've been skiing."

"I figured." He took a platter of pancakes out of the oven. Their smell filled the room. He put the platter down on the kitchen table and pulled out a chair for her, and when she sat down, he leaned over her, pressed his hands lightly on her shoulders, and kissed the back of her neck. "Monday morning with Rach," he said. "Yum yum."

She held onto one of his hands. "I've got something to tell you."

"Wait a minute, I forgot the syrup."

She let go of his hand. He moved to the refrigerator, peered in. *The New Yorker* cartoon she'd taped to the refrigerator a year ago was still there: a husband peering into a refrigerator loaded with nothing but boxes marked *BUTTER*, asking "Honey, where's the butter?" He'd laughed the first time he saw it.

"Not *there*. It's in the cabinet above the stove, where it always is."

He shrugged, moved to the cabinet, opened the door, moved things around while her mild irritation, boring because habitual, turned into a strange comfort for the same reason. He was still the same old Bob who couldn't ever see things right in front of his face, and she was still the same old Rachel who allowed herself to get pissed off because he couldn't ever see things right in front of his face.

At last, he found the bottle of maple syrup and poured some into a bowl and put it in the microwave.

She said, "I ran into the homeless man again."

He turned his head from the microwave. "You did?"

"Yes. It's the same guy. We recognized each other."

"While you were skiing?"

"Yes. By the river. He's made himself a kind of shack. Out of pine boughs. It's pitiful. You should see it. I'm afraid he won't survive the winter."

"Really? He's living in it? By the river?"

She nodded three times.

"Poor guy!" The microwave timer buzzed. He took the syrup out and put it by her plate and sat across from her. She forked three pancakes from the platter. Poured some syrup on. And found she couldn't eat.

"Are they warm enough?"

She forced herself to take one bite. "Yes. Thanks. They're lovely."

"So are you." He put three on his plate, poured the syrup. Sun streamed through the windows, flooding the kitchen, and a steady drip of melting snow on the roof tapped a rhythm outside the windows.

"So what are you going to do about him?" he asked, putting down his fork.

"What am *I* going to do? I told you, this is the same guy who Sylvia couldn't even talk about. She's your daughter too."

"I know. And I'm just as sorry for him as Sylvia is, Rach, but what if he's on school property? The school's land extends for miles beyond the campus, doesn't it? Won't you have to have him removed?" Bob's shoulders slouched. He sounded regretful.

Rachel was stunned. "Did you hear yourself, Bob? *Have him removed*. That's like collateral damage."

"I know," he said, shaking his head. "He'll be dragged off. It's awful. But what other alternative is there?"

She looked away, out the window.

"How would you get him off? The police?"

She snapped her head back around. "How *else*?"

"Well, let's hope they can get him into a shelter."

She heard the sincerity in his tone, that he really did want Sylvia's homeless man—that's how she insisted on thinking of him, now more than ever—to be safe and warm in a shelter. But that didn't stop a bitterness from rising into her throat. "Right," she said, "I'll call Mo Comeau and tell him to have his cops drag him away in the middle of the night so the girls won't know what lengths their school will go to keep the real world away."

"Don't blame yourself, Rach. You didn't make him homeless. And you can always pretend he's not there."

"Is that what you would do?"

"I might. I know I'd have to think twice before I pushed him out into the cold. But if I were you? I don't know."

He seemed so thoughtful sitting there across the table, watching her eyes and nodding his head. "I'll think about it," she said. "Right now, I'm tired. I'm going upstairs to take a nap." She didn't really need a nap. She needed to be by herself to think.

"From skiing?"

"No, *skiing* doesn't make me tired," she said, standing up. "But you should have seen him, Bob. I wish you'd been there with me. Think how cold he must be. How lonely."

"Well, next time invite me. That is, if you *don't* have him removed. We'll bring him some warm clothes."

"Like a down jacket?"

"Exactly," he said, looking straight in her eyes. "Just like the one that was stolen."

She took in a breath and held it.

"Now, while I clean up this mess, why don't you go upstairs and take that nap?"

She let out the breath. "Will you come up when you finish? I could use a snuggle."

"Soon as I'm finished."

She turned to leave.

"I just thought of something."

She turned back.

He shrugged. "For whatever it's worth..."

"Go ahead, say it."

"You wouldn't have to apologize to Syl and Elizabeth if you don't have him removed."

"I know. I already thought of that."

UPSTAIRS, SHE LAY down on her side of the bed on top of the covers. A few minutes later, Bob came into the room. "You'll freeze," he said. He took a down comforter out of the closet, put it over her, and got under it with her. "Remember when Gloria told us that the stolen stuff was returned how surprised I was that Sylvia hadn't told me it was stolen in the first place? That struck me as very strange. I thought then maybe Elizabeth and Sylvia stole it and gave it to that homeless man that Sylvia was worried about. Just maybe, of course. There was no real reason, it was just a passing thought. But then I asked myself, why would they take it back? They're too kind to take a down jacket and other warm clothes away from him when winter's coming, even if he would let them. Then I knew it wasn't true. Actually, that was a little disappointing. I liked thinking of them as latter-day Robin Hoods."

Rachel rolled on her side and put her arms around him. "I had exactly the same thought this morning when I saw him in that shack. Why would they take it back? Especially when I had made it very clear to the whole school that bringing back the stolen things would redeem nothing, that the consequence for stealing was expulsion regardless of the motivation."

"Oh, I hadn't thought of *that.* But wouldn't you have to recuse yourself?"

"Of course I would."

"Well, why don't you start recusing yourself right now?"

"You think I should?"

"I do."

"But suppose—"

He put his hand gently over her mouth. "Shh. Time to sleep."

She pretended to drift to sleep, knowing that he was pretending too. Yes, she would be disappointed too to know that her own daughter didn't care enough about that man to try to keep him warm. And yes, she would recuse herself.

Or maybe she wasn't recusing. Maybe, like all good leaders, she was delegating a responsibility to people she could trust—in this case, Sylvia and Elizabeth—to determine, and self-administer, what consequence justice required of them.

Would she delegate that responsibility to any student who wasn't also her daughter and her daughter's best friend? That she didn't think so was an almost unbearable weight.

Well, she would just have to bear it.

One thing she did know: she and Bob would find out soon enough why Sylvia and Elizabeth returned everything.

TWENTY-TWO

When the cell phone in his pocket vibrated against his leg, Christopher didn't know how many days had passed since he'd been forgiven. He'd been too absorbed in his newfound peace to be aware of time. He'd stopped thinking of what Sylvia had given him as a cell phone. It was what he put his hand around to reassure himself that he wasn't alone. That love was alive in the world. It was the same with the coat.

It was a text message from Elizabeth: *Meet us at grocery store Stop and Shop parking. Today. Noon. Bring phone.* But how was he supposed to know what time it was? Then he saw the time on the phone. Of course! It had a clock! Now it was a cell phone again—a diminishment, but—oh yes, he would meet them!

Wading knee deep in the snow toward the village, Christopher started to sweat. He'd be better off in just his heavy woolen sweater. It had a deep-blue color, "like the ocean on a sunny day," his aunt had said when she'd bought it for him. "You look so handsome in it!" But since then he'd somehow got a smudge of soot from his firepit grill on the front, and the ends of both sleeves had begun to unravel. He turned around and took his coat off and put it back in his lean-to. He'd be back long before late afternoon when it would get cold. In the meantime, his sweater would be enough.

As he headed off again, he heard what he thought were church bells ringing in the village and remembered going to church with his aunt at eleven in the morning not so very long ago. Now there were two ways to know what time it was.

An hour later, sweating hard, legs tired, he came out of the woods onto the road. He hadn't aimed accurately; he had another half a mile to go on the road to get to Stop and Shop. He thought he was a better woodsman than that. It was a surprise to learn that even though he'd been forgiven, he could still be disappointed in himself. He was also worried someone would find his tracks and his hiding place and he'd be attacked in it in the middle of the night, killed in his sleep. Several cars went by. He was sure the people in them noticed him, and wished he'd brought his coat after all. Unlike his smudged and unraveled sweater, it was still new and stylish, and would disguise his derelict state.

Besides, it was getting colder. The sky was clouding over and the air smelled like snow. He was disappointed in himself again: an outdoorsman who couldn't predict the weather.

He heard a car slowing down behind him. He kept walking, looking straight forward, thinking it was maybe police. About to arrest him for walking while homeless. Or maybe it was a bunch of kids slowing down to harass him from the safety of the car. He almost wished that's who it was. He'd yank the car door open, see the surprise and terror, reach in, grab hair. The driver would accelerate to escape, but the kid would be held fast by the seatbelt. The scalp would come right off in his hand.

"Hey, Christopher!" Elizabeth jumped out of a shiny green Subaru station wagon on the passenger side. She opened the back door. "Get in."

"Oh! I thought—"

"What?"

"Never mind." He climbed into the backseat. It was hot in the car. Sylvia was in the driver's seat, turning back to look at him. The little red-headed one, the one called Auda, wasn't in the car. He wasn't surprised. He remembered how scared of him she was in the lean-to. So of course she wouldn't get in a car with him.

Now he was in the cab of his truck, beside his sergeant, staring forward through the windshield at the same girl who was tall and thin like Sylvia, but he shook his head and it was Sylvia again with Elizabeth beside her. Sylvia said, "Sorry we're late," and turned her head forward and started to drive. The seatbelt alarm beeped and beeped and beeped. He thought of the scalp, imagining it still in his hand.

"We got lucky," Elizabeth said, turning her head to Sylvia. "We don't need to go to Stop and Shop now. It's better this way. No one will see us together in the car."

"Yeah," Sylvia said. Then, looking at him in the rearview mirror, she said to him, "Elizabeth doesn't mean what it sounds like. It's because—"

"There's a rule against picking up hitchhikers at our school," Elizabeth said. "That's what I meant."

"I see." If he chose to believe they were not ashamed to be with him, then they were not. He fastened his seatbelt just as Elizabeth did, and the beeping stopped. The image of the scalp in his hand was gone. See? He could make things happen that needed to happen. The peace he'd felt, cupping his hands in the river, washing his face, returned.

"Are you okay?" Sylvia said.

"I'm fine." He wanted to tell her about her mother's visitation, the forgiveness she'd brought, but he didn't know how to explain that two different mothers who lived across the world from each other had become the same mother—*because one of them is yours.* It wasn't as if she actually said, *I forgive you.* She didn't say anything. She just turned around and skied away.

"I'm glad," Sylvia said. "We've brought you some food."

"That's right," Elizabeth said. She leaned down to pick up a red backpack at her feet and held it out for him to take.

He hesitated.

"What? You don't want it?" Elizabeth asked.

He shook his head. "I have some money now. I can buy my own."

"You do? Enough to live on? Where'd you get it?"

"Elizabeth! That's none of your business," Sylvia said.

"It isn't?" Elizabeth said.

He said, "My aunt gave me some. She lives in Hartford. I went there for a while. I lived with her and went to college." Elizabeth was still looking at him like people do when they've asked a question and haven't got the answer yet. "It didn't work," he added, "so I quit."

"Quit?" Elizabeth said.

"Yeah, but maybe I'll go back."

"And try again?" Sylvia said.

"Maybe."

"I hope you do!"

"Well, then so do I," he said. Elizabeth still didn't look satisfied. "I still beg a little," he told her, "but I don't steal, if that's what you're thinking."

"I didn't say I thought you were stealing," Elizabeth said.

"If I was in your shoes, I'd think a lot worse things than stealing. Just a minute or two ago, I was imagining ripping the scalp off a person's head."

Neither girl spoke. The only sound was the tires on the road. Why did he tell them that? They didn't need to know.

Sylvia did a U-turn in the street and headed back the way they'd come.

"You getting rid of me after what I said?"

The two girls looked at each other for a second. Then Sylvia turned forward and looked through the windshield again. Elizabeth kept watching the side of her face, clearly waiting for the answer.

"I was just imagining," he said. "I would never do it."

"I know," Sylvia said.

"I've had lots of chances," he said, thinking of his time in the Allagash when he left so he wouldn't hurt anyone, and the kid in the Stop and Shop parking lot last time. And the VA doctor, and the marketing professor.

"From being over there?" Elizabeth asked, still watching Sylvia's face. "Stuff you saw?"

"Stuff I did too," he said.

"Of course it's from over there!" Sylvia said. "Where else would it be from?"

Very slowly, Elizabeth turned her face from Sylvia's to his. "Ripping a scalp off?"

He nodded. "When you pulled up beside me, I thought it was some boys mocking me."

"Pricks! I'd rip their scalps off too!" Sylvia said.

"No, you wouldn't. You know you wouldn't, Sylvia," Elizabeth said, still facing Christopher, studying him. "You would just laugh at them and walk away and make them feel small."

Sylvia slowed down and pulled the car over to the side of the road opposite the place where she and Elizabeth had seen him come out of the woods.

"But you don't think I could even imagine hurting either of you, do you?" He thought they were stopping here to ask him to leave. He'd never see them again.

"Of course we don't!" Sylvia said.

"That's right. We don't think you can *imagine* hurting us. That's good enough for me," Elizabeth said. Sylvia stared at her. Elizabeth looked mildly back at Sylvia as if to say, *That's as far as I can go.* There was the sound of the engine running, the smell of its exhaust.

Suddenly businesslike, Elizabeth said, "Time to change phones. That's why we're here." She put out her hand to him for Sylvia's phone. He hesitated, disturbed by what she had implied. Elizabeth frowned. "You have it, don't you?" She actually looked scared.

He didn't want to give up what it had become for him, but he took Sylvia's phone out of his pocket and handed it over, watching the relief come to her face.

"Good," Elizabeth said, handing the phone to Sylvia, then reaching into the glove compartment. "We've got a burner for you." She handed him a small flip phone, the kind that opened to dial and snapped shut to end the call. "It's all set up. We're both on speed dial. We've paid ahead plenty of minutes. Try it."

He tried to give it back.

"What? You don't want it?"

"Not if you think I could hurt you."

"Why not, if you think you couldn't?"

"It wouldn't mean anything," Christopher said, holding the phone out to her.

"What do you mean, *mean*?"

"It's hard to explain."

"Christopher, please keep the phone!" Sylvia said.

He hesitated, still holding the phone out to Elizabeth. Elizabeth put up her hands, palms toward him. He looked away from her to the rearview mirror and saw Sylvia watching him.

"Christopher! Please!" Sylvia said.

"All right. If *you* want me to, I will." He pulled the phone back, pressed and held down 1, and Sylvia's phone, just inches away, barked three times like the family dog. He snapped the phone shut, opened it, pressed 2, and from the pocket of Elizabeth's jeans came the sound of crickets. He closed the phone and the crickets stopped. "Thank you," he said. "As long as I have this, I'll be all right."

Sylvia reached down near Elizabeth's feet for a backpack and held it out to him. "There's food in here. When you need some more, give us a call. We'll meet you right here."

"No, not here where we can be seen!" Elizabeth said. She pointed to the woods on the other side of the road. "All we have to do is walk in a few yards and we won't be seen."

"All right. Since you want me to have it, I'll take it," he said, conceding. He took the backpack from Sylvia and got out of the car on her side where the window was rolled down and put the backpack on. She reached and touched his shoulder.

She drove the car away, and he crossed the road toward the woods.

RIGHT AWAY HE saw the footprints, all going the opposite direction from the ones he'd made. At least four people. He remembered the cars that had gone by as he came out of the trees just before Sylvia and Elizabeth stopped to pick him up. He walked into the woods a few strides and saw where one of them had taken a piss, a yellow indentation in the snow, and told himself they were just exploring, just curious. But then they would have parked the car right where they went in, instead of hiding it someplace. He started to run after the prints.

It was hard to run in the snow, even though, there being four of them, maybe more, they had stamped it down. His legs were already tired from walking, and the backpack, laden with what he guessed was canned food, was heavy. Halfway there, he slipped and fell. With the backpack on and the slipperiness of the snow, it was hard to get back up.

He took the backpack off so he could go faster and put it under the lower branch of a pine tree, where he would get it later. After another few minutes he heard their voices over the sound of his own breathing and he rushed on, falling one more time.

The first thing he saw when he came to his clearing was the glint of the river ahead of him, then three boys running away on the trail beside the river. They disappeared around the same bend Sylvia's mother had. He started after them.

Then, between himself and the river, he saw an empty space and stopped running. The lean-to's pine boughs were spread for yards around. Only part of the frame remained, a black skeleton against the white snow. Next, he saw his sleeping bag, pieces of its red outer covering spread near his firepit. Some of the feathers lingered in the ashes. He wondered what they'd cut it with. They couldn't have found his axe. He'd buried it yards away under a fallen tree. He looked around for the coat his aunt had bought him and heard a sound near him to his right where the privy hole was and whirled around to see a fourth kid sneaking away from behind a tree where he'd been hiding.

Christopher lunged, got an ankle, and the kid fell face down in the snow. Christopher knelt on him, both knees in the middle of the kid's back, because that hurts more than just straddling, and shoved his face down into to the snow and held it there, and held it there, and held it there, eager for the moment when the kid would start to twitch and then twitch some more and finally not move at all.

And then, only because he wanted to know where his coat was, Christopher took his hands off the back of the kid's head, grabbed him by his longish brown hair, and dragged him to his feet. The kid, maybe sixteen, pale face, blue eyes, sprouting a thin mustache under the snot dripping from his nose, was no taller than Christopher but bigger around. He was whimpering, a disgusting sound. "Where's my coat?" Christopher said.

The kid started to shake his head. Christopher, his two hands still holding the kid's hair, stood on tiptoes and yanked upwards as hard as he could. The kid stood on his tiptoes too. "Where?" Christopher said. The kid still didn't answer, so Christopher brought his knee up hard into the kid's solar plexus. The kid grunted in pain. Christopher let him bend over. The kid started to cry. Christopher let him cry for a while, then he yanked him straight up. "I'm going to kill you if you don't tell me," he said, speaking the truth, yanking upwards with each word. The kid's eyes darted toward the privy hole. "There!" Christopher said.

The kid gave him a look that could only mean yes. "Well, you'll have get it back, won't you?" Christopher said and let go of the kid's hair so he could nod his head. They walked to the privy hole side by side, like two friends out for a walk, and the kid sat down on the edge of the hole, looking down. "Go on," Christopher said. The kid put his hands on the edge of the hole to support himself and let himself down.

Christopher could barely see the kid down there, ankle deep, but he could hear him crying. He thought he might make a huge snowball, like when he and Uncle Ray made snowmen, and roll it to the hole and drop it down on top of the kid. He thought of the kid down there, drowning in shit, the snowball pressing him down, and all of a sudden he'd had enough of revenge. A surfeit. There was no anger anymore. Just a terrible sadness.

The kid's head appeared a minute later. Then one befouled hand holding the befouled coat appeared too, and the hand placed the coat on the ground beside the hole. Then the rest of the kid crawled out, bringing the stink with him. He stood up. The cuffs of his jeans and his boots were covered with what he'd been wading in. "Put the coat back in and go home," Christopher said. The kid just stared. "Please, just put it back in," Christopher said. The kid obviously didn't want to touch the coat again. "Just kick it in," Christopher said. The kid put the front of his shoe against the edge of the coat, and lifting it like a soccer ball, kicked it back into the hole. "Now go," Christopher said. He stepped way back so the kid wouldn't brush him with shit as he went by. The kid stepped past Christopher and floundered away, as fast as he could.

It began to snow.

CHRISTOPHER GATHERED UP his stuff and brought it back to his naked lean-to. He stepped in the tracks he and the boys had already made, but the effort of adjusting his stride was as exhausting as wading in the snow.

Now what? He was out of breath, sweating hard even in the freezing weather, and his knees were shaking. Without shelter, he didn't have a chance. He should have built a new lean-to before he gathered his possessions. In a new place where the boys couldn't find it if they came back. Then dig a new firepit and move the grill to it tomorrow. Now it was too late. It would be dark soon. He'd have to rebuild the lean-to right where it was.

The sound of the boy crying down in the privy hole stayed with Christopher as he unburied his axe and then labored through the snow, scouting for thin branches to replace the ribs of the frame, chopping them off the trees, trimming them, then carrying them back to the lean-to.

It was midafternoon and the snowstorm blew into a blizzard by the time he'd repaired the frame. The snow was covering up the pine boughs the boys had scattered, making them hard to find, but he managed to gather enough to cover the roof by the time the light had begun to wane. Just as he began to believe he would have enough shelter to survive the night, the roof collapsed under the weight of the snow.

He sat down then, collapsing too. He had nothing now: no coat, no shelter, and even less faith in his own judgment. He hadn't put enough ribs back into the roof!

His butt was getting wet from sitting in the snow. Underneath his woolen sweater, his shirt, dampened by the sweat he was no longer pouring, was cold against his skin. *It's easy to die from hypothermia; once it gets going, you just want to go to sleep*, Uncle Ray had warned him. As if he didn't already know. He started to dig in the snow. He'd build a snow cave and crawl in like a hibernating bear. But his hands were freezing digging in the snow without gloves, and the walls of his cave kept collapsing, and he wasn't covered in fur and inches of fat. So he started to crawl into the jumbled pile of tumbled down pine boughs that had been his lean-to. But he remembered he didn't have his down sleeping bag anymore to keep him warm. *A pile of pine boughs isn't a home*, Uncle Ray would say. *Like a well-built lean-to, snug against the weather. It's just a pile of pine boughs.*

He was homeless!

He took out his phone, punched 1 for Sylvia, not sure whether he was going to ask for help or say goodbye. Then: "Christopher!" sounding as if she were standing right beside him. Then he heard her say, "It's him," and someone, probably Elizabeth, said something but he couldn't make it out. He told Sylvia what had happened.

"They *what?*"

"Yeah, they busted it down!"

"And they took your coat?"

"No, they ruined it."

"*Ruined* it? How?"

"I don't want to say."

An instant of silence and then, "But it's a blizzard out!" Another pause. A tree fell not far away. Then: "Okay. Now listen. I'll meet you at the edge of the woods by the soccer field. All right? You'll recognize it by the goal cages."

He didn't speak, taking it in.

"Christopher? Did you hear me?"

"Yes. By the goal cages."

"Hurry! Leave your phone on."

"I will!" He closed the phone but kept it in his hand for reassurance, and started wading through the snow. After a few paces, he stopped. He should call her and tell her no, stay inside. *The snow will blind you, you'll get lost. You'll freeze to death.* Instead, he put the phone in his pocket, afraid he would drop it and not be able to find it again, and started in the direction of the athletic fields. He hadn't really called her so she could save him. He'd called her because he didn't want to grieve all by himself in the dark for what people do to each other. He would have called her even if the sun were out.

There were so many footprints he was able to find his way in the dark. Soon enough, he came upon the backpack. It was not buried in snow because he'd chucked it under a branch of a tree, but it was empty. The kid must have strewn the cans of food as far as he could throw them, seeking revenge, and now they were buried deep. He picked up the empty backpack and put it on. The least he could do was give it back. Now it was entirely dark and he couldn't see the tracks anymore. He hoped he wasn't walking in circles.

At last, he came out of the woods into the open somewhere on the athletic fields. The wind, unbroken by trees, came right at him, stopping his breath, bombarding his face with snowflakes. He turned sideways to it. Now it blasted the side of his face, numbing his cheek. Snowflakes burrowed into his ear. He didn't have a hat to replace the hood of his coat, so his body heat was leaving through the top of his head. He could be right next to the goal cages and he wouldn't be able to see them. With his arms out in front of him, he waded in the direction he was facing, hoping that was the right direction. His khaki trousers were wet right through to his legs. His woolen sweater, at first resistant, was now soaked through. He imagined his own body slowly reappearing, curled on its side, knees to the chest, as the snow melted when springtime came.

Sylvia must have stepped outside, seen how fierce the blizzard was, and known she would die if she came out in it. He turned his back to the wind; as long as he kept it on his back, he'd be going in the right direction to find the protection of the woods again. Just as he started, the phone buzzed in his pocket. He pulled it out, but his ungloved freezing hands were clumsy, and he dropped the phone in the snow. He bent down, patting the snow around his feet, trying not to panic. His hand finally came upon it.

"Where are you?" Sylvia's voice, ethereal, coming from nowhere.

"I don't know."

"I'm at the goal cages. I have a light. I'm waving it. Can you see it?"

"No."

"I'm coming for you."

"Don't. You won't know where you are."

"I'm in a parka. I'm on snowshoes, with a pair for you. I've got a light. You stay where you are."

He'd stopped shivering, feeling sleepy. His legs wanted to collapse.

"Can you see my light yet?"

"No," he said, peering into the black.

"Now?"

"No. Go home, before you're lost too," he said. He'd just lie down and go to sleep.

"I'm waving the light. I'm walking in bigger and bigger circles. How about now? Can you see it yet?"

"No."

"Now?"

"No."

"Oh shit, where are you?" She sounded scared at last.

"You're lost!" he said. Then a pinprick of light. "I see it!"

"You do! I'll turn in a circle. Now?"

"No. It's gone."

"Now?"

"A little bit of it."

"Now?" It was pointing right at him.

"Yes!" He moved toward it. The light got bigger and bigger and then it shined on his face.

Her parka came down to her knees; its hood was up, hiding her face. She bent down to his feet, put her hands around his leg, helped him pull his foot out of the snow, and guided it down on the snowshoe, and clamped it on. He watched her down there, her rounded shoulders. She moved around to his other side and did the same. She stood and put one hand under his armpit to support him, and they started to walk. He wanted to ask her how she knew which way to go, but he didn't want her to be scared anymore. He put his arm around her shoulders to steady himself.

He didn't know how much later it was when the yellow glow in the windows of the campus buildings appeared in the sideways flying snow. The first building that appeared was the one he'd stood outside of listening to the girls singing. He was safe now, though he heard no singing this time, and no light came through the windows.

"Hurry!" she mouthed at him through the roar of the wind. They moved as fast as he could go, down a row of buildings whose lighted windows made the sideways snowflakes gleam, until they were opposite to a first-floor window. Sylvia knelt down. Unclasping the bindings of his snowshoes, she took them off and her own too, and held all four of them. Sylvia knocked on the window and he saw Elizabeth, sitting at a desk, whirl around, and frown. She came to the window and opened it. Warm air rushed out and he heard Elizabeth say, "You said the equipment shed!" Sylvia pushed him. He went in head first, and Sylvia followed, landing on top of him, still holding the snowshoes. In another second, she was off him. He heard her say, "Screw the equipment shed! He's got hypothermia. He needs a hot shower."

Then he was sitting in a chair, and all he wanted to do was sleep. He was vaguely aware of something Uncle Ray had said about not putting hypothermic people in a hot shower, just warm them slowly and get them dry. There were two desks side by side against the wall to his left and two bunks, one above the other to his right. He raised his arms above his head and Sylvia pulled the empty backpack and then his sweater off his shoulders.

TWENTY-THREE

The sweater, soaked through, was heavy in her hands. It smelled of wet wool and wood smoke, and she was aware of the same rancid odor that had come off him the first time, when Elizabeth had dropped two dollars in his hat. She yearned to help him as he fumbled with frozen fingers to unbutton his shirt, but the intimacy she'd felt when she'd peeled his sweater up over his head disturbed her, and Elizabeth, standing still by the door, pressing a hand against it so no one could enter, was watching her as if to see what strange thing she was going to do next. He finally managed to get his shirt off, let it fall to the floor. His skin was pale, not tanned like when she'd seen him naked in the river, and he had a wiry look, like a long-distance runner. Sylvia put the sweater over the back of her desk chair to dry and took her parka off and draped it over his shoulders.

He bent down to untie the laces of his boots, fumbling again. Doors were opening and closing in the hall, and footsteps and voices. It was dinner time, so girls were leaving the dorm for the dining hall. Impatient with his struggling, Sylvia knelt at his feet, pushed his hands aside, untied his laces, and pulled the boot off his foot. With it still in her hands she looked at Elizabeth, standing at the door. Their eyes met. Elizabeth shrugged. If a friend pushed on the door, she'd have to guess why Elizabeth wouldn't let her in. Dope? Booze? A boy in the room? Sex?

Outside the door, it was quiet now. Elizabeth opened it just enough to put her head out. "All clear in the hall," she whispered.

Sylvia realized she was still holding his boot. She dropped it, making a loud thudding sound. Elizabeth frowned. "Sorry," Sylvia whispered, then giggled. All of a sudden this was funny—a comedy, whatever else it was. Elizabeth still frowned. Sylvia untied the other boot and pulled it off.

One on each side of him, they helped him into the hall. "We'll just have to hope nobody's still here," Elizabeth whispered. Her tone said, *See what you've gotten us into.* Their hands in his armpits, propping him up, they headed toward the bathroom. He seemed almost weightless between them. In the piercing glare of light bouncing from the white tiles of the bathroom, Elizabeth held onto him so he wouldn't fall down while Sylvia ran back to their room and came back with a chair and a towel. She put the chair in the shower stall and hung the towel on a rack and turned on the shower. "You can take off your clothes in there," Elizabeth said, slipping Sylvia's parka off his shoulders. The bathroom was already filling with steam. They helped him to the edge of the shower stall and, leaning in so only their arms got wet, lowered him down on the chair, then stepped back and pulled the curtain closed.

In less than a minute, the shower stopped. The curtain opened and he staggered out, wearing the towel like a skirt around his waist.

"Already?" Elizabeth said.

He nodded his head and mumbled something they couldn't hear.

"Go back in!" Sylvia said, but he shook his head, refusing.

Yielding to him, they helped him back to their room and, closing their eyes so they wouldn't see under the skirt of the towel, helped him up into Sylvia's upper bunk where he would be less likely seen. They pulled the bunk curtain closed.

"We forgot his clothes!" Elizabeth realized. She rushed out of the room, came back a moment later, Christopher's wet khaki trousers, boxer shorts and socks bundled in one hand, the chair in the other. She stuffed his clothes into a laundry bag along with enough of her own clothes so that if anybody did happen to open the dryer, Christopher's wouldn't be noticed. She left for the cellar where the washing machines and dryers were.

While she was gone, Sylvia, still worried about hypothermia, opened her computer to look it up:

HYPOTHERMIA; TREATMENT OF: Warm the victim up slowly. Do not immerse in hot water; this may cause serious disruptions to the normal rhythm of the heart.

Elizabeth returned, closed the door behind her. "I wish there wasn't a rule against locks," she muttered. Her eyes followed Sylvia's to the computer. "So that's why he turned the shower off almost right away!"

Sylvia went down the hall to the common room to make hot tea. She came back, handed the steaming mug to Elizabeth, pulled the curtain open, stood on tiptoes, and propped Christopher up while Elizabeth held the mug to his lips. He still smelled foul. He drank slowly, pushing the cup away several times to get his breath. Some of the tea spilled down onto his chest, wetting the hairs. Sylvia, feeling shy, tender, and repulsed all at once, wiped it away with the edge of the sheet. When there was no more tea in the mug, Sylvia let Christopher's head back on the pillow, pulled the covers up to his chin, and turned away.

Elizabeth slid the curtain closed. "How many times are we going to have to sneak him into the bathroom with all this tea in him?" she whispered.

"So that's why he let us take him to the shower!" Sylvia said, whispering too. "So he could pee without having to ask. He never got under the water. He took his clothes off to fool us."

"Yeah, well, this blizzard better be over by the morning."

"What if it isn't? Suppose it goes on for days?"

"The equipment shed, obviously. Like we planned in the first place."

"I suppose so—until the blizzard ends."

They listened for footsteps in the hall. Elizabeth shrugged. "Maybe we'll get lucky."

Moments later they heard their dormmates returning from dinner: footsteps, doors opening and closing, voices. Then a knock on their door. Elizabeth jumped up from her chair, took one step, and was beside the bunks, pulling the curtain partly open to look at Christopher. "Thank God!" she whispered. "He's sound asleep." She pulled the curtain closed again.

Sylvia opened the door. It was Eudora Easter.

"Aren't you going to let me in?"

"Oh! Sorry." Sylvia stepped aside. Then, trying to sound inviting: "Come on in."

Eudora entered, regal as always. "I missed you at dinner. Everything all right?"

"Everything's fine," Elizabeth said. "We'd already eaten."

"At my mother's," Sylvia said, regretting right away. Suppose Eudora commented on that to her mother? She wished she'd remembered to take her jeans and boots off. Eudora might wonder why they were wet. *Just from walking to the Head's House? Then why aren't Elizabeth's wet?*

"I thought you might have eaten there," Eudora said, glancing at Elizabeth's lower bunk where she frequently sat down when she came to visit, then noticing the closed curtain, looking mildly surprised. "Anyway, in case you hadn't, I brought you these." She pulled two bananas and two apples from a pocket of her fur coat. "There was chocolate cake for dessert, but I didn't bring you any. I knew I would just stop and eat it on the way."

Elizabeth smiled. Sylvia faked a laugh.

"Even in a storm," Eudora said, shaking her head in mock despair. She put the bananas and apples on the desk next to the open computer. "Hypothermia? You studying that in science?"

"No, we just got interested because of the weather," Elizabeth said.

Eudora nodded. "Well, I'll get out of your hair." It was obvious she understood: sometimes kids just don't want the company of grown-ups—frequently when they need it the most, even seniors about to go off to college. She moved to the door, put her hand on the knob. "Next time you decide not to go to dinner, tell me ahead of time, all right? So I won't worry?" Her tone was more like a warning than a request.

"All right, we will," Elizabeth said.

Eudora nodded again and left, leaving the door open.

"DO YOU KNOW how close that was?" Elizabeth whispered, closing the door. All Christopher had to do was turn over. Eudora would have heard. "We'd be getting kicked out of school right now. So shed, shmed! We have to get him off campus."

"Okay. You're right." Sylvia sat down, breathed a great big breath in, and let it out. "I'll call my aunt."

Sylvia dialed Aunt M. She could come first thing in the morning and take Christopher to the VA where they'd try again to help him. Aunt M surely would know how to make that happen. From the phone, Aunt M's recorded voice came on: "I'm unavailable right now. Leave a message. Keep it short."

"Aunt M, this is Sylvia. Please come the minute you get this. It's about that homeless man." Sylvia ended the call and looked away from Elizabeth.

"Why didn't we call your aunt the second we knew he'd come back? We knew he'd be trouble," Elizabeth whispered.

Sylvia turned. Elizabeth really did look curious. "Let's not go there."

"I want to go there. I want someone to tell us we didn't do this just to make ourselves into some kind of heroes."

"Well, that's not going to be my aunt. Maybe you should ask him," Sylvia said, pointing to the upper bunk.

"You're crazy, you know that?" Elizabeth whispered.

"No crazier than you. You're no more about to throw him out into the cold than I am."

Elizabeth didn't answer, just stared.

"Are you?" Sylvia said. "No, of course you're not."

Elizabeth turned back to her desk. Behind the curtain, Christopher groaned and rolled over in his sleep.

"I'm going to take a hot shower too, but for real," Sylvia said. "I'm still cold."

UNDER THE STEAMED, soothing water, it came to Sylvia that she had saved a person's life. Go ahead and punish her for that! No one else would have even tried. And no one else would have figured out how to get home. But she did! *Just face the wind.* It had been directly on her back on her way out. Then, on the way home, the wind blew even harder and she was even more blinded by the snowflakes, but she didn't need to know where the school was. *Just face the wind.* She stayed under the water until she was warm right through to her bones, imagining herself on the stage at Morning Meeting, asking the school, *How many of you would have dared?*

Back in the room, she and Elizabeth agreed: Sylvia would set the alarm on her phone for four in the morning. They'd wake Christopher up and sneak him into the shed. There were warm clothes and plenty of dry food stored in there, the kind for when you don't want to stop and cook: beef jerky, energy bars, and M&Ms, raisins, and peanuts mixed together, otherwise known as gorp. Tomorrow night Aunt M would come, get the key from Sylvia, and sneak him away when everybody was asleep.

Sylvia went to the cellar and retrieved Christopher's clothes from the dryer. The snow hadn't washed all the smell away nor the splatter from the shower, and the remaining heat of the dryer had made it worse. Maybe Elizabeth should have put them in the washer first, but that would have increased the time for someone to discover the presence of a man's clothes in the dorm, and now it was too late to wash and then dry the clothes all over again. Then she realized: he'd have to pee or, worse, take a crap. How? They were going to have to leave the shed unlocked so he could go outside. The security guy would see it! Suppose she hadn't thought of it!

The janitor's equipment closet was also in the cellar. She found a bucket used for mopping the floor and carried it with the clothes to their room, and then put the bucket under Elizabeth's bunk. Standing on her tiptoes, she put Christopher's clothes next to him and shook him gently by the shoulder. He didn't stir. She shook him again, harder this time. "Christopher, wake up!" she whispered. "You have to put your clothes back on!" He stirred, opened his eyes, looked at her, for a second or two, making no sign that he recognized her nor that even knew where he was, and closed his eyes again. "Christopher, your clothes!"

"Not so loud! Elizabeth hissed.

"Christopher! Christopher! Christopher!" Sylvia said, speaking quietly now, not whispering. His eyes opened. "It's me," she said, picking the bundle of his clothes up in both of her hands and placing them on his chest. "Put them on!" She turned away. Elizabeth turned out the light so they couldn't see. They listened to the sound of his putting his clothes back on under the sheet.

Elizabeth turned the light back on. Christopher was lying flat on his back, motionless, the sheet pulled up to his chin. "Well, that's something anyway," Elizabeth whispered. She went to her desk, wrote a note and taped it to the outside of the door: *Tired. Going to bed early. Please don't disturb.* Then Sylvia laid her sleeping bag on the floor, set her alarm for four o'clock—on vibrate only, of course—and crawled into her sleeping bag. Elizabeth turned out the light. Outside the wind still roared, but surrounded by goose down, Sylvia was warm.

Christopher was groaning. He was whimpering too. Thrashing up there in the upper bunk. Sounds of terror and despair in the dark. Sylvia thought she was just having a nightmare. She put her hands over her ears and scrunched herself further down into her sleeping bag, but even with her hands over her ears she heard the sounds of Christopher's nightmare, while in her own she drove a spidery machine with a long, gray gun barrel, like a unicorn's horn, protruding forward, over miles of yellow sand. It was a beach with no ocean. She wanted to hear the sound of surf.

Then she heard Elizabeth jump out of her bunk and woke up to see Elizabeth turned to face the upper bunk. Sylvia jumped up and stood beside her. Elizabeth reached into the upper bunk to lay her hand on Christopher's shoulder and shake him awake.

The instant Elizabeth's hand touched him, he sat up, but he kept on crying out. It was impossible to know whether he was awake or asleep. "It's all right. It's all right, Chris," Sylvia said. "It's just Elizabeth and me. You're safe." The sound of her own words comforted her. She repeated them and reached with both arms and hugged his head to her shoulder, hoping that would silence him, but he kept on crying. So close now, she smelled the rancid smell of him, remembering how he'd fooled them in the shower. "Shh," she whispered, "shh," but he cried out again. She put a foot on Elizabeth's bed to climb. "Don't!" Elizabeth said.

"If I don't, he won't stop," Sylvia whispered, and climbed up, pushing herself through the smell. She lay down beside him, put her arms back around him. He stopped crying out, was totally silent, except for his breathing.

"Oh! All right then. Maybe you better stay up there, if that's what's going to keep him quiet," Elizabeth whispered.

Below her, Sylvia heard Elizabeth getting back into her bunk. The weight of Christopher's shoulders on her arm hurt, but she didn't move it. They'd know soon enough whether anyone had heard.

Minutes passed. No one came running.

"Are you all right up there?" Elizabeth whispered.

"I'm okay," Sylvia whispered. She was getting used to the smell.

Or maybe it was fading. After a while, she fell asleep.

MARIAN BICKHAM'S PLANE landed several hours late that Thursday night, almost midnight. Nevertheless, having heard the urgency in Sylvia's tone, she was surprised that Sylvia didn't answer her returning call. While still at the airport, she made a reservation for the first flight to Bradley Airport in the morning.

It was the last thing she wanted to do. There were a million other things that needed her attention. She had half a mind to call her younger sister and tell her: *You take care of it, you're the boss. So a kid steals stuff from the school and gives it to a homeless person? Give her an A+ for community service and invite the homeless person in for dinner in the dining hall.*

And while we're at it, why should anybody who graduates from your school go on to college? You didn't teach them enough already for all that money? Maybe they should be homeless for a year or two instead. The tuition would be a whole lot less. They could put that in their journal.

She'd known all along she would receive a call for help from her niece, that Sylvia would take her project, the rescue of a helpless person, to a place of crisis where she was helpless too. That she didn't know yet she was doing this to find out who she should be in the world was beside the point. The point was that Aunt M could help.

So of course she would.

ON FRIDAY MORNING, the early light came through the curtain, awakening Sylvia to Christopher's smell. It flashed through her mind, a revelation as stunning as his presence next to her, their bodies touching all along their lengths, that his smell would be offensive only to people who hadn't got used to it. She pushed the curtain open and sunlight poured down on his face. She would get out of bed, but he was still asleep, his head still on her shoulder. The haunted look she had assumed was his only expression was gone. He looked almost tranquil, breathing in, breathing out. And so, though her arm hurt, she kept on cradling him as one draws a puppy into one's chest, or a wounded friend. No sound came from the bunk below her. Elizabeth, too, was still asleep.

Sylvia heard footsteps out in the hall, doors opening and closing. Everyone was coming back from breakfast. Eudora would notice Sylvia's and Elizabeth's absence at breakfast and would be here very soon to see if they were all right. Sylvia looked down at floor from her bunk. Her cell phone was still on the floor in her sleeping bag where, on vibrate only, it couldn't be heard. For all she knew, it was still vibrating.

So why wasn't she leaping out of the bunk, pulling the curtain closed, waking Elizabeth up to figure out what lie to tell Eudora?

TWENTY-FOUR

When the blizzard was over, it was even colder out—below zero, Eudora Easter guessed. The deep snow was crusted so hard on its surface that on her way from the dining hall to Sylvia and Elizabeth's dorm, she could walk directly on top of the snow, a straighter route than if she walked on the cleared path.

A few seconds later, she knocked on the girls' door. Heard a frantic scurrying. Her heart lurched. Waited another second—after all these years, the tension between her respect for other people's privacy and her obligation to supervise still made her uncomfortable. Steeling herself, she opened the door and saw: One, Sylvia leaping down from the upper bunk. Two, Elizabeth reaching for the curtain. And three, a *man* left behind in Sylvia's upper bunk.

Or was it a boy? The sunlight poured down on his face. Even in the instant of her surprise and shock, she was struck by the serenity of his expression. Deep in sleep and innocence.

Christopher couldn't figure out why there was air, just empty space, enough to sit up in, between him and the snow he was buried in.

He did know why he wasn't cold: when you are about to die of the cold it's not the cold you feel, it's the peace.

People who go out feeling peaceful will feel peace forever since they're dead forever too. It's the very last thought you have that counts.

He'd say to Uncle Ray, *The reason you're in heaven is because when you had a heart attack that killed you so fast you were dead before you finished falling down, you were gazing at your favorite view.* It was the same for the girl in his windshield. She hadn't had any more time than Ray had had.

He got up the nerve to ask Uncle Ray if he was right, holding his breath for the answer, but Uncle Ray didn't answer, didn't even appear to him. Because Uncle Ray was dead, and also what was above him wasn't snow anymore; it was the white plaster of a ceiling!

I'm alive, he thought. *I'm not dead and I'm not going to be.* He didn't see anything of all the days ahead, just empty spaces. Still, he felt the same peace he'd felt when he'd thought he was buried in the snow, not knees to chest but face up, after all, waiting to be uncovered by the spring. He knew exactly where he was: where he'd heard those voices singing. It was the only safe place in the world.

NOW THE THREE women were motionless. Eudora felt like one of the figures in a museum's diorama, while Elizabeth and Sylvia stared at her and she stared at the stranger in Sylvia's bed.

"Well, you've caught us," Elizabeth said.

Eudora thought she sounded relieved. They always are. "Who?" she asked, as if the answer would soothe her anguish, pointing at Christopher up there in Sylvia's bed, still asleep.

"I can explain," Elizabeth said.

Christopher stirred. All three watched him slowly awaken, waiting for him to notice Eudora, but he was looking straight up at the ceiling, as if surprised to see it there.

"It's winter. He has no place to stay, so we gave him one," Sylvia said. "Do you have a problem with that?"

Eudora had heard that angry, aggrieved tone lots of times when she had caught a kid doing something wrong—as if it were all her fault, not the kid's. "You didn't have to give him your *bed*," she said.

The boy-man was sitting up now. Looking like a bystander who had happened on an interesting event, stopped to watch it, and fell asleep instead.

"Christopher," Sylvia said. "We've been caught." She gestured toward Eudora. Christopher turned his head that way.

Eudora watched him take her in. She could tell he didn't understand. She could see he was curious about her, welcoming too, glad she'd come to visit. But she also saw, beneath his serene expression, a haggard, exhausted person. She pulled her phone out of her pocket to call the security person on duty. Before she punched the number, Elizabeth touched her hand and shook her head. "He's harmless," Elizabeth said, and started to talk. Eudora hesitated, finger poised, then put the phone back in her pocket as Elizabeth's voice filled the room. Logic told her to call right now; instinct told her to listen.

Elizabeth talked very fast in a matter-of-fact tone, making sure Eudora understood that this man in the room with them was a war vet with PTSD. She made no apology about stealing from the equipment shed. She didn't try to persuade Eudora not to turn them in, she just named the unassailable logic: *He had no other place to go. It's cold outside, and it's warm in here.*

How can you argue with that? How could you argue, too, that these two kids should not be expelled before the day was out? Eudora was not sure anymore whether the logic of that was also unassailable. "All right then," she said. "Who is going to tell—" She paused, trying to decide whether to say *the head of school*, or *Rachel*, or *your mother*.

"We will," Sylvia said.

"Good. Better you than me. When?"

"This morning."

Eudora nodded. She pulled the phone out of her pocket again. "I have to get him off campus. I'm going to call security."

"His name is *Christopher*," Elizabeth said. "It won't kill you to say it."

"But if you call security, it could kill *him*," Sylvia said. "They'll drive him off campus and then just tell him to get out of the car and not ever come back."

"And he won't, you know," Elizabeth added, telling Eudora what she already knew. "Because he'll be dead."

"Frozen to death," Sylvia said.

"So what would you do?" Eudora asked. "If you were me." She heard the complaint in her tone of voice: *Why am I the one who gets stuck with this?* She already knew what they would do. She wanted them to say it. This was their program, their chain of events, not hers.

"Your apartment," Sylvia said. "Until my aunt comes. You've got an extra room."

"Yeah, you're a grown-up," Elizabeth said. "You can have any guest you want."

Unassailable logic again, Eudora decided, ignoring the sarcasm: Call security, maybe he dies. Shelter him in her apartment for a few hours, surely he lives. She'd never done anything so outrageous—nor anything so right. She turned to Christopher, put out her hand to him. He didn't reach for it. She said, "I promise you'll be safe with me."

"Christopher, go with her," Sylvia said. "She's just like us."

Eudora watched him climb down from the bunk. "My name's Eudora, Christopher. I have a nice place for you to stay. It's just down the hall. Will you come?"

He nodded.

"Good. Are you hungry?"

He nodded again.

"I'll make you breakfast." She led him by the elbow out of the room, closing the door behind her.

"IT'S OVER," ELIZABETH said, collapsing onto her chair.

Sylvia turned from the door. Behind Elizabeth, as in the background of an old photograph just come upon, the window framed a view of the campus buried in snow.

"We knew we were going to get caught all along," Elizabeth said. "Maybe that's why I don't feel anything yet."

Sylvia sat down on the edge of Elizabeth's bunk. It seemed years ago that she'd gone out into the dark and the wind and the sideways-flying snow to bring Christopher home.

"Well, anyway, we don't have to whisper anymore," Elizabeth said. She moved from her chair to where Sylvia's sleeping bag still lay on the floor and rummaged in it for Sylvia's phone. Finding it, she held it in her right hand, looked down at it. "Hmm, what's this?" She raised her eyebrows, handed it to Sylvia.

"I know," Sylvia said. "I screwed up."

"We both did."

"Thanks!"

Elizabeth shrugged.

"Will MIT cancel your acceptance now, you think?" Sylvia said.

"I don't know. Jeez, I hope not. But I went right on ahead and did what I did, just like you. Maybe we did it so we'd get caught, who the hell knows? And let me tell you something. You'll find out which college you want to go to when they all say, 'Sorry, but we have lots of applicants who didn't get themselves kicked out of their school.'"

Sylvia shook her head. "Any college that wouldn't let me in for what we did is a college I wouldn't want to go to."

"Yeah? Maybe you better wait and see how you feel when it happens. Meanwhile, let's listen to your voicemail—now that's it's too late."

Sylvia dialed and listened for a couple of seconds. "My aunt will be here at about eleven o'clock."

"Lot of good that will do us now."

"It will do Christopher good. She'll know what to do for him."

"Oh? So does that mean we succeeded? We can go see your mom now and make sure she knows how kind we are, how nice and heroic, before she kicks us out?"

Sylvia had no answer for Elizabeth's sarcasm. So what else was new? It was just veneer.

"All right, let's get it over with." Elizabeth went to the closet and put on her coat.

Sylvia stayed on the edge of Elizabeth's bed, holding on to how right she'd felt when she'd awakened. The storm over. The sun up. Christopher sound asleep. *Where he was safe.*

Elizabeth plucked Sylvia's parka off the back of her chair and handed it to her. "Now that we're no longer Miss O girls, we don't have walk around like it's the middle of summer anymore," she said. Sylvia didn't want to put it on, wasn't ready yet to abandon the ritual, which she'd violated only once to save a person's life, but she also didn't want to argue nor admit to Elizabeth that maybe, just maybe, if she'd jumped out of bed the minute she awoke and pulled the curtain closed...

She put her parka on. Outside, the wind had died. It was so bright she had to squint.

THE BERMS OF snow on both sides of the path to the Administration

Building, where the head of school's office was, came up to their shoulders. It was like walking in a hallway.

When they were halfway there, Elizabeth said, "Why don't I do the talking? It will be easier for her and for you."

"Why do you want to make it easier for her? She gets paid, doesn't she?"

"That's a really dumb thing to say."

"No, it isn't. This shouldn't be easy on anybody."

Elizabeth stopped walking, taking that in.

"I didn't know that until I said it," Sylvia said. "But it's true. Why should it be easy? Suppose we hadn't got caught, and my aunt came and took Christopher off our hands and was making him safe and we went right on and graduated, like none of this happened. Would you feel okay?"

"Are you kidding? It's exactly what I was hoping for."

Sylvia stood perfectly still. Stunned, as if she hadn't known that all along. The sun behind Elizabeth was so piercingly bright, Sylvia couldn't see her face. It was a relief.

"Anyway, let me handle telling your mom," Elizabeth said. "You just be numb. Like you have Novocain in the brain."

Sylvia raised her head, squinting again. "And you be the politician?"

Elizabeth shrugged. "Whatever."

They started walking again. Soon they were close enough to see through the big sliding glass doors that Rachel was watching them approach. Surprise, maybe disapproval even, that they were wearing coats was clear in her expression. Sylvia stopped walking. "You know what? I just had a better idea."

Elizabeth kept on walking. "Come on, let's just get this over with."

Sylvia grabbed Elizabeth's elbow. "Morning Meeting," she said. "Much better place to tell."

"That's crazy."

"Is it? Eudora wanted us to tell my mother. Because we were the ones who did it. So is my mother going to tell the school? We aren't just the ones who did it. We're the ones who lied in Morning Meeting that someone else did."

"So now we're going to un-lie?"

"Why not?"

"You know what? I don't care how we do it since we'll be out of here before the day's over anyway."

"Good. We'll go to classes until then, as if nothing happened."

"Okay, that's what we'll do," Elizabeth said, resigned, exasperated, turning around so her back was to the office. "Gregory van Buren's going to want to know your excuse for being late to his class."

"I'll tell him he'll find out in Morning Meeting," Sylvia said.

"I'VE CALLED A friend," the lady in a long red dress called Eudora said. "I left a message. He'll take care of you."

"I heard them sing," Christopher said, explaining.

"Who?" She turned from the stove to him. It was warm in there, in the kitchen. Pictures all around. The smell of coffee brewing, oatmeal cooking.

"The choir," he said. "There was no other sound. The moon was out. It glistened on the snow."

"Oh?"

"Yes. I did. I heard them sing."

"Do you remember the song?"

"I can hum it for you," he said. She was round and soft and strong, and her face was beautiful to him. So he dared. When he was through, he said, "I wish I could remember the words."

"*I* can!" she said. And reached to touch his hand.

She sang, her voice as round and soft and strong and beautiful to him, her fingers lightly clasping his.

He bent his head and wept.

NORMALLY, WHEN ANYONE was late for one of his classes—indeed not in her seat, ready for work *before* the starting bell—Gregory van Buren would fix on her his famous look of astonishment at her irreverence, and then pursue her with it as she traveled from the door to her seat while a silence descended that he allowed to linger for an eternity *after* she'd found her seat. Only then would he ask, as if overcome with curiosity, for the reason she was late, which, via a very undemocratic Socratic dialogue, he would lead her to the conclusion that such reason was absurdly insufficient. This procedure was so to be avoided that his students would often leave their previous class with a promptness that frustrated any teacher who needed maybe just another minute or two to reach the goal for the day, and then they would actually run across the campus to his classroom.

But that day, when Sylvia entered his classroom, committing the double transgression of tardiness and wearing a parka, his look was of concern, not astonishment, and he didn't even stop talking. After class, he took her aside outside, his hand on her elbow, as he had before on another very cold day. "Are you all right?"

"I'm fine."

"Then why are you late?

"You'll find out at Morning Meeting."

"Sylvia! What's wrong?"

She shook her head and gently removed his hand from her elbow. He saw a considerable sadness flash across her face.

"I only want to say it once."

He watched her walk away from him toward the auditorium. Then he headed that way too.

TWENTY-FIVE

Now!" Elizabeth whispered in the front row, standing up. Next to her, Sylvia stood up too. They stepped into the aisle and headed toward the stage. The boring announcements section of Morning Meeting—*I can't find my blue cashmere sweater; has anyone seen it? The bus to X will leave at*—had just been gotten out of the way so the interesting stuff could begin. The two girls felt a strange relief. In another moment or two, it would all be over.

"No, I'll go first." It was Gregory van Buren's instantly recognizable voice behind them. Sylvia and Elizabeth stopped walking and glanced at each other. It was clear to them why he was going first: so whatever they were about to announce, something so heavy Sylvia wanted only to announce it once, wouldn't take the wind out of the sails of what *he* was going to announce.

Resplendent in his double-breasted blue blazer with the golden buttons, red-striped tie, and fresh-pressed khaki trousers, Gregory passed them without a glance, striding fast. Sylvia and Elizabeth returned to their seats and sat back down. They were going to have to wait some more.

On the stage, Gregory looked straight at Sylvia for a second or two as if apologizing for being so rude. Then he announced, his voice swelling with pride, the outside publication of a poem by Edwina McManis, who was only a junior. "A sonnet no less, in *Glimmer Train*," he said. "Do any of you have any idea how hard it is to get a poem published in a literary journal of that caliber?" Every student at Miss O's knew all there was to know about rhetorical questions by halfway through their first semester, so of course no one answered. "This kind of high accomplishment is what happens at Miss Oliver's School for Girls," Gregory went on. Sylvia could swear he was looking directly at her and Elizabeth—especially Elizabeth—as if he needed to remind them of what they were about to lose. "We learn that we have potential previously unimagined. We learn that we can do it!"

Edwina marched up front and read her poem in her own idiosyncratic voice, catching every subtle sound and sense. It was clear she'd rehearsed for hours under Gregory's coaching. There was a silence and then everyone in the auditorium stood up and cheered and clapped her hands. Gregory and Edwina started to walk to the steps down from the stage.

"No, stay up there!" It was the head of school's voice from the back row where she always sat. Gregory and Edwina went back to center stage and waited. A moment later, Sylvia's mother moved past the front row, her skirt brushing against Sylvia's elbow, and climbed the steps up to the stage. Taking Edwina's hand in hers, she raised it like the winning boxer's above Edwina's head. Edwina stood there, her hand held high, a triumphant smile lighting up her face. When the cheering finally subsided, Sylvia's mom said, "This is a wonderful day. Enjoy the rest of it," and everyone started to leave.

Sylvia stepped out into the aisle, turned, raised her hands. "Wait! There's more." Almost every girl hesitated. "Please. Sit back down," Sylvia said. Some girls sat down again. Others continued to hesitate. It felt wrong. Like an epilogue to a novel that didn't need one, or a joke explained. Many looked to the stage, waiting for the head of school to adjudicate. But the head of school said nothing.

Rachel Bickham being indecisive! What's going on?

Elizabeth stood and joined Sylvia in the aisle and headed forward. Everyone in the audience sat down again.

At the foot of the steps up to the stage, Sylvia and Elizabeth waited while Gregory and Edwina came down. Gregory gave Sylvia and Elizabeth a look of concern, but Edwina looked straight ahead as if Sylvia and Elizabeth didn't exist. "Sorry," Sylvia whispered to Edwina. Then Sylvia turned and followed Elizabeth up the steps. Her mother was waiting there, wearing an expression Sylvia had never seen before: a strange mixture of worry and exultation.

Then Sylvia was standing beside Elizabeth at the lip of the stage, and from the top of the stairs, her mother said, her voice ringing out over the audience as it always did, "Evidently Elizabeth and Sylvia have something to say we need to hear." She went down the steps and walked briskly down the aisle, returning to her seat in the back row. Sylvia watched her all the way.

Sylvia drew a big breath. It was very quiet. Elizabeth nudged her on the hip. Sylvia let out her breath, took another big one.

"As you know, I'm president of the Outdoor Adventure Club. I have the key to the equipment shed." Everyone leaned forward. Just then, one of the big doors in the back of the auditorium swung open. Sylvia stopped talking and stared. Everyone, including her mother—especially her mother!—turned to watch as Aunt M swept through the door and stopped walking, her eyes going straight to the stage, and everyone turned back to stare at Sylvia. "Now you know who stole the stuff," Sylvia said, pointing to herself. There was a collective gasp, then silence, while Sylvia and Aunt M continued to stare at each other as Aunt M took a seat in the back row. "So, you don't have to wonder anymore who it was," Sylvia said. "Or if anybody thinks it was you."

Sylvia watched Aunt M swivel her head to find her sister—who must have felt that gaze on the side of her face. Her mother turned to Aunt M. The two women looked hard at each other across the width of the auditorium, like people do when they come upon each other by surprise in a city far away from home, and Aunt M nodded her head. Her mother swung around and stared across the audience at Sylvia, and Sylvia nodded her head too, feeling a surprising calm.

"Sylvia didn't steal the stuff by herself. I helped," Elizabeth said.

"And don't anybody ask us to apologize," Sylvia blurted.

Elizabeth shot Sylvia a warning look. Then turning to all the faces: "It was for a homeless guy. We brought him food too. From the dining hall."

"And guess what else we did?" Sylvia said. "We brought him into the dorm." She paused to let that sink in, watched the fascinated expressions. "Yeah, we gave a roof to a homeless guy last night. That's our crime."

"It was during the blizzard," Elizabeth said.

"So, you think that's all, just bring him in to where it's warm? Come on, you have to sleep with them when they get cold." Sylvia paused. There was a rage expanding in her chest. "Any of you ever slept with a homeless guy?" She roamed her eyes over the audience, as if waiting for someone to confess. "You should try it." she said. "It warms them right up."

"Calm down," Elizabeth whispered.

"She wants me to calm down," Sylvia said, pointing with her thumb to Elizabeth. "He has post-traumatic stress disorder. And she wants me to calm down? From the stupidest fucking war that ever happened!"

In the second row, Gregory van Buren stood up. "This meeting's adjourned." Everyone stayed transfixed in their seats. "It is adjourned!" he said. "Go, now, to your classes." Still, everybody sat, eyes flashing back and forth between him and the two girls on stage. "Go!" Gregory pointed to the doors in the back. "Now!"

Without a word, everyone stood up and began to troop out. Marian went out the same back door she entered through. Rachel and Gregory looked at each other across the space between them. Gregory mouthed, "I'll bring them to you." Rachel nodded, then followed Marian out, and Gregory came forward and stood beside Elizabeth and Sylvia.

THE AUDITORIUM WAS cavernous now that everyone had left.

"So what happens now?" Elizabeth asked.

"We clean out our rooms, I suppose," Sylvia said, imagining the trudge back and forth across the snow, carrying boxes of stuff to the Head's House. She'd be in limbo, expelled from school, but still living on campus.

The distraught, surprised look on Gregory's face had melted away. He was now wearing his thoughtful look. When that happened, no one ever could figure out what he was thinking, but Sylvia was sure he was asking the same question: *What's it like to be half expelled?* He said, "Let's go see your moth—" and, like Eudora before him, he corrected himself. "—the head of school."

"Why bother?" Sylvia asked him. "The penalty is automatic."

"Because even when it is automatic, as you put it, there is a process." Gregory put a hand gently on each girl's elbow. "Besides, there are mitigating circumstances."

As soon as they were outside, he let go their elbows. *So Elizabeth and I won't look like perps in a newspaper photo being led to jail, and he won't look like a cop*, Sylvia thought, gratefully. She'd known him all her life.

But nobody was outside to watch them go. It was much too cold and windy. Everybody had gone as fast as they could to their classes where it was warm. And where Sylvia knew they were still processing the news. The teachers too.

OUTSIDE, IN THE piercing bright gleam of sun on snow, Rachel said to Marian, "You and I need to talk."

"I reckon," Marian said. "Why don't you start?"

"Not here, where everybody's staring at us!" Rachel started walking fast toward her office. Marian caught up and walked beside her. Neither said a word on the way.

In her office, while her sister watched and listened, Rachel first called the security person on duty and reported the presence of a male intruder who needed to be escorted from the campus—"after being brought to my office," she added.

The security person wanted to know why he should be taken to her office. "Why not just get him the hell out of here? Turn him over to the cops?" Rachel didn't answer, instead told him to start looking for him in Sylvia and Elizabeth's room. "Really! In their bedroom!" The security person was almost shouting now. "This *is* for the cops."

"No! Do as I say. Bring him to *me*," Rachel shouted back, and hung up before he could object anymore.

"Atta girl!" Marian said.

"I'm glad you approve," Rachel said sarcastically.

Marian just nodded her head. "So you want to talk? Those kids will be here in a minute."

"Yes, I do. Because you knew all along, didn't you? You turned to me and nodded your head."

"Like you already knew and we were just agreeing?" Marian's tone was neutral, like she really wanted to know. "Or was I just confirming what I knew and you didn't? You have to answer that before I know whether you really have a reason to be angry with me."

"How do you get the right to tell me whether or not I should be angry?"

"Because you're my sister, sweetie, that's how." Marian glanced out through the big French doors. Rachel followed her gaze. Here came Gregory van Buren, flanked by Sylvia on his right and Elizabeth on his left. The snow piled high on each side of the path towered over them. "You want some advice before they get here?" Marian said.

"I don't know. Depends what it is."

"Well, how about this? Either kick them out because that's what your school is, or give them a prize because that's what it's trying to be. But whatever you do, don't sit in the middle."

Before Rachel could think about that, Margaret Rice, who'd been to Morning Meeting too, poked her head in, her expression studiously blank, and said, "They're here."

"I CALLED SECURITY," Sylvia's mother said. "Is he still on campus?"

Sylvia and Elizabeth looked at each other.

"Please, we have to know. Is he in the dorm?"

"Not exactly," Sylvia taunted.

"Well then, *where* exactly?"

"Eudora's taking care of him," Elizabeth said.

"Eudora!"

Elizabeth nodded. "She gave him breakfast."

"Breakfast! In her *apartment*?"

"That's where her kitchen is," Sylvia said.

Aunt M stood up.

"Where are you going?" Sylvia said. "Stay."

"Nope. You girls are doing just fine. It's Eudora who might need my help." Aunt M left the office, moving fast.

And Sylvia's mother reached for the phone.

"You don't need security, Mom. He's totally harmless," Sylvia said.

"That's not for me or you to decide," her mother said, punching the numbers..

Gregory van Buren said, "Obviously you need to recuse yourself. So I'll take your place at the discipline committee."

She put her hand up to Gregory. "He's in Ms. Easter's apartment," she said into the phone.

"Of course," Gregory said. "First things first." Then he turned to Sylvia and Elizabeth and said, "You two. Go back to your room and wait."

"MY FRIEND JUST got home and called right away," the round, soft lady said. "I knew he would. I've known him forever. He wants to give you a place to stay."

A place to stay? Like here? He was drinking coffee in a *rocking chair.*

"You do know why you can't stay here, don't you?"

There was a knock on the door. She took the coffee cup from him and pointed with her other hand. "Hide in there."

He was only in there a minute, standing by her bed, gazing at a picture of a great big tree, before she said, "It's all right, Christopher, it's another friend," and he went back out.

"This is Sylvia's aunt," she said. "Her name is Marian. She's going to come with us to my friend's house."

THE ROUND, SOFT lady drove. He sat up front in the passenger seat beside her. "Put your seatbelt on," she said.

But he just pretended. If he did as she said, he wouldn't be able to get out of the car fast enough if he didn't want to be there. Keeping his gaze straight ahead, he didn't push the metal thing all the way in past the click, just held it there with his hand. The other lady sat in the back. He forgot her name already. He looked in the rearview mirror. She was looking in the mirror too, watching him look at her. She wasn't round. She was thin and almost tall. "You belong to Sylvia," he said to the mirror. "I can tell."

"Indeed I do. Now put your seatbelt on."

He didn't know how to say no to this one. He clicked his seatbelt in.

The gates to the school were in front of him, down the hill, maybe a hundred yards. He felt the worry rise. They went through the gates onto the road where he'd walked that night, jumping into the snow beside the road not to be hit by the oncoming cars, and he was just as afraid and tense and worried as he had been then—until he'd cut through the campus and heard the girls sing. He put his hands down beside himself and gripped the front edge of the seat. He held on and on, his fingers getting tired.

And then there was a church. Gray stones, shaped like a little castle with a steeple. Smaller than the one he went to with his aunt. Around the back, a house. With a big front porch. "You're going to be safe here," the round, soft lady said. "My friend is the kindest man in the world."

The engine stopped. She pulled the hand brake on and touched his shoulder. A little man, all dressed in black, came out the front door onto the porch. Next to him, a big black hairy dog, wagging his tail. *Doctor Doolittle*, he thought, *all the animals loved him.* He thought of Uncle Ray, reading him to sleep

He got out of the car. The two ladies went first. He climbed the steps behind them. "Hello, my dear Eudora," Dr. Doolittle said. He hugged her and kissed her on the cheek.

"This is Sylvia's aunt, Marian," Dear Eudora said. "And this is Christopher."

"Christopher, I'm glad you've come. My name is Michael, and this is Red. Say hello, Red." The big black dog came forward, still wagging his tail, and shoved his nose into Christopher's crotch. He leaned and scratched the dog between the ears. "Come on in, everybody. I've lit a fire," Dr. Michael Doolittle said.

SYLVIA AND ELIZABETH left the head's office through the sliding glass doors that opened directly onto the campus so they wouldn't have to undergo Margaret Rice's second effort to keep her expression blank. It was uncomfortable to be the objects of curiosity, purveyors of vicarious experience to the cautious. The only company they wanted was each other's.

They were aliens already, returning on empty paths to their dorm, past the classroom building, the science and music buildings, the library, each filled with their schoolmates who would still be there tomorrow. Entering through the big front door of their dormitory, they were hit by silence, like a wind coming at them. All the doors of the rooms lining both sides of the hall were closed.

In their own room, Sylvia picked her sleeping bag up from the floor, stuffed it into its carry bag, and chucked it into a corner. Soon they'd be packing everything up, taking the posters off the walls. What would be left was the barren space they'd entered in the fall and made their own: two chairs, two desks, two bureaus, all in blonde wood, one wastebasket—exactly the same in every room.

Elizabeth threw herself down on her bunk.

Sylvia, restless, remained standing. "What are you going to say to your parents?"

"The same thing we told Eudora. It was cold outside."

"That's it?"

"That's the easy part. The hardest is going to be when they ask me…" Elizabeth's voice trailed off.

"Was it worth giving up so much?"

Elizabeth nodded. "Yeah, that's what they're going to ask. They'll say, *You were about to graduate.* And for once I won't know what to say. How come I didn't know I wanted the Miss O's diploma for its own sake, not just the ticket into MIT? That's what I've been realizing since we got caught. I wanted to show it to my parents. I wanted to frame it and hang it on the wall wherever I lived for the rest of my life."

Sylvia collapsed down beside Elizabeth. "I feel like I dragged you into it."

"I did it just to keep you company?" Elizabeth stared at the wall across the narrow room and shook her head. "No, I was the first, remember? I dropped two dollars in his hat, and you told me what your father would say about that, how you should give to organizations instead, and I was about to say that's too easy, you don't have to look them in the face, but you'd turned around and gone back already and I watched you put *your* two dollars in his hat. It all began right then." Elizabeth paused. "Besides, it's just as bad for you. This is your home."

Sylvia didn't think so. "You wanted to get away from home," she said. "Now they're sending you back. That's what I'm sorry for. But anyway, we still have each other."

Elizabeth smiled a wan smile. She looked out the window at the campus covered in snow. Saying goodbye to it, Sylvia thought. They heard footsteps in the hall. Elizabeth turned away from the window. The footsteps got nearer. "Yeah, we have each other," Elizabeth said.

The footsteps came nearer and nearer. They waited for them to stop and the doorknob to turn, but the footsteps went right on by and they heard a door open to a room down the hall. Sylvia let out her breath. She hadn't known she was holding it. "What's taking them so long?"

"If the discipline committee met for only a few minutes it would look like they didn't think about it," Elizabeth said.

"Nobody expects them to *think* about it. There are only two things you get kicked out automatically for and we did both of them." Sylvia giggled, a small hysteria rising. "Too bad there's not a third thing. We could do that too. Since we're getting kicked out anyway."

"What do you think it would be?"

"I don't know. Propositioning a teacher?"

"That'll do it. Which one do you think?"

"How about old Gregory? Let's tell him he can have both of us. Maybe he'll let us off."

"No, just you," Elizabeth said. "If he does me, he'll be so turned off, he'll kick us out twice."

Both girls laughed. The hysteria melted, and in the silence Elizabeth asked, "So where are you going to go? To your mother's house?"

Sylvia didn't answer.

"You didn't think of that?"

"Of course I thought about it. I thought about it a lot."

"So?"

"I think I'll go to my aunt's house," Sylvia said, deciding as she spoke. The prospect of living in limbo, half expelled, at the Head's House, was even more confusing now that Elizabeth had asked the question. "Yes, that's what I'll do."

"I'd go there with you. But my parents are going to assume you influenced me into being so stupid. They'd send the sheriff to get me out of your clutches."

"Because I'm Black?"

"Why're you bringing this up now? You know my parents and I don't talk about stuff like that."

"Yeah, but you must have told them."

Elizabeth shrugged. "I sort of told them and I sort of didn't."

"And they sort of didn't ask," Sylvia said. Her spirits rose a little knowing she and Elizabeth shared this knowledge together, having navigated it by living together, knowing each other.

Elizabeth shrugged. "It's a different world out there."

"I suppose so," Sylvia said in closing. "I wouldn't know."

New footsteps now, heavier, were coming nearer and nearer.

"Well, I think you are about to find out," Elizabeth said.

The two girls stood up and stared at the doorknob, waiting for Gregory's knock. It was about to happen.

At last the knock came. "Come in," Elizabeth said. The door opened.

Gregory van Buren, his golden buttons gleaming, was framed in the doorway.

"Which news do you want to hear first, the discipline committee's decision or what is happening with your friend?"

"What!" Elizabeth said.

"I think you heard me."

"What is this, a test?" Elizabeth said.

"No, Elizabeth. It's a choice. I didn't want to make it for you."

"That's not fair," Elizabeth said.

"Probably not," Gregory agreed.

"Sometimes I hate you," Elizabeth said. "I'd like to punch you right in the nose."

"I understand. Sylvia?"

"Me too. Just tell us."

Gregory shook his head.

"Oh all right, tell us about him first," Elizabeth said. "You've made your point."

"Yes, tell us," Sylvia said.

Gregory looked like he did in class when he'd reached a goal in his lesson plan. "You'll be pleased to know your friend is now at the Reverend Woodward's house. Ms. Easter and your aunt, Sylvia, have taken him there. A very good decision. He'll be safe and warm.

What better place than a church pastored by such a person could there possibly be? And your aunt will know how to get him help. I hope this news makes you warm too." He paused, nodding his head. "Of course it does. Otherwise, why would you have gone to such lengths?"

"Yes, we're glad," Sylvia said. "Now just tell us we're expelled and get it over with."

"But you're not. As I said, there were mitigating circumstances. You are suspended for two weeks. It was the least unsatisfactory consequence the committee could arrive at, given the unusual situation. Elizabeth, I have informed your parents. You have a reservation on Southwest Airlines. And you, Sylvia, you will leave your clothes here, as you have a supply at your mother's house. Proceed there directly."

"Not expelled!" Elizabeth said.

He put his hand up "When you return, you will both apologize to the school in Morning Meeting. From this moment until after you have made that apology, please refrain from any interaction with the school." He stopped talking and stood very still. "Now I must inform the head of school. I thought I should tell you first." He backed out of the room, a soldier about to salute, closing the door as he left.

Elizabeth collapsed back down on her bunk. The cuff of her jeans slid upward on her leg and it was as if Sylvia could actually see the oil rig, crossed out by the big exuberant X, right through the thick woolen sock, and know how much more desperately Elizabeth had wanted to stay and graduate than even she had realized. Sylvia's own relief was enough to make her collapse down on her chair.

Yet she also wanted to argue with Gregory about suspension instead of expulsion and, even more fervently, about the requirement to apologize. When he'd stopped talking and stood so still, he'd seemed disturbed. Unresolved. *The least unsatisfactory consequence—given the unusual situation.*

But the decision had been made. He would never try to change it. She stayed in the chair, giving in entirely to the huge, overwhelming relief: they were *not* expelled!

Why *not* enjoy it—while it lasted?

"SYLVIA! YOU'RE HOME. How nice!" Bob said first thing when he arrived from the City where he'd been making final arrangements for the sale of Best Sports. "You going to stay here with us tonight?"

Silence from Sylvia and her mom.

"What? Tell me."

"Tell him, Sylvia," her mother said.

Sylvia shook her head. "You tell him."

"No. He's your dad. He deserves to hear it from you."

Sylvia shook her head again.

"Syl, honey. Please. Whatever it is. You can tell me."

"No. It will sound like a confession."

"Okay, Syl. I understand. You have a secret. But it's still nice to have you home."

Sylvia smiled in spite of herself.

"Please," he said. "Just tell me."

So Sylvia told him everything. Right from the beginning. It took a long time. When she was finished, he sat very still.

"Are you surprised, Dad?"

"Not very. Especially now that we know why you returned the stuff. Right, Rachel?"

Her mom flushed.

"Mom?" Sylvia said.

"And anyway, suppose you *didn't* do anything to help the guy," her dad said. "There wouldn't even be a suspension. You'd get off scot-free for doing nothing. How would Mom and I feel about that?"

"Yes, how would we feel? That's the big question, isn't it?" her mom said. "You know what your Aunt Marian told me? 'Either kick them out because that's what your school is—or give them a prize because that's what it's trying to be. But whatever you do, don't sit in the middle.'"

"But you recused yourself," Sylvia blurted. "And look what happened!"

"Yeah, look what happened," her dad said. "Squarely in the middle. No satisfaction for anyone. But for me, the middle has its merits: I get to enjoy your company. The timing couldn't be better. I stop going to the City, and presto, you stay home all day for two whole weeks."

Sylvia didn't answer.

"We'll do stuff together," he said. "Maybe I'll even go with you when you run—if you go slowly enough."

Sylvia looked down at the floor.

"Yeah, I know," he said. "You'd practically have to walk. But I could teach you chess. How about that?"

"That would be great, Dad, but I can't stay here. It would be too weird, suspended from school but still on campus. I'm going to go to Aunt M's."

"Oh?" he said, crestfallen. "Suppose your mother and I ask you to put up with feeling weird and stay with us. We love you. We want you here with us."

Sylvia turned to her mom.

"Bob, she's right," she said. "She's not supposed to have any connection with the school."

"Because, Dad, if I met a student on a path, what would I do? Turn my back?"

"Is that the real reason, Rach?" he asked. "Or is that it is wrong for the head of school to make exceptions for her daughter?"

"Well, of course that's one of the reasons. Elizabeth goes all the way home to Oklahoma, and Sylvia stays right here. How would that look?"

"Sensible," he said. "Sensible. Practical. Reasonable. To people everywhere except at Miss Oliver's School for Girls. What is it about this place? Is it like this in other schools?"

"All the good ones," her mom said.

"Don't be sad, Dad. It's only for two weeks," Sylvia said.

"Well, I am sad. How can I not be? You're my *daughter*."

Sylvia got up from her chair and crossed the room. She kissed him on the cheek and tousled his hair, as if she were the parent, not the other way around, and went upstairs to her room. Of course her parents weren't completely surprised. How could they be? And she'd put her mother in a difficult position. Shouldn't she feel guilty? The truth of the matter was that she hardly felt any emotion at all, vaguely aware too that her numbness was purposeful. After so much drama, she needed the respite from urgent emotions. She wondered if two weeks would be enough, especially since Auda Hellmann's long-anticipated visit from Germany would start the same day as what Sylvia was already thinking of as The Reinstatement, and Sylvia would have to listen to Auda's angry protestations that it was the school that should feel guilty. She didn't want to hear that either.

Right now, she needed to pack a suitcase.

"AREN'T YOU GOING to help her pack?" Bob asked.

Rachel shook her head. "I'm sure she wants to be alone. I know I would."

Bob sighed. "I suppose you're right. And anyway, she's a big girl now."

"Yes, she is. And I just had an idea!" Rachel went to the window, gazed out. "Plant a new copper beech tree."

"Wow, that's a change of subject!"

"No! How can you say that? It's totally related. Look." She pointed across the campus. He got up and stood beside her. "We'll put it there just past the shade the old one makes," she said. "So when the old one dies—"

"Oh yes, totally related," he said. "I love the way your mind works."

"IT'S NICE IN here," Eudora said, sending her smile across the room to Michael.

"So stay for dinner," Michael said. He crossed the room, took Eudora's hand, and led her into the kitchen, leaving Christopher alone with Sylvia's Aunt Marian and the dog, Red, who lay on the floor near Christopher's feet, like all good dogs who always know who in any room is the one most in need of company. Marian sat opposite Christopher in a stuffed chair, regarding him with a calm directness. The sound of Eudora and Michael working in the kitchen floated into the room.

"Sylvia told me about you," Marian said. "Are you surprised?"

"No."

"Well, I'm not either."

Eudora came back into the room bearing a plate of crackers

and cheese. Red thumped his tail on the floor. Michael came close behind, carrying a bottle of red wine and four glasses on a tray. "Beef stew's heating in the oven," he said, pouring the wine. "One of my parishioners brought it to me."

Christopher put a hand over his glass to prove he wasn't crazy and was never going to be. "I have an aunt in Hartford, where I'm going to stay. Will one of you drive me there?"

"You just rest here for a day and get your strength back," Eudora said. "I'll take you on Sunday."

"That's right," Michael said. "You stay right here."

Over dinner, Michael and Eudora continued to look at each other as if they couldn't get enough of the sight, and Sylvia's aunt explained how she and Sylvia had made a friend at the Veteran's Administration for Christopher when he was ready. After dinner, the four of them washed the dishes together while Christopher's spirits went right up to the ceiling, and then Eudora and Sylvia's aunt went back to the school and Michael showed Christopher where his bedroom was. It had a big soft bed with a fat down cover. Christopher got in it and went right to sleep.

TWENTY-SIX

If Jerry Brown can live like an ascetic monk in Sacramento, I can in Detroit," Aunt M said when Sylvia tried and failed to hide her surprise at how small her aunt's apartment was. It was in one of the most neglected parts of Detroit. "It's the kind of neighborhood where I do my work, and I don't spend a whole lot of time at home anyway. Besides, the rent is cheap. And guess where I *own* a house: Grosse Pointe. The tenants pay my mortgage and then some. I need to make some money for my old age, so I invest where the money is."

There was a small living room and kitchen, a tiny bathroom, and a miniscule bedroom. Aunt M pointed to the sofa in the living room. Sylvia was sure it was secondhand, covered in tired brown. "You might have to bend your knees a little to fit," Aunt M said. "But you're young, you'll be fine. Monday night, you'll be sleeping in a gym. Plenty of room there to stretch out that long body of yours."

She went on to explain that she had organized a community presence at a hearing about the proposed building of a city bus parking space in the same low-income area of the city, where there was an epidemic of youth asthma. In the winter, the bus company would have to keep the motors running all night to prevent the diesel fuel from congealing, thus rendering the air even more lethal. Aunt M knew the strategy of the city would be the usual one in such cases: the paid professional advocates of the plan would speak first and late into the night, outlasting the unpaid residents there to fight the plan, who would give up and go home to sleep before they had a chance to speak so they could go to work in the morning, if they were lucky enough to have a job to go to.

"But here's what's actually going to happen," Aunt M said. "The professionals aren't going to outlast us. And they are the ones who are going to be tired. Because after they finish making their case, we are going to bring in the kids from the elementary school and their parents, and they are not going to be tired because they will have been sleeping right up to that moment. I've wangled a gym in a public school not far from where the hearing will be held. The principal is disobeying the law to let them sleep there, of course. That's what you have to do. Your job is going to be helping out the moms and dads and grandparents with the kids. Helping them find the bathroom. Wiping up the mess when they throw up. That kind of stuff." She smiled. "Sounds romantic, doesn't it? Then you'll help wake them up and walk with them to the hearing. That's at night. In the daytime you'll be helping the teachers in their classes." She paused. "You up for this?"

"Sure," Sylvia said, wondering if she really was. "But I don't know a thing about teaching."

"Yes, you do. You've been watching some very good ones for the last four years."

ADELAIDE TRIPLETT, ALREADY dressed for church, heard a car in her driveway and looked out the window to see a Black woman get out of a car. *Another Jehovah's Witness.* It didn't occur to her that it was maybe just coincidence that every person who had come to her doorway to proselytize that faith for the last several years had been Black, but it had occurred to her, each time, that it was important to open the door to their knock and be polite. She had a lot of respect for people who cared so much about other people's salvation.

Thus she went to her front door and opened it that Sunday morning and watched the woman approach, a roundish person, who walked with a kind of waddle in an elegant navy-blue winter coat that came down to her ankles and had shiny brass buttons.

But someone was staying behind in the car. Why? Jehovah's Witnesses always came in twos. "Good morning?" she called.

"Good morning." The woman climbed the stairs to the porch. "My name is Eudora Easter."

Eudora? Easter? It's still the middle of winter.

"I've brought your nephew," this Eudora person said. "He won't get out of the car unless you say it is all right."

Adelaide put her hand on the doorknob behind her to steady herself. "All right?" She was flooded with sadness and anger and joy all at once, in the midst of her surprise. And questions too. Who was this woman? What had she to do with Christopher?

"He told me everything," Eudora Easter said.

"Everything! I don't know *any*thing. I had no idea whether he was even alive."

"I'm sorry," Eudora Easter said. "Shall I tell him he can come in? I'll stay for a little while to make it easier."

"Yes, tell him to come in. I'll be in the living room. I'm too angry to welcome him at the door."

Adelaide turned away and went back into her house and into the living room and sat in a chair with its back to the door, and when she heard his footsteps she still didn't turn around. He came around the chair and stood facing her. She didn't look up at him and he didn't speak and she still didn't look up. She heard his breathing and Eudora Easter's too.

"I'm sorry," he said.

Now she looked up at him. How worn, how old for someone so young, how fragile!

"I really am sorry. And I need a place to stay."

"Your suit's upstairs in your room," she said. "The one I bought for you. You can put it on and come to church with me. Or you can stay away." She was surprised. She had no idea that was her intention until she'd said the words.

"I'd be glad to," he said. "You don't know how glad."

He left to go upstairs and she turned to Eudora Easter. She started to ask who she was, but changed her mind and said, "Will you come to church with us?" She already knew who Eudora Easter was: the person who'd brought Christopher back to her.

"Why not?" Eudora Easter said. "I'm planning to propose marriage to a minister friend of mine. I might as well get used to going to church."

THE PRIEST IN her white cassock looked over her congregation, met Christopher's gaze, and recited the invitation: "Come unto me all ye that are heavy laden."

But *laden*, for Christopher, had a heavy sound. It filled his skull and pressed down on top of his shoulders. His arms, straight down at his sides, felt stretched from their sockets by the bucket of nails—shrapnel from a homemade bomb—he carried in each hand across the street… stepping over the dead girl… toward a building whose windows and doors were all blown out. Dark, empty squares in sun-struck walls, coffin holes in the dirt, uncovered.

He put the buckets down on the other side of the street and returned… stepping back over the girl… to his aunt who sat on his right. Her wool suit smelled like his and she wore her stupid little blue hat on her head that he would have felt sad about if she didn't. On his left, in the pew which smelled like furniture polish, Eudora sat in her gleaming brass buttons.

This morning, on the drive from Michael's house to his aunt's, he'd looked through the windshield of Eudora's car while they were stopped at a red light. A family was crossing the street. He had asked her, "What would you feel if you hit someone?"

The light turned green and Eudora drove on. She said, "That sounds like your question to answer, not mine," and he told her the story of how he killed the girl. He watched the words slide out faster and faster, like snakes from a cave. They pulled into his aunt's driveway as he finished, and all the snakes disappeared. "I'm glad you told me," Eudora had said.

The priest raised up her arms and recited the promise: "And I will refresh you." A few moments later, his aunt left him to go up front and receive communion. She looked almost jaunty, proceeding forward to get what was hers to have.

The choir began the communal hymn. He remembered standing on the glisten the moon made on the snow outside the music building while the girls sang *their* communal hymn.

He watched his aunt put out her hands and take the bread, then the cup. Finished, she stood up from the communion rail, turned around, and came devoutly back. She didn't look any more replete to him than she had before she left, but she sat down on his right, like before, and he was glad for her return. In between her and Eudora to his left, he was safely encompassed again, feeling more hopeful than he had for the longest time, while the choir sang on.

WHEN SYLVIA WOKE up on Monday morning, she didn't know where she was. There was no clue because the shades were drawn, it was entirely dark, and she had no idea where the light switch was. It was frightening in an existential way, the verge of not knowing *who* she was. After what seemed a long time, her memory of all that had occurred to bring her to her aunt's house in Detroit returned and she figured it out, but it was still dark and her panic lingered. So she closed her eyes to control the darkness by making it her own. She lay in that blindness for another moment, marveling that she actually hadn't known where she was in the world, until she heard a door open and footsteps, and her aunt saying, "Up you get, Sylvia," sounding more like a boss on a mission than a loving aunt, and the light went on.

Sylvia sat up and swung her legs off the sofa, relieved to stretch them out, but she sat very still, postponing getting dressed. "You nervous about today?" Aunt M asked. Sylvia nodded. She was eager for the day, but she felt like she did when she was getting up the nerve to dive into the river's cold water for the summer's first swim.

"It's natural." Aunt M pointed at the stove's clock. It was seven in the morning. "We leave in twenty minutes." She gave Sylvia cold cereal and toast. Her own breakfast consisted of two cups of black coffee.

On the way to Aunt M's apartment, they had stopped at a grocery store near the airport and when Sylvia wondered why Aunt M shopped there instead of at a store near where she lived, Aunt M stared at her.

"Oh," Sylvia had said, embarrassed to have been so slow.

"Good. Because you are about to graduate, and I wouldn't give a diploma to anybody who didn't get it. But guess what?" Aunt M had glanced up at the roof of her car as if a new idea were written there. "Maybe we could pressure the city to revoke the permits of the big national groceries to operate in any of the neighborhoods if they don't do in all of them. What do you think of that idea? You could stay on and help me figure it out if you want."

"I can't. You know that. I have to graduate."

"Of course, hon. But what are you doing this summer?"

The question wasn't just about "this summer." Aunt M had really asked, *What are you gonna do with the rest of your life?* "I'll think about it," Sylvia had said. She wasn't prepared to say more.

Now, in the car, driving Sylvia to the school through streets edged with filthy snow left by the plows, past tired-looking single-family houses in various stages of disrepair, some of which were boarded up, Aunt M said, "Don't expect anything to be like what's been planned for the two weeks you're here. You know the old saying, life is what happens when you're planning something else. Just relax and go with whatever happens. Get into it, deep as you can go. You'll be fine." She pointed to the glove compartment. "There's a bus schedule in there for getting yourself home."

Aunt M delivered Sylvia to the school early, before the children arrived. As instructed by her, Sylvia went to the principal's office where the principal's secretary, an almost elderly white woman in a red sweater, greeted her enthusiastically and told her she was assigned to Section C of the third grade. Sylvia walked down a long, dark hall and entered a large classroom. It was decorated with children's work and photographs of notable Black Americans on the walls. But paint was peeling from the ceiling plaster, which sported a brown stain where the roof had leaked, and the windows were streaked with grime. Sylvia wasn't surprised. She'd read plenty of articles about the disrepair of inner-city schools. Nevertheless, it was a shock to be in such a place. It had never occurred to her that buildings where she went to school at Miss O's were actually clean and freshly painted.

"Yes?" the teacher said, a handsome middle-aged Black woman in a navy-blue pantsuit, sitting at a desk in the front.

"I'm Sylvia Bickham."

"And?"

"This is Section C, isn't it?"

"Yes, it is. If you are here to enroll your child, that's not done here. This is where we teach."

"Oh, I didn't come here for that!" Sylvia said, shocked for the second time in as many minutes. "I'm not a mother. I came here to help. I'm here with the project about the buses."

"Buses?"

"You know, the ones they want to park."

"Park?"

"They didn't tell you?"

"Tell me what?"

"I can't believe they didn't tell you."

"Please, just tell me, okay?"

Sylvia explained. When she finished outlining the strategy to defeat the plan by keeping the families well rested and comfortable until it was time, the teacher said, "And you actually think that's going to work? Where do you think they're going to put the buses? Where people don't even *use* them? And anyway, I never heard about your project. I am a substitute teacher. I got the call just this morning. The teacher for this room is sick. She's coming back tomorrow."

"Oh, that explains why you didn't hear about it. My aunt told me stuff like this would happen. But here I am. I want to help."

"But that won't work. With you in the room it would be like *two* subs. I have a routine down for taking over a class of third graders I never have laid eyes on. I actually get a lot done, believe it or not. But if I had to stop and break you in—"

"I'll just watch. By tomorrow I'll know how to help. I can't just turn around and go home."

"I told you, I won't be here tomorrow." The teacher left her desk, went to the blackboard where she wrote *My name is Mrs. Abbott.* Without looking at Sylvia, she said, "Now please, I have to get ready."

Sylvia was surprised by how hurt she was. She didn't even know this woman. "All right, I'll find someone else to help," she said, and turned to leave as the third graders began to pile into the classroom. They came up to her hips, brushing against her on both sides. She felt the warmth of them. Their brown faces, momentarily curious, looked up at hers. "Take your seats, children," Mrs. Abbott said.

Sylvia returned to the principal's office and told the secretary what had happened. "Can you assign me to some other teacher?"

"Who does that Mrs. Abbott think she is, the queen of the universe?" the secretary wanted to know. "You just go back and tell her that you've been assigned to her and that's that."

"I can't do that."

"Yes, you can. You just go back down the hall and tell her."

"I *won't* do that."

The secretary sighed. "You're right. I wouldn't either. The principal will have to assign you to someone else. But he's at a meeting in the district office. He won't be back till eleven."

"But it's only eight-thirty."

The secretary shrugged.

"Why can't *you* assign me?"

"Because I'm not the principal." She pointed to a chair.

Sylvia thought she might call her aunt and ask her to fix the problem. She couldn't remember feeling so unwanted, ignored, useless, and alien. But she'd be embarrassed to have to ask for help. And anyway, Aunt M would tell her to figure it out for herself. So she sat down in the chair, determined to wait, the only way she could think of to fix the problem. She was immediately bored though, staring at the clock on the wall, with nothing else to do, nothing to read. It looked like every clock in every school, even the ones in the classrooms of Miss Oliver's School for girls; they were always the same, she was sure, second hands jerking from one mark to another, round and round all over the world. "The hell with this!" she said, standing up and marching out of the office.

"Where you going?" the secretary called after her.

Sylvia didn't answer. She went down the hall and entered the first classroom she came to.

There were at least thirty children in the room, several years older than the third graders. A huge man bent over a table where four children sat. He was listening intently to what they were telling him. One of the children at the table pointed to Sylvia where she was still standing just inside the door. He looked up and saw her there. He seemed even bigger now that he wasn't bending over. He was bald. A Black man in his forties, in a white shirt and a blue tie and black trousers. "I've been assigned to this room," Sylvia said.

He shot her a doubtful look. "You have?" His voice was deep and rasping.

Sylvia nodded.

He grinned. "Well, come on in then. What's your name?"

"Sylvia Bickham."

"And you are here to do..." He paused, no longer grinning. "What?"

She started to say "to help," then changed her mind. The children were watching her. "Whatever you tell me to do."

"Good. That's the first rule in this classroom. Everybody does exactly what Mr. Carpenter tells them to do." He looked around the classroom. "Now sixth graders, what do we say to Ms. Bickham?"

"Good morning, Ms. Bickham," the children chanted in unison.

"Louder, please."

"GOOD MORNING, MS. BICKHAM!"

"Excellent," Mr. Carpenter said. "Now back to work." He gestured to Sylvia to come to the table of four children where he was still standing.

Sylvia crossed the room. Two boys and two girls looked up at her. She was surprised at how big sixth graders were. Beside her, Mr. Carpenter towered. "Who wants to get Ms. Bickham a chair?" he asked. All four put up a hand. Mr. Carpenter smiled. "Shall we let Charlene?" All four dropped their hands and looked at each other. "Charlene, will you get a chair for Ms. Bickham?" Charlene was tiny, her hair in cornrows. She jumped up and went to a table where one of the chairs was empty and tried to pick it up, but it was too big for her. Sylvia moved to help her. Mr. Carpenter put his huge hand on her elbow and held her back. Charlene pushed the chair across the floor, making a squeaky noise, to where Sylvia was standing. She looked up and smiled at Sylvia.

"Thanks, Charlene," Sylvia said, sitting down in the chair, "but my name is Sylvia."

"No, it isn't," Mr. Carpenter said. "These are *professional* students. Your name is Ms. Bickham. They'll tell you what they are doing. And how you can help." He moved to another table and bent over the children there.

The four sixth graders were silent, their eyes on her, waiting for her to ask what they were doing. Only six years ago she was their age. Her skin was brown too. So why did she feel shy? A square of cardboard was in the center of the table. Placed in the left-hand upper corner of it was a picture of a bottle of Pepsi that had obviously been cut out of an advertisement in a magazine. "What's that?" she said.

"It's science," Charlene said.

"Oh? Can you explain? But first tell me your names."

They each told their names, except Charlene who said proudly, "You already know." Brandon was tall with long arms. Sylvia was tempted to ask him if he played basketball. "I do too," she would have said. Lavinia was a beautiful child, already wearing an assertive look. Sylvia imagined a powerful and glamorous woman ten years from then. Parker wore glasses and was so short, only the top of his chest was above the table.

"We're studying the ingredients," Parker said. "They're written on the bottle."

"Studying?"

"Yeah, what they do to our bodies."

"Like sugar," Charlene said. "See?" She pointed to a composition book. "We're gonna write it all down there."

"Can I see?"

"Got nothing in it yet. We just got started yesterday. Mr. Carpenter gave us the picture of the Pepsi bottle. The other tables got different drinks."

"And you pasted it on the cardboard?"

"Not yet," Brandon said. He put his hand on the picture and slid it around on the cardboard. "We haven't decided where it goes yet. We have to put the statement about what the ingredients do in it too."

"Oh, you're making a poster to show what happens when you drink Pepsi."

They glanced at each other as if she were maybe simpleminded.

"I get it. What a great idea!"

"And we're going to put them up on the bulletin boards in the halls so everybody can see them. But first we're going to talk about them in assembly," Brandon said.

"And then you know what we're going to do?" Lavinia said, leaning forward. "Make an advertisement *for* Pepsi."

"An *advertisement*?"

Lavinia wagged her head up and down. "You know why? So we'll know how advertisements do us."

"Wow!" Sylvia said. "What an amazing project! Tell me how I

can help."

"Maybe when we write the letter?" Parker said.

"Letter?"

"To the boss of Pepsi."

"Oh!"

"We're going to tell him what's in Pepsi," Brandon said.

"And ask him why he doesn't stop," Parker said.

"Maybe you should ask him *when*, not *why*," Sylvia said.

They all looked at each other. "You think?" Charlene said.

"You can decide when you get to that part," Sylvia said.

"Yeah, we have three whole weeks before we get to that part," Lavinia said, pointing to a schedule posted on a bulletin board. "We can wait till then." The three other children turned to see the schedule; they nodded their heads. Then they turned back to face Sylvia.

"You gonna still be with us?" Charlene asked.

They all waited.

"Are you?" Charlene persisted.

"I'm supposed to be here for only two weeks."

"Supposed to be?" Lavinia said. "What's that mean?"

"I have to get back to my own school or I won't graduate."

Lavinia and Brandon glanced at each other and shrugged. The message was clear: they weren't worth three whole weeks of anybody's time. Except Mr. Carpenter's, but he was different. Parker didn't have any reaction at all. Charlene stared at Sylvia. For the rest of the science period, and then all the other periods until the end of day, whenever Sylvia looked up, there were Charlene's eyes on her.

At precisely seven minutes before the three-thirty ending bell, Mr. Carpenter said, "Professionals, its clean-up time. Begin the process." He paused. The children watched him intently. He clapped his hands. "Now!" There was a busy scramble, an orchestrated pandemonium whereby the children cleared everything off the tables, returning each item to its exact and only place. They wiped the tables with rags which they refolded reverently and placed neatly in a drawer at the back of the room. They pushed the chairs in against the tables and stood at attention behind them.

Mr. Carpenter moved to the door. "Ms. Bickham, will you be

here tomorrow?"

"She's gonna stay two weeks," Charlene blurted.

"Charlene, I was speaking to Ms. Bickham."

"Sorry, Mr. Carpenter."

"Charlene's right. I'm staying two weeks," Sylvia said.

"Two weeks." He seemed to be mulling over whether that was too short a time or too long.

"If you want me," Sylvia said.

He smiled. "I've watched you. We do."

The bell rang.

"Table One," Mr. Carpenter said. The four children at the table farthest from the door stood up, marched to the door. He shook each child's hand as they passed him and went out. The pattern repeated itself for seven more tables, emptying the room from the back until the classroom was transmogrified into a hollow space. Mr. Carpenter suddenly looked tired. Or maybe just drained of energy, Sylvia thought. That's different.

He crossed to his desk in the front left corner of the room and folded himself into a chair behind it. "So what do you think?" he said in his dark, rasping voice. "Are we doing all right?"

"Why are you asking me? I don't know anything."

"Yes you do. You went to school."

"I still do. It's different though. It's a prep school. Nobody tells us where to put things. When a class is over, we just walk out."

He made a dismissive gesture with his huge hand and asked his question again. "Are we doing all right?"

"We? I don't know. I've only watched you."

"I know. You were assigned to Mrs. Abbott, but she didn't want your help."

"Oh, you knew."

He smiled. "She never wants help. And you need to practice lying."

She flushed and looked away.

"Mrs. Abbott's a good teacher."

"She is?" she said, still looking away.

"You surprised?"

Sylvia turned to him again "No, I guess not. But she told me she doesn't believe in the anti-bus project."

"Of course not. They could put the buses where she lives, in the suburbs. Would you want that?"

Now she was sure he was mocking her, though gently. It was almost fun.

"So, how are we doing?" he asked for third time. "Are these kids going to make it?"

"They will if all their teachers are like you! Professional students. That's wonderful. And that science project? That's as good as anything we have at our school. It would work just as well for high school kids. I'm going to tell my mother about it."

"Your mother's a science teacher?"

"For just one class. It's all she has time for. She's the head of school."

"Your mom's the head of the school where you go? How's that work?"

"It works okay."

"Really?"

Sylvia shrugged. "Most of the time."

"Well, that's all you can ask for, I suppose." He stood and looked at his watch. "I'm almost late. I tutor in the after-school. You want to come with me?"

Sylvia hesitated. She had planned to go back to her aunt's house and get supper before she went to the gym. She said, "I have to be at the gym by seven to help the kids get organized."

"So do I. I'm in charge."

"That too?"

"Yep. That too."

"Okay, sure," she said, trying to sound eager. "I'd love to help tutor."

"Well, come on, then."

MR. CARPENTER ASSIGNED her to a table of four girls who were doing math in workbooks. Two were doing long division, and the other two converting fractions into decimals. They were sullen with boredom, uncooperative, fidgety, and tired. One look at the workbook format and Sylvia was just as bored as they were. Mr. Carpenter must not have had time yet to design the after-school math program. She planned to ask him about it. She worked hard, though, to help the kids get interested. She failed, struggled on stubbornly, and was enormously relieved when, after an hour, recess began. Out on the playground, which was entirely paved in black cement, not a blade of grass in sight, she broke up a fight between two girls and even persuaded them toward a grudging truce. When recess was over, she was assigned to read to the youngest children. She sat on the floor in a circle with them. One of the little boys kept drowsing off. Sylvia moved across the circle and put the boy's head on her lap and the child put his thumb in his mouth and fell fast asleep. Sylvia felt a rush of tenderness and pride. She knew that Mr. Carpenter would notice.

The after-school program was supposed to end at six, but the last child was picked up at quarter to seven. There'd be no time for supper. She rode to the gym with Mr. Carpenter in his car, a new and shiny Chevy. "It belongs to my wife," he said. "She's a banker. The bank's not far away from where we live. She likes the walk." Then he asked her to tell him about her prep school.

She discovered she didn't want to talk about Miss Oliver's, said only that it's a boarding school for girls, and asked him about his family. "You're very good at the changing the subject. Do they teach that at Miss Oliver's School?" He laughed at his little joke—which surprised her. He didn't seem like the kind of person who ever laughed. He told her about his wife and two boys, one a senior in high school, the other a sophomore at Oberlin.

By the time they arrived at the high school parking lot, it was well after seven. They heard the roar of a crowd and a referee's whistle as they got out of the car. "A basketball game?" Mr. Carpenter said. He and Sylvia ran across the parking lot into the school to discover that the children and their accompanying adults were already there, about a hundred people in the hall outside of the gym, many holding little ones in their arms.

Mr. Carpenter, with Sylvia beside him, moved through the crowd and confronted a very large Black man in a dark suit and red tie who stood in front of the big doors to the gym, blocking the way. "What's happening?" Mr. Carpenter asked him. "We're supposed to—"

"What's happening! You kidding? This is the biggest game of the year."

"But its seven o'clock."

"Yeah, it was supposed to be an away game, but all of a sudden it gets changed to a home game. Why? I'm just the vice principal. What do I know? Ha."

"So we'll use the classrooms."

"You can't do that. You don't have permission."

"Yes we do. You just gave it to us. Remember?"

The vice principal didn't answer, and Mr. Carpenter turned to face the waiting people. "Change of plans, people. Follow me."

He led them to the second floor where, because the lights were out, they milled around in the dark. One of the children started to cry. Sylvia felt along a wall, searching blindly for the light switch while the child's crying became a scream of frustration. "Shh," someone attempted to soothe. The lights came on, someone other than Sylvia having found the switch. The bulbs were dimmed by the dirt covering them, their pallid yellow light revealing a long, tiled, exhausted-looking hall lined with classroom doors. The squares of material forming the ceiling hung down at the corners. No one seemed to notice. Sylvia saw a white-haired woman rock the crying infant in her arms, her long, comely fingers cupping the back of his head. Sylvia felt a rush of tenderness for the second time that day.

Mr. Carpenter's rasping voice sounded over the child's. He asked for two adult volunteers for each of the eight rooms, four on each side of the hall, to move the desks and chairs out of the way. "So the children can sleep on the floor. But, please, before you move anything, memorize where everything is, so we can put everything back right where it was when we leave. I don't want one single teacher to find anything different from the way he or she left it." He paused. "All right?"

The infant's crying had stopped. Every eye was on Mr. Carpenter. People nodded their heads. Sylvia was lifted in a surge of pride for him—and for these people too—as if she'd known them since long before that day.

It took about half an hour to get the children and their accompanying adults into the rooms, the children bedded down on mats on the floor. Many of the adults lay down beside them. Sylvia and Mr. Carpenter each took a side of the hall, popping in and out of the classrooms, assisting wherever assistance was needed. "Just make sure everything is all right," Mr. Carpenter said. He looked at his watch. "About three hours from now we'll get the message that's it time to wake them up and get them across the street to the hearing." After a while, there was no more cheering from the gym. Quiet descended. "It's all good," Mr. Carpenter said. "Go on in to one of the classrooms and take a nap. It's going to be a long night."

Sylvia shook her head. If he was going to stay awake and watch over things, she would too.

At exactly eleven o'clock, Mr. Carpenter's cell phone rang. "Here it is!" he said. "It's time to get the children over there." He pressed the speaker button on his phone and held it up for her to hear.

An agitated male voice yelled over the sound of lots of people talking. "We're screwed, man. Everything's fucked."

"What?" Mr. Carpenter said.

"All the lights are out. Can't see nothing. These motherfuckers are smart, man. I was getting ready to call you 'cause the lawyers' time was about up, and bam, they all go out."

"Well, turn them back on."

No answer from the messenger, just the background noise of angry voices.

"You already tried," Mr. Carpenter said.

"You're lucky you still have lights over there," the man said. "They must have figured you'd take too long to leave and go home if it was dark. Right now, they're telling us the fire department's on its way over here to lead us out. But nobody's waiting. We're using the lights on our phones. We ain't waiting for no fire department."

Mr. Carpenter looked suddenly exhausted. He ended the call and put the phone back in his pocket. "We should have seen this coming."

"What now?" Sylvia asked.

"We get these children home."

"That's it? We give up?"

"Oh no. They have to finish the hearing. They'll move it to some place miles from here. We'll have to organize the transportation."

"My aunt can do that."

"In a heartbeat," Mr. Carpenter said, but he still looked tired. "Now let's wake up these people. You work that side of the hall"—he pointed to his right—"I'll take this. Just say the lights went out. The grown-ups will know why. They won't be surprised. Make sure the kids understand they are still going to have their chance."

He turned and headed for a classroom on his side of the hall. She crossed to her side of the hall, put her hand on the handle of the door to a classroom, wondering why she felt so presumptuous. She was just delivering a message, that's all. She opened the door, walked in, and right away smelled the stuffiness of the air. Why hadn't they opened the windows? Several adults sitting in chairs at the front of the room, looked up at her. One them stood up, an elderly woman still in her overcoat. "Is it time?"

Sylvia shook her head. Several adults who had been lying down with their children stood up. Some of the children stirred in their sleep. How cruel to have to wake them! She gave the message exactly as instructed. As soon as she was finished, she didn't feel presumptuous anymore. She was one of them now.

She made the same announcement in the three other rooms on her side of the hall, and then she helped the children wake up and helped them get their winter clothes back on and all the furniture back in their original places, and when the school was finally empty, Mr. Carpenter drove her to her Aunt M's house. He walked with her to the door of the building and waited there until she was safely in. It was one o'clock in the morning.

TWENTY-SEVEN

It took four days of Aunt M's ferocious insistence to get the city to choose the time and place to continue the hearing. As Mr. Carpenter had predicted, the announced venue was a long distance from the original, and the time appointed was three weeks later. Sylvia was crushed. She wouldn't be there. She'd be back at Miss Oliver's, her two-week suspension completed. She told herself she was making up for that frustration by throwing herself entirely into her work as Mr. Carpenter's aide. But it really wasn't true: she would have done so anyway. Every day Mr. Carpenter gave her a little more responsibility, and at the end of the first week he made her the chief professional consultant not just to the Pepsi study but to all four studies: Coca-Cola, Dr. Pepper, Pepsi, and Mountain Dew.

Her former life began to seem foreign to her, like clothes that didn't fit.

On her last day of the second week, a Friday, two days before her suspension would be completed, Charlene took Sylvia's hand as the class trooped out to recess, and took it again when recess was over and they walked back in. That little palm against Sylvia's larger one, their fingers intertwined, was a palpable gift. When they unclasped and Charlene went to her seat, Sylvia still longed for it. Mr. Carpenter didn't approve of such informality between professionals, but he said nothing, and at the end of the day, he gravely shook Sylvia's same hand and congratulated her for finding her calling: to help kids like his students get the same leg up into the world she'd received at Miss Oliver's School for Girls. His implication was clear: *You have less than half of an academic year remaining to you at that school before you go on to college and finish getting ready for your calling; act like you know how lucky you are.* What would he have said to her if she had told him how she'd risked her place at Miss O's? Would he have approved of the decision not to kick her out? She didn't think so.

The children, especially Charlene, seemed to be sad for Sylvia's leaving, except Lavinia and Brandon, of course, who had known from the beginning they were not worthy of her permanence. When they'd all said goodbye and trooped out past Mr. Carpenter as he stood by the door wishing them a pleasant weekend, Sylvia was already longing for them.

She decided to wait until Sunday afternoon, the very last day of her suspension, to fly home. She wanted another day of Aunt M's company, and she was reluctant to return to Miss Oliver's campus before she was officially reinstated. Maybe she didn't want to return at all.

So on Saturday morning, Sylvia and Aunt M got up when it was still dark and drove north to a cross-country ski area. They arrived midmorning. It was perfect winter weather: blue, cloudless sky, bright sun on gleaming snow, miles and miles of groomed trail. "Don't let me hold you back," Aunt M said. "Go as fast as you want."

Sylvia took off in long, powerful strides. After two whole weeks of no exercise, it was good to breathe deep, to feel sweat coming, muscles loosening. It was also good to be alone. She skied through a pine forest, over the trees' gray shadows on the white snow, through walls of green and the smell of pine sap, then out onto a broad meadow where the sparkle of sun on snow was fiercely bright. She stopped to catch her breath and take in the view as she waited for Aunt M.

In this quiet moment, while she leaned on her ski poles, thoughts of Christopher returned to her with such force that she was in the blizzard again, calling for him through the dark, and then lying on the floor of her and Elizabeth's room, listening to his breathing in her upper bunk. Her work with Mr. Carpenter had pushed Christopher aside. Now that was over, he returned to her mind as unfinished business. Why wasn't she the person who had taken him to Father Woodward's and from there to his aunt's? And why shouldn't she know what was going to happen to him?

Aunt M caught up to Sylvia sooner than expected. Just like when they had skied together to Christopher's lean-to, her aunt impressed her by how easily she kept up. After an hour and a half, they sat on a bench beside the trail and ate their lunches. "This is perfect!" Aunt M said, raising her face to the sun. Sylvia agreed that it was. But it wasn't: her apology to the school on Monday loomed.

Then came Sunday morning. Aunt M took Sylvia to a late breakfast at Connie and Barbara's, her favorite soul food place in West Detroit, where they both had the salmon croquettes, scrambled eggs, and rice "because that's what I always eat here," Aunt M said. She went on to repeat her promise to take Christopher from his aunt's house when he was ready, back to the VA where that savvy woman would take him under her wing again. "You should absolutely take a day off from school and come with us."

"It's like you're reading my mind," Sylvia said, wondering if she'd be able to think about anything else while she waited for that day.

Later, at the airport curb, just as Sylvia was about to get out of the car, Aunt M said, "I've been talking to Mr. Carpenter. I hope you don't mind."

"I don't mind at all."

"You did well, hon. Very well indeed."

"I know."

"You proud?"

"Yes!"

Aunt M smiled, and they got out of the car. "Good luck tomorrow. I know you'll do the right thing," she said, reaching out her arms. Sylvia stepped into the hug. "Whatever that is," Aunt M added, then turned away and got back in her car. Sylvia watched her drive away. She wished she could have seen Aunt M's face when she said, "Whatever that is." But their two faces were side by side.

"I'm here," Sylvia said, her phone held up to her ear. Her parents were waiting for her in the Bradley Airport cell phone parking lot.

"Wonderful! We'll be there in a sec," her father said. She wished she could be as happy as he was that she was home again. She didn't feel like a person returning to her home. Home was where you went when the school suspended you.

She waited at the curb by baggage claim. It was a bright, sunny day that, except for the smell of car exhaust, felt like spring, even though it was only February. Several cars approached that she was sure were her father's BMW, but each went right on by, driven by a stranger. After what seemed forever, she saw him through the windshield of a car she didn't recognize. He was waving at her and blowing the horn. Of course he wouldn't have his company car. He'd sold it when he sold Best Sports. Had he sold his New York City apartment yet? Or would he ever? This news that she wasn't the only person in the family who was changing, coming at her now, as if she hadn't known the fact of it before, unsettled her even more. Everything was changing all at once.

The car pulled up to the curb. Elizabeth was in the backseat, her plane from Oklahoma having arrived a few minutes earlier. Their eyes met and Elizabeth's expression lighted up. She would stay at the Head's House tonight rather than the dorm for the same reason Sylvia would: her suspension wasn't over yet—not until tomorrow morning when they would apologize.

Her mother got out of the car and put out her hands for a hug. Sylvia responded with a tiny squeeze.

"What's wrong?"

"Nothing, Mom."

"Well, hop in," her mother said, sounding distracted too.

Sylvia's father came around the car, and Sylvia stepped into his arms and hugged him hard. He grabbed her backpack and threw it into the trunk of the car, and he jumped back into the driver's seat.

Sylvia got in the back. The two girls hugged. Sylvia's father started to drive. "It's so great to have you two with us again!"

Sylvia hardly heard him. She was taking note of the snow piled on the sides of the road, sprinkled with twigs and pine needles fallen from trees, and remembering the snow in Detroit, sprinkled black with what had fallen from the air.

"How was Aunt M?" her father asked, glancing at Sylvia in the rearview mirror.

"Fine, Dad."

"Did you have a good time? Was it interesting?"

"Bob! Give her a moment to breathe," her mom said. "She just got home."

He turned his head to her, frowned, then turned forward again.

She stared straight ahead too.

"How come nobody around here wants to talk about anything?" he said. "Don't you like clarity? All I want is a clear picture of what it was like for Sylvia in Detroit. What's wrong with that?"

"Bob, all I said was give her time to breathe."

Sylvia nudged Elizabeth's hip. "Say something," she whispered.

"I had a great time, as a matter of fact," Elizabeth announced.

Sylvia nudged her again.

So Elizabeth, speaking very fast, told how she wrote three whole drafts of her history paper which she'd been able to finish early because of all the free time she'd had with no classes to go to and her parents both at work. Sylvia knew she was just making stuff up to soothe the tension in the car—and also because it's fun to bullshit parents every once in a while. Hers were in Oklahoma, she couldn't bullshit them. Elizabeth never even did a *second* draft. She always got it right the first time, which was practically against the rules. She always said that she did two or three, to keep the teachers happy. And she always got an A. She was still talking when the car pulled into the Head's House driveway.

And Elizabeth did the same thing at dinner that evening, managing to get Sylvia's dad to tell the whole history of Best Sports, from his founding to his decision to sell it. The lights were low, candles flickered, a vase full of flowers centered the table to welcome the two girls' home, and Elizabeth asked just the right questions. Sylvia was well aware she could learn new things about her father, know him better, if she were not so distracted, but she hardly heard a word. When dinner was almost over and his story finished, he congratulated Elizabeth. "I understand," he added. "Nobody wants to talk about tomorrow until it's all done and everything's back to normal." He looked down the table, "Right, Rach?"

"It seems that way," she said.

"Except for me," he said. He looked first to his right at Elizabeth, and then his left at Sylvia. "What I want to know now is, are you two ready for tomorrow? Because it will be hard, won't it? Would be for me."

"You should ask if we are *willing*," Elizabeth said. "That's different."

He looked hard at her. "You're right, Elizabeth. As usual. Willing. That's what my question should have been."

"Well, the answer is yes. And by ten o'clock tomorrow, I'll be ready."

"To get it over with?"

"That's it. Just get it over with and move on."

"You sound a little bitter."

"I *am* a little bitter."

"Well, you sound very matter-of-fact about being bitter."

"I am very matter-of-fact about it. It's just the way it is, that's all."

He turned to Sylvia. "And what about you?"

"I'm ready."

"And willing?"

Sylvia shook her head. "Just ready."

He glanced down the table at his wife.

She shook her head and said nothing.

Sylvia stood up then and began to clear the table. Mr. Carpenter had told her to act like she knew how lucky she was to be getting ready for her calling by finishing at Miss Oliver's and going to college. That's what she was doing: acting like she knew how lucky she was. That's why she would apologize tomorrow.

TWENTY-EIGHT

Elizabeth and Sylvia waited until just before ten the next morning to start crossing the campus, so that everybody would have already arrived at the auditorium, thus reducing the time they would have to endure the fascination they brought everyone at Miss O's, including the faculty. "We have created a paparazzi all our own," Elizabeth said. "Here we are, headed toward our re-initiation ceremony," she added, bathing the term in acid, "to be watched on our way, let alone talked to. That would be torture."

When they were a hundred yards away from the doors, Elizabeth said, "Since you're not willing and I am, would you lower yourself enough to nod your head while I apologize for both of us?"

Sylvia stopped walking, so Elizabeth did too. "Really?" Sylvia said. "You'd—"

Elizabeth shrugged. "Why not?"

"Oh! Yeah, I suppose? All right. Thanks!"

"Don't mention it," Elizabeth said in her most ironic tone.

"You sure?"

"I just said I was. Come on, let's get it over with."

At one minute before ten, Elizabeth and Sylvia climbed the steps up to the big auditorium doors, already hearing the silence. They paused, glancing at each other. Getting there late wasn't going to work. Everybody was waiting for their entrance, too focused on the impending drama to make the usual buzz of many conversations.

Elizabeth sighed and walked through the doors. Sylvia followed a half step behind. Some heads were already turned to catch their entrance. Gregory van Buren sent a small smile to the two girls as they passed where he was sitting, right next to the aisle. His smile seemed to say, *Hang on, it's almost over.*

Sylvia looked past everybody to the stage up front. She followed Elizabeth up the aisle toward the nearly empty front row as the auditorium grew even quieter. Better to sit there than toward the back and have to walk all the way up to the stage when they were called. Sylvia wondered where her mother was sitting. Elizabeth took the second from the aisle seat in the front row. Sylvia sat in the aisle one. Both girls were aware of the door across the aisle from them to their right. Above it in lighted green letters: *EMERGENCY EXIT.*

Mary Callahan, the student in charge of Morning Meeting that week, stood up from her seat on Elizabeth's and Sylvia's left in the front row and climbed the steps up to the stage. She was dressed for winter in a red sweater and jeans, so different, Sylvia remembered, from the crop top and sandals she had worn when she stared through dark glasses at a homeless man in September and looked away as soon as he looked at her. "Any announcements?" Mary looked straight at Elizabeth and Sylvia.

Sylvia turned her head away to her right. She kept her eyes there, tempted by the emergency exit, until Elizabeth's legs brushed against her knees. Then she stood up too and followed Elizabeth.

Up on the stage, it was exactly as she had imagined: all those eyes staring. She looked for her mother and found her all the way in the back, sending her a private gaze across that very public space that seemed to be asking a question, and Sylvia realized that her mother didn't know whether her own daughter was going to apologize, or not. *I said I was ready*, she thought. *Wasn't that enough?*

Beside her, she heard Elizabeth say in a monotone, "We apologize for stealing." Sylvia turned to Elizabeth and nodded her head as she had promised. Then, already moving toward the steps down from the stage, and speaking slowly and clearly, raising her voice, still in monotone, Elizabeth said, "and for bringing a man into the dorm so he wouldn't freeze to death." She continued toward the steps, mission accomplished.

Sylvia started to follow Elizabeth. It was that easy? Really? For the first several steps she felt light, unburdened. It was over! Then suddenly heavy with a vague dissatisfaction.

"Wait!" Gregory van Buren stood up from his seat.

Sylvia and Elizabeth stopped walking.

Gregory walked up the aisle toward them in his blue blazer. He stopped at the foot of the stage and looked up at them.

"Two things," Gregory said loudly for everyone to hear. "First, you need to say those words in a different tone of voice. Second, you need to be more precise as to where in the dorm you allowed that man."

"Why?" Elizabeth challenged.

"You know why, Elizabeth. So does everybody in this auditorium. Don't pretend you don't."

"I'll say it then," Sylvia blurted, to save the day. Besides, Gregory was right: it shouldn't be so easy. "We apologize for stealing."

"And?"

"For bringing the man into our room."

Gregory nodded, apparently satisfied. "Thank you, Sylvia."

To Sylvia's left, Elizabeth took one more step down from the stage.

"Would you tell us the man's name, Sylvia?" Gregory asked.

"What?"

"We all have names, Sylvia. What was his?"

"Christopher."

"Christopher," Gregory repeated. He turned his head to the audience. "A real person, with a name, like you and me." He turned back to Sylvia. "And why did you and Elizabeth bring him into your room?"

"So he'd be warm, obviously," Elizabeth said, halfway down the steps. "Why else?"

Gregory nodded, unperturbed. "A good reason—for both transgressions. There was a blizzard outside on the night you brought him into your room, if I remember correctly."

"That's right," Sylvia said, raising her voice. She was catching on.

"Was there a reason for giving him your bunk?"

"So he wouldn't be found," Sylvia said, slowly and clearly, and even a little bit louder. "So he'd be safe."

"Of course. Behind the curtain. And where did *you* sleep?"

"On the floor, at first."

"At first? Then where?"

"In my bunk."

"With him?"

Sylvia paused.

The audience waited.

Sylvia glanced at Elizabeth.

Elizabeth shrugged.

Yeah, who cares, Sylvia thought. She turned her face from Gregory to all those staring, fascinated eyes, feeling a sudden and unwanted pulse of contempt. Maybe she would make up a story, tell them she'd had sex with Christopher. Describe it in detail. That would give them something really to be fascinated by.

"Sylvia?" Gregory said.

"Yes, with him," she said, pushing the temptation aside, determined to help Gregory out. "I got in my bunk with Christopher."

"To keep him quiet?"

"Yes, he was crying out," Sylvia said, still facing the audience.

"Crying out?"

"I put my arms around him and he stopped."

"And then what happened?"

"We both went to sleep."

Gregory waited, letting that sink in, while he and Sylvia looked across all the faces to her mother's in the back. Her mother nodded her head: her daughter would never lie to her.

Gregory moved on then and asked, "When did you wake up?"

"In the morning."

"In the morning," Gregory repeated.

"Yes. I woke up and he was still asleep, and he looked so peaceful I didn't want to wake him up, and then Eudora came in and caught us."

"If you had woken him, could you have hidden him from Eudora?"

"Maybe."

Gregory was silent. It was clear to everyone he was giving Sylvia a chance to change *maybe* to *yes*. Then, seeming relieved—even happy—that she had not, he said, "Is there anything else I should ask?"

"No. That's all there is."

"Good." He turned to Elizabeth, still halfway down from the stage. "Have Sylvia and I covered everything, Elizabeth?"

"Yes. Everything," Elizabeth said, loud and clear, and not combative anymore. She leaned forward, ready to go the rest of the way down.

Gregory nodded again. "Well, then, thank you both."

He turned to the audience and drew in a big breath and everyone knew he was going to explain, wisely and justly, though in ponderous syntax, what they already understood—and were grateful to him for. "I hope we all understand that the reason I have invaded the privacy of these two by asking them so many questions was not only to protect their reputations by clarifying what actually happened, and what did not—I emphasize, *what did not*—but, equally important, to reveal their kindness, empathy, and compassion extended to a fellow human being when it was most needed as the reason for their continued inclusion in our community, after the apology you have just heard, as opposed to their being expelled." He'd run out of breath, so he took another. "I hope you find this a satisfying conclusion to this event so that we can all move on."

There was an instant of silence, then a collective sigh, and then applause began. Gregory turned his face up to Sylvia and Elizabeth. "Welcome back, ladies," he said, raising his voice. "You are now reinstated."

But Elizabeth was turning around, climbing back up the steps as the applause continued. She moved past Sylvia and shoved Mary Callahan aside.

"There's more, there's more!" Elizabeth shouted over the applause. "You don't know the half of it."

The applause stopped.

"Kindness and empathy?" Elizabeth shouted. "You think that was all? You think Christopher came to us? He knocked on our door? We said, 'Oh you look cold, come on in.' Do you? Is that what you think? No, Sylvia went way out there where he was wandering around at the edge of the woods and rescued him. He was lost. He would have died. Remember how cold it was? How hard the wind was blowing?" She paused again. "How many of you would have done that? Raise your hands. Come on, raise your effing hands!"

"Elizabeth, be careful," Gregory van Buren said.

"Shut up, Gregory! Just shut up and listen for a change, okay? I'm talking, you're not." Elizabeth turned back to the audience. "That's right, she saved his life. He was dying of hypothermia. Hypothermia! He had about another minute and he'd be dead. But that girl there," turning and pointing to Sylvia, "she found him. In the pitch dark. Anybody else would have gotten lost. No one else would have dared. She could have died. And then she led him back. She found the way. The wind had been at her back on the way out; so she kept her face straight into it on the way home. Do you understand how hard that is?"

Mary Callahan turned to Sylvia. "Maybe you *shouldn't* have apologized," she blurted. Her hand flew to her mouth.

"I know, I shouldn't have," Sylvia said, sounding surprised.

Silence. Everyone waited.

"I'm not sorry for what I did," Sylvia said. "So how can I apologize?"

Another silence. Elizabeth stared at Sylvia.

"Be careful, Sylvia," Gregory said. "Think hard."

"I don't apologize. I can't and I won't."

"You're retracting?"

"I am," Sylvia said, instantly feeling the clarity.

Gregory's face fell. "And you, Elizabeth?"

Elizabeth turned to Sylvia.

Sylvia shook her head.

Elizabeth turned back to Gregory. "No, I don't retract."

Gregory nodded and soldiered on. "And you feel that's right?"

"I don't have to answer that. How I feel is nobody's business but my own," Elizabeth said, and burst into tears.

Sylvia watched her mother stand up and cross the small space to the doors in the back and push one of them open. There was the gleam of sun on snow, then the door closed again, her mother was gone, and in the enormous silence in which the only sound was Elizabeth's sobs, Sylvia also fled, crossing the stage, going down the steps, leaving Elizabeth on the stage.

At the emergency exit door, Sylvia looked back over her shoulder at Elizabeth. Elizabeth stared back, still sobbing. "Why?" she called across the space. Sylvia burst out into the glare of the sun on the snow.

The siren screamed. She'd forgotten all about it! It went on and on and on and on.

TWENTY-NINE

The alumnae of Miss Oliver's School for Girls who were in attendance at that famous Morning Meeting can still call up the sound of that siren. And some who'd graduated long before had heard about it so often, described so vividly, they felt as if they, too, remembered the moment when Gregory van Buren's performance was suddenly rendered absurd. Everybody had seen Sylvia rush out through that door. A fire hadn't started. A bomb had not been planted by an angry employee. Everyone just sat there, some with hands over their ears, waiting for someone to do something about it.

And finally someone did: a freshwoman, one of the youngest members of the community, who hadn't paid much attention to the proceedings on the stage because she was doing her math homework due the next period, strolled up the aisle and closed the door, and the siren stopped. In the silence, she looked quizzically around at all the people in their seats, and then returned to hers.

And in all the endless conversations, no one criticized Gregory van Buren for letting Mary Callahan proceed to the next thing on the agenda, as if nothing had happened. What was he supposed to do, rush out through the emergency door, setting off the siren again, and drag Sylvia back in so he could beg her to retract her retraction?

RACHEL HADN'T THOUGHT about fleeing. She'd just run.

And here she was, standing perfectly still, the glare of sun on snow so bright it hurt her eyes, thinking, *I should go back in and rescue everyone.* Then a siren went off and here came Sylvia, out the side door, fleeing too, not thinking either.

They rushed toward each other, legs sinking to their knees in snow, and embraced, holding tight, swaying together. "Why didn't you tell us?" Rachel said.

The siren stopped. There was the sound of a truck downshifting on a hill, miles away.

"Well, anyway, now you know," Sylvia said. Then they crossed to a cleared path and headed together toward the Head's House.

"Your father will be so proud of you!" Rachel said.

"SO PROUD I'M about to burst!" he said in the Little Room when Rachel finished telling him how brave their daughter was. He jumped up from his chair and almost tripped on the rug crossing the room to hug Sylvia where she was still standing shyly. He'd stayed home, waiting for a call from Rachel to tell him that yes, Sylvia and Elizabeth had apologized and everything was back on track, but the minute his daughter and his wife appeared in the doorway together, he guessed that had not happened.

"You would have done the same, Dad," Sylvia said, still in his embrace. "You wouldn't have just let him stay out there and freeze."

He stepped back and glanced at Rachel. "Yeah, I would have called 911. By the time anything happened, the guy out there in the woods would be dead." He turned to Sylvia. "But *you* went out there! Jesus!" His face was flushed. His voice quivered. There were tears in his eyes. Sylvia stared. The last time she'd seen him cry was when Sylvia's grandfather died, her mother's father. Her dad just let go, shoulders shaking, his head in his hands, a grievous wailing.

This time though, he contained his weeping. You can only cry so long about a loss that didn't actually happen, and tears of pride are very different from tears of grief. By the time he'd returned to his chair, flopping back down into it, no trace of tears remained, only the flush on his face. "Of course it was *wrong* to apologize," he said. "Everybody knew it was *wrong*. But just the same—"

"You would have retracted, Dad. You might not even have apologized in the first place, like I did."

"Here we go again," he said.

"Would you have?" Rachel asked him.

"Apologized?" He nodded. "Yes, I would. So I could graduate."

"So would I," Rachel said.

"Like Elizabeth did," he said. "I'm glad for her."

"And me, Dad?"

He shook his head. "No. Not glad. How could I be? But proud. That's better."

THEY ATE LUNCH together on trays in the Little Room—the first time Sylvia remembered her mother eating lunch on a weekday during the school year at the Head's House rather than the dining hall. As they finished, her dad said, "I guess this means you're going to leave us again and go live with your aunt?" He sounded resigned.

Sylvia just nodded her head.

"She knew everything all along, didn't she?" he said. "What you and Elizabeth were doing all these months? I get it. I understand. At least, I think I do. Still, it hurts." He glanced at Rachel, but she just looked back at him and said nothing. Surprised, he turned to Sylvia again. "Speaking of your aunt, she called this morning. Said she has some news for you about your homeless man. She said you won't be surprised. Something tells me she won't be surprised when you tell her yours."

"I'll call her now," Sylvia said, standing to leave. Both her parents glanced at her back pocket where she always kept her cell phone—as if to say, *Why not call her right here?*—then quickly away.

"Don't worry," she heard her dad murmur as she started to close the door behind herself. "There'll come a time when we'll all tell each other everything, won't we, Rach?"

Sylvia closed the door before her mother answered. She knew her mother's answer was a yes. She wasn't really surprised that her parents had known something all along, and trusted her enough to refrain from asking the rest. She stood still for a second, overwhelmed by love and gratitude. Then she went upstairs to her bedroom and called Aunt M.

"CAN YOU GET off school tomorrow?" Aunt M asked.

"Easily," Sylvia replied.

"Easily? You'd think a school that charges what that school does would make it hard to skip a whole day."

"Yeah, you'd think so, I guess. So, Christopher's ready?"

"Yes, his aunt called me. I didn't need to tell her you'd be in the car too when we take him to the VA. She beat me to it. She's going to stay home and let us take him. She's going to have lots of time with him and you won't."

"She said that?"

"Yup. She figures you'll want to say goodbye to each other without her around. So I'll fly tomorrow morning, rent a car at the airport, and pick you up at your dorm and we'll go straight to his aunt's house and get him to the VA. She's right, you know. You started it all."

"Actually, Elizabeth started it, Aunt M. And don't pick me up at the dorm."

"Starting isn't what counts. It's finishing," Aunt M said. "What? Not at the dorm?"

"No, not at the dorm."

"Oh? Where? The Head's House?"

"Yes."

"Why? Don't tell me you—"

"That's right. My dad said you wouldn't be surprised."

"So you *didn't* apologize?"

"I did, but then I retracted it."

"You did! Well, I'll be. What did your mother say?"

"She said she was proud that I went out and saved Christopher."

"You did what?"

"I went out and found him and brought him back."

"He didn't just come asking to be let in? You went out there in that storm? Why didn't you tell us?"

"I don't know. I just didn't."

"Well, I'll be," Aunt M said again. "You glad you retracted?"

"I'll see you tomorrow, Aunt M," Sylvia said, and hung up the phone.

SYLVIA SPENT THE rest of the afternoon and evening waiting for a visit from Elizabeth. Elizabeth would understand why Sylvia couldn't come to the dorm: she'd be the object of everyone's curiosity. But Elizabeth didn't come. Sylvia went to bed remembering looking back just before she escaped through the emergency exit and seeing the look of shock and abandonment on Elizabeth's weeping face. She might as well have yelled, *Don't leave me!* That image played and replayed all night long. Sylvia hardly slept.

IN THE MORNING, Sylvia's parents suggested that the least painful way for Sylvia to separate from the school would be for her mother to announce an open house for goodbyes at the Head's House that evening. There would be good munchies. Sylvia had thought she would return for graduation and say goodbye then, but her dad pointed out that she might not want to when the time came. "I don't think you will enjoy sitting in the audience watching everybody get a diploma while you don't."

"And Auda's arriving today. She'll be at the party," her mom said. "Everybody will want to greet her. That will take some of the focus off you. Besides, you don't want to just sneak away."

So Sylvia agreed.

Would Elizabeth come?

A FEW MINUTES later, Sylvia looked out the kitchen window for her aunt's rented car to appear in the driveway. Instead, she saw Elizabeth walk among a group of girls across the campus to their next class in a drizzle of rain that, landing on snow, caused a mist to rise, and Sylvia was flooded with sadness and regret. She watched Elizabeth to see if she would turn her head toward the Head's House, but Elizabeth hurried on and disappeared into the Science Building. *If she doesn't come to my going-away party tonight, I'll go find her and we'll talk*, Sylvia decided. No way was she going to leave without telling her best friend she didn't mean to abandon her. They'd explain things to each other. They'd be friends forever.

Just then, Aunt M drove into the driveway.

THE LAST TIME they'd made this trip, it had been raining too, as if certain kinds of weather were always assigned to certain kinds of errands. Aunt M turned the windshield wipers up a notch as the rain increased and the pure white snow on the lawns in Fieldington turned to mush. They passed Rose's Creamery, bedraggled in the rain, and the corner where they'd first met Christopher. "Aren't you glad Christopher isn't in his lean-to in all this?" Aunt M said.

"No," Sylvia said. "He'd be dry in there. He knows how to weave the branches tight." She was proud of him for that and visualized him sitting in the lean-to, up straight like a meditating Buddha in a black down jacket, listening to the purr of the rain and the burble of the river. Did he know she was coming for him now? "It's not winter, it's black fly season; that's the hardest time to live outdoors," she said, wondering why she wanted so much her aunt to know, "and after that, the second hardest is June and July when the mosquitoes are the worst."

"Well, you're the expert. But winter or summer, our job is to make sure he never has to live in that lean-to again."

"Right!" Sylvia said.

That morning, Sylvia had dressed for this occasion first in a wool skirt over black tights and a light blue sweater. Then she had changed her mind and put on what she was wearing now: jeans and her L.L. Bean boots and a red-and-black checkered lumberjack shirt. What would he be wearing? What could they possibly say to each other? Which look would he have on his face: the serene one she'd woken up to in her bed, or that lost, haggard, crazed one that, though she was sure he would never hurt her, scared her nevertheless?

A few minutes later, when they climbed the steps of the porch of Christopher's aunt's house, the front door opened before they rang the bell and Christopher's aunt was framed in the doorway. Around her eyes she looked just like Christopher. Her gaze went first to Aunt M and then to Sylvia. She looked surprised. "So *you're* the one."

"She is," Aunt M said.

Christopher's aunt stood up on her tiptoes and put out her arms. Sylvia hesitated for an instant, then stepped into the embrace. His aunt's arms were bony and thin as they squeezed her tight. "Thank you for what you did," she said.

"You're welcome," Sylvia replied, embarrassed that she couldn't think of anything more appropriate to say. She stepped back out of the hug and her eyes wandered, seeking Christopher. His aunt took her hand and led her into the living room. Aunt M followed closely behind.

Christopher stood up from a chair that was facing the other way and turned around. He was wearing a brown suit with a white shirt and red tie. He'd grown a small tidy beard, blond, like his hair, which didn't come down to his shoulders anymore, his face was fuller, and his shoes were polished.

"Say hello to Sylvia," his aunt said.

"Hello, Sylvia." He spoke so slowly she could tell he had tranquilizers in him.

"Hello. You ready to go?"

"I am," he said, and she could tell, even in his haze, he was glad to see her.

His aunt opened the hall closet door and took out an overcoat. "Don't forget this," she said, "it's cold outside," and held the overcoat open for him to put his arms through the sleeves. When he had it on, she patted his shoulders. The coat was a handsome gray, brand new, an ivy-league cut. It wasn't lost on Sylvia how different it was from the down jacket she'd stolen for him. He looked like a young businessman in it, or maybe a professor. "Now you're ready," his aunt said, and moved to the front door, opening it, gesturing them out.

Outside in the driveway, Christopher headed for the backseat of Aunt M's car, but Aunt M put her hand on his elbow "No, sit up front with me." Sylvia got in the back. "Put your seatbelt on," Aunt M said. She waited to start the car. A second or two went by before Sylvia realized Aunt M was talking to her. Christopher had put his on without being reminded.

For most of the drive, Sylvia stared at the back of Christopher's shoulders, trying to think of the right thing to say. She didn't want to make small talk. She wanted to ask him what his plans were, what he hoped for, but he seemed too drugged to tell. It seemed forever before they arrived at the Newington VA building. Aunt M drove straight to the entrance marked *MAINTENANCE.*

The elderly white men in baseball caps were sitting there again, as if permanently enthroned. This time they looked even more interested as the two women walked in with Christopher between them and Dorothy got up from the information desk and came out to greet them, wearing the same brown suit she'd worn before. She took Christopher's right hand in both of hers, held it for a moment. "I've been waiting for you." She led him down a hall. He looked back over his shoulder at Sylvia and her aunt, and disappeared around a corner, surprising Sylvia by the likeness of the moment to all those times she'd watched new girls delivered to the campus for the first time, looking back over their shoulder to watch their parents drive away. Sylvia and her aunt took chairs at the end of the row of baseball caps to wait. The man next to Sylvia smelled of cigarette smoke. He had an artificial left hand. It looked like a robot's claw. He rested it on his knee right next to Sylvia's. She stared straight ahead, away from it.

Only an hour later, Christopher emerged carrying in a big folder the papers for his restarting at Southern Connecticut State U under the GI Bill. Dorothy must have eased the way. And whatever drugs he was taking seemed to be working. He was calm, but no longer in a haze. Sylvia thought that maybe, with the drugs inside him, he'd succeed at college this second try.

The sun was coming out on the drive back to his aunt's house. Christopher, reviving more each moment, spoke of his plans to study retailing and to borrow some money from his aunt to open a store in a place called Saranac. "To sell canoes," he said, "and kayaks, fishing equipment, tents, sleeping bags, hiking boots." He listed everything that anybody who loved the outdoors could ever want—except guns. "No guns," he repeated. "No guns, ever." He'd have one of those signs that reserved the right to refuse service to anyone he didn't want to serve: people who wore camouflage suits and talked too loudly and never looked at the view and couldn't light a fire and got drunk in the evenings at campsites. "They can go to Walmart," he said, turning to smile at Sylvia in the backseat. He would think of a name for the store that honored his Uncle Ray. He began to tell stories about Uncle Ray, mostly funny ones, in spite of his elegiac tone that sounded to Sylvia as if he were saying goodbye to her too, the distance between them of age and condition—and what he had lived through—too far to travel. He ended with the story of how his

Uncle Ray died while looking at his favorite view.

"How about calling the store Uncle Ray's Outdoors?" Sylvia said. "Something direct and simple like that to honor him."

"You think so?"

"I do."

"All right, if that's what you think I should name it, that's what I'll name it. Uncle Ray's Outdoors."

"Thank you," Sylvia said, utterly inadequate words for the pulse of joy she felt. They were silent the rest of the way. There was nothing more to say.

Except goodbye, a few minutes later on the front porch of his aunt's house, where they hugged each other, shyly.

SYLVIA WAS GRATEFUL—AND not at all surprised—that her aunt knew enough not to say anything on the drive back to school. Nor was she surprised, when, about halfway there, her aunt took her right hand off the steering wheel and patted Sylvia's left knee twice before returning her hand to the steering wheel, all the time staring straight ahead.

A few minutes later, when Aunt M turned the car into the head's house driveway, Sylvia exited reluctantly. She wanted to continue the silence she and her aunt had shared, not go to a party, especially one in which she was the center. Would Elizabeth come?

As she walked toward the front door, it swung open and Auda Hellmann stood on the steps, hands on hips, frowning, looking even smaller than Sylvia remembered, her hair even redder. "I've been watching out the window for you to get back. I wanted to be the first to tell you how crazy you are." She ran down the steps and hugged Sylvia. "You could have graduated and *then* made your point," she said as Aunt M came up to them. Auda released Sylvia from her hug. "This must be your aunt."

"It is. She's crazy too, by the way," Sylvia said.

"It runs in the family," Aunt M said. "Call me Aunt M. And you must be Auda. I've heard good things about you."

Auda, looking slightly surprised, and very pleased, glanced at Sylvia.

"Oh yes!" Aunt M said. "Very good things." Then, pointing into the house: "Has the party started?"

"Yes. Everybody's in the big room."

"Well, go on in, Sylvia. I'll go upstairs and get out of the way."

THERE WAS THE noise of many conversations as Sylvia and Auda entered the house, but when they entered the big room, everybody turned to them and the air went silent. There were about thirty girls, all standing up, like at one of her mother's fundraiser cocktail parties. Sylvia felt Auda's hand on her elbow as if Auda were presenting her as an interesting specimen to a curious audience. One of the girls started to clap; several joined, tentatively. "Oh please! Don't!" Sylvia said. The clapping stopped. The room was silent again. Nobody seemed to know how to act. Brown boxes of pizza, exuding their greasy smell, were piled on a counter, waiting to be opened.

Sylvia was glad her parents had the good sense not to be present. Especially her mother. She imagined them sitting on the sofa in the Little Room, waiting for this to be over. They'd make a quick appearance near the end.

But where was Elizabeth? Sylvia roamed her eyes around, and finally found her talking to a group of girls, way across the room. Their eyes met. Elizabeth turned away. Sylvia crossed the room to her. Nobody seemed insulted that she didn't stop and talk to them on the way.

One of the girls talking to Elizabeth saw Sylvia approaching. She said something to Elizabeth and then drifted away. The other girls followed, leaving Elizabeth by herself, her back to Sylvia. Knowing that everybody in the room was sneaking glances, Sylvia was embarrassed by all this unwanted attention and that made her angry at Elizabeth, to whom until a second ago she'd wanted to apologize. She took another step toward Elizabeth and in a perfect imitation of her sarcasm whispered, "You can turn around now."

Elizabeth whirled around. "Where did it say what kind of tone of voice was required—or how precise?"

"Huh?" Sylvia stepped back.

"Where did it say?" Elizabeth asked again. "That's what I would have asked him. He would have had to sit down and shut up for once. And don't tell me you *had* to retract. You just wanted to. We were in this together! We had a deal. I'd apologize. You'd nod your head. That was all there was to it."

"I didn't plan it," Sylvia said. "And I *did* have to retract."

"No you didn't."

"What do you mean, I didn't?"

"Just what I said. Do you really think it was easy for me *not* to retract? You made me have to choose between us staying together and me graduating. All of a sudden we weren't partners after all. No, we were each on our own. Right there in an instant. You completely changed the rules just so you could keep yourself nice and pure and feel good about yourself," Elizabeth said. "So let's just get this ridiculous party over with, okay?"

"That's it?"

Elizabeth nodded. "That's it."

"All right, let's," Sylvia said, crestfallen. "But thanks for coming."

Elizabeth shrugged.

"Really," Sylvia said. "I mean it. Thanks."

"How else was I going to say goodbye?" Elizabeth said, her lip quivering. "I knew you wouldn't come to the dorm." She stepped abruptly away from Sylvia and headed for the counter where the boxes of pizza were piled.

Sylvia joined Elizabeth behind the counter, a kind of protective wall between them and everybody else in the room, and they became partner hostesses, serving the pizza in spite of the hurt between them. No one seemed to know what to say to them. Neither of them was in the mood to help them out. So they hardly said anything at all. And to those who wanted to know why she had quit the school, Sylvia answered that she hadn't, she had retracted an apology—an answer she knew was as perverse as it was indirect. To those who said they admired her and Elizabeth for doing what was only right to help the homeless guy, she and Elizabeth said almost nothing.

After a while Bob and Rachel made their appearance. "Hello, everybody," Rachel said. "Thank you so much for coming. I know you all wanted to say goodbye to Sylvia—and she to you." Next to her, trying not to look sad, Bob nodded his head, and turned to leave.

Rachel turned too, a second later.

"But, Rachel, there's something I don't understand," Auda said, speaking very loudly.

"Only one, Auda?" Rachel said. "You're way ahead of me."

"Yes, only one. You want to hear it?"

Rachel smiled. Everybody could see she wasn't worried. She'd been doing this job for twenty years. Nothing phased her anymore.

"Well, do you?"

"Fire away, Auda."

"All right, it's this. How do you explain kicking someone out for providing shelter in the dorm to a homeless person?"

"Leave my mother out of this, Auda," Sylvia said. "I knew what I was doing."

"Leave her out? Are you kidding? She's the head of school."

"You're right, Auda. I am. And your question is a good one," Rachel said. "But you know the answer as well as I. So I invite you to answer it."

"Well, I'm not going to. It would seem like I agree with it. And I have another question: why don't you guys start a homeless shelter right here on campus? The students could help run it. What are you waiting for?"

"That's two questions," someone murmured. There was a collective giggle, and some of the tension went out of the room

"I'm serious. You've got the land. It goes all the way to the river where Christopher's lean-to was," Auda said, and now everybody in the room remembered Auda hadn't returned in time to be at Morning Meeting. So how did *Auda* know?

"Yeah, I know, it's politically impossible," Auda went on. "The trustees would never approve. It's not in the mission. But screw the mission, and their politics too. Who gives a damn?"

"As I said, that's a very interesting idea," Rachel said.

"Yeah, and I have another *interesting* idea for you, Rachel." Auda's voice was trembling now. It was clear to everyone how satisfying to her was her righteous anger. "Un-recuse yourself. You're the boss. You've got the power. Just do it. Declare the decision that Sylvia needed to apologize invalid. Because it is, and you know it is. That fixes the problem." She snapped her fingers. "Just like that. So people will say you did it because she's your daughter. What do you care? You can take the heat. You've been here for years."

Rachel stood very still, appearing to be considering Auda's proposal.

"Well, are you going to do it or not?" Auda said.

Rachel shook her head. "No, Auda, I am not." Then, addressing everybody: "Ladies, it's time to eat the ice cream. Who'll help serve it?"

"I will," Sylvia said. She headed for the refrigerator. There, she turned and looked at Auda. "This my house. If anyone starts to talk any more about me, I'm going to kick you all out of it."

Several girls moved toward the counter. Auda stayed back for a while, then she shrugged and moved there too. Soon more girls were at the counter to serve than there were girls to be served. No one knew what to say, especially to Auda now. Was she in on the stealing; was it all her idea? A triumvirate? No one wanted to ask her directly, at least not there.

After another little while, the girls began to drift away. There was homework due in the morning. They came up to Sylvia one by one and in little groups to say goodbye, administering hugs. Sylvia was stone faced through all of this, showing nothing of her grief, only that she wanted to get this over with.

Elizabeth and Auda were the last to leave. Sylvia walked with them to the door and opened her arms to Elizabeth for a hug. But Elizabeth just said goodbye and started to walk away. "Don't worry, she'll come around," Auda said, trying to sound convinced, and then did her best to make up for what Elizabeth had refused by hugging long and hard.

Sylvia refused to weep as she watched Elizabeth and Auda cross the campus, as familiar to her as her own face in the mirror. It didn't even occur to her that Auda might say goodnight to Elizabeth and continue walking toward the dorm she'd lived in. The two girls disappeared into Elizabeth's dorm where Sylvia was sure Elizabeth would still be at her desk studying when Auda climbed up into the upper bunk. Auda wouldn't need to change the sheets. She had what it takes to get used to the smell.

BACK INSIDE, SHE found her parents in the Little Room. Her mother was talking fast, words flying out, and her father was nodding his head. They turned to her when she came through the door. "Guess what," her father said. "Your mother really does think Auda's idea is interesting."

Sylvia stopped in the doorway. The ground was falling away beneath her feet.

"I was giving myself time to think," her mother said.

"No, Mom! It's too late. It's over."

Her mom frowned, uncomprehending "Why not? We *do* have plenty of room on campus. And the girls *could* help run it. All we have to do is have our lawyers set it up so the school won't be liable."

Sylvia stood utterly still, taking this in. Her dad was still nodding his head.

"We were in the parking lot and your homeless man was standing by a white Prius, remember?" her mom said.

"Yes, I remember," Sylvia said, also remembering her father coming toward her at Bradley Field in his brand-new car, honking and waving his hand.

"And Auda asked why are there so many homeless people in America?"

"I remember, Mom."

"And your dad said, 'We better damn well figure it out.'"

"I remember, Mom. But, Mom, the board will never let you do that."

Her mother put her hand up. "And you asked, 'If we don't, what?' And he turned and looked out the window like he was talking to the whole wide world and said, 'We won't like ourselves very much, I guess. Some of us already don't.' Do you remember what you said then?"

"I said I was glad he said that."

"Well, I was glad too!"

"I'm glad you were glad, Mom, but still, the board won't let you build a homeless shelter."

"Well, then I'll follow you out of here," she said. "We'll both be gone. I'll resign and start a school that will."

No one spoke. The news seemed to float in the room while the tick tock of the clock on the mantel grew louder and louder.

"And we have something else to tell you," her father said. He glanced at his wife.

"Go ahead, Bob," she said.

"We could have figured it out, but we didn't want to," her father said. He seemed relieved, like a person confessing a sin. "Your mother would have had to ask you next if you and Elizabeth did steal that stuff—and then get up in front of the school and indicate someone else did. Suppose you *hadn't* stolen it? Would you ever forgive her for thinking you were a thief? It's time that your mother and I admit to you that we are complicit."

"Yes, it's time," her mother, the head of Miss Oliver's, said. "The reason I didn't ask if you and Elizabeth were the ones who stole that stuff is because if you were, I knew why you were: so you could help that helpless man."

"And she didn't want you to stop," he said. "I didn't either."

"And if it turned out you weren't the ones, I'd have been disappointed," she said. "Isn't that strange?"

"So now we've each told each other everything," her dad said. "Nothing's hidden anymore. That's good. Isn't it?"

"Yes, Dad, that's good." Sylvia said.

UNAWARE OF RACHEL's plan to found a homeless shelter for the likes of him, but soothed by his meds as he prepared for bed in his aunt's house, Christopher was hearing gentle voices again while planning his future: he'd try again at the university to focus his brain and learn. If that didn't work, he would retreat to where he'd lived in his lean-to and build another one. He'd rest there for a while. Sylvia would visit him. And then he'd try again. If again he failed and couldn't trust himself not to hurt anyone, he wouldn't stay in his lean-to. He'd walk right past it, stopping long enough to pick up the grill from his firepit. Then holding on to it, he'd walk into the river. He'd wade to his knees and turn around to see her on the bank. He wouldn't hear what she said, over the sound of the voices, but he'd read her lips: *I forgive you.*

He'd turn around again then, and walk the rest of the way.

On the following Saturday, Rachel's hour of meditation was more akin to prayer than it had been all year. She spent it entirely on her plan for the advent of spring, when a sapling copper beech would be planted in a ceremonious Morning Meeting held outdoors. The students would encircle the grand old tree that had kept Rachel calm for twenty years. Alumna and board member Sarah Warrior, the first Native student at Miss Oliver's, would remind the girls that her ancestors had sat in its shade and how fitting it is that this little one will follow it. Then Rachel would spade the earth and plant the tree.

She would not know whether this was an inaugural planting for her, or a farewell one. The board would not have voted yet on her proposal to include the welcoming and caring for the homeless in the curriculum, empowering young women by their empowerment of others. But she had decided that such a school would exist, either Miss O's, or one she would found. So, she did not ask herself, as she had before: *Is this all?*

What had been missing had been found.

Acknowledgments

I am grateful to:

Julie Chagi, Linda Lancione, Ed Mcmanis, Kira Petersons, and Joana Davenport for their insightful critiques.

For the superb editing by Olivia Ngai and Catherine Adams.

And to the staff of West Margin Press: Jen Newens, Rachel Metzger, Angie Zbornik, and Olivia Ngai.

WEST MARGIN PRESS

Book Club Guide

The Encampment

Stephen Davenport

Discussion questions for *The Encampment*:

1. Miss Oliver's School for Girls is a prestigious boarding school in Connecticut, with acres of land to its property and only the highest caliber of teachers employed there. How would you describe the school community's general view of themselves? How do others view the school?

2. Consider the culture and perspective of people in Miss Oliver's School as represented in the book, from the tradition of not wearing jackets in the cold to the ritual gathering and conversation practice at dinner. Do you consider the school and its values to be progressive or conservative? Why?

3. Sylvia and Christopher both feel like outsiders in their community. Discuss how Sylvia and Christopher can relate to each other in the role of an outsider. In what ways are their experiences shared? In what ways are they different?

4. Though she and Sylvia are generally in agreement about things, Elizabeth is often at odds with her friend throughout the book. Why do you think Elizabeth and Sylvia are best friends? Where do they differ in their beliefs and in their actions? Why do you think Elizabeth and Christopher personally feel more comfortable with Sylvia than with each other?

5. According to the National Institute of Mental Health, post-traumatic stress disorder (PTSD) "develops in some people who have experienced a shocking, scary, or dangerous event." As a veteran of war, Christopher's PTSD manifests in tangible ways that express his fear, anxiety, and trauma that have carried over since being deployed in Iraq. Recount the times Christopher's PTSD inserts itself in the book. How often was he noticed when he experiences the symptoms of the disorder? What is his reaction to himself during these times?

6. Homelessness affects a great number of people in America, including veterans like Christopher. Christopher's personal situation illustrates how even having family with homes may not necessarily protect someone from becoming homeless. What are some factors that may lead to homelessness? What resources do you think are available to homeless people?

7. Compare Christopher's life as a homeless person to his life at Adelaide's house, and the change in his thoughts and feelings. Neither

the street nor Adelaide's house is a comfortable choice, so what drives him to go to Adelaide's in the first place? Why do you think he leaves and then later returns to her house?

8. Reread the passage on page 15, when Sylvia thinks of Christopher while in class and asks herself, "Did he see another girl in her face?" Then reread the passage on page 53, when Christopher dreams Sylvia visits him and asks, "What do you want? Who do you want me to be for you?" How do these two passages drive the novel? How do they contribute to the theme of identity and forgiveness that Sylvia and Christopher struggle with?

9. Rachel and Sylvia's relationship is filled with deep love yet also great tension throughout the book. Why do you think Sylvia lies and hides certain things from her mother? How does Rachel react, especially since she suspects Sylvia's not being completely truthful?

10. Think about your own relationship with a parent figure. How would you feel in that person's position, and what would you do?

11. During her suspension from school, Sylvia goes to Detroit with Aunt M and helps out with small community-organized movements. What insight did she gain from her time there? How does her experience clash with her life at Miss Oliver's, considering she came from and later returned there after Detroit?

12. Sylvia and Elizabeth's actions for Christopher eventually leads to a forced public apology in front of the entire school during Morning Meeting. If you were in their place, would you have apologized? Why?

13. At the time, Elizabeth and Sylvia both believed in their actions to steal and lie for Christopher, yet the outcome of the Morning Meeting with their public apology ended differently for the two of them. How do their decisions affect their lives? Do you think they regret their decisions? Do you think they see each other differently after the meeting?

14. *The Encampment* touches upon several subjects, from social issues of race and ethnicity, socioeconomic class, gentrification, homelessness, education, and mental health, to more personal struggles with identity, family, and friends. Which of these, if any, were you concerned about in high school? What are some issues that are important to you now, and how have you contributed to or actively engaged with them?

Q&A with Stephen Davenport

Q: Where did the idea for *The Encampment* come from?

A: One of the starting places was the horror of homelessness—of human beings, like you and me, sleeping on sidewalks, getting their food in dumpsters, in the richest country in the world. What is it like to be that person, especially when he or she is remembering the life before whatever happened to make that person a castaway? We stop at red lights and try not to look at them. Or we give them some money, maybe say Hello or God Bless. But it rarely goes further.

The book began with Christopher Triplett, the uninvited guest who changes everything simply by showing up, by being there, by not going away. I was sure someone from the school would step up, do what's right, and help him. I was sure it wouldn't be the school itself. Helping the homeless wasn't the school's mission—at least no one thought it was. And when I got the idea that the way two girls would feed and clothe the homeless person would cause them to break the only two school rules for which the consequence was expulsion, the story came to me.

Q: What made you decide to bring homelessness as a forefront issue of this novel about teenagers in a wealthy school?

A: Living in Oakland, I see homeless people every day, almost everywhere I go. There are degrees of connection and disconnection that immediately happen between people who are homeless and people who are not. We naturally take on a perspective that agrees most with our own circumstances, but novels can explore more fluidity in the role the reader and writer can take. For Sylvia, she has the marvelous ability to continue to be herself and at the same time be Christopher, thus charging herself with empathy for him. If there is any disgust, it won't be hers for him—it will be his self-disgust, which she will have sufficient distance to understand empathetically.

Q: After writing two novels set in Miss Oliver's School for Girls, what is it that made you want to revisit the world?

A: There are so many facets on a school to explore still. Through a long career working in schools whose clients are ambitious families, I grew increasingly disturbed by the harm done to students and the education they were receiving by the obsession about getting into the "right" college. I had finished writing *The Encampment* months before the recent scandal of parents manufacturing bribes and falsifying their children's credentials, and though most parents would never step that far out of bounds, the scandal does signify the power of the obsession. I'd like to ask every parent that if, God forbid, you knew your son or daughter would live only a little while after graduating from secondary school, would you deny him or her the experience of that school? What would you want that experience to be? I believe the answer would clarify that secondary school, let alone middle and elementary school, is too early a stage in life to be a careerist.

Q: Tell us a little about your writing process. Do you use outlines, or do you just write as you go?

A: No outlines. I have a general idea of where the characters are heading. When I come to the end of a chapter, I will sometimes outline the next. But when I actually start to write that chapter, I lose the outline. It becomes a way of getting me started, and that's all.

I actually didn't know what the story required, nor what I wanted to do, until I actually started writing—that is to say, recording the visualization of someone doing something, or thinking something, or saying something to somebody else. I knew eventually, but I didn't start knowing.

Q: Do you have any advice for writers?

A: I feel presumptuous giving advice, but here it goes. When you are stuck, write something anyway. Power through. The results will probably be terrible, but you will have something to work with the next day when you return. Get hard-headed, severe criticism of your work before you submit. Expect that criticism to be harsh, that it will reveal critical flaws. That attitude will enable you to write a better next draft, without first having to feel defensive. If you can afford it, hire an outstanding freelance editor so that the acquisition editor to whom you submit receives your very best work. If accepted, that editor will do another edit and help you make it even better.

How to Help the Homeless

Most organizations whose mission is to help homeless people are local. Search the web for organizations in your area to which you can volunteer your time and/or donate. One national organization that does a lot of good is the National Alliance to End Homelessness: www.endhomelessness.org

To help homeless who are war veterans, check out Volunteers for America: www.voa.org

Also, many of us have the opportunity to stop and speak to a homeless person as we go about our routines. Saying hello is an easy way to communicate that you care and that you value the person. Most homeless people have been rendered homeless by a combination of events, a perfect storm, so ask what he or she needs before offering. The most helpful items to give are gift cards for food, granola bars, water, socks, clean underwear, even sweaters.

In the end, homelessness is a national problem that can be resolved through kindness, education, and reform in laws.

CPSIA information can be obtained
at www.ICGtesting.com
Printed in the USA
BVHW040459230520
580162BV00006B/17